GIVING UP THE GHOST

BY

STACY-DEANNE

Giving Your Soul a Rise...One Page at a Time

ISBN-13: 9780982967256
Library of Congress Control Number: 2010935328

PUBLISHER'S NOTE

PEACE IN THE STORM PUBLISHING, LLC.
P.O. Box 1152
Pocono Summit, PA 18346

Visit our Web site at
www.PeaceInTheStormPublishing.com

GIVING UP THE GHOST

BY
STACY-DEANNE

Acknowledgments

<u>Special Thanks:</u>

To my Mother (RIP): There is not a minute of my life I don't think about you.

To my Dad: I love you and you've supported me from the beginning. I wouldn't be where I am today if not for your belief in me and concern for my happiness.

To my family: Thanks for the endless support. I know you're all proud of me and that makes this journey even more enjoyable.

<u>Shout Outs:</u>

To my girl Pam: You've been my biggest cheerleader and we've shared a lot. We're sisters in my eyes and the kindness and love you've shown me could never be measured. Here's another one, Miss P! Enjoy it!

Shout outs to author pals **Sheila M. Goss, Heather Convington, Marsha D. Jenkins-Sanders, Ruth Ann Nordin, Charisma Knight, Dyanne Davis, Cydney Rax, Dee Dee M. Scott, Serenity King, LaVerne Thompson and Stephanie Williams.**

Thanks to all the literary bloggers, book reviewers and media professionals who have supported me or thrown me some promo one way or another. I appreciate the love!

Special thanks to the entire Interracial Romance and Multicultural writing community, fellow IR authors, supporters and readers. You make life fun!

I'd like to thank my mentor and agent, **Maxine Thompson**. Funny how much you think you know until you meet someone that knows just a little more than you do. I've learned so much from you in the short time we've worked together. You are a gift in this business and I am very lucky to have your guidance and support.

Very special thanks to **Elissa Gabrielle** for supporting me. We came up in the game together and the minute I met you, I knew you'd hold a special place in my life. You've shared in my accomplishments by always supporting me and even in my hardships by just being there in the few times I vented. I see so much of you in me. We're both kind people who do our best to support other writers. That's something no one can learn and something you definitely can't teach. Your heart shows through everything you do and it's a pleasure to work with you and join in your vision.

Thanks to Peace in the Storm's authors and the many PITS supporters.

Saving the best for last. Thanks to all the readers and book buyers out there. It's you that remind me to stay tough and be the best writer I can. It's been a pleasure to share my work with all of you.

Praise For Giving Up the Ghost

If it's a great book you want, Stacy-Deanne is making sure that it's a great book that you will get with Giving Up the Ghost! For Detective Brianna Morris, the serial rapist known only as The Albany Predator has just been ousted as her worst case ever. A new attacker is targeting African-American women, and Brianna's best friend Cheyenne Wilson was unfortunate enough to be one of his victims. In Giving Up the Ghost, Stacy-Deanne pushes the limits to which Brianna must navigate a lecherous world of lust, logic and elusive lurkers.

~Joey Pinkney, author of The Soul of a Man

Giving Up The Ghost is a riveting and engrossing psychological thriller which grabs you from the beginning and refuses to let go until the very end. This fast-paced mystery is an intriguing love triangle of Mayhem, Lust and the Obsessions that inspire the two. Through captivating twists and turns, Stacy Deanne keeps you on the edge of your seat with a suspenseful, "Who Done It" which is a must read for the sheer enjoyment of figuring out the reasons "Why."

~Lorraine Elzia, Author of *Mistress Memoirs* and *Ask Nicely and I Might*

CHAPTER ONE

S he could die tonight because she'd never seen anything this beautiful. The April breeze swept against Cheyenne Wilson's face when she walked onto Simon Watts' terrace. She hadn't appreciated the aura of Albany, New York's nightfall in years. She remembered a game she played as a child. She used to stare out her bedroom window at night and try to count the thousands of headlights moving up and down the lanes.

Her frizzy ringlets danced in the breeze. Her gold nail polish caught the light in the corner of the terrace every time she moved her hands. She dug an inch of her peach dress from underneath her bosom. Seemed like every time she moved the humidity glued another part of the flimsy cloth to her caramel-brown skin.

These days Albany citizens had two choices where weather came into play. Either bitch or moan and curse Mother Nature or deal with the wrath of humidity left from the constant thunderstorms. Calm skies were a luxury.

Simon lived in Albany's richest neighborhood cut off from the rest of the city. He still dealt with the nuisance of loud music, barking dogs and car horns from blocks away.

Cheyenne chuckled. So even the rich weren't immune.

The best restaurants in the city surrounded Simon's neighborhood. Cheyenne smelled every aroma from the fried fish at the Asian restaurant to the tacos and enchiladas from that award-winning Mexican restaurant the Mayor raved about.

Crrrraacccckkkkk!

Glasses broke.

"Ahhhh!"

Simon screamed from the kitchen.

"Simon you okay?" Cheyenne ran into the living room. Her heels sunk into the thick carpet the faster she moved. The objects in the room thrust into her vision with the speed of a tornado.

Black furniture, white walls, glossy fixtures, portraits, the conventional, classic-style lamps...

"*Ahh!*"

"Simon!"

"Ahhh! No! No! Uh!"

"Simon!" Cheyenne scampered to the hall. "Simon what's going on?"

"Cheyenne! Uh! Stay away! Get away!"

"Simon!" She laid her hand on her mouth. "Oh god. Simon are you all right?"

She heard him tussling in the kitchen. Could someone else be here?

"Cheyenne go! Run! Leave now!"

"Simon? Simon answer me please!"

Silence.

"Fuck." She spun in circles around the living room. "Oh god, oh god, oh god." She chewed the side of her hand. "Where's the fuckin' phone?" She searched the room, sweating and wheezing.

Big ass room and no fuckin' phone?

She got her cell from her purse.

Something moved in the hallway.

She turned around. Her breath locked in her throat.

Footsteps.

"Simon is that you?"

The footsteps stopped.

"Hey I got a gun!" She lied. "You come near me if you want to!"

Bree had helped Cheyenne through some of the roughest times in her life. But right now, none of that outdid the bluffing tactic she'd taught Cheyenne.

When cornered, say you have a weapon especially when you *don't.*

Shit. It paid to have a detective as a friend.

Cheyenne dropped the cell phone. It plopped underneath the couch.

"Shit!" She got on her knees and dug for it.

Thunder.

The electricity flickered.

"No, not now. Don't go out now." She moved her hand under the couch.

Rain sprinkled into the room from the terrace. Cheyenne flattened her body to the carpet to get a better grip on the phone. One of her fake nails broke off. She snatched the phone. She sat up on her knees and started to dial.

The electricity went out.

"God damn it! Shit! Not now!" Cheyenne crawled and fumbled through the darkness. "Shit!" She heard breathing in the room. She laid her shaking hand on her chest.

"I...I have a gun." She closed her eyes. "*Fuck*."

Someone grabbed the front of her dress. Still on her knees, she slid towards them.

"Ahh!"

She dropped the phone. Her knees burned against the carpet.

She broke free. She got up and tried to run to the terrace.

If she couldn't see *them*, maybe they couldn't see her.

Or maybe they *could*.

Her arms were snatched back.

"Ahhhh! Ohhh!"

They snatched her by the hair and tossed her.

"Ohhh!"

She landed on the couch, tumbled and flipped onto the floor.

Lighting sparked the room.

Her knees tingled from being scratched on the carpet. Her arms felt like they'd been popped out their sockets. Her head pounded. She squinted, desperate to see the person in front of her but it was too dark.

They moved closer.

A speck of lightening allowed Cheyenne to see the shimmer of something gold in front of her.

The footsteps got closer. She couldn't see who held the object, but definitely recognized it. She'd fallen in love with Simon's little golden angel statue the first time she saw it.

Now she was afraid of it.

The lightening stopped. The room went pitch black again.

"Please don't hurt me." She coughed from a lack of breath. Vomit swirled in her stomach. Thick drool lathered between her lips.

The little angel dangled over her.

She clawed and kicked through blackness.

"No...please." She threw her arms up. "Someone help me! Help me! He..."

The statue cracked the base of Cheyenne's skull.

"Detective Brianna Morris?"

"Yes?"

The tall black woman's eyes locked on the man with the white coat and clipboard standing in the hospital waiting room. She moved from the soda machine. Her fingers left prints in the Styrofoam coffee cup. Her ponytail shifted until a few curls escaped the rubber band. Humidity banded the loose strands to the back of her neck.

"I'm Dr. Walden." He shook her hand. "It's nice to meet you."

"Yeah I wish it was under other circumstances."

Her curvy lips and sleek nose turned an otherwise plain face into one worthy of being painted by Monet.

She sipped the last drop of her coffee. "How is Cheyenne? May I see her?"

"She just came out of surgery and she's in intensive care right now."

"Intensive..." Brianna stood against the vending machine. "So I can't see her?"

"Follow me and I'll gladly fill you in on the details."

They went down three long halls and turned right towards the elevator.

"Doctor what can you tell me? Is she gonna be all right?"

"It's too soon to comment on that."

They got on the elevator.

"Well isn't there something you can tell me?"

"She pulled through surgery but Cheyenne suffered extensive blows to the head. Her skull was severely fractured. We didn't see any significant brain trauma but we're still running tests so we don't know if her recovery will be the success we hope. With head injuries, things can crop up after the fact."

"Is she in a lot of pain?" Brianna propped the back of her foot on the elevator wall. "I just don't want her to suffer anymore than she already has."

"We're keeping her heavily sedated so she's able to rest." Walden studied his clipboard.

"We looked through her things for next of kin or someone to contact but your name and number was the only thing in her billfold."

Brianna chewed the side of her cup. "She doesn't have any family."

"Really?" Walden held the elevator door for her to get off first.

"That's one of the reasons I promised I'd always be there for her. She doesn't have many people in her life."

"It's sad to hear that, Detective Morris."

They walked down the freezing ICU hall. The walls, floor, everything shined an eye-blinding white. She'd been up here many times thanks to her occupation. Always felt one step closer to death whenever she came down these halls.

She peeked through the corridors and doorways as they passed.

He could be here right now. He always stayed a step ahead.

"Detective?"

"Huh?" She almost bumped into Walden.

"Are you all right? Did I lose you?"

"Oh." She felt her forehead. "Sorry I had something else on my mind. Just worried you know? What were you saying?"

He moved aside for a male nurse to pass.

"I was just inquiring about your relationship with Cheyenne. I mean…" He switched the clipboard from under one arm to the other. "You two must be very close since you were named as her emergency contact."

"Uh yes." She walked with her hands locked behind her back. "I met Cheyenne when I was investigating a serial rape case."

"Ah yes." He plucked his chin with the end of his clipboard. "I remember, the Albany Predator case right?"

"Yes."

"He was raping African-American women and killed some didn't he?"

Brianna held her breath. Desperate not to remember the fear she felt when she almost became one of the Predator's prize victims.

Of course over the last few months, she'd become accustomed to living in fear. A new predator claimed Brianna as his victim. And this man could teach the Albany Predator a thing or two about elusiveness.

She couldn't avoid him and she couldn't stop him. She didn't even know where to look or who to look for. Going after other criminals were easier because after months of studying them, she always picked up on vital clues. Not this time. This man not only played the game like a skilled pro but Brianna began to believe he might have even invented it.

"You should be congratulated, Detective Morris. No one thought the Predator would be caught but you did it."

She smiled. "I appreciate that but I don't think of it as any different than any other rape case I've worked on."

"But surely you have to. Shoot I remember how scared everyone was." Walden pushed up his glasses. "My wife's not black but even she didn't wanna leave the house. Remember the Mayor had everyone in the city on curfew."

"Yeah well that's…"

"He broke into your home and attacked you didn't he? I remember that from the papers."

She closed her eyes.

"He almost killed your partner and…"

She stopped in mid stride. "Can we just get back to Cheyenne please?"

Walden stepped back and dropped his shoulders.

"I'm sorry. How insensitive of me? You probably wish you could forget that case everyday don't you?"

"Just understand that Cheyenne means a lot to me. I promised her I'd always protect her and I vow to keep that promise. I'm not gonna let the person who did this get away with it."

"I can tell you care."

She touched his arm. "Just be up front with me okay? What happens if she has trauma to the brain after all? Are you talking about something that can't be fixed?"

"Don't know until we see the remaining tests. Her head was cracked open."

"Jesus." She counted the little lines dividing the squares of the floor tile as they walked.

"Yeah I gotta tell you I'm shocked she even survived, Detective Morris."

They walked past a row of beds with privacy only provided by thin curtains.

"I assumed she had her own guardian angel ya' know?" Walden led Brianna to Cheyenne's bed and pushed back the curtain. "Now meeting you, I know for sure she does."

"Believe me if I were her guardian angel, this wouldn't have happened." Brianna froze at the sight of the battered woman. "Oh god."

Bandages and tape covered eighty percent of Cheyenne's face and head. She lay so still Brianna couldn't tell if she were breathing. Tubes hung from her nose, mouth and arm.

"See the discoloration underneath her right eye?" Walden pointed to the swollen, purple area.

"Uh-huh."

"She was hit so hard that the blows caused the discoloration. She had fluid building in that part of the face but we're giving her something to drain it off. If she hadn't gotten to surgery when she did she would have definitely died. Just a minute later could have made the difference."

"That son of a bitch." Brianna's eye caught a tear. "He's not gonna get away with this." She twisted the curtain in her hand. "I don't care what I have to do, he's not getting away with this."

"Detective Morris, do you know who did this?"

That would be the question of the hour. Her new predator would do anything to get to her. He'd said that many times. Would attacking her friend be a way to get her attention?

"Detective Morris?" Walden touched her shoulder.

She had to be objective. She needed to think like a cop and not a woman fighting every day for peace of mind. Yet she'd become both. Anyone could have done this to Cheyenne but only one person seemed to have a motive.

Was he really this twisted?

"Detective Morris?" Walden pulled her from the curtain.

"Huh?"

"Detective, you sure you don't need a check-up yourself? You don't look well at all."

"I'm fine." She tugged at her blouse. "This could cause permanent damage couldn't it?"

Walden nodded. "The good news is that she's stable and her vitals are good. She lost a lot of blood but we're getting a handle on that. Like I said, we'll know more when the tests are all done."

"So you guys didn't call the police, only me?"

"Yes. We would've called the police but since you were a detective, we decided to call you first and go from there."

"You should have called the police, Dr. Walden."

He shrugged. "You're right I suppose. I was with another patient when it happened. The nurses should have called the police."

"So how did Cheyenne get here in the first place? Obviously she didn't drive." Brianna touched Cheyenne's freezing hand.

"She was brought in. That's what the ladies in admittance say."

"By who?"

His glasses tilted off his square nose. "I haven't a clue, Detective."

"You didn't ask?"

"Well no…"

"Dr. Walden wouldn't you say this isn't your average situation where a patient is concerned? The first thing I'd have done was ask for all details."

"Detective Morris it's been very hectic around here and the place has been a zoo. We have patients in and out of trauma I guess…" He looked at Cheyenne. "You're right. I have no excuse. I guess we were so focused on helping Cheyenne we didn't worry about anything else."

"No, look I apologize. It's the cop in me. We're always thinking of the details. I suppose it's a little different for doctors."

"Just different type of details I guess. I'm sorry, Detective Morris."

She straightened the curtain. "Here's my card and everything. Give me a call if you learn anything else."

"I definitely will."

Brianna walked backwards through the curtain. "I'll be back tomorrow."

"Uh, Detective? Before you go there's the matter of insurance. We didn't find that Cheyenne has any type of policy."

"Cheyenne could barely afford her rent let alone health insurance."

"Well there has to be arrangements."

"Don't worry about it okay? I'll take care of everything. Put my name on anything that has to do with her bills."

"Detective Morris uh, you sure you wanna do that? Put yourself out like that?"

Her eyes shifted to the curtain separating Cheyenne's bed.

"Well you said it yourself right? I'm her guardian angel."

◆◆◆◆◆◆

Detective Steven Kemp's doorbell rang for the fourth time.

"Hold on!" He ran downstairs with his bed sheet around his waist. Bang! Bang! Bang!

"I'm comin'!" He fumbled with the sheet. "Moron."

His body flushed with intense heat when he saw the beautiful woman in the peephole.

He opened the door. "Hey, Bree."

His short blond hair absorbed the sweat from his forehead and neck. He tried to read her thoughts but he'd need a psychic to do that these days.

He closed the door behind her, taking a whiff of her peach perfume along the way.

"Hmm, what a surprise."

15

"I need to talk to you, Steve."

"Really?" He lowered his blue eyes to her shivering fingers. "I kinda got that feeling."

His nipples hardened when her eyes stroked his naked chest.

She pointed to the sheet. "Are you *naked*?"

He wrapped the sheet tighter. "Duh, I was asleep."

"When did you start sleeping naked?"

He scratched his chest. "Why you worried about it?" His blue eyes lit up. "You don't sleep with me anymore."

"I'm not worried about it. I could care less how you sleep." She went into the kitchen. She'd poured a glass of milk before Steven got into the room.

"What's up, Bree?" He sat at the table. "You're not the kind to drop by late at night for no reason." He rocked his legs. "Unless I'm still dreaming?"

"Yeah you wish." She finished the milk and put the glass in the sink.

"Hey, don't put the glass in the sink. Leave it on the counter."

She moved the glass.

"And did you forget you're lactose intolerant?"

"I needed something to calm my nerves." She leaned over the counter. "My heart's beating so fast."

"Bree, honey you can talk to me about anything. You know that."

She hid her tears underneath her palms.

"Bree, what's happened? You okay?"

"Cheyenne she…" She folded her arms. "She was attacked tonight."

"What?"

"Steven she looked horrible." She sucked in tears. "I can't get it out of my head. I keep seeing her lying in that bed all wrapped up, struggling for her life."

He passed her a paper towel.

"She was beaten on the head and left for dead." She walked around the table. "No one knows shit. The doctor didn't know anything and the nurses didn't know anything."

Steven's sheet slid from his waist.

"Someone's gotta know something. They just don't know they know it."

"It's all my fault." She leaned over the kitchen table.

"The hell it is. Don't go blaming yourself for this too, Bree."

"I promised I'd protect her, Steven! And I didn't."

"What the hell could you have done? She was attacked. It's not like anyone knew it would happen."

"It doesn't matter." She moved from his touch. "I told Cheyenne I wouldn't let anything else happen to her. I didn't keep that promise."

"The woman was attacked. You're not psychic, you didn't know it would happen."

"Funny it doesn't make me feel any better."

"Maybe not but you've done a lot for Cheyenne and I'm not gonna let you beat yourself up over this."

"I just can't believe this you know? How much bad luck can one person have? She's a great person, Steven. She's never hurt anyone but she can't seem to catch a break. You know how long it took her to finally get over being raped."

"Yeah I know."

"And now this? Forget physically. She might not ever recover mentally. She could be scarred for the rest of her life."

"Cheyenne is tougher than you think she is."

"Oh come on, Steve. Who could take all this shit and come through it like nothing happened?"

"I didn't say she'd ever forget, but she'll get through this. You'll be there to help her like you always have been."

"Right." She ran her finger across the stove. "Like I was there for her tonight huh?"

He caressed her shoulders. "She's always known she can count on you. But you can't keep trying to save the world. When are you gonna realize you're human too?"

"I should have been there." She moved to the sink. "I'll never forgive myself for this."

He stood in front of her. "I can't tell you how to feel. All I can say is that you shouldn't beat yourself up about this." He took her hands. "You've been a great friend to her, Bree. She's not gonna blame you for any of this."

"But I blame myself."

Ring! Ring!

"Ahh!" Brianna hovered in Steven's arms.

"Bree? What the…"

Ring! Ring!

She crept from his embrace. Her fingers dug into the counter behind her.

"Bree it's just the phone."

17

Her eyes stayed on the kitchen doorway.

Ring! Ring!

"Bree look at me all right?" He shook her. "What's going on?"

"Aren't you gonna answer it?"

"No."

The ringing stopped.

Brianna inched to the doorway.

"Bree, you practically jumped outta ya' damn skin now what's going on?"

Sweat filled her face.

"Bree look at me."

She did. Her eyes were on him but she didn't seem quite there.

"Bree?" He grabbed her arms. "I'm worried about you. You jump when the phone rings at work and now you almost had a heart attack."

"It's nothing." She shoved his hands away.

"Bullshit. Tell me what's going on with you."

"Just seemed strange that you'd get a call this late." She tangled her fingers together.

"Isn't it strange to you?"

"Not really. What's strange is how you've been acting lately."

"I'm just under pressure." She dabbed her face with the paper towel. "So much is going on. That molestation case we just wrapped up and now Cheyenne."

"No this is about you, Bree."

"Just leave it alone, Steven. Please."

"I can't." He put his arms around her. "I care about you too much to look the other way."

"Steven."

"And you know that. I don't have to tell you. You know how I feel." He brought his mouth to hers. "I can't stop caring about ya', Bree. I don't want to."

"Steven stop it." She turned her head. "I have a lot on my mind right now. This is the last thing I wanna think about right now."

"I won't stop trying to get us back to where we used to be, Bree. Where we both want and need to be."

"I gotta go."

He blocked her. "But you don't really want to do you?"

She pried his hands from her waist. "Bye, Steve."

"You can't run from this, Bree. I won't let you."

She left.

CHAPTER TWO

Ring! Ring! Ring!

Brianna set the carton of milk on her kitchen counter an hour later. She took a deep breath and counted to ten. That familiar, alarming chill fell through the house.

"Meow!" Davis sat on the edge of the stairs licking his paws.

Just thinking about the caller's maniacal voice scared her before she answered the phone. She tiptoed into the living room. Everything stood silent except the taunting chimes of the clock in the upstairs hallway.

She stared at the phone beside the couch. She could ignore him but that didn't work with stalkers. He knew she was home. He knew everything. She knew nothing. She couldn't dissuade him. She couldn't control him. But she danced to *his* tune like a puppet. No amount of surveillance, tracing and threatening had brought any answers.

He kept the same anonymity he had from the beginning. She rubbed the front of her pink top. She straightened the ends of her blue shorts. Her mind ran through every horrid thought she could have imagined.

She picked up the phone.

"Hello?"

"Mmm. That's something I've been missing. You don't know how much I needed to hear your pretty voice today." Brianna shut her eyes. "What? You got nothing to say to me, sweetie? Nothing to say to the love of your life?"

"I've taken all the shit I'm gonna to take from you. You're not gonna continue to do this to me."

"You say that all the time but you haven't stopped me yet."

Davis slipped into the living room. The brownish-tan feline stopped by Brianna's feet.

"I keep telling you this just gonna keep happen', love. What do I have to do to show you I'm the boss and there's nothing you can do about it."

"And that's what it's all about isn't it?" She turned in a half-circle. "You having control over me. It's that simple."

"Hmm, not really."

She gazed in midair as if he stood right in front of her.

"You're not in control like you think you are. You're a coward. If you weren't you'd face me and stop hiding."

"Ohh, baby."

He breathed so deeply into the phone she almost felt it.

"Oh honey is that an invitation?"

She twisted the phone cord between her fingers. She burst into a horrid sweat that drenched her from head to toe.

"See, I've wanted that from the beginning, Brianna. You'll never know how much. But let's not play games okay?"

"Oh no?" Her voice caught in her throat. "Thought you liked to play games."

"What I meant is, you already see me all the time. You see me in your dreams and every time you try to forget me, I'm always there. I know that. We're bonded, honey. Not even I can stop that. There's just no way."

"I will find you. And I won't hesitate to take the law into my own hands when I do."

"Oooh you promise, Brianna?" He sucked his tongue. "See this is what excites me. Every time you threaten me and get upset, you show your fear. That's when I know I got you."

"And what if I told you I'm not gonna let you get to me anymore? Would that make you go away?"

"Ahh, you don't really want that, Brianna. Deep down you like playing my little reindeer games. It makes our relationship all worthwhile."

"We don't have a relationship. I *am* gonna find out who you are."

"You gonna find out what happened to your friend too?"

"What?" She almost kicked Davis when she moved. "What did you say?"

"You heard me."

She backed into the table.

He laughed. "Now I know you can't be surprised! I know everything about you. I know your friends. I know where you work, where you live, who you talk to, when you leave the house. I even know about the guys you've fucked and the ones who wanna fuck you."

"Stop it." Her knees quivered.

"Mmm but there's something I don't know. I don't know what you look like when you come."

"Stop it!"

"But I plan to know real soon. You can count on that, baby."

"You shut your fuckin' mouth." She pressed her palm over the receiver. "If you had anything to do with Cheyenne's attack I will kill you." Sweat dribbled down her lips. "You understand me? I will fuckin' kill you."

"I love you, Brianna."

"You don't know how to love anyone! You stay away from the people I care about."

"Hey, you've got it all wrong. I didn't attack your friend."

"Like I'd believe you. You'd do anything to get my attention!"

"I already own your attention. I didn't have nothing to do with Cheyenne's attack."

"Bullshit."

"You can believe it or don't. But the fact is looks like someone was trying to make her pay attention. Take a lesson from that, Brianna. Because like the person who attacked Cheyenne, I don't like being ignored either. Ever."

Click.

"Okay Morris, we're alone now." Captain Jersey closed her office door the next day. Brianna watched her older, pale superior than continued her thoughts. Jersey's green eyes glittered like Christmas lights against the red in her glasses. She stuffed a loose strand of her reddish-gray hair back into her bun.

"What did you want to say about Cheyenne's attack that you couldn't mention in front of Kemp?"

"I know that as cops we aren't supposed to jump to conclusions.

I also know that in this line of work, things don't come easy. Clues I mean."

"True. Morris why are you talking in riddles? Can't you just spit it out? We both have a lot of work today."

"I got another phone call last night. From *him*."

"Oh, no." Jersey scratched underneath her glasses. "Well what did he say this time?"

"Look it's bad enough he's forced himself into my life. He's not going to hurt the people I care about. I won't let him." She paced. "Captain I've been up all night trying to see why someone would hurt Cheyenne. We don't know the why or even the where concerning this. But maybe the major points aren't all that's important."

"What are you getting at?"

"It's a chain reaction, a domino effect. He's...he's been toying with me. He's been a step ahead. He wanted me to think he stopped but he hadn't. He lives on playing with me and jerking my emotions. What better way to get my attention than to do something like this right?"

"Wait, wait, wait." Jersey propped up on her desk. "Are you saying that the man who is stalking you might be the person who attacked Cheyenne Wilson?"

Brianna turned from Jersey's somber expression. She tried to block out noise from the rampant detectives down the hall.

"Morris I want to catch this guy more than anything and we're doing all we can, and being discreet. But what makes you think your stalker did this? It makes no sense to me."

She chewed the tip of her finger. "None of this makes sense. I don't have any proof or anything but I know he has something to do with this. I know it."

"What would be the motive?"

"Damn Captain you know what it would be! To get back at *me*! To make me pay attention to him! All he wants is to have me jump through hoops and play this game with him. Wants to see how far I'll let him push me. He's playing with me like I'm on a fuckin' Monopoly board! It's one thing to bother me but when he tries to hurt people I care about, I can't let that happen." She stood behind Jersey's chair. "We have got to find him *now*. It's not just about me anymore."

"Easier said than done. We've been on this man for months, Brianna. Nothing has worked. We can't trace his calls. You don't even know what he looks like! You can't even tell what his voice really sounds like because he talks so low on the phone." Jersey sat at her desk. "You got all this crap to deal with. Cheyenne's attack is the last thing you need to worry about."

"I don't give a damn. I'm gonna find out who did this to her. It connects to me, Captain."

Jersey dug through her drawer. "I heard this morning they're giving it to Homicide downtown."

"Who?"

Jersey filled her cup with coffee. "Our beloved Jayce Matthews."

"Homicide? Why? There was no murder."

"It was an *attempted* murder, Morris."

"It was an *assault*. That's Steven and my neck of the woods. Look I like Jayce but he's not gonna put the time into this case that I would."

"It's Jayce's case. You can't do anything about that."

"Well Steven and I are gonna work on it too."

"Morris."

"We don't have another case right now, Captain. You got something for us?"

Jersey shook her head.

"Well then. And even if I did have another case I'm not leaving this up to Jayce. Cheyenne's my friend. I didn't stop her from being attacked but I damn sure will do all I can to find out who did it."

"You gotta start thinking about your own life. You gotta take this nut seriously."

"I am taking it seriously!" Brianna bent over the desk. "I deal with this every damn day, no one else, me."

"Everything we've tried hasn't worked. I think we'd be a lot better off if we pull others in."

"No."

"Morris."

"I don't want anyone else to find out! I sure as hell don't want Steven to know. I don't want folks hovering over me and treating me like some victim."

"You are the victim." Jersey stood. "Maybe it's time you accept that. Jumping into Cheyenne's situation isn't gonna change yours. Sooner or later you're gonna have to face that this is really happening."

"You promised me this would be between us."

"We can at least tell Kemp. I don't feel right keeping this from him."

"I don't mean to be rude Captain but let me handle this the way I want to."

"There's something you're not addressing, Morris."

She grabbed the doorknob. "What?"

"If this man really did attack Cheyenne, he could do the same thing to Steven."

"That won't happen."

"Please. How do you know that?"

"Because I won't let it happen, Captain. He won't hurt anyone else I care about."

"You can't promise that, Morris."

"The hell I can't."

◆◆◆◆◆◆

Brianna and Steven squeezed their way through the crowd blocking the entrance doors of the hospital. Police cars sped towards the building with their sirens blaring. Fire trucks, including the Fire Marshall's vehicle parked by the side entrances and exits. A van from *Channel Five News* drove through the gathering onlookers.

People who weren't included in the latest firefighter accident rushed inside before paramedics brought two firefighters in on gurneys. The firefighters were rushed down the hall so fast that a cloud of smoke followed. People covered their noses as the harsh stench of smoke and soot clouded the front of the hospital.

Brianna pushed her nose in her blouse.

"It's from that fire downtown." Steven covered his nose with a tissue. "I heard about it on my way to work."

They approached the ladies at the admittance desk.

"Aww, man." Brianna stretched. "I swear if I had the chance, I could sleep a month."

Steven flicked her ponytail. "You didn't sleep well last night did you?"

"No." She put her hand on her hip. "But that's not unlike any night lately."

"So we gonna keep dancing or are you gonna tell me what's going on with you?"

"Don't start, Steven. Leave it alone."

"What that you've been jumping outta your skin lately? Bree let me help you."

"I don't need your help." She lowered her voice when someone passed.

"You in some kinda trouble?"

"We're here for Cheyenne, Steve. Not me."

"Yeah you say that but I'm not convinced."

A chubby woman in a blue smock walked behind the counter with a Coke.

"May I help you?" She sat down with her side rolls hanging out the chair.

Steven showed his badge. "Detective Steven Kemp and Detective Brianna Morris with the Albany Police Department." He put his badge up. "Need to ask some questions about a patient, Cheyenne Wilson who was admitted last night. She'd been attacked, beaten on the head."

The lady shoved a McDonald's sack off her keyboard. "Uh, Cheyenne Wilson?"

"Yes," Brianna said. "Someone brought her in last night and we're hoping someone around here got a name of the person or can tell us anything that will help."

The lady picked her teeth with her pinky nail. "Okay let me check for you."

She scrolled through a list of names.

"Okay here she is I see. She's in ICU?"

"Yes." Brianna leaned to see the computer screen.

"Well it doesn't have a name for anyone who brought her in." The lady checked another list. "Nope, no name was given."

"So you can't tell us anything? I was here last night and Dr. Walden said you guys saw who brought her in."

"I wasn't working last night. Marsha was."

"Well?" Steven smacked the counter. "Could you please get Marsha then?"

"Sure." She dialed the phone. "Let me uh see what floor she's on right now."

A petite woman with limp blond hair and her arm in a cast walked up.

"Marsha's not in yet, Ruth."

The blond smiled at Brianna but seemed to find it hard to take her eyes off the handsome officer beside her.

"Oh she's not?" Ruth hung up the phone.

The blond rested her injured arm on the counter. "Is there something I can help with?"

"Were you here last night?" Steven asked.

"Why yes." Her eyes scanned Steven from head to toe. "I'm Janet. You are?"

"I'm Detective Steven Kemp and this is my partner Brianna

Morris."

Brianna waved.

"Detectives?" Janet stood up straight.

"We're trying to find out who brought in a patient, Cheyenne Wilson last night." Brianna tapped her palm with her fist. "On the computer it doesn't have a name but I spoke to Dr. Walden last night and I know someone brought her in."

"Yes I remember her. She was beaten right?"

"Right." Brianna sighed. "Now we're finally getting somewhere."

"Hopefully." Steven scratched the back of his neck.

"Yeah a man brought her in but he ran off before we could get him to sign in or tell us his name."

Brianna took out her notepad. "What did this man look like?"

"Uh." Janet's head fell to the side. "He got my attention quick. Not just because he was with this injured lady, but because of how he was acting."

"And how was he acting?" Steven asked.

"A little jumpy. I thought it was just because he was worried about the lady but when he left the way he did, I found it suspicious."

"Yet no one bothered to call the police." Brianna got her pen out her back pocket.

"Tell us what you can about this man okay?"

Janet nodded at Steven. "He was a white guy. He was tall."

"How tall?" Brianna scribbled on the pad.

"About as tall as both of you are. Very tall."

"Bree's six-feet and I'm six-three. Which one did he seem closer to?"

"About your height." Janet slunk against the counter. "I'd say six-three at least."

"Okay." Steven rubbed his chin. "What else?"

"He was about early thirties I'd say."

"Early thirties?" Brianna jotted.

"Yeah."

"What about clothes?" Steven asked. "Can you remember what he was wearing?"

"Hmm." She bit her fingernail. "Well you guys know it was raining very heavy last night. He had on a raincoat. I couldn't tell what else he had on because his coat was closed. He had on a hat too."

"What kind of hat?" Brianna waved the pad. "Baseball cap, knit cap, rain hat, what?"

"No it was a small hat. Like a tam or something. Dark color, I don't remember if it was black or navy or brown. There were so many people in here, walking in and out I couldn't tell the exact color."

"Any other distinctions?" Brianna flicked her ponytail off her shoulder. "Did he have an earring, tattoo, facial hair? Anything that made him stick out?"

"I couldn't tell if he had an earring or tattoo but he did have a goatee. I guess he had brown hair because the goatee was brown but I couldn't see his hair because of the hat. He had very pretty eyes but they looked kind of sneaky."

"What color eyes? Blue like mine?" Steven pointed to his eyes.

"No." Janet blushed. "They weren't as pretty as yours."

Steven smirked.

"I'd never forget that shade of blue."

Brianna tapped the pad. "What color did the man's eyes look?"

"They were light. I'd say gray or maybe hazel. At least that's what they looked like from a distance."

"Is that all you can remember?" Steven slid in behind Janet.

"Yes." She stiffened. "If I think of anything else I'd be more than happy to tell you guys."

Brianna closed the pad. "I bet you will."

"Oh uh, he looked like he had money."

"Why you say that?"

Janet faced Steven. "I swear that hat was Armani. Fashion magazines are my life. Oh yeah and he had on sneakers. I think Sean John."

"Sean John sneakers huh?" Steven sucked his lip.

"And his watch was probably a Rolex at least. It was very elegant. I can't be sure of the brand but it looked very expensive."

"Call us if you think of anything else all right?" Steven passed Janet their cards.

She shoved them inside her smock. "I'll call you even if I *don't.*"

CHAPTER THREE

S teven and Brianna piled behind the crowd in front of the Flamingo strip club that night.

Usually Brianna avoided the Flamingo like the plague but seeing how Cheyenne's place of work might hold the answers they needed, she couldn't be picky.

Men ran from all directions and headed straight to the gyrating strippers on stage. People raced up and down the parking lot waving cans out the window and yelling. Brianna and Steven were swept inside by the typhoon of loud patrons.

Brianna couldn't take safety for granted no matter how crowded the place was. Any one of these men could be her stalker. She studied faces and body language. Made a mental note of every man in that room.

Yet still had no idea whom to look for.

"Owwww!"

A gang of young guys danced in front of the stage. Others grabbed at the strippers only to be thrown back by the bouncers. Men dropped beer on the floor and fondled the passing waitresses.

Brianna moved back and forth to save her feet from being trampled by the human traffic.

Springsteen's "Adam Raised a Cain" echoed from the speakers across the room.

"Steve!" Brianna covered her ears. "Damn it's more crowded than usual in here!"

"Huh?"

"I said it's more crowded than usual!"

"Whoo! Hoo!" Men danced between the detectives.

"I think I know why, Bree!" Steven pointed to the sign over the bar. "They're having a discount on beer tonight!"

"Oh great! The last thing anyone in here needs is cheap beer! God I hate this place!"

"*What?*"

"I said I hate this place!"

A leather bra flew over Brianna's head.

"Whoa, Bree." Steven pulled her out the line of fire. "Almost got'cha there huh?"

"I tell you my patience is running out!"

A bucktooth man with two king-sized beers bumped into Brianna.

"I hope someone here can tell us something, Steve. I can't take much more of this!"

"I told you to let me come by myself!" He danced and snapped his fingers.

"Yeah right! Something tells me you wouldn't have been able to keep your mind on business!"

He laughed.

"Oww!"

"Yeah!"

"Whoo, baby!"

"Steve!"

"Huh?" He laid his hand on Brianna's back.

"This place makes me feel like a piece of meat."

"Ha, ha! Come on, it ain't that bad."

"Yeah I'm sure it's heaven for you!"

"Hopefully Juney's working tonight!" Steven stretched to see over the crowd.

"Oh god let her be here! I'm serious, Steve! I'm two seconds from leaving!"

"You know you wanna find out what happened to Cheyenne." He pushed her out of the path of raging men. "If anyone knows anything about Cheyenne it would be Juney." He nudged her. "Hey, Bree. Check it out."

"What?"

"Hey ain't that Ryan from work?" Steven pointed to the young man with the coal black hair and blazing blue eyes. He wasn't holding the same enthusiasm as the other guys in the club.

"Yeah that's him." Brianna jumped up and down. "Ryan!" He turned around in the booth.

"Ryan over here!"

"Hey, guys!" He galloped to the detectives with a half-empty glass of beer.

"Ryan, dude!" Steven slapped his back.

"Hey, Steve. Bree."

"Hey, Ryan." She crossed her arms. "Didn't expect to see you here."

"Oh yeah?" He looked towards the stage. "What man wouldn't wanna be in a room full of beautiful semi-naked women?"

Steven play-punched him. "Well shit when the fellas asked you to come here with us last week you said this wasn't your thing. Makes me think you didn't wanna hang with us."

He blushed. "No nothing like that. I got a little lonely you know? It's not easy being new in the city and not having any friends."

"Oh now you know that's not true." Brianna put her arm around his shoulder. "You're one of us."

"Yeah, man." Steven jabbed Ryan's chest. "You know we stick together."

"You mean you cops stick together." He sipped. "I just work at the station, getting mail and running errands. Not exactly on you guys' level."

"Ryan it's not like that believe me, " Brianna said. "We think you're a great kid."

He looked into his glass. "Kid?"

"I didn't mean anything by that."

"No I…I get it."

She touched his shoulder. "I didn't mean to offend you."

"Oh!" He laughed. "Come on, Bree. You could never offend me."

"Well you can hang with us anytime you want."

"You mean that, Bree?"

"Of course I do."

He finished his beer. "Well I'd better go. Gotta be up bright and early. Oh by the way." He snapped his fingers. "What are you two doing here?"

"On official business, can you believe it?" Steven chuckled.

"A case or something?"

"Yeah. A friend of mine was attacked and Steven and I are doing our part to find out what happened."

"Oh man that's horrible, Bree. I hope they're okay."

"I hope she'll be but to be honest, not sure yet. She's in ICU."

"I really hope she's okay. I'll keep her in my prayers for you."

Brianna smiled. "I appreciate that."

"Yeah." He broke his stare. "Well I gotta get outta here. It was great seeing you guys."

"Oh hey, man!" Steven raised his arms. "Debra's been bragging about you. Said you put in a new alarm system in her place."

"Oh yeah." Ryan shook his glass. "It's a hobby of mine. I know a lot about alarm systems and locks. Always interested me."

"Well Debra was impressed," Steve said. "Said you did a great job and she's never felt so secure."

"I was uh…thinking of getting an alarm system."

"Since when, Bree?"

"Does it matter, Steve?"

"No just surprising that's all. You always said you didn't like alarm systems."

"Well uh…" She cleared her throat. "A woman can never be too safe can she?"

"She's right, Steve. A lot of things can happen to a woman living alone, cop or not. Tell you what, Bree. If you ever wanna talk about getting a system then let me know. I'd love to help you. I'd get you a good price."

"That's very sweet, Ryan."

"Well I'll see you guys." Ryan dissolved into the crowd.

"Cool guy if only he'd relax."

Brianna fidgeted. "I still don't see Juney."

"If she's not here we might have to try another time."

Brianna massaged her temples. "I can't take much more of this noise."

"Hey, Steve!" Tim, the bartender slid drinks to the end of the bar.

"Tim! Hey, man!" Steven and Brianna burrowed through the crowd at the bar.

"Steve what's happen' huh?" The men bumped fists. "Didn't expect to see you here. Oh and hello to you too, Detective Morris."

She tugged on her ears. "Hey, Tim."

"So what'cha two drinking? Sit down!"

Tim shooed men off the center stools.

"Anything you want is on the house."

"We'd love to take you up on the offer but I'm afraid we're here on official business, Tim."

He wiped off a glass. "Really? I don't like to hear that. The last time you guys came here on business something horrible happened to Cheyenne."

The officers exchanged glances.

"Oh no." Tim set the glass down. "What's happened now?"

"Why don't we talk over here huh?" Steven gestured to the other end of the bar.

Tim crossed his arms underneath his flabby chest. "What's going on, guys?"

"Cheyenne was beaten last night," Brianna said. "She almost died."

"What?" He slapped the hand towel over his shoulder. "I don't believe this."

Steven leaned in. "All we know is she was brought to the hospital by some guy. We don't know if Cheyenne knew him and we don't have any idea who he is."

"We were hoping maybe someone around here could tell us something."

"I sure as hell don't know anything. I can't believe this. Is she gonna be all right?"

"I don't know. She's in ICU and she's not looking too good."

"Yeah Bree and I were hoping you could tell us anything that's changed with Cheyenne lately. Like, someone she might have started hanging around or anything."

"I haven't seen Cheyenne in weeks. She doesn't work here anymore."

"What?" Brianna looked at both men. "She didn't tell me she'd gotten a new job."

"I don't know if she got a new job. She just said she didn't wanna work here anymore. You know she was fed up with this place."

"Why wouldn't she tell me?"

"Is that really a big deal, Bree?"

"Could be. It's strange for Cheyenne to just quit her job. And where the hell is she getting money from?"

"Maybe Juney can help you out." Tim pointed. "She's over there somewhere."

"Yeah thanks, Tim."

"No problem, Steve. I wish I knew more." Tim went back to the bar, shaking his head.

"Hey, Detective Morris! Detective Kemp!" A frail brunette perched a tray of drinks on her shoulder.

"Juney! Hey." Brianna hugged her.

"Hey, Juney." Steven kissed her cheek.

"Oh man this is a surprise." Juney chewed bubble gum. "It's a jungle in here tonight as I am sure you can see."

"*Can* we." Brianna fanned.

"Whoo it's hot!" Juney fanned her blouse. "Sweating like a pig in here. It's good to see you guys." She lowered the tray. "That is of course unless you're here on business."

"We need to talk to you, Juney," Steven said. "We need your help."

Juney handed her tray to another waitress and followed the detectives to the restroom area.

"What's going on? Something's happened hasn't it?"

Brianna exhaled. "Cheyenne was beaten last night."

"What?" Juney covered her mouth. "Oh no. No."

Steven held her. "She's in ICU at Central West. She's doing okay."

"Oh no." Juney buried her head in Steven's chest. "What the hell happened?"

"Tim told us she doesn't work her anymore."

"Yeah she quit her job a few weeks ago." She stared at Brianna. "You didn't know?"

"No she didn't tell me. I doubt she could find another job so fast so how is Cheyenne paying her bills if she's not working?"

"I don't know, Detective Morris. All she said was that no one needs to worry about her and that she finally has her life under control."

Steven pulled trash out his pants pocket. "What the hell does that mean?"

"She just said she's finally happy without any worries. I'm guessing it had something to do with this guy. Her new friend."

"New friend?" Brianna raised an eyebrow. "What new friend?"

"Some guy she met through Havana Horizons."

"The dating service?" Steven asked.

"Uh-huh."

Brianna sucked her lip. "Cheyenne used a dating service?"

"Something else she hadn't told you huh, Bree?"

"Juney what's this guy's name?"

"I don't know. She never told me. I haven't seen her much lately."

Steven watched a stripper come out the ladies' room. "So you never

33

met him?"

"No. I told her I had a strange feeling about this. Things she told me about this guy made me think he's kinda controlling you know?"

Brianna got her notepad. "Juney think okay? Did she ever tell you what he looked like? Anything that might help us?"

"Wait what does this have to do with Cheyenne being attacked?"

"That's what we're trying to find out," Steven said. "See a man dropped Cheyenne off at the hospital and didn't leave his name or anything. All we know is he's a tall white guy with a goatee and he wears Sean John sneakers."

"Sean John sneakers?"

"Yes does that ring a bell?" Brianna got her pen ready to write.

"I never met him and she never told me his name but she did say he was a white man and he had an accent."

Steven stooped in front of her. "What kind of accent?"

"British."

Brianna wrote the information. "And this is the same guy she met through Havana Horizons?"

"I assume so yes." Juney sighed into her palms. "Oh god I can't believe this has happened. I gotta get to the hospital."

"Wait." Steven grabbed her. "Think, is there anything else at all Cheyenne said about this man? Anything?"

She slithered from his hold. "She said he was always trying to buy her stuff. Jewelry and things like that. Said he offered to take her to Venice."

"Venice?" Brianna lowered the pad.

"Yeah. And from what Cheyenne says, he wasn't exactly hurting for money."

"Holy shit…Steve."

"Juney, hmmm!" Steven kissed her. "Thanks."

"Did I help?"

"Oh you bet." Brianna put the pad up. "You helped a *whole* lot."

◆◆◆◆◆◆

The man watched inside the Flamingo from the parking lot. He stretched against the building to see past the men that went in and out. Another group of guys strolled inside the bar. He spotted Brianna. His shaft tore at his zipper. No stripper in the world could compare to her fully clothed.

He gripped his crotch. "Mmm."

He rushed to his car. His vision blinded by lust and sweat. He yanked the door open, got inside and unzipped his pants. He shoved his hand in his underwear.

"Uhh *ahhh*." He came before he shut the door.

CHAPTER FOUR

A Week Later

Steven drove through the sophisticated homes of Madison Hills. The elite neighborhood housed some of Albany's most prominent residents from upper middle class to wealthy. A resident had to make at least ninety thousand just to rent in the area. Doctors, lawyers, politicians, executives, local celebrities and socialites made Madison Hills a gold mine.

Brianna wiggled in the passenger's seat admiring the perfectly trimmed yards, serene atmosphere, and the soaring town homes and mansions.

Thanks to Havana Horizons they'd gotten a list of men who could fit the so-called description of Cheyenne's new friend. So far their search led them to one hundred and fifty men. Now they were down to the last one. They'd gotten nowhere with the others. All of the men had solid alibis and no accents. They also hadn't heard of Cheyenne Wilson.

"There's your house, Bree."

They passed the Spanish-colonial mansion that had become Brianna's favorite. She'd fallen in love with the animal-shaped hedges and white iron fence.

"Well it must be nice huh?" She turned her head upside down to see the top of the house.

"Wonder how much they paid for that place."

"Shit, I missed the turn." He did a U-turn in a culdesac. "Uh-oh." Steven stuck his head out the window. "Security cameras all over the damn place. I bet you fart around here and they throw ya' in jail."

"Usually money doesn't mean much to me, you know that." Brianna searched the radio stations. "But a place like this makes a girl wonder what it's like to have a little extra change."

She sat back. "Know what I meant?"

"What the hell ya' talkin' bout, Bree? You're rich ya' damn self."

"I'm not rich."

"You are too rich." He laughed.

"My stepfather's rich." She waved at a little girl walking down the street with flowers.

"It's not the same thing."

"Your stepfather's rich, your momma's rich, you're rich. You ain't gotta bullshit about it, Bree."

"My stepfather was rich before he married momma. I'm not rich."

"Yes you are."

"No I'm not."

"You are too. Rich by association."

"I said I'm not rich." She punched him.

"Oww!" He stroked his arm. "Jesus I'm driving. What's your problem? Like being rich is a put down."

"Look I work hard for my money. I don't sponge off my stepfather. If I was rich would I be struggling to pay bills from month to month?"

Steven's shades slid off his head. "That's got nothing to do with you not being rich, that's you having fucked up credit."

"Shut up. I got great credit. My credit was good enough to co-sign for this heap of shit you call a car."

"Kiss my ass, Bree. And you love this heap of shit car."

"Yeah you wish. Steve your credit's so bad you couldn't even get Internet service in your own name."

"Whatever."

"Now that's fucked up credit."

He squinted at the orange street signs. "What's the name of the street again?"

"Perri View."

"This is it." He made a left. "What's the address?"

"Thirty fifteen."

"Thirty fifteen?"

"Yeah see it? The one by the brick house."

Steven cruised in the middle of the street. "The white one?"

"Yep."

A sculptured yard and pebble walkway offset the deluxe two-story. Elegant patio furniture sat in a circle on the front porch.

They parked behind the black Mercedes parked crooked in the driveway.

"Whoo wee, Bree." Steven turned the car off. "Look at that Mercedes. Man she's sweet."

"Maybe we should park on the street."

"I'm not parking on the damn street for someone to steal my car."

"Uh judging by the look of the cars in this neighborhood Steve I think yours is the last to worry about."

"Well let's hope Michael cooperates." Steven closed his door and followed Brianna up the walkway.

"Think he might be Cheyenne's friend?"

"Let's hope because we've run out of options."

Brianna rang the doorbell. Steven stood so close he could have inhaled her.

"Mmm." He propped his hand on the door.

"What?"

"Nothing you just smell so good."

"Steve." She looked down.

"What? Is it my fault you smell good?"

"Stop looking at me like that."

"Like what?"

"You know like what." She fondled her ponytail. "Get your mind on what's important."

He swept his arm behind her back. "Believe me it is."

"Stop it." She knocked his hand down. She checked the peephole. "Shit what's taking him so long?"

"Maybe he ain't here."

Brianna rang the doorbell again.

"Maybe he can't hear the bell." Steven banged on the door. "Michael Buchanan are you in there? It's the police! We need to ask you some questions!" He knocked again. "Michael!"

"Arf! Arf! Arf!" A black Chihuahua flew from around the house and landed at Brianna's feet.

"Aww, Steven look. " She scooped him up. "Hey, baby. Isn't he cute?"

Steven hooked his shades on his shirt. "If that's Michael's dog he's gay."

"What?" Brianna bounced the dog.

"No straight man would have a dog that little."

"You don't know anything."

"I know about the rules of being a man." He knocked. "Michael! I know he's in there."

"Wait back up." The dog licked Brianna's face. "The rules of being a man?"

"Yep there are rules every straight man follows. That's how you know he's straight."

"Steven I would say that's the dumbest thing you've ever said but I know you're gonna start talking again so I won't."

"Look straight men don't buy little dogs and they don't buy cats. A surefire sign they're gay." He kicked the door. "Michael Buchanan!"

"So Michael's gay?"

"If that's his dog he is."

Steven fell back when the door opened.

A tall man walked onto the stoop. He was shirtless and his slacks sagged off his slim waist.

"I assure you I'm not gay."

His short brunette hair held the trend of the '60s with a modern twist. Long sideburns with bangs that hid his eyebrows. Every strand submerged in mousse. He presented a cunning grin that probably hid and betrayed his secrets at the same time.

His goatee couldn't have been neater if it had been painted on. Faint wrinkles appeared under his nose every time he blinked.

His firm body wore small signs of maturity but his youthful face stood still in time. Eyes so gray they turned silver in the sunlight. He wore a diamond stud in his right ear.

He slid a paint-stained towel in and out his long fingers. His stare sent a deadening chill down Brianna's spine.

That and of course his British accent.

"Well hello there." Michael swung the towel, drawing attention to the black charcoal on his fingers. "What can I do for you?"

"Bree he's British." Steven whispered.

"No shit."

"Aye?" Michael scratched his six-pack stomach, leaving a trail of blackness on his bellybutton.

"You are Michael Buchanan right?" Brianna kept her distance.

"Why yes I am." A tiny dimple poked from his chin. "And you are?"

They introduced themselves and flashed their badges. Michael put his hand over Brianna's as he overlooked the information. She got the feeling he used it as an excuse to touch her.

"Detective Morris huh?"

He made that sucking sound with his teeth that all men seemed to when they met a woman they found attractive. This didn't feel right. Brianna had the instinct to turn around and run but couldn't risk it. Michael, bizarre or not might be the one who could shed light on Cheyenne's attack. If he didn't know anything Brianna would be more than happy to leave and never come back. But if he did...

"You like my dog?"

"What?" Brianna exhaled.

Michael wiggled the dog's paw. "He seems to like you a lot. I knew he had good taste."

"Yeah well uh, here you go." She held the dog out to Michael.

"Oh no, you can hold him. Believe me I don't mind at all."

Brianna secured the tiny pile of black fur in her arms. "He got a name?"

"Coal." Michael's eyes leapt from her face to the line leading to her cleavage.

She stood back.

"I named him that because he's so black."

"Oh."

"You can hold him as long as you want, Brianna. He loves being in the arms of a lovely woman."

"Is that right?" Steven asked.

Brianna had forgotten Steven was there until he spoke.

"Of course. Don't most men?"

"Whatever." Steven gestured inside the house. "We need to ask you some questions about a case we're investigating. We'd appreciate your cooperation."

Michael's eyes stayed on Brianna. "Am I under suspicion or something?"

Brianna transferred Coal to her other hand. "Why would you think that? Should we be suspicious of you?"

"Well no but usually when cops show up on your door it's not because they want to exchange recipes." He widened the door. "Come on in. I hope I can help you."

"Thanks." Steven went in first.

Michael stood so close to Brianna when she walked in she had to touch his chest to keep her balance.

"Excuse me, Mr. Buchanan."

"Hmm." He sniffed her hair. "You smell good, Detective."

"What?"

"You smell like peaches."

Steven rubbed the inside of his palms.

"That's not a very appropriate thing to say, Mr. Buchanan. This is a very serious visit."

"Call me by my first name." He sandwiched her between the wall and his chest.

"Mr. Buchanan, please move."

He did but acted as though he didn't want to.

"I'm confused, Brianna. Is it against the law for an officer to be complimented?"

"No. I'm just not used to men smelling me."

Steven chuckled. "Got an interesting place here." He scoped out the lavender furniture set in the den.

Michael's home wasn't dripping in fine paintings and antiques like Brianna pictured. His den looked like an upgraded college dorm room.

Steven came back into the hall. "You got a fetish for purple or something, man?"

"Got many fetishes." Michael's stare hit Brianna's face again. "Purple just happens to be my favorite color."

"It's Bree's too."

"Oh is it?"

"It's one of my favorite colors."

"So we have something in common?" Michael leaned into her. "Wonder if we have anything else in common."

"I hope I don't have to tell you again, Mr. Buchanan." She stepped back. "Please stay out of my personal space."

"I'm sorry. I meant no harm. I wonder what else we like that's the same."

CHAPTER FIVE

"Shit, man." Steven picked up a miniature crystal statue of a naked woman. She bent over with her gigantic breasts hanging down her knees. "Now this is the kind of stuff that makes a guy appreciate art."

"I'm sure it does, Steve."

"Ah." Michael got the statue. "You like it, Detective Kemp?"

"You see the front of my pants? I *love* it."

"I got that from Mia's." Michael put it on the shelf.

"That's that place that sells erotic art isn't it?"

"Why yes it is, Brianna." Michael's eyes widened.

"Should've known Bree would know. She loves art."

"Oh really?" Michael crowded her again.

"Steven." Brianna stood against the wall.

"So we do have something else in common huh?"

"I don't shop there I just know about it. What would I want erotic art for?"

"Oh to appreciate it of course. Art is art isn't it?"

"That's not my kind of art, Michael. Sorry."

Steven grinned. "I think I'll give this Mia's a try after work."

"Please, Steve. You couldn't afford to park there. It's for rich people."

Steven raised his head. He wore an expression Brianna couldn't decipher.

And she knew *all* his expressions.

"Well, well." He sniffed. "You had a woman here earlier, Michael?"

"Why you say that, Detective Kemp?"

"Come on, we're all adults. Bree I know you smell it too."

"I don't." Course she'd smelled it and it got louder each second.

Michael took a deep whiff. "You trying to say my house smells like pussy, Detective Kemp?"

"Ha, ha, ha, ha!"

"Jesus." Brianna sighed. "Steven, shut up!"

"God well I wasn't trying to say it out loud, man. Ha, ha! But yes. That's what it smells like."

"Sorry if this uh, embarrasses you, Michael."

"I'm not embarrassed, Brianna. We're all adults aren't we? We all know what women smell like."

Brianna stroked Coal. "Can we just get to the reason we came?"

"I had a female over earlier and we made love."

"Whoa." Steven sucked in laughter.

"Look that's too much information, Mr. Buchanan."

"Does this offend you, Brianna? Speaking so openly about a woman's natural smell?"

"Look…"

"It's natural isn't it? Women smell and that smell gets more intense during lovemaking."

"Holy shit!" Steven leaned over, holding his stomach. "Michael I mean it when I say this is the most fun I've *ever* had questioning someone."

Brianna walked towards the stairwell. Michael's gaze reached her destination before she did.

"You don't have any servants or anything?"

"No. I value my privacy."

She turned from his stare. "Are you an artist?"

"Yes I am."

"Is that how you got your money? Are was it inherited?"

"Guess you can say it was inherited by someone very close to me."

"What part of England are you from?"

"That's funny." Michael scratched the back of his neck. "See I'm really American but I lived abroad for a long time. That's the reason for the accent."

"Ah I see." Brianna took the opportunity to observe *him*. "Interesting."

"Okay since we all know one another let's get to the point," Steven said. "Do you know a woman named Cheyenne Wilson?"

"Cheyenne? That's a pretty name but no I don't. Why?"

"She was almost beaten to death a week ago. Wednesday, April twelfth."

"Oh my goodness."

Brianna showed him Cheyenne's picture.

"Well she is a beautiful woman but I don't know her. How did this lead to me?"

"She has been seeing a man she met on Havana Horizons, the dating service. We got your name off a list from there. We were told this man also had an accent and imagine our surprise when you did."

"Detective Kemp I understand that but I swear I've never heard of Cheyenne Wilson."

"Hmm." Brianna snuggled Coal. "Did you ever meet any women from Havana Horizons?"

"Look I didn't even wanna join the damn thing to be honest. A friend of mine suggested it." He swatted his towel. "Said it would help me settle down and not be so wild you know?"

"Uh-huh." Steven nodded.

"But I like being wild. Anyway, I never met anyone from Havana. I didn't participate that long. I talked to some women online but it never went further."

"Why not?"

He smiled at Brianna. "They weren't my type."

"And what's your type?"

He threw his arms behind his back. "It's, hard to explain, Brianna."

"I'm listening."

"Let's just say the women on Havana were a little too ordinary for my taste."

"And what does that mean exactly?"

He moved closer. "I'd probably have to show you for you to understand."

"Back it up, Michael." Steven got in front of him.

"Sorry. I meant no harm. She just smells so good you know?"

"Yeah we've established that," Steven said. "Stick to business."

"I could get lost in that smell."

Brianna put Coal down. He scampered to the den.

"Okay the ladies just weren't my type. Can we leave it at that?"

"You're a weirdo or something?"

"I don't consider myself one, Detective Kemp. What others might think, well I can't control that."

Brianna got her pencil. "Where were you the night of the twelfth if you don't mind me asking."

Michael scratched his arm. "At a restaurant. I'm sure. I eat out a lot."

Steven put his hand on the railing of the stairs. "What restaurant?"

"Well, honestly I don't remember."

"You don't remember?" Brianna chuckled. "How can you not remember when it was just a week ago?"

"I lead a busy life. I pick up something to eat or go to a restaurant all the time. I don't always remember where I am every night." He twirled his finger. "Maybe my brain's warped from sniffing all this paint and stuff. I have my head buried in a canvas all the time. I live in my own world."

Brianna paced. "Well think, Michael. I mean do you have a place you regularly eat at? Maybe that's where you were."

"I don't remember."

"Michael that doesn't seem to make any sense," Steven said. "I don't eat out as much as you probably but I can remember where I ate. Can't you break it down to a favorite restaurant or something?"

"No." He groaned. "I cannot and I don't know why you're asking me. I told you where I was. I was eating."

"Not all night though right?" Brianna played with her fingers. "What did you do after that?"

"I came home."

Steven perched his shades on his head. "And what did you do when you came home?"

"I...look I came home and probably watched a movie and went to sleep. I was tired that night."

"Oh you were?" Brianna looked at Steven. "You can remember that you were tired but you can't remember where you ate that night?"

He exhaled. "I'm always tired after I eat, Brianna."

"I see."

"Look I never heard of Cheyenne Wilson and I don't have anything to do with her attack."

"Well..." Brianna touched her chest. "Did we say that? Steven, did we say that?"

"No I can't remember us saying that."

A crooked smile tore through Michael's lips. "You like this don't you, Brianna?"

"What are you talking about?"

"Playing games. You're playing with me and you like it."

"Michael this is serious."

"Oh I know. I'm serious too. I don't know Cheyenne Wilson. I cross my heart and hope to die."

Being in Michael's presence alone made Brianna wanna throw up. But she wouldn't let anxiety stop her from getting the answers she needed. Michael had lied with such ease it scared her. In fact she doubted everything he'd said before he opened his mouth.

If he wanted to play games, they'd play.

"Uh Steven can I speak to Michael alone please?"

"What? What the hell you talkin' 'bout, Bree?"

Michael licked his lips.

"Can you just wait for me in the car?"

"Why? What's going on?"

She shoved Steven to the front door. "This guy's pulling my chain so I'm gonna pull his."

"What?"

"Shh. Just go wait for me outside. I think I can get more out of him if you're not here."

"Bree he might be lying or he might not but he's obviously not gonna tell us anything."

She opened the door. "I know what I'm doing. He's playing with me. I'm gonna play with his ass too."

"But…"

"Please wait for me in the car."

"What are you gonna do, fuck him?"

"Go wait in the car." She pushed him outside.

"Shit Bree we don't have time for this."

"I'll be out in a minute." She closed the door.

"Is Bree your nickname?"

"Yeah."

"Hmm." He pursed his lips. "Well I'm flattered you wanna talk to me but I don't know how else I can help you."

"I think you might be able to."

Ring! Ring!

Even the phone didn't interrupt Michael's stare.

"You gonna get that?"

"Huh?"

"Your phone's ringing, Michael."

Ring! Ring!

"Oh is it? Just a second." He went to the den.

Brianna checked out the kitchen and living room. Michael's phone conversation had become quite heated when she got back to the hall. Since it didn't seem like he'd be done soon she took the chance to look around upstairs.

Nothing stood out. You could hardly tell Michael had money by his home. Brianna had more antiques than he did.

She walked down the hall, peeking inside the darkened doorways. She came to the room in the middle of the hall with the door parted open. The red walls beckoned her. She put her hands on the door and listened for Michael. He still spoke on the phone downstairs.

She might have been better off listening in on his conversation but something told her to go into this room.

She'd walked into the pit of perversion. Red velvet had been stapled to every inch of the walls, hiding their natural color. The carpet had been torn away, exposing a scuffed up floor. Whips and chains dangled from hooks. Satin material, probably blindfolds were folded on the dresser. Hats, gloves and kneepads with assorted spikes were piled in front of a box fan. Brianna got the feeling that fan wasn't there just for cooling off the room.

"Jesus Christ." She turned in circles but couldn't absorb the madness to save her life.

The room was bare except for the dresser and the wide table in the middle of the room.

Spiked chokers and wooden paddles of assorted sizes were strewn over the table. Rows of thick belts were hung on the walls by nails.

And that smell. A sour, indisputable stank of sweat and musk. She became engulfed in body heat as if she stood in a room of a hundred people.

She covered her nose with her blouse but she now wore the scent.

Explicit cartoons and pictures of naked women and men in various, painful positions were all over the walls. Women had gags in their mouths while the men whipped them with cattle prods and posts.

Over to the side was a wrinkled picture of a woman with enormous breasts, tied to a table and being beaten by several men and women. The caption, "More!" sat between her spread legs.

"See anything you like?"

"Ahh!" Brianna whisked around.

Michael didn't move or smile. Just stared with that same keen expression.

He closed the door.

CHAPTER SIX

"M...move."

He kept his place. "What's your hurry?"

"Move, Michael. I'm not playing with you."

"What's the problem? You came up here on your own."

"I said move. That's an order."

"You're no stranger to giving orders are you, Bree? I knew that immediately."

"Don't call me that." She reached for the door. "Get out of my way."

"But you said you wanted to talk to me didn't you?"

"You think this is funny and cute?"

"What do you think about my room?"

"I..."

He stepped up to her. "Wondered where the bed is didn't you?"

"No I..."

"It's down the hall. I moved it out recently. It was..." He gazed at her chest.

"In the way."

"I *want* you to get out of my way right now. If you don't I'll arrest you."

"You can't arrest me. If anyone is going to be in trouble it's you for snooping. You can't come in here and look around without a warrant."

"I wasn't snooping."

"Yes you were. You thought you'd find something that tied me to Cheyenne Wilson didn't you?"

"And maybe I have." She pointed to the walls. "Looks like you got a taste for violence, Michael. I wouldn't be surprised if the person who attacked Cheyenne did too."

"I don't hurt women."

"Oh right." She chuckled. "Only when they want you to right?"

"What are you so afraid of, Brianna? Yourself?"

"Get outta my way."

"You're a Domme aren't you?"

"Excuse me?"

"A domme. You like to be in control don't you?"

"Move damn it!"

She grabbed the doorknob. His hand stopped her from twisting it. "Move!"

"I didn't do anything to Cheyenne Wilson."

"Oh really? Judging by your attitude and this room I find that pretty hard to believe."

"I'm telling the truth."

She put her hand on her gun. "I'm giving you one more chance to get outta my way."

"Your gun?" He raised his hands, chuckling. "Do I intimidate you that much?"

"Move. I won't tell you again."

He opened the door. "I think we have a lot in common, Brianna."

"Go to hell."

"You smell so good." He followed her downstairs. "What's that perfume?"

"Don't play with me, Michael." She yanked the front door open. "You understand me?"

She stomped down the driveway.

"Oh yeah I understand just fine!" Michael stood on the stoop. "Hey, Bree? If you need anything, anything at all you make sure you let me know!"

◆◆◆◆◆◆

Simon Watts stared up at a bundle of odd-shaped stars from his terrace. The humid breeze swept his long brown hair across his back. Moonlight covered the sky like a sparkling sheet. He treasured the burning sip of Cognac. Not much else soothed his anguish these days.

"Simon?"

He drowned in the breath of the woman behind him. Her fingers felt light as cotton on his face.

"Tell me your thoughts." She stroked his goatee.

"You really want to know?" His British accent shaded his words.

"Yes."

"Really? I thought you already knew everything before I told you." He slurped liquor.

"Don't you?"

"Don't be angry. I only wanna protect you." Her hands clenched his waist.

"It has to stop, Clara."

"It'll never stop. We're one." She laid her head on his back. *"I hate it when you're upset with me. I never want you to be upset."*

"Then why do you do it, Clara? Why do you continue to hurt people?"

"We both know I do it all for you."

"You promised me that after Olivia Delcie you wouldn't hurt anyone else."

"Olivia Delcie was trouble. No woman will ever care about you the way I do."

"Ahh!" He threw the glass over the terrace. "Don't use me as the reason, Clara. You do these horrible things because you want to. No one forces you to."

The bottom of her white dress cascaded in the darkness.

"Do you love me, Simon?"

"Do you love *me*?"

"After all I do for you, you have to ask that? What's it gonna take for you to believe it?"

"I can't do this anymore. Cheyenne was the last straw."

"I had to get my point across didn't I? What's the big deal? She's just one woman like all the others."

"No she's different damn it." He sat in the chair in the corner. "She doesn't care about my money, just me."

"Load of shite Simon, the money's what they all care about."

"It's the truth." He sobbed. "She was the light behind the tunnel. Someone I could spend time with and just talk to. She needed that too."

Clara knelt in front of him. *"And what the hell am I then?"*

"I keep telling you no one will ever take your place in my heart. If you love me then you'll stop it, Clara." He cried into his arm. "You'll

51

stop being so jealous and hateful."

"Stop loving you?" Her blond hair blew against her face. *"I can't do that, Simon."*

He raised his head. "I'll stop you myself if I have to."

"Oh don't threaten me." She stood. *"You're nothing without me, Simon. Look how pathetic your life would be."*

"I mean it this time. I'll stop you before you hurt someone else."

"Oh what are you gonna do, Simon?"

"Anything I have to."

"Don't you dare threaten me. I run the show, not you."

"Not anymore. I'm taking control over my life again. Cheyenne is the last time you're gonna hurt someone."

"Oh really? Ha, ha, ha!" She held up her dress and twirled. *"You wanna blame me for hurting those women? Wanna blame me for you being fucked in the head?"*

"Shut your mouth!"

"Let me tell you something and don't you forget it. If you wanna act high and mighty and play Romeo to damsels in distress be my guest, Simon. But don't you dare put the blame on me."

"What?"

"You heard me. Want someone to blame for all this? Why don't you go look in the mirror? We both know the face you'll see is where the blame really belongs."

♦♦♦♦♦♦

A Week Later

Brianna waited at the front counter of Jayson's restaurant. It wasn't as crowded as usual during lunch. Ten people occupied the side booths. A decrepit Asian man wearing flooding slacks and a faded cardigan sucked soup at the center table. Sign of the times. Before the economy collapsed there'd be so many people in here you couldn't see the carpet.

Brianna inhaled from the base of her stomach.

Ooh wee. All she could think about was planting her ass at a table and devouring those chicken enchiladas she loved so much.

Damn Cheyenne's case right now.

She licked the roof of her mouth. See this is why Jayson's would always be her favorite restaurant. They used three different varieties of cheeses on those damn enchiladas and she could mentally taste every one of them.

"How are you, ma'am?" A waiter walked by with food spilling off the tray.

Oh no. He had a bowl of another of her favorites; pickled tomato wedges. Oh god. She'd kill for one of those heavenly slices. Just to taste the salt of the seasoned tomatoes rounded out by the sour sauce. If she dared to indulge her feverish appetite, she'd throw in a bowl of that long-grain Cajun rice too. Shoot Jayson's lemonade alone could drive her to multiple orgasms.

"Detective Morris?"

A short brunette in a brown pants suit ran up with her arm ejected.

"Yes I'm Detective Brianna Morris. You called the station for me?"

"Yes I did." She shook Brianna's hand. "I'm Ms. Tyne, the assistant manager. I'm glad you weren't too busy to shoot by. I can imagine how it is being a cop and all."

"Believe me nothing would deter me from coming here if you know something about Cheyenne that could help."

The food didn't hurt either.

"Uh, we can talk back here."

They squeezed through the busy bodies in the kitchen. Ran up the corner stairs by the employees' restroom and ended up in a musty room with packages of paper stacked everywhere. A table with a Dell computer and HP printer stood by the grubby window. A fax machine with an "out of order" sign had been shoved in the corner.

Dust flew up wherever Brianna stepped.

"Sorry for the mess. This is where we do all our business." Tyne moved boxes to get to the trapped chair behind the table. "Please sit down, Detective."

"No that's okay." Brianna sneezed. "Ooh excuse me."

"I am so sorry about the dust." Tyne opened the window. "It's hard to keep this room clean with so many folks in and out you know?"

"Yeah I...ahh choo!" Brianna took out Kleenex. "Oh." She rubbed her nose.

"I'm sorry. If you have allergies we can go into the hall."

"If I didn't have allergies before, I sure would now."

"I'm sorry."

"No it's okay." Brianna parted her mouth, feeling another sneeze coming on.

"False alarm."

Tyne smiled.

Brianna grabbed for her notepad while fumbling with tissues.

"Okay uh. What...oh goodness. Ahh choo! Man."

"You sure you don't wanna go outside?"

"I'm fine." Brianna sniffled. "I think if I stood by the window it would help. Ahh choo!" She slid on a loose piece of paper. "Oooh shit!" She held onto the table.

"Detective, you all right?" Tyne helped her.

"Yeah."

"God this place is a mess." Tyne threw the sheet away. "It's a lawsuit waiting to happen if you'd hit your head on that table."

"You ain't lyin' there." Brianna took the top off her pen with her teeth. "And I sure as hell would've sued."

Tyne grinned.

Brianna sat on the windowsill and rested her foot on the table.

"What did you wanna tell me?"

"Well I've been outta town for two weeks. My mother died."

"Oh I'm sorry to hear that. I'll keep you in my prayers."

"Thank you. Anyway, I just got back last night and I saw Cheyenne's story in the paper. I recognized her picture immediately."

CHAPTER SEVEN

"You did?"

"Yes. I remember the last time she came in, there was a problem with her order."

"Uh-huh."

"And I had to help her and her date get things straight. They'd been overcharged or something. Well, she stuck in my head and I couldn't believe that was the same young woman who was attacked."

"Yes?"

"Well, the man she came in with that night fits the description of the man they described in the paper. Uh, it sounded like this could be the guy you're looking for."

Brianna dropped her foot.

"Uh, the man was very good-looking. He was white, tall and he had a goatee."

Brianna's mouth dropped.

"Had funny-colored eyes. They could have been green or some kind of clear, or gray."

"Gray?"

"Yeah and uh, he had on a designer suit, very expensive looking. Uh..." Tyne looked at the ceiling. "A very expensive looking watch. Might have been a Rolex."

"Wait a minute."

"And uh, he had an accent."

Brianna moved from the window.

"A British accent just like the description of the man you guys are looking for."

"Wait a minute here. Hold on. Are you sure about all this?"

"I'm positive. He was very polite and kind. Very gentlemanly like old-fashioned you know? He ordered for her. He held her chair for her and he even offered to pay for her. They kinda got in a little argument. Ms. Wilson didn't seem to want him to pay but I guess she gave in."

"Hold on okay?" Brianna dug in her pockets. "I want you to look at this picture and tell me if this is the guy you remember with Cheyenne okay?"

"Okay." Tyne clasped her hands.

Brianna showed her Michael's picture from his Havana Horizons profile.

"Now Ms. Tyne, is this the man you saw with Cheyenne?"

"Umm."

"Concentrate. Does it resemble him at all?"

"Definitely a resemblance."

Brianna exhaled. "You sure?"

"Well yeah but the hair."

"What about it?"

"Well the man who was with Cheyenne had long hair. It went down his back. All the women were swooning over his hair. I'd never forget it."

"But could this be the same guy with a haircut?"

"Uh…" Tyne studied the photo. "Yes I think it could be."

Brianna looked up and mouthed, "Thank you."

"I mean it's the same color eyes, same color hair, goatee and earring. I mean he looks different because he has short hair in this picture but I think that's the man." Tyne gave Brianna the picture.

"Oh Ms. Tyne you don't know how much I wanna kiss you right now."

"Uh." She raised her hand. "That won't be necessary, Detective."

"Can you remember about when they came in?"

"Oh that was probably about the last of March or probably the first week of April. Had to be around that time."

"Cheyenne was attacked on April twelfth, a Wednesday night."

"No it was before then, at least a week. Also I don't come in on Wednesdays. I only work weekends, Tuesdays and Fridays."

"Michael." Brianna squeezed the photo. "I knew it."

Ring! Ring!

Tyne patted her sides. "Is that me or you?"

"It's me." Brianna answered her cell. "Steve, I got some big news! It's about Michael."

"What a coincidence because I got some news about our friend Mike too."

"What are you talking about?"

"Just got off the phone with Janet from the hospital."

"You mean your admirer."

"Whatever, anyway she said Michael was just at the hospital. He just left a few minutes ago."

"What?"

"Yep and get this, he was visiting Cheyenne. Brought her some flowers and everything."

"Wait is Janet sure this was Michael?"

"She remembered how he looked from when we showed her his profile picture last week. Said it was definitely him today and now that she saw him again up close, she's sure he was the man who brought Cheyenne in when she was attacked. She said it was him down to the British accent."

"Yes!" She jumped.

Tyne scooted to the wall.

"I told ya', Steve. I knew Michael was involved."

"Let's not get too excited but I'd love to see what Michael has to say about being at the hospital."

◆◆◆◆◆◆

Brianna's stomach flip-flopped during the ride to Michael's. She'd spent her career studying and catching criminals. Interrogated some of the city's most vile offenders.

She studied a suspect's thoughts and actions. Channeled the truth underneath the bullshit. She recognized details others didn't think to look for. She listened to the tone of the voice instead of just the words they spoke.

She watched and took in everything they said or did.

Minus the gun and badge she was still a woman. She wasn't immune to the type of fear that would make any sane woman wanna run and hide or second-guess becoming a cop in the first place.

She'd sat alone in rooms with men who'd mutilated and raped. Rode in the car with psychopaths who'd converted their basements to sex chambers. Chatted for hours with sadists who spoke of how good it felt to inflict sodomy and torture on children and women they'd been trusted to care for and love.

Yet out of all the twisted and intimidating bastards she'd encountered over the years, not one set her on edge or produced the multitude of anxiety inside her that Michael Buchanan did.

Well except for the stalker.

Brianna lost breath when they got to Michael's door.

Steven knocked. "You okay?"

"Huh?" She stared at the maroon mat on the porch.

"Yeah I'm…"

"Hey." Steven held her hand. "You're shaking."

"Am I?"

"Oh come on, Bree. Can't you be honest with me? I know you better than anyone."

"I don't know what you mean." She rang the doorbell.

Why did it always take Michael so long to get to the door?

"Bullshit you know. You been jittery for weeks and now you look like you're gonna split in two."

"I'm fine. Let's just get this over with."

"Did something happen the last time we were here? When you sent me outside?"

"No."

"You been acting strange for weeks anyway, but you really started acting funny after you were alone with Michael."

"I'm fine for the last fuckin' time." She banged on the door. "Michael it's Morris and Kemp! We know you're in there!"

"I ain't letting this go, Bree. What's up with you?"

"He gives me the creeps okay? You happy?"

"And why does he give you the creeps?"

"Gee I don't know. Maybe it's because he's a fuckin' weirdo."

"Okay I'll buy that about Michael but that doesn't explain why you've been acting funny from the beginning."

"It's nothing okay, Steve?"

"You know you can come to me with anything."

"Oh fuck this!" She started back to the car.

"Bree get back here. What the hell's the matter with you?" He pulled her back. "Wait!"

"Just get off my back, Steve! I got enough shit to deal with. I don't need to put up with these stupid questions from you too."

"Well fuck you then." He let her go. "Go fuckin' crazy. I don't care."

"I didn't ask you to care did I?"

"No and from now on I won't!"

"Fine!"

"Fine!"

Michael popped out. His fingertips once again stained with charcoal.

"Let me guess. Lovers quarrel?"

Steven took his shades off. "Why does it always take you so fuckin' long to answer the door?"

"I'm sorry, I was drawing." He leaned to see Brianna. "When I'm focused on art I'm in my own world. How are you today, Brianna?"

She rocked with her arms crossed. "Been better."

"Oh really? Something I can do?"

"Why don't you start by cutting the bullshit?" Steven wiped the lenses of his shades.

"Neither of us are in the mood for your shit today."

"Whoa. Have I done something, Detective Kemp?"

"Let us in and we'll tell you."

"Come on in. I was just working on my latest masterpiece." His eyes stayed on Brianna.

Steven peeked into the den. "I don't see nothing in there."

"No I do all my drawing in the kitchen."

"What the hell for?"

"Has the best lightening and I don't know, just like the atmosphere." Michael gestured down the hall. "I'm glad you two showed up."

"Are you really?" Brianna followed the men.

"Yeah I'd love to get your opinions on my work."

"Good luck 'cause I know shit about art." Steven went into the kitchen. "Whoa look at the size of this place. You could fit my whole living room in here."

Michael blocked Brianna with his shoulder.

"You still smell good."

If any room echoed its owner's personality it was this kitchen. The lavender walls reminded Brianna of his chic style while the shiny black tile floor displayed an eerie tone that was Michael a million times over. He'd covered the kitchen table with a plastic sheet.

He offered them some fancy tea that smelled like pinecones and apples.

They declined. The charcoal drawing on the easel stole their attention.

"So?" Michael straightened the easel. "What do you think? Be honest."

Brianna loved art to the point where she'd taken classes just to get inside the head of artists. She'd drooled over the work of mesmerizing artists like Georges Braque and Georgia O'Keeffe.

But she hadn't seen a portrait as enchanting as this.

The structured precision and detail proved how much Michael paid attention to the naked female form. Not only had he captured the flaws of this woman's body he beautified them.

There wasn't a face. The silhouette began after the neck. She bent over in a seductive pose. The masterful strokes heightened the undeniable sleekness in her chest and the lopsided sway of her breast. Forced your eyes on that succulent dip that started above her hips, went down her thighs and curved to the front of her crotch.

Brianna's nipples tore at the confining satin of her bra.

Michael's skill as a lover showed through his art. He'd made love to this woman. Only a portrait from an artist who'd navigated his way around his subject's body could affect innocent eyes this way.

His zeal for sex and women oozed from every line of charcoal.

And he seemed damn proud of it.

CHAPTER EIGHT

"Wow." Steven wiped sweat off his neck. "I think I came."

"Well I'll take that as a compliment, Detective Kemp." Michael traced the drawing with his finger. "And what do you think, Brianna?"

"It's beautiful." It would have been easier swallowing nails than admitting she found him talented.

"Is that it? You get anything else from it?"

"I'm guessing this is a woman you've been intimate with. Am I right?"

"Touché'." He titled his head. "And how did you know that?"

She touched the easel. "By the attention you've paid to her body. How you drew it. Something tells me you might even be in love with her."

He cleared his throat.

"Reminds me of Georges Braque. He's one of my favorite artists."

"Really?" Michael moved closer to her.

"Yes." She backed up.

"Well it just so happens that Braque is one of my favorite artists too. So I guess I was right before huh? We do have things in common."

She shrugged.

"What's your favorite portrait of Braque's?"

"Why? So you can say you like the same one too?"

Michael bumped Steven with his elbow. "She's very sly isn't she? Loves to play games hmm?"

"Would you stop talking about me like I'm not in the room, Michael?"

"Well come on then. Tell me what's your favorite portrait of Braque's."

She sighed. "*Fruitdish and Glass* and *Woman with a Guitar*."

"You're kidding? *Woman with a Guitar*?"

"Yes."

"That is my absolute favorite portrait."

"Right." She rolled her eyes. "Why doesn't that surprise me?"

"No I mean it, it is. I love Braque's work and that painting is what brought my passion for art."

"I think you're just trying to impress me."

He leaned into her. "Is it working?"

"Uh, hello." Steven whistled. "Can we get to the reason we're here?"

"Sorry, Detective Kemp. But Brianna I am telling the truth. That is my favorite portrait."

"Let's just get to what Steven and I came for."

Michael sat on the end of the table. "Are you angry with me, Brianna?"

"No." Her jaws filled with air.

"Hmm, looks like it."

"Yoo hoo," Steven said. "Am I missing something here?"

"No I think it's a misunderstanding between us." Michael put the easel by the fridge.

"I think I offended Brianna the last time we were alone."

"Oh really? Is that true, Bree?"

"You did a little more than offend, Michael."

"What did he do?"

"He trapped me and wouldn't let me leave."

"What?"

"Oh, Brianna." Michael swung the towel. "That's not exactly the truth."

"The hell it isn't. He's a pervert, Steve."

"I'm not a pervert."

"Whoa, whoa, hang on. What the hell really happened between you two?"

"Well Brianna decided to take a fieldtrip into my bedroom."

"You were in his bedroom?"

"It's not how he's making it sound. I didn't believe a word he said and I wanted to look around."

"In his bedroom?"

"Yeah in my bedroom? Why in the world would you think there would be something in my bedroom?"

"Uh Bree I think you need to explain."

She stood beside Steve. "Why are you acting like you're accusing me of something?"

"You had no right in his bedroom, Bree. Besides we didn't have any kind of warrant."

"She was curious."

"I was not." She turned toward Michael. "I went in there because I knew you were lying then about Cheyenne, and I know you're lying now!"

"Wait, is this why you were so wound up when you came back out?" Steven sat on the table and dangled his leg. "Something you saw bothered you?"

"Not as much as the way Michael was acting. He wouldn't let me outta the damn room."

Steven glared at him.

"That's not true, Detective Kemp."

"The hell it's not. He's sick. He's into that rough sex. You know BDSM."

Michael felt the bridge of his nose. "I'm not sick and I don't have to explain my hobbies to anyone."

"Hobbies?" Brianna laughed. "Hobbies? I think they're a little more than hobbies, Michael. Steven he's got all types of shit in there. Uh, whips and chains. Spikes, blindfolds and all these disgusting pictures."

"You had no business in his bedroom, Bree."

"Steve?"

"You had no right sneaking into his things. You could've gotten us into a lot of shit by doing that. You wanna help Cheyenne, then don't jeopardize getting us banned from this case."

She rocked from side to side. "If I hadn't gone into that bedroom, I wouldn't have learned what I have. What I saw speaks way louder than words."

"Brianna can I ask you a question? If you were so offended by what you saw in my bedroom why didn't you leave?"

"I *tried* to."

Michael massaged his hand. "You had to be there at least five minutes before I got off the phone. If it all disgusted you so much, why did you stay in there?"

"This isn't about me, Michael."

"She's right." Steven hopped off the table. "And this is getting way off track. I don't care what the hell you do in your spare time and who with, Buchanan. I only care about Cheyenne. Which finally brings us to why Bree and I are here."

"Shoot."

"You lied about not knowing Cheyenne," Brianna said. "Course I knew you had anyway. Now I know for sure."

"What's she talking about?"

"Well where should we start first?" Steven pressed his hands together. "You know Jayson's restaurant?"

"Of course."

"The assistant manager there told Bree that Cheyenne came in there with a man who looked an awful lot like you."

"That's a lie."

"I showed her your picture, Michael. She says it's you but when she saw you in the restaurant with Cheyenne, your hair was longer. Everything else seems to fit."

"Wait this is a load of crap. I wasn't at Jayson's and I wasn't ever with Cheyenne Wilson. I told you I don't know her."

"But you claim you can't even remember where you ate right?" Steven leaned on the food cabinet. "How can you be sure you weren't at Jayson's? With or without Cheyenne?"

"Because I don't eat at Jayson's at all. I don't like the food there. The last time I ate there everything was so greasy I almost threw up."

"So you're sticking by your claims?" Brianna circled him.

"Yes I am. I don't know Cheyenne."

"You know her well enough to take her flowers?" Brianna playfully punched his shoulder. "We heard you were at the hospital earlier. Or is that not true too?"

"I was there." He shrugged. "So what?"

"And we were told you went to see Cheyenne," Steven said.

"Well yes I did."

"Why?" Brianna scoffed. "Why would you go see someone you don't even know?"

"Because I have a heart. I've been reading about her in the papers. I thought it was sad that she didn't have any family and was alone."

Brianna looked at Steven. He shrugged.

"I took her some flowers and I wanted to see how she was doing. I feel really bad for her."

"Oh please."

"I don't expect you to believe me, Brianna. You already have your mind made up where I'm concerned don't you?"

"Say that was true." Steven observed the fancy appliances. "Why did the lady at the hospital say that you were the guy that brought Cheyenne in the night she was attacked?"

"What? That's insane!"

Seeing Michael squirm became the highlight of Brianna's day so far.

"That's what the lady says."

"I don't care what she says, Detective Kemp! It's a lie! I don't know Cheyenne Wilson."

"Michael this just don't add up here." Brianna's ponytail swung as she paced.

"I mean, how would it look to you if you weren't the man in the middle?"

"I don't care how it would look. The lady at the hospital is full of it."

"We've shown her your picture and she was the one who gave us a description in the first place."

"You know Brianna, I was happy you'd come back until now."

She grinned.

"I want you two to leave. If you have anymore questions I'll relay you to my lawyer."

"Oh come on, Mike." Steven teased. "Just calm down and take a breath okay? We're all friends here. I mean, we're not saying you beat Cheyenne. Are we, Bree?"

She remained silent.

"I'm telling you for the last time." He dug his finger into the plastic on the table.

"I don't know Cheyenne. I won't say it again. Did it ever occur to you both that these people have gotten me confused with someone else?"

"And who would that be, Mike? They've seen the pictures and even before we had your picture, the description fit you."

Brianna motioned to Michael's feet. "Except we haven't seen your Sean John sneakers yet."

"Oh is that why you went into my bedroom? To look for sneakers,

Brianna?"

"No to look for the truth because you obviously wasn't giving it to us."

"Stop fucking with us, Mike. You've been identified. You can't deny that."

"The only difference was that the lady at Jayson's told me the man had long hair."

"*Hello*?" He touched his head. "Do I have long hair to you, Brianna?"

She displayed a mocking grin. "Ever heard of haircuts?"

"I've never had long hair! Even in my profile picture I don't have long hair."

"Yeah and that picture's at least five years old, Michael," Steven said. "You think we're idiots?"

"Yes I do if you think I was the one who beat Cheyenne Wilson."

"Michael we are not saying you did it." Brianna's arms dropped to the side.

"We're saying we know you knew her. Why can't you just admit that?"

"Ha, ha, ha." Michael leaned over. "Oh, ha, ha, ha!"

"What the hell's so funny?" Steven put the football-shaped cookie jar down.

"Oh why am I even entertaining you two? You've got nothing. I've been reading the papers. You got a flimsy description of someone who knows Cheyenne." Michael counted on his fingers. "You guys don't know what Cheyenne was hit with which means you got no weapon, no DNA. You guys don't even know where it happened! Ha, ha, ha!"

"It's not too funny to us."

"It is to me, Brianna. You think that me being a part of Havana Horizons, someone saying they recognized me and me taking Cheyenne flowers is enough to try to link me to Cheyenne's attack? Ha, ha, ha! And from what I've read in the papers, this is not even officially your case. It's Detective Matthews'."

"One thing you're forgetting, Michael," Brianna said. "You still can't tell us where you were that night."

Color left his cheeks.

"What's the matter, Mike? Got knocked off ya' high horse there?" Steven put his arm around Michael's shoulders. "You lied didn't you? You remember where you were that night don't you? Tell us something we believe and we might cut you some slack."

"*Might*." Brianna muttered.

CHAPTER NINE

❝I lied because I was trying to protect someone I care about.❞ Michael sat at the table.

"See the night Cheyenne was attacked, I was with Stephanie James." He lowered his head.

"She's married and we'd been having an affair."

"Really?"

"It's the truth, Brianna. I didn't wanna say anything before."

"So let me get this straight." Steven propped his foot on a chair and leaned over.

"You'd rather us think you were involved with attempted murder than to admit you've been banging some guy's wife?"

"Yeah it's a little hard to buy, Michael."

"It's the truth."

"Oh so now you're big on the truth?"

"I can't make you believe me, Brianna." He swallowed. "It's the truth. We were at her place that night, watching a movie. Her husband was out with the kids. They have two little girls."

Brianna laughed. "Oh please come on. Steve?"

"He could be telling the truth, Bree."

"It makes no sense at all."

"Well we'll check it out."

"Steve…"

"Why are you so determined to pin this on me, Brianna?"

"Because you're a liar, Michael. And I know if you're involved with that BDSM crap that you have the capacity to be violent. How do we know you weren't the man dating Cheyenne, something happened and you took it to another level?"

"Look." He jumped up.

"Back it up, Mike." Steven laid his hands on Michael's chest.

"I didn't say anything about Stephanie because she's married to Gene James."

"Gene James?" Steven squinted. "The psychiatrist?"

"Yes." Michael broke free from Steven's grip. "If you've heard of him then you know he's very successful and prominent. If my affair with Stephanie got out Gene would take everything from her. He'd divorce her, take the kids and she'd have nothing. I couldn't let that happen. I care about her."

"You must if you're willing to have someone think you're involved in Cheyenne's case before mentioning the affair."

"Detective Kemp you ever loved a woman so much it scared you?" He looked at Brianna. She turned away.

"I mean, to the core of your being? Well that's how I felt about Stephanie."

"Felt?" Brianna asked.

"Yeah, until she broke my heart." He slumped into the chair.

Steven played with his shades. "Stephanie's the woman in the charcoal portrait isn't she?"

"She's the woman in all my portraits." Michael clasped his hands. "Steven you buy this?"

"For now I do."

"Well I don't. I think he's just trying to throw us off."

"Well if he is, we'll find out. Michael we gotta talk to Stephanie."

"No." He stood. "You can't."

"We have to. You just provided her as an alibi."

"But if our affair got out, it would ruin everything!"

"I don't buy that you care so much about Stephanie's well-being." Michael walked around Steven to reach Brianna.

"What?"

"I doubt you care about anyone more than yourself."

"Well that's interesting Brianna seeing how you don't even know me."

"Oh I know you more than you think."

"Is that right?" Michael flexed his jaw. "I think there are some things about me that would surprise you."

"And what do you mean by that?"

Steven got his notepad. "Cool it, Bree. Michael we need Stephanie's information so we can check with her about this."

"I can't let you do that."

"You don't have a choice, Mike. Now we're not gonna disclose the affair. All we're gonna do is talk to Stephanie and see if this checks out. Right, Bree?"

"I still wouldn't buy it. Besides if this woman had something going with Michael she probably can't be trusted anyway."

Michael smirked. "Boy if I didn't know any better Brianna, I'd say you were jealous."

"Excuse me? Why would I be jealous?"

"You tell me."

"What's Stephanie's number and address?" Steven tapped the pad with his pencil.

"You don't give it to us then we'll go look it up ourselves."

Michael gave the information.

"Thanks for cooperating, Mike. Come on, Bree." Steven left the kitchen.

"I don't buy this, Michael. I know you're lying and I'm gonna prove it."

He presented that sickening grin that chilled her bones the last time.

"Has anyone ever told you how pretty you are when you're mad?"

"If you had anything to do with Cheyenne's attack…"

"Bree let's go!" Steven hollered from down the hall.

"I swear Michael, if this doesn't add up you'll be seeing me again." He smiled.

"And the meeting will be anything but pleasant."

"Brianna?" He grabbed her arm.

"Let go of me."

"I'd love it if you'd let me draw you too."

◆◆◆◆◆◆

"Yes. Michael Buchanan was here with me on April twelfth."

The statuesque Stephanie James showed Brianna and Steven into her spacious home office.

Brianna tried to ignore her envy but it rocked her like a thunderstorm.

69

What woman wouldn't be jealous of a gorgeous blond who obviously hadn't worked a real job in her life?

She probably manipulated the most powerful men with one smile. She'd gotten Gene James to marry her. Brianna didn't even have to guess why. He was fifty-six and Stephanie was thirty-five. He was looking for someone to pamper and Stephanie wanted to be kept like a rare jewel.

She pranced around in designer clothes and high heels, backing up Michael's claim.

But Brianna didn't believe either one of them. In fact she got the same suspicious feeling about Stephanie she'd gotten from Michael.

This would definitely be an interesting visit.

"And then he left around ten-thirty." Stephanie sat in the leather chair in front of her computer.

"And you're sure this was the twelfth?" Steven asked.

"Yes. I know for sure because Gene always takes the kids out for pizza on Wednesday nights." She placed her hands between her thighs. Those red colossal nails caught the light at every angle. "It's like his quality time with them so I never go."

"At the risk of getting too personal..." Brianna tilted forward. "What did you and Michael do while they were gone?"

Stephanie tangled her fingers. "We just watched television. *Sleepless in Seattle* was on uh, TBS and I love that movie." She smiled.

Brianna doubted the truth of her cheerfulness.

"So you don't think Michael could have beaten Cheyenne Wilson?"

"No, Detective Morris."

"Why don't you look into my eyes when you say that, Stephanie?"

She lifted her head. She acted like looking Brianna in the face caused pain.

Guilt perhaps? Or was she the type that couldn't lie to a person and look at them at the same time?

"It's the truth." Stephanie walked to the black file cabinet.

"Michael said you broke his heart." Steven propped his foot on his thigh. "Is that true?"

"I guess if he says it."

"We saw a portrait he drew of you." Steven doodled on his notepad. "It's very intimate to say the least."

"That's all he does. Sits around drawing pictures of me. He can't move on. He's so intense."

"You don't seem too flattered." Steven bobbed his foot. "Most women would find that kinda stuff romantic. Wouldn't you, Bree?"

"In what ways is Michael intense?" Brianna straightened up in the chair.

"You really wanna know?"

"I asked didn't I?"

Stephanie pursed her glossy lips. "I broke it off with Michael because being with him was killing me. Not just the guilt of cheating on Gene but the affair was draining me physically and emotionally. I couldn't take it anymore and I broke it off."

"I take it he wasn't too happy with that."

"You can say that, Detective Kemp. He refused to accept that I didn't want anything else to do with him. He started calling me and writing me letters. He sent me flowers almost everyday. I was lucky Gene didn't see them."

Brianna crossed her legs. "So Michael's been stalking you?"

"What would you call it?" Stephanie swatted her hands. "He follows me to the frigging grocery store! He's always around. I confronted him and told him I was gonna get a restraining order if he didn't leave me alone. Well he didn't like that. No he wanted to teach me a lesson."

Brianna glared. "How?"

"He stopped sending me gifts and started threatening me. He sent all these weird emails."

She gestured to the computer. "Sent my photo with my face scratched out and he'd drawn squiggly lines on it in red marker. He sent me a Trojan virus. He's even hacked into my Facebook account and put up naked pictures of me." She laid her face in her palms. "So I met with him because I wanted him to see I meant business. I wanted my life back."

"And what happened?" Steven tapped the arm of the chair.

"I went to his place." She inhaled. "I tried to tell him it was over again but he got so mad." Her voice weakened. She put her hand on the computer table. "He kept saying he loved me and wouldn't let me go."

"Go on." Steven said. "What happened?"

"I went to leave and he grabbed me." She fidgeted. "I kept telling him to let me go but he wouldn't. He started kissing me."

The detectives looked at each other.

"And he was holding me tight and I couldn't move. I tried." She sucked in breath.

"I tried but couldn't. I begged and pleaded and he finally let go. But then he told me if I left that he would tell Gene about the affair."

CHAPTER TEN

Steven pulled on his pants and looked at Brianna. "Stephanie did Michael rape you?"

"In my mind he did. And in my heart he did but it was my choice. I could've left. I chose to do what he wanted to save my marriage."

Brianna shook her head.

"I love Gene more than anything. I can't lose him and my kids or I'd have nothing. Michael told me to sleep with him one last time, just to bring closure." She chuckled between tears. "And I did." She wiped her eyes with her fingers. "I hated every minute of it. He was so rough. He ripped my clothes off like some animal. I was so scared."

"I'm sorry." Brianna passed her a tissue. "Did you love Michael at all?"

"God no. It was just sex for me, an attraction you know?" She sniffled. "Michael knew that from the beginning. When I realized his feelings were getting serious, he'd become possessive. He actually thought I'd leave Gene for *him*. Never would that happen. Gene's my world. I don't exist without him."

"Stephanie you can't let Michael terrorize you and get away with it," Steven said.

"He's stopped. I mean, I haven't heard from him in weeks. I broke up with him right after the twelfth."

Brianna stood. "Stephanie, are you really telling the truth about Michael? He was here that night?"

"Yes."

"You don't have to be afraid of him." Steven touched her arm. "Has he threatened you? Is he making you say this to us?"

"No. It's the truth. He couldn't have beaten Cheyenne Wilson." Stephanie's face went red. "He was here. I swear on everything I love he was."

"Hmm." Brianna studied her notepad. "Well thank you."

"You do believe me don't you, Detective Morris?"

"If you say it's the truth, then it's the truth right?"

"I'll get Marta to see you out."

"That's okay we can see ourselves out." Steven laid his card on the table. "Call us if you need to okay?"

"Okay."

"Thanks for the cooperation."

Steven met Brianna at the top of the stairwell.

"She's lying, Steven." They walked downstairs.

"I'm not saying she is and I'm not saying she isn't."

"But you know she is. If Michael was stalking her, she could be lying because she's afraid of him."

They got to the front door.

"I don't trust either one of them, Steven."

"Maybe not but she backed up his story. Until something else comes up, looks like Michael's outta the picture."

"Not in my book." They left.

Stephanie watched them drive off from the upstairs window. She ran to the table and snatched up the phone. Michael answered on the first ring.

"Stephanie." He breathed.

"I did it."

"What? You told them what I said?"

"Yes."

"Did they buy it?"

"That's not my concern. I only wanna get rid of you and I'd do anything to do it."

"I love you, Stephanie."

"You twisted fuck." Tears fell on her blouse. "Now you promised me if I backed up your story you'd leave me alone for good."

"Yes." He lowered his voice. "I did say that. But is that what you really want?"

Her fingers turned red from gripping the phone.

"I'll never want anything else as bad as I want that."

"We belong together, Stephanie. Gene can't satisfy you the way I can. You'll come back to me because you know it's where you really belong. You're just scared."

"You sick son of a bitch. You get this through your head! I don't wanna *ever* see you or hear from you again for the rest of my life."

"You know you don't mean that."

"I do mean it. If you come near me again I'll go to the police."

"What about Gene? You go to the police and he'll find out for sure."

"I'll risk it. I want you to stay away from me, Michael. If you don't I'll take back everything I told Kemp and Morris."

"And why would they believe you after you've already lied?"

"You're afraid they will?"

"No."

"I don't know what happened to Cheyenne Wilson but after how you've treated me, I wouldn't be surprised if you beat her."

Click.

◆◆◆◆◆◆

Ring! Ring! Ring!

"Mmm."

The clock by Brianna's bed struck three a.m. as she awoke. She'd slept with one arm pinned behind her back. Davis had curled into her other arm during the night.

Ring! Ring!

She checked the caller ID. Her heart deflated when she saw, "unknown number".

She hadn't heard from him in at least a week. She didn't know what felt worse. That he'd called again or that she'd been stupid enough to believe he'd moved on.

Ring! Ring!

She couldn't control his actions but she wouldn't entertain his sickness. She knew it killed him not to talk to her.

She pushed the speaker button on the phone.

He could talk all he wanted but she wouldn't give him the satisfaction of hearing her voice.

"Hello, love."

Brianna sunk into the sheets and laid Davis on her chest.

"So you're not going to answer huh? You put me on speaker? I can tell. Well okay, I'll keep it short and sweet. Probably been wondering where I've been haven't you? Why you haven't heard from me?"

She sipped her cup of lukewarm water and frowned at the taste.

"Well I've been around. I knew you were busy so I wanted to respect that and give you space. That's what you do when you love someone, Bree."

"Yeah right."

"But I'm always there for you in case you need me. You know you do need me right?"

She scooted against the headboard.

"You might not know it, but you do. I wanna help you with what's happened if I can."

"Sick asshole."

"Wish I could make it go away too. I'd never want you in any pain. I know how much you care about Cheyenne Wilson. I visited her in the hospital by the way."

She jerked up. "What?" She stopped before she grabbed the phone. *Don't give him the satisfaction.*

"I hated seeing her in that kind of pain you know? She didn't deserve that. Some people might but not Cheyenne. She always seemed so sweet."

God how much *did* he know about the people in her life?

"I called because it's so hot tonight. So incredibly humid that I couldn't sleep."

Brianna stroked Davis' ears.

"But I can't lie." He chuckled. "The humidity wasn't what was so uncomfortable.

I couldn't stop thinking about you. My dick's so hard I feel like I got a semi automatic attached to my crotch."

She shivered.

"So I got in the shower. Oh, man. You won't believe how cold it was. Had to make it cold to wash this hard on away and it didn't even work. No." His breathing held a low growl as he spoke. "Because when I was in the shower, all I could think about was you."

She shut her eyes.

"Your perfect skin underneath my hands. When I was washing, I started to touch myself."

She went to push the button to hang up on him but for some funny reason, didn't.

Even though she hated his voice he had the power to make her wanna listen.

Maybe she just wanted to know how far he'd really go. If she knew that maybe she could finally gain the upper hand.

"I touched myself...ahh. Like I'm touching myself right now."

She lifted her knees under the covers.

"I touched myself like I was touching you, Bree. Like I was touching all over your body. Oh. All I could think about was you hot and sweating. Just to feel you and smell you and drink your sweat."

"Stop it." She whispered.

"Just to feel you. Oh...ahh...feel you sweating."

"Stop it!" She knocked the machine on the floor.

"Raaaaarrr!" Davis hopped off the bed.

"Come on be honest." He breathed heavier. "Don't you sometimes think about me the way I think about you?"

She got on her knees and stared at the toppled answering machine.

"Come on...ohh. I'm rubbing my cock now, Brianna. Rubbing it and imagining it between your lips. You sucking it and rubbing my thighs. Oh."

She brought Davis to her chest.

"Come on pick up, Bree. Tell me do you think about me like I think about you? Ohh, mmm. I know you do. You might think about me even more. I know you're curious."

"Stop it."

"Curious not as to who I am but how I'd feel inside you."

"Motherfucker!" She covered her ears. Yet she took her hands down again.

Why she had this desire to hear what he had to say disgusted her.

"I know you want that in your heart, Bree. We have a bond, an attraction no one else can compare to. You're mine and there's nothing either of us can do to stop that. Oh...oh yes."

Vomit locked in Brianna's throat from the image of him coming.

"Oh ahh...let me get a towel, honey." He made noise in the background. "Ah that's it. I'm wiping myself off now. I came so hard it hit the wall from across the room."

A tear fell from her right eye.

"*I* came hard this time, Bree. When we see each other again, maybe you will too."

She threw Davis on the bed. "See each other again?"

"Rrr!" Davis hoisted his tail in the air and stretched on the pillow.

"*Again*?" She snatched the machine off the floor. "Again?"

Did she know him? Who was he? Who the hell was he?

"You'll be hearing from me again real soon, sweetheart. Count on it."

"Wait!" She knocked the receiver on the floor. "Shit!"

"Always remember darling, I'm closer, much closer than you think."

"No don't hang up!" She screamed into the phone. "Hey! Heeeey!"

Click.

"Ahh fuck!" She tossed the machine.

CHAPTER ELEVEN

Brianna rushed into the station the next morning. She'd received a message from the lady at the front desk. A man named Simon Watts had called for her and left his number.

She wouldn't have found it such an emergency if he hadn't mentioned Cheyenne *and* had a British accent.

She hopped off the elevator and zipped onto the detectives' floor. She burrowed in between roving officers who flung folders and swung coffee cups.

She leapt behind her desk and snatched the phone receiver.

She dialed Simon's number.

"Hello?"

"Uh, hello. Is this Simon Watts? This is Detective Brianna Morris. You left a…"

"Yes. You called."

"Are you okay? Your voice is shaking."

"Just wanna make sure I'm doing the right thing."

Brianna brushed rubber bands into her drawer. "If you know something that can help us find out who attacked Cheyenne, you're definitely doing the right thing."

"I guess I'm a little afraid."

"You don't have to be afraid, Mr. Watts."

Unless you were the man who attacked Cheyenne.

"What I have to say is important information. We need to talk in person."

"Okay why don't you come to the station?"

"No."

What in the world was he hiding?

"I'd feel better if we talked somewhere else."

"Look Mr. Watts I'm not in the mood for games. If this is some kind of joke..."

"No you don't understand I care about Cheyenne very much."

"So you know her personally?"

"I just want you to know I'd never hurt her."

Brianna scooted up in her chair. "Do you know who did?"

Silence.

"Mr. Watts?"

"No but, look I can tell you more if we meet. It doesn't have to be somewhere private or anything. I just don't wanna come to the station."

"I don't like this, Mr. Watts."

"I know you don't know me but you can trust me."

"And why would I believe that?" She gathered paperclips. "All right then where do you wanna meet?"

"You know that Jamaican place with the live reggae band?"

"The one on Dante Street?" Brianna smiled. "It's one of my favorites."

"Really?" He breathed into the phone. "Mine too. Meet me there at two o'clock. Is that okay?"

"I'll be there." She got a sheet of paper and a pen. "What do you look like? So I'll know who you are."

"Don't worry, Detective. I'll know who *you* are."

◆◆◆◆◆◆

Brianna bopped in her chair to the jazzy Caribbean music. The restaurant resembled an island hut you'd find in a Jamaican village. Imitation bamboo and fake vines dangled from the ceiling and walls. Plastic palm trees hovered in the corners. Fake coconuts decorated with glitter draped the top of the entrance doorway. They bounced from the wind of two tall fans sitting on opposite sides of the room. The trashcans by the door were shaped into shiny pineapples.

The car horns outside were the only thing to remind her she wasn't on a real island.

She'd ordered her favorite coconut and pineapple smoothie. The tangy drink rippled down her throat.

Just when she thought Mr. Watts had forgotten their meeting, a man walked inside.

She caught his stare. Her hand titled, spilling her drink over the glass.

"Shit." She got a napkin. She'd been lucky to catch the mess before it hit her lap.

This man, Simon Watts or whoever had a presence that would leave an impression in Brianna's memory forever.

He looked like one of the Musketeers got trapped in a time machine. His brown hair flowed down his back like a model in a shampoo commercial. Some of the luscious strands landed on one shoulder. His goatee wasn't of the modern style. Reminded her of the beards you'd see on one of the Knights of the Round Table.

Wow. The more Brianna watched him, the more engrossed she became. Maybe she should stop reading those damn Harlequin romances.

He walked toward her. The sexy men in those Harlequin books didn't hold a candle to his gallant face. He'd make any storybook hero jealous. He was the real thing.

He stopped at her table. Had the stare of a wild animal. Piercing and daunting.

He dropped his hands to his sides in a rigid stance of a monarch.

The small stud in his ear added to his allure.

"Detective Morris." He took her hand. "It's nice to meet you. I'm Simon Watts."

"You…uh…uh…" Her hand stayed in midair seconds after he'd let it go.

"You're even more beautiful in person than in your photo."

"My…my photo?" She stirred the straw in her drink.

"Yes." He sat across from her. "Cheyenne showed me a photo of you two at the beach. But it doesn't compare to seeing the real thing."

He watched her just like Michael had except she didn't mind Simon doing it at all.

"So the photo is why you said on the phone that you'd know me when you saw me."

"Yes." He tilted his head, staring.

She touched her cheek. "I appreciate the compliment, Mr. Watts."

"Call me Simon, please." He clasped his hands. "I didn't mean to embarrass you."

"No." She crossed her legs at the ankles. "No it's fine. I'm not embarrassed."

"Maybe *I* should be." He hooked his arm on the back of the chair.

"Excuse me?"

"For not being able to turn away from you."

Oh my.

"I'm making you uncomfortable aren't I?"

She placed her hands under the table. "I told you, you aren't. Maybe we should uh, talk about what we came here for."

He looked at the floral tablecloth. "I was with Cheyenne the night she was attacked."

"Is that right?"

"Please let me explain."

"Oh I wouldn't think of not letting you explain."

"I wasn't with her *when* she was attacked. I'd been with her earlier that night. We'd gone to the opera. Afterwards I took her home and the next day I heard she'd been beaten."

"So you were with her that night just not when she was attacked?"

"That's correct."

"And I should believe that because…"

"Why would I lie?"

She laughed. "Oh I could think of a reason. Maybe you attacked her and you're trying to cover your tracks. Maybe you knew we would close in on you."

"Oh please, Detective. I've been reading the papers. I know you guys don't have anything. You have no weapon, you don't even know where the attack happened. They already said her place was ruled out."

"Simon if you were me, what would you think right now?"

"Probably the same thing you are. But I have the truth on my side. I'm also not stupid. Why would I contact you if I'd beaten Cheyenne?"

"Maybe you're extremely clever and thought this might throw us off."

He shook his head. "I wish Cheyenne was able to talk right now. She'd tell you I'd never hurt her. Look at me."

She did.

"What do you see in my eyes?"

"Sincerity. Something tells me you do care for her."

"Yes."

"But that doesn't mean you didn't attack her. You could be a damn good liar, a charmer. Maybe that was your plan from the beginning, to charm me."

"It's not. I came forward because I want to help. I know I shouldn't have waited but I was afraid that the police would accuse me just like you are now."

She stood.

"Where are you going?"

"I'm taking you down to the station."

"The station?" He jumped up. "I didn't beat Cheyenne. I swear it. I wouldn't do something like that."

"Simon you just told me you were with her the night she was attacked and you hid that."

People abandoned their food to observe the scene.

Brianna lowered her voice. "Simon you've got to come down to the station and we've gotta talk to you. There's no way around this."

"If I wanted to be arrested I would have gone to the station in the first damn place."

"I'm not arresting you." She pushed her chair under the table.

"'Yet' you mean."

She hung onto his shirt. "If you are telling the truth than you don't have to be afraid."

"What about my car?"

"We'll bring you back to get it."

"Unless I'm detained right?"

She led him to the door.

"I'll go to the station, fine. But will you tell me one thing?"

"What?" She caught the spark in his eyes.

"Do you believe me?"

"I can't answer that."

A smile she couldn't tell the meaning of covered his lips.

"You already did."

She watched him walk out.

CHAPTER TWELVE

❝I think Watts is full of shit." Steven sauntered around Captain Jersey's office. "And if you believe he's not you need a brain transplant, Bree."

"Who needs a brain transplant? I admit Simon did the wrong thing but the more he explained the more he made sense."

"Uh…" Jersey tapped her desk.

"Bree how can you stand there with a straight face and defend Watts after the bullshit story he laid on us?"

"What's so bullshit about it, Steve? He didn't come forward before because he was scared. Is that so hard to believe? Everybody doesn't deal with this shit everyday, the average person would be scared and might not react the right way all the time." Brianna slapped her palm with her fist. "But he came forward to help. He deserves credit for that."

"Credit?" Steven scratched his ear. "You're not being fair, Bree."

"How the hell am I not being fair?"

Jersey gave up getting their attention and sat down.

"You were ready to hang Michael even though he has an alibi for that night. But Watts walks in here with some lame ass story, admitting he was with Cheyenne that night and you wanna congratulate him."

"Steve…"

"No listen. You're being prejudiced, Bree."

"Where the hell you get that?"

"I'm talking about Michael. You don't like him or his lifestyle or whatever and because of that you'd do anything you can to pin this on him."

"Oh. How dare you, Steven?" Brianna marched in behind him. "I am an officer of the law. I would never try to pin something on someone or accuse someone of something if I didn't think they did it."

"Bullshit." He bumped into Brianna when he turned around. "You hate Michael and you like Simon obviously and that's all you need to know huh?"

Jersey poured a cup of coffee and hummed.

"Why are you turning this around on me? You don't think Michael's innocent either."

"I might not but at least I'm willing to be fair about it. Michael has an alibi and someone who backs it up. What the hell does Simon have?" Steven turned and crossed his arms. "Except long hair and charm apparently."

"Oh I see. You're trying to say I like Simon or something?"

"Hey?" Jersey fanned.

"Well I don't know, Bree. Hell you were sitting up in his face so close when we were talking to him I thought you were gonna ask me to leave the room so you could fuck!"

"Kemp!" Jersey banged the desk with her fist. "That's enough."

"Well what am I supposed to think?" He laughed with his arms out. "Shit she's eating everything Simon says with a spoon."

"Oh fuck you, Steve. People are innocent until proven guilty."

"Oh, ho, ho!" He threw up his arms. "Except those with sexual preferences you don't agree with right, Bree?"

"Fuck you!"

"No, fuck you! Watts is lying and if you weren't so wet between the legs you'd know that!"

"Kemp!" Jersey stood.

"How dare you talk to me like this, Steve?"

"Because I don't know what the hell's your problem. Watts could have beaten Cheyenne and you're taking up for him!"

"I believe him, Steve. I can't explain why I do but I believe him." She caressed her knuckles. "Something tells me he wouldn't have hurt her."

"Well I don't believe it no matter what your "women's" intuition is saying to ya.'"

"I'm confused about something." Jersey walked from behind her desk. "Simon's the guy Cheyenne was seeing from Havana Horizons right?"

Brianna nodded.

"How come his name didn't come up as a match for that list like Michael's did?"

"Simon didn't use his real name," Brianna said. "He said he was being cautious about the kind of people he'd meet if they knew he was rich."

Steven yawned. "Isn't that a coincidence huh? He has an answer for everything."

"It makes sense to me, Kemp," Jersey said. "I mean it's hard enough going through these sites not knowing what kind of weirdo you might meet. Imagine the creeps a rich person would attract. It'd be stupid to go advertising how much you got like that."

"That's why he didn't even tell Cheyenne he was rich until they'd gone out a few times." Brianna pushed loose strands behind her ear. "Until he trusted her."

"You gotta be careful these days." Jersey sipped coffee. "You be too careless and you might end up with a stalker." She caught Brianna's expression. "Uh, I mean...it can happen."

Brianna sighed into her palms. "Doesn't matter what we say makes sense or doesn't. Steve's got his mind made up about Simon so why bother."

"You are so damn two-faced, Bree. When you give Michael the benefit of the doubt, I'll do the same with Simon. But I'm sure that's never gonna happen."

"I don't know why you two are fighting like idiots." Jersey reclined in her chair. "We'll know the truth in a little while when Watts finishes the polygraph." She put her feet up on the desk. "He's already been in there three hours. Shouldn't be long now."

"And that's another thing, Steve. Why would Simon agree to take a polygraph if he attacked Cheyenne? And without a lawyer if he was guilty? You got an answer for that, Colombo?"

"I don't care if he has a video tape that proves he didn't do it, I still wouldn't believe it."

Knock! Knock!

Ryan popped his head in. "Excuse me, Captain Jersey?"

"Yes?"

"Hey, Steve. Hey, Bree."

"Ryan." They muttered in unison.

"Uh, they told me to bring these up." He held out a printout. "Polygraph results for Simon Watts."

"Give me those." Steven snatched them.

"Thank you, Ryan," Jersey took the results from Steven.

"Uh, who's Simon Watts?"

"It's not your concern, Ryan." Jersey scanned the results with Steven breathing down her neck.

"He's just someone who has some information about Cheyenne," Brianna said.

"Oh really?" Ryan beamed. "Well that's good news. I know you're pleased."

"I'd be pleased if I know Simon was telling the truth or not."

Steven scoffed. "Thought you already knew."

"What do the results say?" Brianna stood beside her superior.

Jersey peeked at Ryan over her glasses. "Ryan would you excuse us?"

"Oh yeah." He backed up to the door. "I uh, hope you guys find out what happened to Ms. Wilson."

"Thank you, Ryan." Brianna smiled. "I'm sure she'd appreciate that."

He inched out the door. "Keep me informed on her progress?"

"Ryan." Jersey gestured for him to close the door.

"Oh yeah. Well uh, I got things to do."

Brianna waved. "Bye, Ryan."

He blushed. "Bye." He left.

"Well looks like you lose, Kemp. Watts passed the polygraph with flying colors. He's not lying."

"Let me see that." He read the results. "I don't believe this. He must know how to trick the machine."

"Oh please, Steve. Just admit Simon's telling the truth. What we need to do is bring Michael in here." Brianna headed for the door. "I bet the results would be much different."

"Well we don't have authority to bring Michael in since you got nothing on him." Jersey took the results from Steven. "And remember this is still Jayce's case. Don't step on his toes."

"Believe me Jayce is more than happy that we're taking some of the load off him. I'm gonna go tell Simon he's free to go." Brianna left.

"I don't care about no damn test, Captain. I know Watts is hiding something. I'm gonna find out what it is."

◆◆◆◆◆◆

"Simon?" Brianna entered the sparse interrogation room. A uniform officer stood in the corner. "You're free to go. You passed the polygraph."

"Thank you, Detective Morris."

"I didn't do anything. You passed on your own. Anyway you said you were telling the truth and you proved it."

"No I meant..." He came from around the table. "Thank you for believing me. That means a lot."

"I was just doing my job."

"But I know that you believe me. You do don't you?"

"Yes I guess I do."

"I've felt so guilty for not coming forward. I want to help you anyway I can with the case."

"I don't see how you could help unless you know who attacked Cheyenne."

He rubbed the back of his neck. "If I knew that the police needn't get involved. I'd take care of the person myself. Cheyenne didn't deserve what happened to her. Someone has to pay."

"It's good you wanna help. If we need you then we'll let you know." He smiled.

"I've arranged for an officer to take you back to get your car. Thank you for being so cooperative. Call us if you know of anything else that would help." She turned to leave.

He grabbed her hand. "And what if I don't know of anything else? Can I still call you?"

The officer in the corner grinned.

"Excuse me?"

"I'd like to see you again, Detective Morris."

She loosened her hand from his grip. "Why?"

"Why not?"

"I uh, I'm flattered but I don't think that would be a good idea, Simon. All on my mind is helping Cheyenne. I have enough distractions in my life."

"Distractions? So I have the capacity to be one?"

"I didn't mean it that way."

"Let me take you out to dinner."

"Why?"

"Why not?"

She sucked in her amusement. "Goodbye, Simon."

"Brianna?"

She turned from the door. "Yes?"

"Shall I ask again?"

She smiled and left the room.

CHAPTER THIRTEEN

Brianna arrived at Jayson's a few nights later. She'd gotten another call from Ms. Tyne and high tailed it to the restaurant after work. She dumped her umbrella outside the door and went to the front counter. After rushing down here in a flash flood Brianna wasn't too happy to see Tyne had gone home just moments before she got there.

At least she'd left someone there to take care of Brianna. Ms. Tyne had offered to let the police look over some security tapes to see if they could see the man who'd been with Cheyenne. Steven said it was a waste of time because the videos would just show Simon. Brianna had a spark of hope that Mr. Michael Buchanan would be on one of those tapes with Cheyenne.

Steven could rant about her being unfair to the elusive artist all he wanted. Brianna's suspicion towards Michael grew each day. She wasn't giving up.

The man dashed to the back of the restaurant to get the tapes. She'd never seen Jayson's so empty during dinner. She dabbed her forehead. Back in the day there could be a tornado or terrorist attack and this place would be crowded. She wasn't sure what caused Jayson's drop in customers but it saddened her. She'd kill to be able to enjoy one dinner here these days and erase the pressures she faced.

She was kinda glad there were only a handful of people in here. It made it easier to keep an eye on everyone. She'd be damned if she ended up like those pathetic stalking victims on those Lifetime Movies. Sure she might be out alone at night but she had a gun and common sense. She was on an important mission. She stared out the windows across the room. A man shuffled down the sidewalk with an umbrella. A lady ran in front of parked traffic with two kids struggling to keep up.

Nope Brianna wasn't dumb like some women.

Yeah right.

But what if he'd been the man with the umbrella? Or the man sitting in the corner booth eating spaghetti? The busboy, one of the waiters, or even the man who went to get the videotapes?

Everyone and their momma knew this was Brianna's favorite spot. Maybe that's where she'd attracted him. He could work here. She glanced around. It made sense. She peeked at the door of the kitchen area. He could be anyone and anywhere.

"When we meet again."

That's what he said.

"Damn it." She chewed her thumbnail. "Who are you?"

The employee popped back out to ask Brianna to wait a few more minutes because he'd gotten tied up with something.

She thought of ordering something but was still full from the large lunch she'd had.

She strolled onto the back patio. When she got a chance to come here she got an outside table.

She loved eating outside and watching the people and traffic.

She leaned over the railing. The hectic streets contrasted with the vacant restaurant.

Inside the people moved in slow motion. Out here it was like someone sat on the fast forward button on the DVD remote. Everyone moved as if they were trying to outrun their shadows.

Brianna got tired just from watching.

"Brianna?"

She didn't have to turn around. She recognized the cologne faster than his voice.

British accent or not.

"You following me?" Wind spit rain into her face and brushed her ponytail.

"No." He hung across the railing. "Why would you think I'm following you?"

"So is this a coincidence?"

"I could ask if you're following me." He smiled. "I was here first."

"Were you?"

"Yes." The wind sent Simon's hair above his shoulders. "I was eating at the back table. Guess you didn't see me."

"Doesn't mean you weren't following me."

"And I ask again, why would I be following you?"

She crossed her arms on the railing. "I don't know."

"Is something bothering you, Brianna?"

"I missed when I said it was okay for you to address me by my first name."

He smiled and threw his hair off his shoulders. "I wonder how much rain heaven has left for Albany. Don't you?"

"What do you want from me, Simon?"

"Want?" He cupped rain in his hands.

"You want something and I think it's more than a date."

"Why are you so suspicious of me? I passed the lie detector. You know I didn't beat Cheyenne."

"Cheyenne's gotten better. They took her off some of the medicine and she's talking now. I went to see her earlier."

"I know. I just came from visiting her."

"They're moving her from ICU and into a room tomorrow. From there, we'll just have to see."

"So, did you ask her about me?"

His eyes were so beautiful.

"Yes."

"And what did she say?"

"The same thing you said, that you'd never hurt her."

"And what else?"

Brianna shielded her eyes from light across the street.

"She doesn't remember anything about the attack."

"Yeah I know." He took a breath.

"She doesn't remember where she was, what she was hit with, nothing. Dr. Walden doesn't know if she'll ever get that part of her memory back. Just my luck huh?"

"I'm sorry but it doesn't mean it's over."

"You said so yourself, Simon. We got nothing. Shit let's not sugarcoat it. We have shit. Cheyenne's the one person around here who knows what happened that night."

Simon let the rain drizzle over his open hand. "Cheyenne and the attacker."

"Yeah well I don't think he'll be confessing any time soon."

"What makes you think it's a he?" He shook his hand dry.

"You saying it's not?"

"I don't know who it is. You look like you know something though. I could tell when you interviewed me the other day."

"Mind your business, Simon."

"Hey if you know the person who might have done this, I have a right to know."

"You don't have any rights. You're the one who didn't admit you'd been with Cheyenne that night. You're the last one to throw around demands."

"And you know I care about her."

"Actions speak louder than words."

"Damn it what do I have to do to convince you?"

"It's not me you need to convince."

He looked away. His exhausted expression turned to amusement.

"What's so funny?"

"Anyone ever told you that you're a very stubborn woman?"

"Maybe." She half-smiled.

"Oh Brianna I was hoping that the other day proved that you can trust me."

"I just don't understand why it's so important for me to trust you, Simon. I'm not even the chief officer on the case. You should be talking to Jayce."

"You and I have a bond because we both care about Cheyenne and know her personally. No disrespect to Detective Matthews but this is just another case to him. I came to you because I know if we work together, we can find out what's going on."

"I don't know if that's a good idea. I've got a lot of question marks where you're concerned."

"Well give me the chance to answer them."

The double doors opened. The man from the counter walked out.

"Someone told me you were out here, Detective." He gave Brianna three security tapes.

"Those should give you what you need."

"Thanks."

The man went inside.

"Those are security tapes?"

"Yeah I know it's a long shot."

"I'm afraid the only one you might see on them is me."

"And how would you know that?"

"I don't."

"I might see something else."

"And I hope you do." He ran his hand down his face. "Look can we start over? If I've offended you in anyway or..."

"It's not you. I'm having a rough time right now that's all. Going through some things."

"Other than Cheyenne?"

"Yes."

"What? Maybe I can help."

She swatted rain from her eyes and chuckled.

"And is that what you do? Go around helping damsels in distress?"

"Sometimes. But you definitely don't fit in that category, Brianna." He swept his hand across her backside. "In fact when it comes to you, the only one who needs to be rescued is me." He kissed her.

She pulled back. "Simon."

His hand remained on her ass.

"Why did you kiss me?"

"I wanted to."

"Simon uh, look that's not what's happening here."

"What do you mean?"

"I think you're getting the wrong idea. I'm not interested in anything with you. I don't know you from the man down the street."

"I invited you to get to know me."

"This feels weird."

"You still doubt me after what Cheyenne said? What in the world can I do to prove that you can trust me?"

"Simon you can start by not scaring the hell out of me. You don't grab a woman you barely know and kiss her. You crazy?"

"Well I'm sorry. Sue me. I wear my heart on my sleeve. I can't help that."

"How do I know you're not trying to get close to me to keep tabs on the case?"

"I'm not."

"How do I know?"

"Because it's the truth damn it."

She stared into his guarded eyes.

"I've liked who you are ever since Cheyenne first told me about you. She always said how wonderful you were and I wanted to meet you just because of the things she said."

"Simon that's sweet but this is strange to say the least."

"If it wasn't for the current circumstances, would you still think that?"

"But these are the circumstances, Simon. If you really wanna help Cheyenne then keep your mind on her and off me."

"Don't be afraid of me, Brianna." He opened the double doors.

"I'm not."

"We'll see."

"And what does that mean?"

"Nothing." He smiled. "Nothing at all."

He walked through the restaurant and out the entrance.

CHAPTER FOURTEEN

R ing! Ring!
 Brianna dropped her purse at the front door. She hadn't even gotten in and he was calling.

Ring! Ring!

She threw her keys on the table in the den.

Ring! Ring!

"Meow." Davis darted to his mistress' feet.

She picked up. "Unknown Number" graced the caller ID.

She inhaled all the breath she owned. "Aren't you bored yet?"

"Never. I live for you." A lump caught in her throat.

"I'm kind of glad you called."

"Really? Why is that may I ask."

"You're not surprised that I'm happy to hear from you?"

She felt his apprehension.

"It's like a dream come true. But I don't know what would bring on this change of heart."

"We need to settle this." She curled the phone cord in her fingers. "Once and for all."

"And how do we do that?"

"We meet."

Had she lost her damn mind? Even Davis looked at her like she was crazy.

"Oh, ha, ha, ha. Oh. You don't mean that do you, darling?"

"Yes. How long are you gonna keep doing this from a far? You said you wanted to show me you love me right?"

"Mmm, yes."

"You can't do that over the phone. Can you?"

"Stop this, Brianna. Mmm stop playing with me."

"I'm not playing with you."

"You have no idea how much I want you. I can't be led on and be disappointed."

"You won't be." She sat on the couch. "I want us to meet face to face. Don't you think you owe me that?"

"I'd do anything for you. You wanna meet? Okay we can meet, darling. I'd want nothing more. Alone right?"

She patted the gun on her waist. "All alone. How about tom…"

"Hmm tonight sounds good to me."

"Tonight?"

"Is something wrong?"

"No but…"

Davis hopped on her lap.

"What? You do really wanna meet me don't you? You're not setting me up right?"

"No I really wanna meet." She crossed her fingers.

"You sure? You sound nervous."

"I'm uh…" Her hands trembled. "Trying to think of a good place for us to meet."

"Oh I'm closer than you think."

She went to her window and opened her blinds. She didn't see a car or anyone walking outside.

"Where are you?"

"Guess."

"Down the street?"

Her body ached from terror.

"Mmm, closer."

She tiptoed to the front door. "I don't see you in the yard."

"No, a little closer than that."

"Where?"

"Upstairs. In your bedroom."

"Ah!" She dropped the phone. "Oh…oh shit." She raised her gun. He laughed from the receiver.

She didn't hear laughing upstairs. She got the phone.

"Just kidding," he said.

"You bastard. You won't keep playing with my life."

"Oh but I was there earlier. Got in as easy as pie."

"You're a liar. You're just mind fucking me."

"Go upstairs and find out."

Click.

◆◆◆◆◆◆

"Okay, Brianna." The officer read over the report. "I think that's all for now."

"All right." She escorted him to the porch. "I appreciate you coming out."

He patted her shoulder. "It's my job. Besides you're a cop. We look after each other."

"Thanks. You promise you'll be discreet at the station?"

"Scout's honor. Even though I don't agree with you keeping this a secret, I respect you not wanting to tell."

"I just wish I could make it stop. He's stealing my life."

"You know what to do if it happens again. Take care."

"You too." A car sped up her driveway. "Bree!"

"Is that Cummins?" The officer looked back and forth.

"Bree!" Ryan ran up the walkway. "You okay?"

"Cummins." The officer left.

"Bree?" Ryan struggled to catch his breath. "I rushed over."

"What are you doing here?"

"I heard the dispatch at the station when you called in."

"Oh jeez. I didn't want the whole world to know."

"That's what they said but I'd heard anyway." He peeked inside. "Are you all right?" He hugged her. "I was so worried."

"Ryan. Ryan?" She broke loose. "I'm fine."

"You're shaking."

"I'm okay. You didn't have to come."

"Are you kidding? We're friends aren't we? That's what friends do."

"Does Steven know?"

"No." He coughed. "I'm sure he'd been right here too if he knew. Why you don't want anyone to know?"

"I just don't. It's private and I don't wanna talk about it okay?"

They went into the living room.

"What happened?" His shoes snagged on the carpet.

"Just a break in. They didn't take anything."

"Brianna we both know that's not the truth."

"Ryan please."

"Look I won't tell anyone. I promise."

"Okay but you better keep this between us."

"I wouldn't betray you."

"I know the person who did this. He's been bothering me for a while."

"Bothering? Like what?"

"Calling me, following me and watching me."

"A stalker you mean?"

"He got in and left a dress and a pink rose on my bed."

"A dress?"

"Yes see, I've been saving up to buy this dress. It's very fancy and I fell in love with it." She put her hand on her face. "I guess he knew that like he knew everything else. I guess he bought the dress, broke in and left it on my bed."

"That's completely insane. And you hadn't told anyone?"

"Only Captain Jersey knew until tonight. I sure as heck wouldn't tell Steven. He'd overreact and well it's best he doesn't know. I don't want him worrying."

"How did the guy get in anyway?"

"He broke into the back window in my guest bedroom."

"Whoa."

"I can't take much more of this. I gotta find out who he is." She looked out the window.

"He's gotta slip up soon and I'm gonna have him when he does."

"You sure about that?"

She faced him. "Why wouldn't I be?"

"These people are very dangerous and delusional, Bree. You need to take him seriously."

"I am but I'm gonna get his ass too. I promise you that."

"So you think he'd slip up so easily?"

"He's human isn't he? He'll make a mistake."

"I bet I can't imagine how scared you are."

She wrapped her arms around herself.

"I mean to have someone have so much control over you. To know your every move and thought while you know nothing about *him*."

She closed her eyes.

"I mean, he holds all the cards. No matter what, it all comes down to who he is and you might not ever find that out."

"Ryan are you trying to freak me out even more?"

"No of course not." He rubbed her back. "I just hope you'll be more cautious from now on."

"I've been cautious. I got it under control."

"But he was in your house, touching your things and in your bedroom." His pupils stretched into slits. "I'd hate to think what would have happened if you'd been here. He'd have raped you. I know he would."

"Ryan stop it. I don't wanna hear about what he could've done. I don't wanna talk about this anymore."

"I'm sorry. I didn't mean to scare you more."

"I'm a cop okay? I know how to handle myself."

"You're a woman first, Bree. You're not invincible."

"Neither is he."

"Well let me do something for you to make up for me putting my foot in my mouth huh?"

"What?"

"Let me put in a security system for you? It wouldn't take me but a couple of hours. I could do it tomorrow."

"No, Ryan."

"You gotta make sure your home is secure, Bree. You don't know what this nut is capable of. He broke into your house. If you don't stop him now it'll get out of control."

"I don't wanna feel like a damn prisoner in my own home."

"You wanna come home one night and see this guy sitting in your kitchen?"

She shuttered.

"If it's the cost then don't worry about it. One of the best security systems around is the DX-five thousand. Everyone's getting it. I'll put it in and do the code for you. You don't have to do anything but learn to set it." He smiled.

"Well they say it's the best system around these days."

"It is."

"But it's so expensive. No way I could afford it."

"You're my friend." He nudged her. "I'll do it as a favor."

"Oh Ryan I couldn't let you do that."

"I want to."

"Ryan?"

"Shh." He ran his hand down her arm. "I'd do anything to keep you safe."

CHAPTER FIFTEEN

A Week Later

Captain Jersey thought the plan was stupid but Brianna didn't have a choice.

She wouldn't catch the stalker hiding from him. For the last week she'd thrust herself into public activities hoping to draw him out. She went to crowded movie theaters and ate in the most popular restaurants. She went shopping, more like *pretended*. She just shifted around in the stores trying to look nonobservant.

She checked newspaper listings and did her best to be at every showcased event in the city. She'd attended a Cancer fundraiser, hotdog eating contest and even a rollerblading tournament. She memorized the face of every man she saw. If he showed up at more than one place she'd been, he was the stalker.

She came up empty but wouldn't give up. He might be clever and slicker but Bree didn't just get out the loony bin herself. She had some evidence of a brain in her head.

"Yaaaay!" The people in the bleachers went wild as the softball player made his way to a homerun.

"Yeaahhhhh!"

A man's lime snow cone toppled in his hand.

"Woo! Hoo!"

Brianna covered her ears. She'd gotten this Saturday off. The annual charity softball game became today's event of choice.

People overflowed the park. Couples in love. Singles on first dates. Families having a weekend outing. Kids ran in every direction. Vendors sold hot dogs, ice cream and candy across the field. Volunteers beckoned for donations.

Even the Mayor had attended.

Brianna sat on a blanket in the grass sucking her cherry snow cone. She didn't pay attention to what team had the lead. She just sipped and scanned, sipped and scanned.

The bastard had to be here. She could *feel* him.

"Yeah!" A fat man danced when the blue team hit a homerun.

"That's how you gotta do it! Ha, ha!"

A shadow blocked Brianna's view.

"You're in my way. I can't see."

"I didn't peg you as the softball type."

Simon stood over her. He had an apron bounded around his small waist. He wiped mustard off his hands.

"Simon?"

"Hi, Brianna."

"What the hell are you doing here?"

"Volunteering." He pointed to the corndog stand. "Been helping with the corndogs."

"Oh bullshit."

"Excuse me." He sat down.

"Get off my blanket." He laughed. "What's the problem?"

"You know what it is. You think I'm stupid? You been following me." She grabbed his collar. "Are you the one who's been calling me huh?"

"What?" He pulled her hands away. "No I haven't been calling you."

She dabbed sweat off the back of her neck. "Simon this isn't funny."

"I swear I always volunteer for charities. I didn't know you were here."

"I've been here since one."

"Well I've been here since ten this morning. There's no way I could be following you."

"Right."

"Hold on." He jumped up and dusted off his jeans. "I'll prove to you I was here before you."

He brought over a woman from the corndog stand. She verified Simon's claim and went on her way.

"See?"

"Strange that's all I'll say." Brianna sucked her cone.

He reclaimed his seat next to her. "You owe me an apology." His eyebrows lifted. "But I'll settle for a kiss."

"You wish."

He laughed.

"You were right about the security tapes from Jayson's."

He picked a leaf out her hair. "Hmm?"

"We did see Cheyenne on those tapes and you were the only one with her."

She fanned with her napkin. She could deal with the rain and the mosquitoes after it. But these humid days were a bitch. She got up every few minutes just to keep her sweat pants from sticking to the blanket.

"I wish you could've found something helpful."

"If we at least knew where the attack happened." Brianna swatted a fly off her knee.

"You have any suspects at all?" Simon curved his ponytail over his shoulder.

"No." She twirled her snow cone.

"Something tells me that's not entirely true. You were looking for someone specific on those tapes weren't you?"

She moved one leg from under the other. "And why you think that?"

"Because of how disappointed you are."

"I'm disappointed because we're not coming up with shit. And Jayce knows less than we do."

He propped his legs up and laid his arms over his knees.

"I told you to let me help."

"And how could you if you don't know who did it, Simon?"

"Feel free to pick my brain if you want to."

"Oh please."

He swung at flies.

"You might be able to help with some things." She bounced her Dripping icey.

"It's obvious Cheyenne is very close to you."

"No closer than with anyone else."

"Yes she is. Obviously closer than I thought she was with me since she didn't even tell me she quit her job."

"She didn't wanna bother you with her problems. She said you'd been stressed lately. Like something had been bothering you."

She chewed ice. "She also never mentioned you to me. Why didn't she?"

"Yes!" The fat man threw his fists in the air at another homerun.

"Brianna Cheyenne's a very private person." He dabbed sweat from underneath his baseball cap.

"Shit you're telling me? But she didn't seem so private when it came to you. I know she told you things."

"Well sometimes you're more comfortable confiding certain things in some friends than you are others." He smiled at a couple that walked by.

"Maybe it could be a positive side to that huh, Simon? She might have told you something important that's the key to her assault and you don't even know it."

"Why did you ask me if I'd called you?"

"Huh?" She licked her cone. "Oh no reason."

"Is that the reason why you've had so much on your mind?"

"This is about Cheyenne. Not me."

"Maybe but I wanna know what's going on with you. Looks like you need a friend."

"Look save it all right? I know what you're doing."

"Ah. And what am I doing?"

"This "damsels in distress" thing might work with other women and it might make Cheyenne get goose bumps but you'll have to try a lot harder than that to get to me."

"Does there always have to be an underlining reason for someone to be concerned about you?"

"When the man's a perfect stranger, yes."

"You're not a stranger to me, Brianna."

"Let's get back to Cheyenne. Think okay. She ever mentioned other people to you besides me?"

"Just her friend down at the Flamingo. You know Cheyenne has only a few friends and no family."

"Right but I can't let it go how secretive she was about you. So I'm wondering if she was even more secretive about someone else."

"Do you ever stop being a cop?"

She winked. "Not when my button's on automatic."

"If you're asking me if Cheyenne mentioned someone who might

Stacy-Deanne

be the person who assaulted her to me than the answer is no."

"Think, Simon. Maybe during all those bonding sessions you guys had, she told you something." She poked his forehead. "Search that British brain and concentrate."

"She didn't mention anyone else to me. If she had I'd have told you before. I have a very good memory."

She pushed her cone in and out the side of her mouth.

"Would you stop looking at me like that? I don't know anything. I'd do all I could to help Cheyenne. I'm sick of singing this song for you."

"Fine."

She enjoyed getting a rise out of the well-contained Mr. Watts.

"So you got a temper huh?"

"Oh here we go." He sighed. "Doesn't everyone have a temper when they're pushed?"

"Sure."

"So I'm no different. Don't try to turn this back around on me, Brianna. I came over here to shoot the breeze not be interrogated. You keep this up and I'm going back to the corndogs."

"I was just asking."

"No you weren't."

Two Latino girls wearing apple-bottom jeans strutted past with ipods.

"I know you feel you can't trust me but I'm gonna prove you can."

"Why did you say that I shouldn't be afraid of you the last time?"

"Because it's the truth." He played with grass. "I'm not gonna hurt you. I don't hurt people."

"Cheyenne says you helped her out when she quit her job. Gave her a loan. And it never was romantic between you two?"

"Course there was an attraction but we realized we clicked better as friends."

"What kinds of things did you talk about? If you don't mind me asking."

Simon touched her chin. "You."

"Me?" She uncrossed her legs. "Why me?"

"Cheyenne started telling me about you and from then on I wanted to know more. You interested me so much. I admired you I guess."

"Why? I'm nothing special."

"You are to Cheyenne so you are to me."

"She said you had a hard time growing up."

He winced.

"Said you don't like to talk about your childhood."

"She was right." He picked another blade of grass. "Some things are better left in the past."

"Trouble with your parents or something? Did they hurt you?"

"Just like you don't wanna talk about the person who's calling you, I don't wanna talk about my childhood okay?"

"She told me about your sister Clara."

He stretched his arms out behind him.

"Said you two were very close."

"Clara is the only person in my life who has been there for me when I needed someone. Other people have come and gone but she's always been there."

A plastic cup blew on the blanket. Brianna flicked it off.

"Don't litter." Simon retrieved it.

"How can I be littering when it's not my trash to begin with?"

"You should've picked it up."

"Okay sue me." She propped her chin on her knee. "Are you and Clara still close?"

"Guess you can say that."

"Where is she? Does she live in Albany?"

"Why? So you can go talk to her about me?"

"Well, should I?"

"No. I have nothing to hide."

"For a man who has nothing to hide you sure act like you got something to hide."

He ran his finger down her face, catching sweat.

"You're so beautiful."

"Simon?"

"Maybe I shouldn't have kissed you the other day but I won't apologize for it."

"It wasn't appropriate."

"Maybe not but you gotta understand I feel like I know you, Brianna. Cheyenne has shared so much about you that I can't possibly see how I can know more."

She moved a curl out her face. "Are you saying you have a crush on me, Simon?"

"Look I care about Cheyenne but I gotta be honest, sometimes it was like I just wanted to see her to talk about *you*. I had this wonderful picture in my head about the kind of person you'd be. I was so enamoured. Then when she showed me your photo something clicked inside."

She wiggled on the blanket.

"I made up my mind I had to meet you."

"So you used Cheyenne's attack as an excuse?"

"Sounds kind of callus when you say it like that."

"Well Simon that's a little fucked up don't you think? Using Cheyenne's attack to come onto me."

"I wasn't doing that. I respect you too much."

"Owwwww!"

People jumped off the bleachers and ran onto the field.

"Yaaaaaaaaaaaah!"

"The game's over, Simon."

"I don't care. I wasn't paying attention anyway."

"I don't know what it is about you but I wanna know more," she said.

"I still don't know for sure if I can trust you."

"Well in order to trust me you can't be so afraid of me."

"Please. I'm not afraid of you."

"Uh-huh."

"It's the truth."

"Prove it." He tweaked her nose. "I bet you won't."

"How?" She threw her snow cone in the grass. "

Come home with me."

"What?"

"Come to my place. I think we need to be alone."

"Why?"

"See?" He laughed. "Just as scared as you can be. Like a frightened little dove."

"I am *not* scared of you, Simon."

"Okay." He stood and held his hand out to her. "Come home with me then."

"Uh fine."

She sounded confident but her nerves did summersaults.

"But with one condition."

He helped her up.

"That we only talk and that's it." She straightened her pants.

"Fine." He bowed. "But I'll hold you to that same promise."

Brianna smirked.

CHAPTER SIXTEEN

S imon lived in a luxurious two-story home on Courtland Avenue. Nicknamed "Court A" by anyone not rich enough to live there. The swank homes on Courtland made Madison Hills look like Skid Row.

You could smell the money in the air. Just minutes ago Brianna watched soft ball and slurped a snow cone. Now she stood in a house that made her feel like a bum scrounging for pennies. *Damn.*

Had she caught a ride on a thunderbolt into another dimension?

"Be my guest and take a look around."

"Are we alone?"

"Yes."

"You don't have any servants?"

"No I like my privacy." He dug in his back pocket. "I had a maid that came in once a week but when I weighed how much I was paying her to what she actually did, I didn't need her."

"I see." She picked up a picture of a lovely blond standing beside a tree. "Is this your sister? Clara?"

"Yes. When she was a teenager." He pointed around the corner. "I'll be in the kitchen okay? Make yourself at home."

"Oh…okay."

He disappeared down the hall.

She set the picture back beside the orange vase.

Did anyone else feel slapped in the face when they first walked into this palace?

She had no business being here. Steven would have choked her if he knew and she couldn't blame him.

She didn't know Simon Watts enough to be at his place. She wouldn't be caught dead doing something like this and while being stalked? Shit Simon could be her stalker. She didn't think he was but he could be. Anyone *could* be.

But hell she didn't care right now. Her mind told her not to get involved but her hormones didn't agree.

She got lost in antiques and statues sitting on the mantle by the stairs.

"Brianna!"

"Yes?"

"I'm making some drinks! What would you like?"

"Oh no! I shouldn't drink!"

"Why not? You're not working today!"

She picked up a multicolored container of jellybeans.

"I'll make something weak! Is that all right?"

She put the jar down.

"No! Please, I'd just like something else!"

"Okay! I got some tea! Would you like that?"

"Do you have lemonade?"

"Okay I'll make you some lemonade!"

"Thanks! I'll be there in a minute!" She wandered into the living room. The modish furniture and beautiful view of the terrace hadn't taken her mind off the confusion she felt towards Simon.

This wasn't your average attraction and it wasn't common to Brianna. She always listened to her mind but her curiosity for Simon overruled sensibility. She wouldn't categorize it as lust but animalistic all the same.

She had a mental scoreboard where she rated her attraction for a man. She'd have to raise the highest score from ten. Simon had her zooming to a *hundred*.

She went to the white fireplace on her way to the terrace. The choice of color scheme stuck out. While the walls were either beige or white, his furniture and other items were dark.

Dark lamps and dark lamp shades. Dark picture frames and dark portraits inside of them. Dark chairs with dark tables that accented dark rugs.

It didn't take away from the home being amazing, but why did it seem like he tried to hide that? She walked onto the terrace. The one chair over to the side caught her eye.

Brianna wriggled her lips. She couldn't let go of that detail.

"Brianna!"

"Oh coming!" She ran down the hall. She stumbled before she got to the kitchen.Two polished wooden stands sat on both sides of the kitchen doorway. One showcased a sparkling miniature stature of a swan. She'd never seen anything so polished and immaculate.

It had diamonds for eyes and the wings so detailed you could count the feathers.

But the other stand...had nothing.

What had been on this other stand?

"Oh there you are." Simon stepped out with two glasses of lemonade. He'd stuffed a decorative straw within the ice.

"Two lemonades?"

"Yeah I decided to make me one too. You're right. It's too early to be drinking."

She sipped.

"I didn't think it was polite for me to drink and you didn't."

She sucked lemonade from her lips. "That statue is breathtaking."

"Oh the swan?" He sipped. "Yeah I got it at an auction in Southeast Asia. A man makes them by hand with gold, silver, anything. I'd tell you how much it cost but wouldn't wanna be rude."

"Where's the other one?" She pointed to the vacant stand.

"Excuse me?"

"The other statue? This stand doesn't have one."

"Oh there wasn't ever one there. Come on, let me show you the rest of the place."

"Never one there? Why would you have the stand then?"

He chuckled. "What can I say? I like stands."

Brianna got on her tiptoes and checked out the top of the stand.

"Uh...what are you doing?"

"Just looking."

"Why?"

"Oh just blame it on my detective nature I guess. See I knew there'd been something up here."

"What?"

"Yeah you got a clear spot up here." She got off the stand. "You know how when something's been sitting somewhere for a long time then naturally a spot forms."

"Uh-huh. So?"

"Well there's a spot there. Something was there."

"Oh yeah." He snapped his fingers. "Now I remember. I set a plant here the other day but didn't like it so I moved it."

"No that wouldn't leave that spot."

"Course it would."

"No it wouldn't."

"Brianna."

"See that spot's been left by something that's been there a long time. Maybe even years. You putting something up there the other day wouldn't have left that spot."

"Okay well I don't know where the spot came from then. It's not important anyway."

"No but I was just curious."

"I don't see why it would make a difference if something was up there or not."

"You never had another swan up there?"

"No."

"Something else?"

"*Brianna*. It's just a space."

She grinned. "I'm sorry. It's the detective in me. I'm so used to looking at details and stuff that I guess I go overboard. I always wanna know why something is the way it is. I'm sorry."

"So you were telling me you love art huh?"

"Very much." The lemonade got sweeter towards the end.

"Well let's see if you like this." He pulled her arm.

"Simon!" She laughed and spit lemonade. "What are you doing?"

"Wanna show you a portrait I just got."

They flew upstairs. Brianna paused at the antiques in the hall but had no time to ogle.

Simon ran to a set of double doors at the end of the hall.

"Come on." He whisked them open and dissolved inside.

"Simon?" She stopped at the doorway.

Simon stood inside a huge bedroom.

Bright tan walls with thick off-white carpet. A long dresser holding an old-fashioned oval mirror accented the modern décor.

"Brianna you all right?"

A colossal circular bed with tan sheets sat on a five-inch platform. Six fat pillows were stacked around the heart-shaped headboard.

"Brianna honey? Something wrong?"

"Uh, maybe I should let you bring the portrait out to me."

"Don't be silly."

"Well it's just that the last time I went into a man's bedroom I hardly knew, got in a little trouble."

"I didn't bring you up here to seduce you."

She tugged on the end of her tank top. "And I know that how?"

"You think I'd insult your intelligence and mine by doing that? After all that would be a very flimsy excuse to get you up here wouldn't it?"

"But it got me up here. Isn't that what matters?"

"Got you up here…" He walked to her. "Maybe because you want to be."

Thank god for the view of his window to save her from whatever the hell she would have done just now.

"Wow!" She got on her knees to see out the window behind his bed. "Oh this is heaven."

"Is it?" He climbed beside her.

"Yes. Shit you can see all of Albany from this angle. Oh it's beautiful."

"Here let me take this." He got her drink.

"Oh, man. I bet it's great to wake up, turn around and see the city." She lay on the headboard.

"Yeah sometimes it's too beautiful for me to get up." He moved closer. "I lay here in the mornings for hours sometimes."

"Simon have you ever heard of a man named Michael Buchanan?"

"Michael Buchanan? No. Should I have?"

"No. I was hoping you had. I asked Cheyenne and she said she didn't know anyone by that name. Even showed her his picture."

"Who is he? Is he uh, someone you guys are looking at?"

"Forget it." She scooted from the headboard. "I shouldn't have said anything."

"Wait. If this guy's a suspect…"

"He's not a suspect. I was just curious. We came in contact with him during the investigation and he's kinda weird. Forget it okay?"

"Well now you got my gears ticking. I can't just forget it. You make me wanna go speak to him myself."

"Leave it alone, Simon. This is police business."

"So he is a suspect?"

"Stop it. Please."

"All right."

"God that view is so lovely. Makes me wanna stay in here forever."

He pressed his hand on the curve of her back. "You should see it at night." His hand slid down her sweat pants.

"Uhh." She got off the bed. "Your home is amazing. Really beautiful."

"You okay?"

"Oh of course." She giggled. "I'm fine."

"You always giggle and move your fingers like that when you're fine?"

"I'm fine, Simon."

"Sure?"

He stood so close his chest touched hers.

"Kinda close there aren't you?"

"You sure you're not uncomfortable?" He caressed her arm.

"No." She tightened up. "I'm fine."

The only thing uncomfortable is how much I want you right now. If you don't stop touching me...God help us all.

How could a mere touch on the arm feel this good?

"Hmm? So this doesn't make you uncomfortable or nervous?"

"I told you no." She looked at everything in the room except his eyes.

"What about when I do this huh?" He put his arms around her. "Does that make you nervous?"

If she got wetter she'd flood the room.

"Brianna?" He inched his mouth to hers. "You look like you're about to crumble in my fingers."

"Oh..." She felt lightheaded. "Do...do I?"

"If I wasn't so sure I'd say I had quite the effect on you."

"I bet you'd love to think that." She respired. "But you don't."

"Why are you shaking then?"

"I'm not." She switched and turned in his grasp.

One part of her desperate to be out of his arms the other dying to be buried inside them.

"I guess I fell for the oldest trick huh?"

"Umm." He locked his fingers in back of her. "I didn't trick you, Brianna. You wanted to come to my place and you wanted to be in my bedroom. That's why you are here."

"I only came up here because you asked me."

"Really? You always come up to men's bedrooms just because they ask you?"

She felt that vein bulging out her forehead.

"You know damn well why I came up here. I thought you were gonna show me your portrait."

"And I will." He lay his finger under her chin. "Right after I make love to you."

CHAPTER SEVENTEEN

"What?"

Whoa.

"Brianna?"

"Huh?" She clutched his shirt.

He dropped his arms. "I'm just kidding."

"Wh…what?"

"Ha, ha, ha!" He twirled and pointed at her. "I had you didn't I?"

"Oh go to hell, Simon."

"No I did! You should see your face right now." He opened the double doors of his closet. "Man I wish I had a camera right now. Ha, ha! It's priceless."

"Yeah well your idea of a joke is very sick, Simon."

"Ah but if you trusted me you'd know the kind of man I am and what I'd really do."

"I didn't appreciate it. I don't like being teased like…"

"Teased?" His hands stood in midair. "You mean you *want* me to make love to you?"

"No. Hell no." She crossed her arms and rocked. "I just don't like your sense of humor."

"Jeez I thought it was funny." He wrestled with a huge brown sack. "How would you feel huh? If I'd done that to you?"

"You mean got me all hot and bothered and stopped? Isn't that what women always do anyway?"

"Yeah. I mean no. You didn't get me hot and bothered. Don't flatter yourself."

"You're sweating, Brianna." He put the sack on the bed.

"No I'm not."

"What's that running down your nose huh?"

"Just show me the damn picture."

"You're adorable when you're flustered. Hold the bag for me while I slide it out."

"Oh my goodness."

"I knew you'd know it since you're into art."

"*Do* I? That's *Dance in the City* by Renoir."

She absorbed the portrait of a pale couple dancing. Pink roses dangled from the lady's pint-up red hair. She wore a satin white evening gown with thick ruffles that dipped down her back. She danced with a man with coal-black hair. His tuxedo tails fluttered at the ends.

A green plant lay in the background. Brianna always found it the most telling detail in the piece.

"I love it because it's romantic." Simon stared with a slight smile. "I love anything romantic. This couple makes you wanna fall in love don't they?"

"The couple's not the reason I like it. It's the plant."

"The plant? Why the plant?"

She shrugged. "It sets the mood to me. Brings you into the atmosphere."

"More than the couple does?"

"To me." She turned her head to the side. "Besides the whole thing about this portrait is that the woman isn't smiling. She's not in love with that man."

Simon bucked his eyes.

"Why you looking at me like that?"

"Because you're the only person I know who ever pointed that out. Most people just look at the dress or the fact that they're dancing. They don't pay attention to the woman's face to see that she's unhappy."

"I guess it goes back to my detective nature." She swatted a gnat. "Why haven't you put it up yet?"

"Well I had the hardest time figuring out where to put it."

"I think you should put it in the entrance hall. That's a portrait someone should see the minute they enter your house."

"You think so?"

"Yes. It's too beautiful to hide away in here."

He laid his hand on her side. "A lot of things are too beautiful to hide."

"I don't understand."

He pulled her into his arms. "It means you don't have to keep hiding…from me."

♦♦♦♦♦♦

Dr. Gene James pushed up his glasses as he overlooked papers in his office. His degree hung off the wall in a frame. The office smelled of strong cologne that Simon couldn't name.

"Gene?"

The slender psychiatrist twisted his narrow-face. The lights cascaded against his balding head.

"Oh, Simon. I'm glad you came on such short notice. I think you'll like what I say."

"Really? Your invitation was quite a surprise since you barred me from your office."

"Simon I did no such thing." Gene bounced in the leather recliner. "I told you, I kept warning you that I could no longer be your doctor if you refused to take your medicine."

"I did take my medicine."

"But you didn't *keep* taking it."

"Gene?" Simon shut the door. "You said you were my friend. I've told you things I haven't told anyone. Things that I'm ashamed to talk to even God about."

"I understand that. You gotta know I care about you very much. I've tried my best. I can't keep up with you and it's getting too hard."

Simon sat in the suede chair in front of Gene's desk. "What did you call me for anyway?"

"I've been talking to a colleague of mine. She wants to work with you."

Simon muttered.

"No listen. She's writing a book on people with your condition."

"Condition?" Simon dragged his fingernails down his thighs. "There is no condition. Nothing's wrong with me, Gene. Just get a little more stressed than others that's all."

"You've outgrown what I can do for you."

116

"How the fuck can that be? You're one of the best psychiatrists in the state of New York. Don't treat me like I'm stupid. If you wanna pass your leftovers onto someone else just be honest about it. I'm used to being thrown away." Simon picked lint off his pants.

"Heard from uh, Clara lately?"

"What do you think?"

"She's still around." Gene's eyes peered over his glasses. "Isn't she?"

"Nope."

"Simon this is me you're talking to. Did she flush your medicine down the toilet again?"

"No!"

"Calm down. You can't let her do this to you. I wanna stop it, Simon."

"She doesn't like me on that medicine. Says it comes between us."

"It does and that's the point."

"I really want to take them but she doesn't let me. I…I try to hide them but she always finds them. I never could hide anything from her."

"I told you before." Gene scribbled something on a paper. "You have to choose. Is Clara worth you throwing your own life away?"

"Gene?" Simon leapt on the desk. "I can't take this anymore."

"What?" He slid his chair back. "I'm out of control." He snatched Gene's shirt. "I can't live like this anymore."

"Simon, calm down okay?" Gene pulled Simon's hands off his collar. "Shh. Take a deep breath. You're in control, Simon."

"I'm not."

"You'd be in a lot better shape if you take your medicine."

"I'm in a war, Gene." Simon bucked his eyes. "A fuckin' war and I don't know how to win. I don't know if I *can* win."

"Simon sit down please. Come on, sit down."

"Gene."

"Shh sit down. You know I care about you very much. Stephanie even asked about you the other day to make sure you were okay."

"Why? Why were you talking about me?"

"See how you get without your medicine? You get paranoid. You start doubting everyone in your life."

"I can't stop it." Simon gripped his head.

"That brings us to the colleague of mine. You heard of "Roots of Hope"? In Washington?"

Simon shook his head.

"It's a facility."

Simon shut his eyes.

"But it's a lovely place. I've been there many times. The people are happy there, Simon."

He rubbed his hands until they turned red. "Facility?"

"We've been talking and she's very interested in working with you. They're having long-term success with their patients."

Simon exhaled.

"They use a very nurturing therapy and support system. Uh, and it's a beautiful place too. I have some pamphlets I could show you. Uh, it's a very admired facility by those who've participated and my colleague thinks you'd be a great addition and that they can help you conquer some of the things I haven't been able to help you with."

"No."

"Simon listen."

"I am listening I just don't like what you have to say. You tricked me. You could've told me this on the phone. That's why you didn't 'cause you knew I'd have no part in it." He got up.

"Simon sit down and listen to me. This is about you being able to truly lead a normal and productive life."

"Funny Gene but I think I do just fine."

Gene twirled his pen, shaking his head.

"You could do better and we both know that."

"I'm fine, Gene. I went through all that before and I'm not going through it again!"

"You can trust me. This is what you need."

"I'm not going back into a hospital, Gene."

"It's not a hospital, it's a facility!"

"Look when I started seeing you, you promised me you'd help me. That I wouldn't ever have to be locked up again. You promised!"

"You've got the wrong idea. It's not gonna be like that this time."

"I don't care. I'm *not* going to a hospital and I am not taking any tests. You can go to hell."

"You're being unfair. I've done many things to help you, Simon. I cannot do it on my own. If there is something better for you I want you to have that experience."

Simon paced. "See I knew I couldn't trust you. I can't trust anyone can I?"

"Oh jeez." Gene touched his forehead. "You know that's not true."

"I wanted to believe you were on my side, Gene." Simon stopped by the desk.

"You said you were on my side."

"I am damn it." Gene exhaled into his palms.

"You're not listening to what I mean. It wouldn't be like the other times. This is to help you cope in life forever. They'll show you techniques and be a support system for you." Gene picked up the phone. "Just talk to Dr. Kellogg okay? I told her I'd call her when you came in so she could talk to you."

"No." Simon pressed his hand on Gene's.

"Simon you're hurting me."

"I'm not going into another hospital! I won't be put away again, ever!"

Simon ripped the phone cord out of the wall.

"Simon no!" Gene covered his head. "Simon! Ahh!"Gene ran from his desk.

Simon chased him, waving the phone like a weapon.

"Simon I'm your friend!"

He lifted the phone.

"Please. Stephanie and I both love you. You know you're more than a patient, you're a friend."

Simon lowered the phone. "I'm not going into another facility. You get that through your head and things will be fine."

"Simon?"

"You got that?"

"I don't want you to get hurt or hurt anyone else."

"I'd never do that."

"Not on purpose no. You don't have a harmful bone in your body."

Simon put the phone on the desk.

"But we both know sometimes when you're vulnerable you can't control your actions. How can you live a real life if you can't? How can you be happy?"

"I can't stand to be in a place I can't get out of. I hate not being able to make my own decisions."

"Of course everyone does." Gene patted his shoulders. "I know you're afraid but I'd never let anything happen to you."

"You tell me one thing. Is this a place where I can just leave if I want to? No strings attached?"

Gene slumped against the wall.

"Gene?"

"It's not a hotel, Simon. It's a place to help you get the treatment you need."

"So the answer is no. I'd be trapped."

"Come on Simon it isn't Bellevue. You'd have your own little place to stay. You'd have your privacy. They have tons of recreational activities and wonderful people to interact with. You'd have friends you have things in common with."

"Uh huh." Simon pushed his hands through this hair."

The only thing you'd have to do is observations, therapy and…"

"Medicine right?"

"If needed yes."

"Wow yeah it's just like Disney World isn't it?"

"All of that's to get you better."

"I'm fine."

"We both know your issues aren't resolved, Simon. You're much better than before but I don't want you to go back to where you were."

"I won't go into a place where I don't have control."

"Simon you're not in control now. You won't be unless you get the help you need."

"I uh, gotta go."

"You can't do it on your own, Simon. This is about *your* life. Not anyone else's."

"Not even Clara's?"

Gene's expression hardened. "Especially not Clara's."

CHAPTER EIGHTEEN

Brianna watched the couples drift in and out the entrance of the Jamaican restaurant Sunday night. Phase two of her plan. She'd continue her mission to force out the stalker until she got something.

She sat at the center table in the spotlight, by the dance floor. She'd picked this spot on purpose to be the center of attention. So far it worked. Every man in the room checked her out at least once. She'd worn that thin black dress that always made men look at her like they were thirsty.

She didn't wear a slip this time. She enjoyed how the material felt on her skin. Plus she was trying to entice the stalker so the more revealing the better.

She'd scooped her curls into a bunched up French roll. Wore a sleek gold necklace around her neck and a bracelet that sparkled in the lights from the ceiling.

The waiter brought her another pineapple drink with a hint of liquor.

Couples swerved on the dance floor to the live reggae band. Brianna wiggled so much in the seat her panties rode up.

"Jesus." She maneuvered to get comfortable again. Trying to be sexy made her feel like fish outta water. She'd been a tomboy since she got out her mother's womb. She didn't mind wearing make up *sometimes* but she hated dressing up, wearing stockings and fancy shoes that pinched.

The band began to play an instrumental slow song. The couples who hopped around in frenzy only moments ago now held each other tight.

Brianna bobbed her sore foot. She'd burn these shoes when she got home.

She closed her eyes, settling into the smooth tempo of the song. Felt as though she were floating. It took her back to the times she came here with Steven. How he'd secured her in his arms and swayed her to the music. They used to come here any chance they could.

Her eyes landed on the crushed ice in her drink. Sure would be nice to be whisked by someone again. She might not have felt the way she used to about Steven but she missed being in his arms.

Being in anyone's arms.

"Oh this is pathetic." She got her purse and started to get out the seat when the gorgeous man she'd tried so hard to forget crept into the door.

Her train of thought shut off. She didn't think Simon could look sexier until she'd seen him in that black blazer. His hair lay on his back in a silky ponytail. His suit molded to his shape like he'd been poured into it.

Brianna fell back into the seat. Just the way he walked got her wet. She couldn't control this attraction and he probably knew it. Another man who'd pulled that trick Simon had in his bedroom yesterday would've gotten dropkicked. But she couldn't stop wondering what making love to him would be like.

He went to the bar. Hadn't even seen her. She didn't know whether to speak or leave it alone. Which would be best? He was like a necessary evil. She could stay away but didn't want to.

He ordered some kind of drink she couldn't figure out then began a conversation with a big-boned woman sitting on a stool.

Oh god the way he looked in that suit. She imagined her hands slipping underneath that gray shirt. She wanted to feel his chest, stroke his stomach and suck his nipples.

Sweat swiveled down her neck. People looked at her like she was crazy but she didn't care.

He turned around and stared right into her face.

"Shit." She put the purse on the table and covered her eyes. She couldn't fight the desire to look again so she did. He lifted his glass to her.

Damn him. He knew how much she wanted him. His smug smile

confirmed it.

His eyes searched her body. Maybe undressing her in his mind. The table didn't seem to interfere with the attempt either.

He walked to her.

She took a breath and lay her hands in her lap.

Stop being so silly, Bree. He's just a man. That's all.

"Don't worry, Brianna." He set his drink on the table. "I'm not following you. I swear it."

"What?"

Oh that. She hadn't thought about that and right now wouldn't care if he had been.

"What are you doing here?"

"Well." He watched the people dancing. "I thought this beat staying at home all night. Needed to get out and get some fresh air I guess."

She caressed the material of her dress.

"You look amazing."

"Thank you, Simon. You do too."

"Your hair." He ran his finger down the back of her neck. "I love your hair this way."

"Thanks." She gobbled her drink.

"So what are you doing here by yourself? Too beautiful to be alone."

"I'm used to being alone."

"I see." He bobbed his head. "Are you used to dancing too?"

Wetness seeped her panties.

He bent in front of her. His cologne overtook the nagging smell of cigarette smoke.

"Dance with me, Brianna."

"All right." That searing heat between her legs wouldn't allow her to say no.

She placed her hand in his and followed him to the dance floor. He put his hands on her hips like he had in his bedroom. He swayed her back and forth, doing fancy turns in between. She was impressed. She hadn't pictured Simon dancing like this. His hips twirled to the rhythm, so wild and free.

"Wow."

"Wow what?" He did a fancy two-step.

"Wow I mean." She chuckled, trying to keep up. "I didn't think you could dance like this."

"Oh really?" He turned her around until her back faced him. Pulled her close and bent her over.

"Simon." She laughed. "Stop it."

He swerved his middle against her backside.

"Simon, people are watching."

"So." He swung her around. "You thought I was some uptight Brit that didn't have an ounce of rhythm to his name didn't you?"

"Well."

He pulled her arms over her head and moved his hands down her body.

"Well, I'm not."

"I see that."

He hooked her arms under his and swung his crotch against her middle.

All she thought about was how he moved in bed. They said if a man could dance, he was great in bed. It'd proved factual with Steven. He'd been a wonderful dancer and he could write a book on making Brianna come before she even knew it would happen.

Wonder how Simon worked it.

"Having fun?" He breathed in her ear.

She moved her body in tune with his. "Yes."

The bright lights blurred her vision from time to time. It made it easy for her to pretend they were the only ones in the room.

"You smell so good." He kissed the back of her neck. "I love peaches."

She faced him. He pressed his body to hers. Her breasts flattened against his chest. They moved up and down, causing a type of stimulation she had no power to control.

"You like this?" The breath of his words hit her mouth. He slipped his hand underneath her dress in a way others couldn't see.

"Simon." She slapped her hand over his but he didn't stop.

"What huh? We're just dancing." He moved his hand in between her legs. Swerving against her as if nothing changed. Why she didn't stop him, she had no idea.

"You're a great dancer, Brianna." He dropped to his knees in front of her.

"Simon?"

He stared up at her. He pushed his hand up her dress again.

"Mmm." Her nipples peaked. "Don't."

She didn't know if he didn't hear her because of the music or if he chose not to.

His hand nestled her sweaty thighs. His eyes remained on hers. He stood and pulled her close. He lifted her leg and lapped it around his waist.

"Simon!" She hit his arm.

He flashed a sneaky smile in return. People took notice at the sexy dancing style.

"Simon." He moved back and forth until Brianna forgot she was dancing instead of making love.

"Simon." His movements knocked the wind out of her. She sucked her lip, fighting an orgasm here and now. She wanted him to put his hand back up her dress and catch this fire she would unleash.

"Mmm." He rocked her. His chest rubbed her nipples as they rocked.

God he felt so damn good. She imagined them in his big bed. Him spreading her legs to the ceiling, plunging inside of her until she broke from pleasure.

She licked salty sweat from her lips. He pulled her leg up higher.

His hard crotch stabbed her center.

"You…you like this?"

Oh they were making love. They were fully clothed but they were definitely making love. It might have been the danger of it all that enticed her but Brianna hadn't ever felt this good in her entire life. She wanted to rip her clothes off and let him fuck her right here in the front of all these people.

They moved faster with the music. Men and women gaped and pointed from their tables.

But Brianna didn't give a damn.

Make me come. Oh yes. Yes.

She'd never been this wet. Her panties were so thin that when he moved a certain way his dick hit her sweet spot. She chewed her lips to keep from moaning.

Had he unzipped himself? It was as if nothing even stood between his cock and her clit.

He swerved deeper. His hardness began to hurt as if he really were inside of her.

The wetter she became, the more he gyrated.

"Stop." She breathed.

He continued, prodding her with his erection. He felt so hard and tender.

"Simon, stop." She held onto his shoulders as he gyrated.

She wanted him but not *here* like this.

"Simon stop, please."

He watched her as if he'd forgotten they were in public. He looked at her risen dress. She studied the expression when he noticed her panties.

He lowered her leg and fixed her dress.

The couples beside them whispered and giggled.

She straightened her shoulder straps. "We could've gotten arrested."

He almost ripped her skin from her hand when he grabbed it.

"My place." He pressed his forehead to hers. "Now."

"No." She put her hands on his chest. "No, Simon."

"Yes. We gotta do this, Brianna. You think this kind of passion will just go away?"

"Simon."

"This is bigger than both of us."

"I said no." She tried to push him but he wouldn't budge. She didn't want him to.

"Brianna I could take you right here and now. That's how much I want you. I don't care who's looking."

"Simon this is happening too fast."

"No it's not. This is fate." He curled his arm around her waist. "Can't you feel how much I want you?"

His dick poked her stomach.

"Yes."

"Does it feel good? You like the way it feels?"

"Yes."

"I know you want me too. I knew it in my bedroom yesterday. We should've made love then."

"You're just seeing what you want to see."

"No I feel it. I felt it a few minutes ago. You wanted me inside you. You were begging for it."

"I'm going home, Simon."

He held onto her. "Then I'll come with you."

"No you won't."

"Why are you doing this? You know you want this as much as I do."

"Good night, Simon."

"Brianna?"

She went to her table to leave a tip. Simon rushed in behind her.

"Brianna wait."

But she didn't pay him much attention. She couldn't stop staring at the pink rose on her table.

"Oh my god." She picked it up.

"What is it?" Simon stepped in front of her. "What's that?"

"Damn it. He was here."

Brianna ran around the room asking people if they'd seen the person who laid the rose on the table. No one had.

"Shit!"

"What is it?" Simon followed her to the door.

"Damn it I lost him!"

"Who?"

"It's all your fault, Simon. If I hadn't been wasting time with you then I would've seen him!"

"Brianna?"

"You ruined everything!"

He followed her into the parking lot. "Brianna what did I do?"

She unlocked her car. "Just stay away from me, Simon. You screwed everything up and I'll never forgive you!"

"But…"

"Never!" She drove off.

CHAPTER NINETEEN

A Week and A Half Later

Brianna gathered the folders off her desk and headed to the file room. The one night in weeks she decided to work late and the biggest storm of the month brewed outside.

She tiptoed down the hallway, checking out every desolate corner she passed. She was the only detective still in the building. The uniformed officers were downstairs. Probably not even aware she'd been in the building.

The lights blinked on and off every two minutes. Just let them stay on long enough to put these files away so she could go home.

Another roar of thunder made her stumble. She hadn't realized she'd made it to the file room. She placed her hand on the doorknob and took slow breaths.

That excruciating fear she fought to ignore slashed her into pieces. Breath lodged in her throat. She touched her chest but it didn't calm her breathing.

"Damn it, Bree. Settle down." She raised her hand to her face.

Her forehead felt like it could melt ice.

She'd sworn from the beginning that she wouldn't let the stalker take over her life.

Who was she kidding? He had the upper hand and she didn't know what the hell to do to change that. *If* she could do anything at all.

Like a disease he spread from one aspect to her life to the other.

She hated the vulnerability the most. She hated being someone's victim and he knew that. He preyed on it. Breaking her down got him off. He'd said that many times.

Her knees quivered. Her stomach bubbled with fear.

Thump.

She jerked. That sound. Came from the end of the hall somewhere. She shook it away.

"Just calm down, Bree." She opened the door. "It's okay. No one's here."

Thump.

She closed her hand until her fingernails dug into her skin.

Thump. Thump.

Sounded like footsteps from soles heavy with rain.

"Hello? Is someone there?"

It could have been one of the officers. Why didn't they answer?

Thump...thump...thump.

Thunder, sounded like a plane fell on the building.

"Jesus."

Thump. Thump. Thump.

"Is someone up here? This is Detective Morris!"

Thump...thump...thump...

"Shit." She ran into the file room and shut the door. She threw the folders on the computer table.

BOOM!

The lights went out.

"Shit." Her chest ached from the forceful breathing. "Damn it."

BOOM! BOOM!

She covered her ears from the deafening thunder. She stuck her arms out to feel through the air. She couldn't reach the door. She bumped into file cabinets and tables. She slipped on a piece of paper.

BOOM! BOOM!

"Hey! Can someone hear me? It's Detective Morris! I can't find my way out! Hey!"

She fumbled around chairs. "I'm in the file room! Hey can someone hear me?"

"*I* hear you."

"Oh!" She swatted, grabbing nothing but air. "Who is it?" She spun around. "Who the *fuck* is it?"

Silence.

"Who's in here?" She felt her waist to get her gun. Too bad she'd left it on her desk.

"Shit!" She stayed in place. "Who the fuck is in here?"

"You're so smart. Why don't you tell *me*?"

She couldn't scream. She couldn't move. She couldn't breathe.

"Hmm? Guess who."

"Ahh!" She shoved the closest table across the room. She didn't know where he was but she'd do her best to hit him.

"Ohh!" He rummaged through the darkness.

"You stay away from me!"

"Nice try with the table. But not good enough."

She squeezed between two file cabinets. "They know I'm up here. You must be a bigger idiot than I thought to come to the police station."

"No I just wanted to show you that I hold all the cards."

"You stay away!" She found the folders and pitched them through the air.

"Ahh!" He moved through the file cabinets.

"Leave me alone! I'll kill you!"

"Oh now what kinda way is that to talk, Brianna? When I care about you so much?"

She crouched beside the cabinets. She sniffed to pick up a scent. Nothing helped her pinpoint where he stood.

"Hey, Bree? This is very exciting isn't it? Why don't you come out so we can play?"

"Go to hell!"

"Ahh come on, sweetie. I thought you wanted to meet face to face."

She fought tears.

"Isn't that what you said before? Oh let me guess. Was it only when you wanted to?"

"I got my gun you motherfucker! I'll shoot you!"

"Be hard to when you can't see me right?"

"You're a fool. They know I'm up here."

"You have any idea how huge this place is?"

He sounded closer. Brianna snuggled further between the cabinets until her back touched the cold wall.

"Huh? Even if they did know you were up here and needed help, you really think they could make it up here in time huh?"

"Look. You're threatening a cop. You're…you're smarter than this. I know you are."

"You didn't answer my question. Do you think they could get up here and save you before I did whatever I wanted?"

"Stay away." She threw fists up. "I might not have my gun but I'll still kick your ass."

"Hmm. I see my job's not nearly done yet."

"What are you talking about?"

"Well you're still talking shit. Obviously you're not scared as I thought you'd be."

That's what he craved wasn't it? To make her so afraid she'd turn a wreck and never trust herself or anyone else again. Yes, that's what he'd wanted all along. He'd been dead wrong. She'd never been so scared in her life.

He'd already won.

"You still there? Did you faint?"

Tears sprinkled her cheeks.

"That's what you want isn't it? To scare me beyond comprehension?"

"Amongst other things."

"Why?"

"Because you need to be broken. Need to be shown you're nothing but a woman like all of 'em and stop walking around here like you're better than everyone else."

"Is that what I do?" She placed her hand on the side of the file cabinet. "Act like I'm better than everyone else?"

"Better than men. Better than me anyway."

"Do we really know each other? Or is what you said on the phone just something you said to throw me off?"

"Oh Bree don't analyze me, please. You're not equipped to understand how my mind works."

"I'd believe that. I'd say I needed a couple of diplomas and PHD behind my name to understand how your mind works."

"Oh see? You're still just as smartass as always. Nothing breaks the great Brianna Morris does it?"

"Let's talk this over okay? If I've done anything to offend you in anyway, I'm very sorry."

"Really?"

"Tell me what I can do to make you go away forever."

"Relinquish yourself to me physically, spiritually and mentally. I want to own every part of you. Want it all under my control. You need to be put in your place."

"What did I do to deserve this?"

"See? You're so dense you can't see that it has nothing to do with you or me specifically. We're just actors in a movie. Chess pieces if you will."

"What?" Tears stuck to her face.

"See this isn't something I started. Don't you get that? I'm just playing a role. This is God's doing, fate. He wanted this to happen."

"I can't believe that."

"Yeah? And what would you know about God? When's the last time I've seen you in church?"

Church? Did she attract this psycho at *church*?

"We go to the same church?"

"Not originally. Nice try though. Anyway I spoke to some of the members of your church. You haven't been there in at least a year."

"I work hard. I don't have time."

"You barely work on Sundays. Stop lying."

"This has nothing to do with church! What do you expect to gain from all of this?"

"I told you what I want for the long term."

"Okay. What do you want right now?"

"Oh to have a little fun I guess."

Thunder.

"Always room for fun. Besides all work and no play makes Brianna a dull little girl doesn't it? You need some excitement in your life."

"I got all the excitement I can handle I promise you."

He opened something in his hand. She couldn't tell what.

"This is the first main lesson, Brianna. When you leave here tonight you'll realize I mean business."

"I already realize that."

"You're gonna be punished for your sins."

"What sins?"

"That filthy display a week ago. Dancing in that place like some little slut. Like some whore!"

A table flew towards her.

"Ahh!" She ducked on the floor.

"Man I couldn't believe it! You acted like you'd lost your fuckin' mind! Wearing that trashy dress!" He kicked the table.

"Oh!"

"Gyrating and twisting like you got no common sense and embarrassing the hell outta yourself! And making a fool of me!"

"It had nothing to do with you."

"I got so mad I wanted to take you out right then and there. I was there."

"I know. Left your calling card."

"And I was in the parking lot when you left and I followed you home too. I was gonna kill you that night, Brianna. Had it all planned out in my head but you're lucky God stepped in."

"I didn't mean to make you mad."

"Bullshit! You live on it!"

"Like you live on scaring me? Huh?"

"See? A match made in heaven if we'd get our shit together."

"Stop this. Please."

"Not until I get what I came for tonight."

CHAPTER TWENTY

❝*What* do you want?" She punched the cabinet. "You wanna kill me? Wanna rape me?"

"I want you to pay attention."

"I am! You're ruining my life! How can I not pay attention?"

"I want you, Brianna. That's the ultimate goal. To break and bend you until you realize I'm the only person you'll ever need."

"No!" She ran in the direction of the door. "I won't let you do this!"

"You ain't going nowhere!" He snatched her by the blouse." Ahh! Let me go!" She swung her arm back to hit him. He locked it behind her.

"Get off of me!"

"You're scared now huh? Are you?"

"Stop! Let me go! Help!" She kicked at the door but couldn't reach. She screamed until she thought her throat would bleed.

He covered her mouth. "Settle down, Bree."

"Mmmm! Mmm!"

"I'm gonna have you. Right here on the floor."

"Mmm! Mmmm!"

"I said settle down, cunt. Now this is gonna happen and it ain't nothing you can do to stop it."

She pushed her backside into his stomach to try and throw him off. Nothing worked.

"Those defense moves don't work all the time do they?" He laughed. "Lucky for me."

"Mmm! Mmmm!" She bit at his hand but he held her mouth too tight.

"I'm gonna fuck you, Brianna. Then I'm gonna leave you here unclothed and vulnerable for all to see. Then just maybe you'll understand what I mean."

"Brianna?" A voice sounded from the hall.

"Mmm!"

"Shit." The stalker placed a small knife underneath her chin. "You even mutter and I'll gut you like a fuckin' fish."

"Mmmm!"

"Quiet." He shoved her to the back.

"Brianna?"

It was *Simon*.

She struggled.

The stalker pressed her against him. "Shh good girl."

"Mmm. Mmm!"

"Brianna they said you were up here!" Simon knocked on the door. "Are you all right? You in there?"

She couldn't let Simon leave.

The stalker wouldn't just rape her. He'd kill her. She knew it. She plunged her foot into his.

"Owwww!" He let her go.

She slammed her elbow into his face.

"Ahh shit!" He fumbled, swinging the knife. "You bitch! You're not getting out of here!"

"Oh I think I will!" She slung around and kicked him in the face.

"Ahhh!" He fell over.

Simon busted in. "Brianna?"

"Simon!" She ran to him.

The stalker grabbed her and threw her back.

"Ohh!" She rolled over on the floor and landed under the table.

"Brianna!"

"Simon be careful he has a knife!"

"Motherfucker!" The stalker threw Simon against the wall and punched him in the stomach. He drove his elbow into Simon's groin.

"Ohhh!" Simon landed on the floor. The stalker hopped on top, delivering punch after bloody punch.

"Leave him alone!" Brianna dug in her jeans. Shit she didn't even have her *pepper spray.*

"Simon are you okay?"

She couldn't tell who landed the punches and who cried out in pain.

The electricity popped back on. Brianna adjusted her eyes. The man had Simon pinned in the corner between the cabinets. He bashed his head into the wall.

"Oh…oh!" Simon clawed at the black ski mask on the stalker's face.

He wore gloves, black jeans and leather lace-up shoes. His pale skin shown from under the mask.

"Simon get outta the way!" Brianna hooked her arm around the stalker's neck.

"Rrrr ahh!" She tore at his mask.

"Brianna!" Simon jumped on the stalker to hold him down. "Go get help! I'll hold him!"

"Can you?"

"Yes, just go!"

Brianna ran down the hall and through the detectives' area. She pushed the alarm by the elevator and headed back to Simon.

"Get off me!" The stalker swung his knife.

"Ohh!" Simon flipped off him.

The stalker grabbed Simon by his shirt. His punch threw Simon into the hall.

"Simon!" Brianna got to the hall. She'd gotten her gun along the way. "Hold it!"

Chilling eyes stared at her from the mask. "You won't shoot me, Brianna."

"I will! Get off him!"

"Unnnn!" The man threw the knife at her face.

"Brianna!"

"Ohh!" She reared back. Her gun flew out her hands.

The stalker jumped up.

"No!" Simon grabbed the stalker's leg. "You're not going anywhere!"

"Get off me!" He swung his other foot and kicked Simon on the side of the face.

"Simon!" Brianna got her gun and crawled to him.

The man ran down the hall and into the stairwell.

"Simon stay here all right!"

"No!" He coughed and clenched his middle. "Don't go after him!"

"I got to! I'm not letting him get away!"

"No, Brianna!"

She leapt over Simon's legs and headed to the stairs.

"Detective Morris!" An officer ran up holding his gun.

"What's going on?" Another officer came around the corner.

"What the hell happened?" The first officer watched Simon heaving on the floor.

"He was here damn it!" Brianna wheezed. "I gotta go find..."

"No don't let her go!" Simon reached for her. "He's dangerous!"

"Who the hell are you talking about?" The second officer asked.

"The stalker damn it!" Brianna pointed her gun to the stairwell. "He was just here and he's getting away! He went down these stairs! I have to go!"

"No." The second officer pulled her back. "I'll check it out."

"Hurry! He might be gone by now!"

He ran down the stairs.

The first officer knelt beside Simon. "Are you all right, Mister?"

"Yes...yes. He punched me in my ribs. Ah." He lifted his knees. "I'll be okay."

"Simon you're breathing hard." Brianna took his hand. "You need to go to the hospital?"

"No I'm fine. Are you all right?"

She shook loose strands from her face. "Physically I guess so. Don't know about mentally."

"Why didn't you tell me this was going on?"

"It wasn't your business."

"It is now." Simon touched her cheek.

The second officer came up the stairs ten minutes later.

"What is it?" Brianna rushed to him. "Where is he?"

"I didn't even see him. It was even harder with all the rain."

"Fuck." Brianna whispered.

"Some of the guys are patrolling the block. There wasn't anyone in the parking lot."

"You think he could still be in the building?" Simon asked.

Brianna shook her head. "I was this fuckin' close. I can't believe I let him get away."

"Maybe you didn't." Simon stood with the officer's help.

"Of course I did. How could I let this happen? Damn it!"

"Brianna."

"What?" She huffed.

Simon gestured with his head. "He left his knife."

◆◆◆◆◆◆

An hour later Steven marched around his desk. He'd jumped out of bed, thrown on some clothes and had arrived at the station before Brianna finished her call to Captain Jersey.

Officers scrambled down the hall and searched the file room multiple times for clues.

Unless his DNA landed somewhere nothing they'd find would be more important than the knife.

Brianna hadn't moved from her chair since she sat down. People asked her how she felt every five minutes. They kept bringing her cups of coffee and staring at her. She hated that the most. She'd been afraid that once her secret got out her co-workers would look at her like they did right now.

Simon sat beside her in Steven's chair with his hand on hers. He didn't stare or ask her how she felt. That's what she needed, space. Too bad the others didn't understand that.

"Kemp why don't you sit down?" Captain Jersey took off her rain bonnet. She set her dripping umbrella against Brianna's desk. "Stomping around like a buffalo isn't doing anyone any good."

"That's what I do when I think. You know that."

"Or when you're angry right?" Brianna looked up from her coffee. "You obviously have something to say Steve so let's hear it."

"I'm trying not to be insensitive right now, Bree."

"I wanna know what you think."

"Wanna know what I think? I'm thinking how can the woman I've known for so long act like she doesn't have half a brain in her head!"

"Wait a minute."

"Stuff it, Watts." Steven lunged at him. "This is between us. Bree how the fuck you think I feel? I'm so mad I don't know what to do! You been walking around here, being terrorized, the whole goddamn station knew it and I knew shit! How is that supposed to make me feel?"

"Oh I don't know, Steve. I just got attacked tonight so it might take me a while to think about how you're feeling at the moment."

"Morris has gone through something horrible tonight, Kemp. The last thing she needs is someone shouting at her."

"You're just as bad as she is, Captain!"

"Excuse me?"

"You knew this shit was going on and you hid it from me."

"It wasn't my place to tell. I had to respect her decision."

"Right. So much for us sticking together and looking after each other right?"

Brianna slammed her cup on the desk. "And you wonder why I didn't tell you, Steve?I need compassion right now and all I'm getting from you is attitude."

"Compassion? You didn't trust me to be compassionate before obviously so why the hell should I be now?"

"I didn't say anything to you because you have a way of making me feel guilty when things aren't my fault!"

"Oh please, Bree." He fanned. "You chose to hide this and that's why you almost got killed tonight! It's your fault!"

"My fault?"

"Kemp!"

"Don't take up for her, Captain! You know it's the truth."

Jersey looked at Brianna.

"If she hadn't been too busy trying to save the world on her own and realize she's a human being then she would have come to me and I could've helped her."

Brianna chuckled. "So you could have stopped the stalker, Steve?"

"Maybe not but I'd have been there for you and protected you!"

"I don't need anyone to protect me!"

He scoffed. "Well judging by tonight Bree, you do."

"You son-of-a-bitch."

"Morris," Jersey said.

"Who do you think you are Steven to pass judgment on me? You've never gone through something like this! You can't tell me how I should've reacted!"

"You saying you aren't to blame for almost being killed tonight?"

"So I grabbed myself and stuck a knife to my own face?"

"No but you might as well!"

"Stop it!" Jersey jumped between them. "Just stop it right now."They sized each other up and turned the other way.

"No one can say how they would be in a situation like that Kemp, not even you. I don't agree with Morris' choice to hide it but that was her choice. There are more important things to think about. That maniac was right in this building." Jersey pounded her fist on Brianna's desk."If he's got the guts to attack her at the station, he's more warped than we think."

CHAPTER TWENTY-ONE

"I agree with Captain Jersey," Simon said.

Steven sat on the edge of Brianna's desk. "Who gives a fuck?"

"Kemp shut up." Jersey touched Simon's shoulder. "Mr. Watts you should be proud of what you did. You risked your life to save Morris and on my behalf thank you. If you hadn't shown up no telling what would've happened."

Steven groaned.

"I'm just glad I got here in time before he could really hurt her."

Brianna smiled at him.

"I care about Brianna a lot already. She knows that."

"What the hell were you doing here anyway, Watts?" Steven bounced his leg.

"I had to talk to Brianna. We had unfinished business to discuss."

"What kind of unfinished business?"

"The kind that's none of your business."

"Oh?" Steven reared back. "Is that so?"

"Stop it, Steve." Brianna sat down. "You're mad at me. Don't take it out on Simon."

Steven got off the desk.

"I'm sorry I didn't tell you sooner but I have my reasons. It's over and done with and I'm not gonna explain it to you again."

"You didn't trust me, Bree." Steven tapped his chest. "*That's* what's so hard to accept."

"Oh god do you have wax in your ears? I keep telling you that this had nothing to do with you! I do have things in my life that don't revolve around you."

Steven cut his eyes to Simon. "I'm starting to get that feeling."

"Instead of being an asshole to Simon you need to be thanking him."

"For what, Bree? Letting the fucker get away?"

"I didn't *let* him do anything, Detective Kemp. I fought him as best I could but he was stronger and he had a knife."

"Mmm hmmm. Well if I'd gotten here you can believe his ass would be in a cell downstairs but because of you he's probably snuggled up in his bed."

Simon inhaled.

"Oh Steven stop it." Brianna massaged her forehead. "This isn't the time for you to challenge Simon to a penis measuring contest okay?"

"You saying I'm jealous of him?"

"No." Brianna sat back. "Your behavior is."

"Can we please get back to what's important here?" Captain Jersey stopped in front of Steven's desk. "The bad thing is that Morris didn't see a face so we still don't know what he looks like or who he is. But the good thing is the knife. We can get fingerprints off of it and we can go from there."

"But he was wearing gloves," Simon said. "You might not be able to get prints."

Jersey got her coffee from the edge of Brianna's desk. "I'm willing to bet that he's probably had that knife for years. You see how old it was. I know he's touched that knife once in his life and left prints."

Brianna yawned. "It's better than nothing."

"You're tired." Simon patted her back.

Steven cursed under his breath.

"I am."

"Go home and get some rest, Morris," Jersey said. "And why don't you take tomorrow off huh?"

"Oh no that's not necessary."

"See?" Steven shook his head. "Still trying to be Miss Big Shot huh?"

"Me sitting at home isn't gonna help anything." She got up.

"Besides I'm not deserting Cheyenne's case for a minute."

"You're amazing." Simon passed Brianna her purse. "Even after what you went through tonight you're still concerned about Cheyenne."

Steven rolled his eyes.

"I won't stop being concerned until I find out who attacked her."

"Bree." Steven jumped in front of Simon. "I don't think you should be alone tonight." He looked at Simon. "You can stay at my place."

Simon's lips curled.

"That's not necessary. I don't mind being alone."

"No come on, Bree." He caressed her arms. "You don't need to be alone."

"I think she said it's not necessary, Detective." Simon smiled.

"And I don't remember asking you what you think either."

Jersey pulled Steven back. "She said no all right?"

"Fine then. Excuse me for being concerned." He stomped away.

Brianna and Simon said goodnight to Captain Jersey and went to the elevator.

"You really didn't mean that did you?" Simon pressed the button.

"What?" Brianna straightened her purse.

"That you don't mind being alone tonight."

They stepped into the elevator.

"What is it to you?"

"Let's just say I got a better idea." He locked his arm in hers. "You're coming to my place tonight."

"No, Simon. I'm fine, really."

He touched her chin. "There's something you need to remember, Brianna. I'm not as easy to dissuade as Detective Kemp."

"Davis?" Brianna snapped her fingers. "No. Shoo!"

Davis ignored his mistress and continued his game of clawing at Simon's dresser.

"Davis?"

Simon walked into his bedroom with a bottle of wine and two glasses.

"Maybe I should've left him at home."

"It's okay. He's not bothering anything."

"Thanks for following me home to pick up some things."

Simon winked. "Hey I'd done anything to persuade you to come."

"Aarrr." Davis rolled over and kicked his paws into the air.

"I don't want him to scratch up your furniture."

"He can't scratch that type of wood. It's fine." Simon poured her a glass of red wine.

"This should help you relax okay?"

Davis explored the luxuries in Simon's bedroom as if he were at a feline wonderland.

"Ha, ha. Let me guess." Simon sat beside her on the bed. "You never take your cat out do you?"

"I don't get a chance to much these days you know?"

"You okay?"

"More mad than anything else. I could've socked Steven. Such a jerk."

"Ahh don't be too hard on him. He cares a lot about you. Anyone can see that."

She shrugged and sniffed her wine.

"So how long were you together?"

"How did you know we had been?"

"By the way he looked at you. Like he's a man in love."

"He means the world to me. I'll never have a friend like Steven but I've moved on from anything romantic with him."

"You sure you have? I'm sorry. Obviously you don't wanna talk about Detective Kemp."

"I shouldn't be drinking."

"Nonsense. After what you went through tonight you deserve the entire liquor cabinet."

"I do love red wine."

Simon suckled the wine from his lips. "Never met a woman that didn't."

"And we both know you've known a lot of women haven't you?" She sipped.

"I'm a Cognac man myself."

"Ooh." Brianna stuffed one leg underneath her. "Sly diversion tactic, Mr. Watts. I notice that about you."

"What?"

"You're talented at switching the subject in a way people wouldn't notice."

"Well we both know you would huh? You notice all the details."

She twirled her glass.

"I'm sorry." He touched her leg. "Did I offend you?"

"No. Obviously I don't notice enough of the details do I? I still don't know who the stalker is."

"Brianna I am so sorry you've been going through this. Must be awful but I could tell something was bothering you." He poured her more wine even though she'd only had one sip.

"He's jealous of me, Simon. That's what fuels his anger. He said I think I'm better than everyone else is. It's almost as if he resents me more than admires me."

"At least now I understand why you always accused me of following you. Did you think I was the stalker?"

"Simon you gotta understand this shit gets to you. You start second-guessing who you can trust and who you can't. I didn't know you so I had to be sure and when you kept popping up everywhere, what was I to think?"

"I just hate you'd assume I'd have the capacity to do something like that."

"I didn't after I first came here that day." She glanced at the old jewelry box on his dresser. He used it to store his seashell collection. "After then I didn't feel like it could be you."

"Why not?"

"Because if you were him I figured you'd have made a move on me when we were alone or started acting weird. You were a complete gentleman."

"Did you want me to be?"

The wine trickled down her throat, easing her anxiety little by little. "Honestly? No."

"Why not?"

"Rrrr." Davis stretched and clawed the carpet.

"Simon."

"Answer the question. Did you want me to be a gentleman that day or not?"

"No all right. I wanted you to make a move." Her voice trailed. "You happy now?"

"Well I know that must be hard for you to admit that. I wasn't asking to embarrass you."

"How do you figure I'm embarrassed? I lack the capacity to blush."

He laughed. "I love your sense of humor. So quick."

"Uh-huh."

"And I knew you wanted me to keep going that day. When I supposedly teased you. I could feel the heat from your body. Feels kind of like it does now."

They stared into each other's eyes for what seemed like forever to Brianna.

"Do you trust me now?"

"If not I wouldn't be here. Anyway you saved me tonight. If I can't be safe with you, who can I be safe with?"

"I'm so glad you feel that way, Brianna. I want you to feel safe with me more than anything."

The thrill in his eyes disintegrated.

"What's wrong, Simon?"

He dragged his thumb across his glass.

"I know this might seem like shite but it's the truth. I haven't felt this connected to a woman in a long time. That's what makes this so amazing, Brianna. I felt like I knew you before I met you. I know it was fate for us to meet."

"I understand."

"I don't think you do." She watched him.

He took his eyes from hers the first time since he sat down.

"I don't wanna hide anything from you. That's a first for me. I don't trust a lot of people at all. I'm always guarded."

"I think we all are to a point right?"

"Some more than others though."

"Simon you don't have to…"

"I had a very difficult childhood. It's left me bruised and a little broken but I think I bounced back okay."

She smiled.

"I learned about emotional pain at a very early age and I fight everyday to forget it."

Brianna leaned back on the pillows.

"I grew up in Manchester. I never knew my father. From what my mum said he was some bloke who'd passed through the flat like all the others. She wasn't exactly a Christian woman if you get my drift. I doubt you'd know anyone poorer than us. We'd go days without eating and sometimes mum wouldn't come home so we had to fend for ourselves."

He scooted further onto the bed.

"I did all I could for change to keep in the house. And that house." He chuckled. "The worst thing you'd ever see. The walls were practically unattached. We literally, Clara and I had to stand up when it rained and hold our hands into the holes in the wall. That's how big they were."

"Oh my goodness."

"Yeah. I couldn't explain the smell around there because the entire neighborhood was poor. I'll never forget that rank smell of dead rats and excrement. People would walk up and down the streets taking shits and pissing everywhere. On someone else's walkway, in the yard. Clara and I were so dirty at times we had to go to the hospital for the simplest of diseases."

"I'm sorry."

"I bet it's hard to imagine me like that and now having so much money huh?" She scratched her shoulder.

"It's true what they say, Brianna. We are products of our surroundings and our childhood. No matter how rich or old I become I sometimes still feel like that little barefooted dirty boy who ate outta cans and spent his time daydreaming because he didn't have any friends."

"Why didn't you have friends?"

"The other kids didn't like me."

"Because you were poor?"

"No in that part of Manchester, everyone was poor. I don't know why they didn't like me. I always did things to get folks to like me. It didn't work. That's how Clara and I became so close. We were only a year apart. She was a year older and I looked up to her so much. She was my guiding light. Our bond is what got us through the hardest times."

CHAPTER TWENTY-TWO

"I don't have any siblings." Brianna touched the ends of hair. "I can relate to the part about your father though. I know my father but he was never in the picture. He left my mom and I when I was a kid. I guess I can't blame him."

"Why?"

"Ol' George Morris just didn't have it in him to be somebody's daddy. He tried to play the part of a good husband and father but no. It never worked."

"How did you feel when he left?"

"Oh." She sat Indian-style. "Hurt and confused. I wondered what I did for him not to be there. But as I grew older I realized it was his problem and not mine. I don't regret it to be honest." She finished her wine and poured more. "Momma never would've met Edgar and he's the best thing that ever happened to her."

"He's rich right? Your stepfather?"

"Yes."

"You two get along?"

"Oh absolutely." She gobbled wine. "He's treated me like I was his from the beginning. I couldn't ask for a better father. He'd give me anything I needed if I'd take it."

"Well stepfathers are a touchy subject with me. See my mother got married to the first man who'd pay her some attention. Didn't say nothing to us, just did it."

"She didn't tell you she was getting married?"

"No. She'd been gone for days and came back with a ring on her finger. He seemed okay at first. Had a nice house we moved into and a good job. He was a welder so he worked at the steel plant. Made a good living for us. He had a daughter of his own that was Clara's age."

"How did this man treat you?"

"He killed my mother."

"Wh…what?"

"My mother never loved him. She treated him like dirt. They fought all the time. At first it was okay but everything quickly turned sour." He closed his eyes. "Oh Brianna if you lived in that house you'd be scared of your own shadow. They both turned to drinking and drugs. Soon Clara and I were in the same fix as before. My stepfather lost his house and job. Can you believe we ended back up only blocks down from the flat we used to live in?"

"Oh, Simon."

"We ended up even poorer. Lost everything to their habits. The more they drunk and did dope the more abusive they got."

"Just to each other or to all of you?"

"We all got slapped around a few times but they took it out on each other mostly. That heroin is a demon."

"Man they were on heroin?"

"He did heroin and coke. Probably just to put up with my mum."

Brianna shook her head.

"She took to prostituting again to get money. Of course Clara and I didn't know she'd been doing that all along when we were home alone all those days. One day when Clara was nine and I was eight, my stepfather busted into the living room."

Brianna sat up.

"Clara and I didn't know what was going on. We didn't know my mother had a man in there. She always told us to go to our rooms and "do something". That's what she said and we knew to stay out of her way. We thought one of her pushers was coming or something because the drug men came in and out anyway."

Brianna held his hand.

"I remember exactly what I was doing when it all happened." He wiped a tear. "Clara was lying on the floor, looking at a magazine. I was sitting on the bed. It was raining. I remember because there were holes in the ceiling over my bed and it always leaked. I remember the cool water dropping over me and I thought then, "This is a sign." Brianna I really felt that. Like something was about to change forever."

"You don't have to go on."

"Heard some arguing. We ran to the hall and...bang!"

Brianna jumped.

"We didn't know what it was at first but it shook the house. Then we heard it again and we knew it was a gun."

Brianna stroked his arm.

"Two shots and then nothing." His pupils stretched. "So I told Clara to wait in the hall and I ran to the other room. My stepfather was standing over my mum." His hands shook." She was...was gasping and holding her neck." He put his hand on his neck. "And she was reaching to him, crying and begging. He looked her in the eyes. Oh." He closed his eyes." And I remember trying to breathe but not being able to. I was gonna beg him not to shoot anymore. To leave her alone."

Brianna sobbed.

"Before I got the words out my mouth, he shot her. Right in the head."

"Si...Simon. You don't have to say any..."

"I tiptoed to the couch. I bent down. Her eyes were still open and her hand was shivering. He pushed me outta the way. I crawled backward to the hall." He licked tears. "Clara ran into the room and I grabbed her so roughly my fingerprints were left in her arm."

"It's okay." She brought his head to her shoulder.

"He turned the gun on us."

"What?" Brianna shivered.

"Said that he wished we'd never come into his life. My stepsister was outside and she came running in then. She said, "Daddy stop! Please!" She fell to her knees and screamed so loud when she saw my mother." His eyes darkened.

"You said he turned the gun on you? The...the children?" She felt his ponytail.

"He said he was gonna kill us and say someone broke in and killed everybody except him and my stepsister."

"Shh. It's okay."

"So he...he lifted the gun on Clara. Then everything went white. I don't even remember doing it, Brianna. I swear I don't. It was like I wasn't even there."

"What did you do?" She moved from his arms.

"I just remember me coming back from wherever I was and holding the gun. Clara and my stepsister were screaming. And he was…my stepfather was…"

"What?"

"Dead."

Brianna covered her mouth.

"On the floor with a bullet in his chest."

"Oh. Ohh."

"From me, Brianna." He stared into his wineglass. "From me."

"Shh. It's okay." She kissed his forehead. "Don't say anymore."

His hand went up her back. "I didn't mean it. I…I didn't mean it, Brianna."

"Shh. I know you're a good person, Simon." She pecked kisses down his cheek." I understand. It wasn't your fault. I'm so sorry you had to go through that." She curled his ponytail in her fingers. "It's okay. You can let go of it now."

"Hmm?" He touched her lips.

"Shh." She kissed his nose. "You can let go."

"I wanna let go with *you*." He captured her mouth in his. Slipped his warm tongue on top of hers. "You're so beautiful."

She put her hands on his shoulders. He wrapped his arms around her. This kiss unleashed an ache of sexual urgency she could no longer ignore. She didn't want to ignore.

"You smell so good." He nudged his nose into her neck. "Do you like this? Being this close?"

"Yes."

He moved her hair and sucked her earlobe. "Want me to stop?"

"Mmm." She moved her head along with his mouth. "No. Please don't."

"You want me to make love to you?" His fingers tickled the crotch of her jeans.

"Hmm? Do you want that?"

"Mmm. I…"A tingle shot through her nipples.

"Say it." He sucked her neck. "Say you want me to."

"I…oh I want you to."

"Say my name." His lips made a sucking sound on her skin. "Say it again and say my name."

"I want you to…" She melted in his arms. "Make love to me."

"Say my name."

"I want you to make love to me. Simon."

♦♦♦♦♦♦

Brianna stretched out naked on Simon's bed. He dipped a tiny amount of massage oil in his palm and lowered over her. She licked that warm spot behind his ear. Enjoying the salty taste of his skin. She slid the rubber band off his head. Freeing his hair from the tight ponytail. She pushed her nose in his hair, feeling the silky strands within her fingers. His cologne smelled like the aftermath of fresh rain mixed with mint.

His scent intensified throughout the room the more he sweated. The delicious odor got her clit so wet she could've engulfed a baseball in it.

He dampened his palms with oil and lifted her leg. He massaged the bottom of her foot.

"Mmm." She wiggled on the sheets.

"Oh those pretty toes. Mmm." He separated her big toe from the others with his fingers. He sucked it, working his sticky tongue against the curve of her toe.

"Oooh. Yes." She caressed her nipples. "Yes. Oh, that feels so good."

He tickled her toe with his tongue. He moved his hand down her ankle in a circular motion.

Brianna wasn't easy to please in bed. But if she had a tail she'd be wagging it like a dog right now. Steven used to complain about how long it took to get her off. She needed a man to take his time more than the average woman. She loved being teased, massaged, nibbled and groped. She judged a man's lovemaking on how hot he got her *before* penetration.

So far Simon passed the test.

He smoothed oil down her legs. He swept his hands underneath her and polished her ass with the soothing ointment.

"You like that?"

She sucked her finger. "*Yes.*" He stroked her breasts and brushed her nipples with his damp thumbs.

"How about this?" He slapped his tongue over her tight black nipple. "You like that?" He tugged on her nipple with his teeth. "Huh, darling? You wet yet?"

"Oooh." She wrapped her thighs around his waist.

Simon pulled the covers over them. He eased his breath down that spot between her breasts that got her so hot.

"Oh yes."

He wrapped his tongue around her nipple and plucked it with the tip.

"Ohh." She arched her back for him to take her entire breast into her mouth.

"So beautiful." He dragged his tongue past her stomach and to her center.

She chewed her lip. Tangled her fingers in the sheets.

If he felt this amazing *before* penetration she figured she'd split in two from the override of orgasms he'd force out of her.

"I've wanted you like this since the first time Cheyenne told me about you."

He spread her thighs. His hair flowed across her legs.

She wanted this. She *needed* this. She'd wasted too much time fighting him. She couldn't believe giving in felt so good.

Sweat beaded on her breasts and stomach but flowed like a waterfall under her back and ass.

He sucked her clit.

"Ohhh."

He lashed at it with his tongue. "Should...I...stop?"

She shivered and kicked. "No...uh...no!"

He leaned up.

"No please." She heaved. "Don't stop."

What the fuck are you doing? Get your head back down there!

Sweat ran down his chest and dissolved in the patch of hair on his crotch. He had a mammoth cock. Long, bulky and wide. Stood straight out like a meaty sword. She'd had a clue of his size when they danced at the club. His dick had gone straight through her panties and it seemed like there were inches left.

"Simon?"

He flicked his hair.

"Why did you stop?"

"Because I need to be sure."

She propped on the pillows. "Sure of what? This isn't the time for this shit."

"Meow."

"See even Davis knows it ain't fair to stop in the middle of giving head."

"I wanna make love to you more than anything. Never wanted a woman so much in my life."

"Then what?"

"I gotta be sure that it's me you want and not anyone else."

"It is. I'm attracted to you, Simon. I can't fight it and I don't want to. If I didn't want this I wouldn't be here."

"For me this is destiny. I really believe we were meant to be."

"It's over between me and Steven. I swear it."

"Are you sure? Does he really know that?"

"I can't control how he feels. He'll have to get over it." She kissed him. "The only man I want is the one right here in this room."

He maneuvered himself between her legs. "Look into my eyes."

She did.

"If you want me inside you." His hardness poked her thighs. "Say it."

"I want you inside me."

He lifted her legs above her head and placed her ankles on his shoulders.

He grunted. "Say it again."

Her walls shuttered as she felt the tip of his dick.

"Ahh. I want you inside of me, Simon. All of you."

"I promise you darling, you'll never regret it."

He plunged inside of her.

"Uhhh!" She dug her fingernails into his back.

"Show me, Brianna." He pumped with urgency and expertise. "Show me."

"Yes. Ahh!" Her body bounced with his. "I'll show you. I'll show you."

CHAPTER TWENTY-THREE

"Ahh." Simon stretched out on the hammock in his gazebo the next day. He couldn't get Brianna out of his head and he had no complaints. He closed his eyes and let his hands travel down the tall glass of lemonade. Everything smelled of peaches in and outside the house. Her scent stayed in his nose from the lovemaking. *He had no complaints.*

He crossed his feet at the ankles and put his free arm behind his back. He imagined the curvy glass to be her body. He'd fixed her breakfast. They enjoyed the aftermath of more lovemaking then she'd taken off.

What he felt for her scared him. He didn't know where it would lead but he wasn't letting her get away. He'd do whatever it took to keep her. He'd fight anyone he had to. He loved her. It began the first time Cheyenne told him about her and it had grown into something he had no hope of controlling. That he didn't wanna control.

"Mmm." He imagined her naked body on top of him. Could feel the skin under his hands it seemed so real. "Just don't run away from me." He sipped from his straw. "Let me love you always."

"Aww isn't that sweet?"

"Ahhh!" Simon flipped outta the hammock.

"Ha, ha, ha!" The guy took off his shades and crossed the yard.

"What the hell are you doing here?"

"I don't know. Guess."

"What the?" Simon struggled with the hammock. "You scared the hell outta me! How'd you get in here?"

"Come on, dude." The man relaxed in the hammock. "I got a key remember."

Simon knocked the man's feet off the hammock.

"Whoa!"

"Get the hell outta here now!"

"Now." The man touched his chest. "Is that anyway to talk to your best friend, Simon?"

He clenched teeth. "You are not my best friend. You're a nightmare I can't get rid of."

"Really?" The man swayed in the hammock. "If it hadn't been for me you wouldn't be outside here relaxing. And you sure as hell wouldn't be enjoying these riches."

"My money has nothing to do with you."

"I enable you to keep it don't I? Oh come on, Simon. We're friends. You know that."

"You have no business here. You can't just come around whenever you feel like it. What if someone sees you here?"

"Who the fuck's gonna see me all the way out here?" The man sipped from Simon's straw. "You got a thousand fuckin' acres of land and no neighbors."

"Still we gotta be as safe as possible. People cannot know we're connected at all!"

"Would you calm the fuck down?" He belched. "Ahh."

Simon grimaced.

"Shit you're usually begging me to come over here. Now I'm not invited?"

"It's too risky."

"Look no one knows we know each other and they won't so calm down." The man sat up in the hammock. "Anyway." He dug in his ear. "Don't act like you didn't expect to see me. I've been calling all morning."

"You did not call this morning."

"I called your cell phone. I didn't know who was over here. You think I'd call your house and have you bitch more than you are now?"

"Oh." Simon rubbed his hair. "I turned my phone off last night."

"Why'd you turn your phone off? And why you have that goofy, I-just-had-the-greatest-sex-of-my-life look?"

"Go to hell."

"So that's it huh? You had company? That's why you turned your phone off."

"What is it to you?"

"I gotta make sure you're thinking straight from now on. You already almost got us locked up. You had no business going to the police in the first place."

"I told you I felt guilty."

The man snickered. "But not the other times? I don't recall you feeling so guilty when you asked me to dump Olivia Delcie's body in that shed."

"Shut up!"

"Ohh what? The guilt too hard to handle, Simon?"

"I got nothing to be guilty for. I didn't do anything wrong."

"Right. I think the cops would see it differently. Imagine how they'd feel if they knew what really happened to Olivia."

"Are you threatening me? You must be outta your mind to threaten me after all I've done for you."

"And I've done a hell of a lot more for you the way I see it." The man stood and pulled up his pants. "Now I love you like a brother, Simon."

He scoffed.

"But I'm telling you right now. I'll send your ass up the river if I get an inch of suspicion that you're about to do the same to me."

"I'd never do that. You're being paranoid."

The man exhaled. "Look why are we jumping down each other's throats? We both need each other anyway. So what?" He put his arm around Simon's shoulders. "I love you man. But you gotta stop being so soft."

"I am not soft."

"Yes you are. You got a good heart and it makes you stupid."

"Well excuse me for having a moral compass. I feel horrible about Cheyenne."

"I know. But I didn't come to talk about that. I need some money."

"How can you need money? You're fuckin' rich thanks to me!"

"My money's tied up right now. I can't get any out of the account. Some issues going on. Anyway, I just need some dough okay?"

"If you didn't spend it on casinos and those disgusting women then you'd have money."

"There haven't been a lot of women in a long time you know that.

I don't care about anyone but her."

"Oh this sad story again?"

"Simon I'm dying here."

"Dying?" He laughed. "You look pretty damn good to me, man."

"I mean without her."

"And you talk about me getting us in trouble with the law? You keep chasing after this woman then that's it. I told you to leave it alone."

"I can't, Simon. I love her. Don't you understand that?"

"You gotta get it through your head that she doesn't feel the same way."

"Yes she does. She's just afraid of me. I fucked things up and got mad."

"You can't have her, man. And you never should've wanted her."

"Can you talk to her for me? She likes you."

"Absolutely not."

The man grabbed Simon's arm. "You got to."

"No."

The man's face fell.

"You're starting to scare me when it comes to her. It's like you're obsessed."

"She loves me." He put his shades back on. "And I'm gonna show her that."

"Leave her alone."

"Can I have that money?"

"How much you need?"

"About one hundred grand."

"A hundred grand? What the fuck did you do?"

"I don't need a lecture, just give me the dough. Cash of course because we can't risk things being traced to us."

"I'm not stupid remember?" Simon sat on the hammock. "If that's all you wanted, please leave."

"Okay."

"Wait a minute."

"What?"

"I need a favor."

"Simon I've done you enough favors to last you a million years."

He smiled. "I need you to do me one more. It's for a new friend."

◆◆◆◆◆◆

"Stephanie come on." Steven sat on the couch. Brianna studied the family pictures around the James' living room.

"I don't understand why you don't believe me, Detective Kemp." She picked toys off the floor and stuffed them under her arms. "Michael and I spent the evening here together the night Cheyenne Wilson was beaten. So there's no way he's connected."

She called for the maid. The antsy young woman took the toys and ran out of the room.

"Blame it on Bree."

Brianna glanced from a photo of the James family on a boating trip.

"See I had your back Stephanie but Bree wasn't convinced that you were telling the truth."

"Steve." Brianna faked a smile when Stephanie looked at her.

He stretched. "Stephanie we know you lied."

"I have no idea what you're talking about." She held her robe closed. "I'm not feeling very well today and the house is a mess. Will you two please just leave?"

"We can't do that." Brianna stepped over boxes of board games and jigsaw puzzles. She slid next to Steven. "We know Michael wasn't here that night. Do you really wanna lie for Michael?"

She laughed. "I'm not lying." She motioned to the television. "He was here and we watched *Sleepless in Seattle* just like I told you."

"Yeah and you said it was on TBS right?" Steven asked.

"Yes so?"

"Only it wasn't," Brianna said. "We checked the listings on the Internet. *Sleepless in Seattle* hasn't been on TV in a year and it certainly wasn't on TBS the night Cheyenne was beaten."

Stephanie trudged up and down the carpet. "Oh uh." She gathered stuffed animals off the television. "Oh you know?" She chuckled. "I was wrong."

Steven and Brianna looked at each other.

"I don't know how I could make a mistake. See I watch TBS a lot and I guess I got confused. We watched the movie but it was on DVD."

"DVD huh?" Steven plucked the roof of his mouth with his tongue.

"Yes." Stephanie dumped the animals into the hall. "So I didn't lie on purpose. I made a mistake."

"Let me see the DVD." Brianna held out her hand.

"What?"

"Let me see the DVD, Stephanie."

"Uh." She twisted the ends of her hair. "I don't have it. It was my sister's and I gave it back to her."

Steven smirked.

"Stephanie we only wanna help you but you're only getting yourself into trouble when you lie."

"I'm not lying, Detective Morris. It was my sister's movie. I swear it."

"Stephanie that's not the only reason we know you're lying." Steven spread his legs and hung his arms in between them. "See we talked to your neighbors."

"My n…neighbors?"

"Uh-huh. Because of what they told me and Bree, we know there was no way Michael Buchanan was over here."

"It's a lie. Whatever they said." She crossed her arms under her bosom.

Brianna recited what she'd written on her notepad. "Both of your neighbors said that Gene and the girls were home that night. They both remembered because Gene came home early because of the weather. One of them even spoke to him."

Stephanie's face went flour-white. "They have the days mixed up. Gene was gone that night with the girls."

"With the weather being that bad?" Steven tapped the arm of the sofa. "Stephanie."

"I'm telling the truth! Michael was here right where you're sitting and we watched *Sleepless in Seattle*!" She burst into tears. "It's the truth."

Brianna slapped the notepad on her thigh. "No see one of your neighbors is recovering from an injury isn't she?"

"Yes."

"Well she said the physical therapist comes every Wednesday. The therapist cancelled because of the weather. So your neighbors didn't get mixed up." Brianna leaned forward. "Maybe you did."

"She's crazy."

Steven grinned. "Ahh you don't have to tell me that."

"I'm crazy if you think I still believe you're telling the truth. Stephanie you could be in big trouble."

"I didn't do anything, Detective Morris. Not one damn thing."

"Michael could've attacked Cheyenne and if you're covering for him that's a crime."

"No!" She marched, gripping her head. "That didn't happen! He was here."

Brianna jumped up. "You ought to be ashamed of yourself."

"Bree calm down."

"Don't tell me to calm down, Steve! Cheyenne is lying in a hospital fighting for her life and Michael might've put her there!"

"Get out of my house!"

Brianna charged Stephanie. "I'm not going anywhere until I find out the truth!"

"Bree cool it!"

"Cheyenne might not mean a damn thing to you but she's my friend and she didn't deserve what happened to her!"

"I wouldn't ever hurt anyone, Detective Morris!"

"Then stop lying!" Brianna shook her. "You tell the truth right now!"

"Bree stop it!" Steven tussled with the women.

"Tell me the truth! Michael wasn't here that night was he?"

Stephanie broke free. "No he wasn't!"

CHAPTER TWENTY-FOUR

Stephanie sobbed into her hands.

"Stephanie what's going on?" Steven helped her to the couch. "We got the feeling that you were forced to say what you did the last time."

"I just wanted it to be over with." She sniffled. "I was so tired of Michael and what he was doing to me. He kept threatening to tell Gene. I couldn't let him do that. Gene's my world."

"We know you love him."

"Not just that, Detective Kemp. You don't understand. Without Gene I have nothing. I have no place to live, wouldn't have my children, nothing. I'd lose everything. If he ever left me I'd rather be dead. I can't make it on my own. I just can't."

"Wait." Steven sat beside her. "Come on, you're the mother of his kids. He loves you. I'm sure he wouldn't throw you out just because you had one affair."

"It wasn't just one affair."

Brianna rocked. "Say what?"

"I had an affair before." Steven stopped caressing Stephanie's shoulder.

"It was a huge mess. Before I got pregnant with our second daughter. I had to tell Gene because I didn't know if the baby was his or not."

"Oh no." Brianna sighed.

"It almost ruined my marriage. Gene was so cold to me. He hated me. I worked my ass off to get him to love me again. He told me then he'd leave me and take the children if I ever looked at another man again."

"Well why did you do it?" Steven asked. "Why would you risk things for an affair with Michael?"

"Especially when you didn't love him," Brianna said.

"That heat." Stephanie stared mindlessly.

"Heat?" Steven leaned in.

"Come on, Detective Kemp. I know you understand. The heat of an attraction you just can't fight."

"Well uh." He cleared his throat. "Of course. But…"

"I love my husband more than anything. But it never stopped the desire I had to just be myself."

Brianna squinted. "What do you mean?"

"Ever been in a situation where you weren't in control? So full of fear that you didn't know what to do?"

"We all have." Steven put his feet on the table.

Stephanie licked her lips. "Ever liked that feeling?"

Brianna knelt in front of the couch. "I don't think we understand what you mean."

"Course you do, Detective. Whether you're a man or woman that heat's always the same. The heat that's only cured from having a good hard fuck."

Steven's jaws puffed out.

"There's a big difference between fucking and making love. I make love to my husband. I like to *fuck* other men." A tear hit her cheek.

"Stephanie that's none of our business."

"That's the problem, Detective Morris. I've been making excuses to myself for too long. When I met Michael, I didn't have to. There were no boundaries and in the real world, there's nothing but." She relaxed against the pillows.

"What kind of boundaries are you speaking of?" Steven whispered.

"The kind that don't exist. Being wrapped in passion. Being sucked on every part of your body, beaten until being hit is the only way you want to take it."

Brianna stood.

Steven stared at Stephanie with his mouth opened.

Stephanie made a fist. "Being thrown against a building or tree, struggling and fighting while he rips your panties off and fucks you in broad daylight for all to see. And not giving a damn if someone's watching." She brushed her fingers through her hair. "Being fucked all over the house, so good you don't care what happens until you nut. The whole world could be burning down but you don't give a damn. Getting to the point where the pain you experience gets you high as a drug."

"So that's why you were attracted to Michael?" Brianna couldn't shake Stephanie's vivid words. "You like that lifestyle."

"Yes." She wiped her tears on her robe. "What's so bad is that I'm not ashamed. I could always look myself in the face afterwards. Is that a good thing? I'm not sure."

"Uh." Steven rummaged in his back pocket. "We appreciate you telling us the truth."

"I didn't wanna lie but Michael promised he'd leave me alone if I did. You don't understand how desperate I was. I can't explain how it feels to have someone else try to control your life."

Brianna scratched her elbow. "I think *I* understand."

"Uh Stephanie we're gonna tell Jayce what you said."

"Huh?" She stood.

"And then he'll probably talk to Michael again."

"No." She grabbed Steven's arm.

"Stephanie it's okay."

"Detective Morris you guys can't say anything! If Gene finds out I won't have anything. Please don't tell Detective Matthews."

"We have to, Stephanie." Steven pried her fingers away. "We can't not tell him. This is an attempted murder case."

"Damn it! No!"

"Calm down all right?" Brianna held her. "Jayce won't tell Michael you told us okay? All he's gonna do is question him again. Michael won't suspect anything."

"I'm begging you please." She touched Brianna's blouse. "I can't lose my husband. My whole family."

"It's gonna be okay," Steven said. "Michael won't know."

"I'm not letting him take my life away from me."

Steven and Brianna exchanged glances.

"I'd kill Michael before I let him ruin my life. I swear I will."

◆◆◆◆◆◆

"Mmm, damn." Steven scraped the corner of the fruit cup to get the last chunk.

"Hey these ain't half bad I gotta say."

"They are when you gotta eat three of 'em everyday." Cheyenne touched her head.

"You all right? Need me to get the nurse?"

"No it's okay just getting a headache. Dr. Walden said I should get used to those for a while."

"Hmm." Steven pitched the cup into the wastebasket across the room. He hopped around like a basketball star afterwards. "Yaaaa! He shoots and he scores! Yaaaa!"

She laughed.

"I'm silly huh?" He sat on the chair by her hospital bed and put his leg up.

"No I welcome the silliness believe me, Steve. Thanks for coming to visit me."

"You don't have to thank me."

"Ha, ha, ha, ha!"

"What's so funny?"

"I'm just thinking about when we first met."

"Oh yeah." Steven loosened his watch. "When you chased me around your house with that knife huh?"

"Yes! Ha, ha!"

"Boy that was something huh?"

"Well I really did think you were the rapist."

"Yeah I know. It wasn't your fault I looked like him though."

"Yeah." Her mouth settled into a slight frown. "Why in the world did I have to bring that up?"

"Hey it's okay all right? You got through that and you'll get through this."

"Steve?"

"Hmm." He turned the television on *Judge Judy*.

"Why are you really here?"

"To check on you." She stared at him.

"Okay that was part of the reason. I wanted to see how your memory was coming along."

"It's exactly the same. I don't remember anything about the attack. I don't even remember going out with Simon."

"Cheyenne you gotta remember."

"Well sorry I don't."

"All right." He patted her arm. "I know it's hard but just try."

"I can't. Raise my bed up please."

He pushed the button on the side.

"All right that's good. Thank you."

"Cheyenne you gotta remember something deep down. You gotta concentrate."

"I've been doing that and I don't remember anything, nothing. Matthews and Bree keep telling me all this stuff that supposedly went on and I don't remember it."

"Okay let's focus together then." Steven strutted underneath the wall television. "Simon said he brought you home after you'd gone out."

She nodded.

"So that means you had to have gone out again because they found no signs of an attack at your place. Cheyenne is there anywhere you would've gone?"

"I can't imagine going back out after getting home with it raining so bad. I hate being in bad weather."

"Okay." He bent over the foot of her bed. "Say you did. Anyplace you think you would've gone?"

"The only thing I could say is maybe someone called me and I left. But who the hell would that be and the few folks I know wouldn't have kept quiet about it. It would have to be Bree or Juney. No one else."

"No we checked your phone records and you had no calls."

"Steven I don't know what to say."

"Have you ever been to Simon's place?"

"Sure lots of times." She opened her little carton of milk.

"You think you were there that night? Like maybe he took you to his place?"

"No."

"Why not?"

She wiped her milk mustache. "Because Simon wouldn't lie."

"Oh please."

"I'm serious, Steve. If I had been at Simon's any time that night he would tell the truth. He wouldn't hide something like that."

"So Watts is so trustworthy right?"

"I know you don't like him but he is. Simon's the sweetest man I've ever met."

He cleared his throat.

"Next to you of course. He wouldn't hurt a fly and he wouldn't hurt me."

"I didn't say he hurt you. I'm just saying he could be lying about the events of that night or confused."

"Not Simon. He's always on top of things."

"Think damn it. Cheyenne you had to have left that night."

"Well where the hell would I've gone? I can't begin to think."

"Okay calm down. Don't get yourself upset."

She set her milk down. "I'm just frustrated. I wish I could remember."

"We still don't know who took you to the hospital that night."

"Bree thinks it was Michael."

"Shit Bree thinks Michael's responsible for Nine Eleven."

"Do you think he was the man who brought me to the hospital?"

"Well he did lie about his alibi but when Jayce questioned him Michael's lawyer shot holes in every theory Jayce thought of."

"You think he did it?"

He didn't answer.

"Oh you think Simon did it don't you? Even though he passed the lie detector? I keep telling you he wouldn't hurt me. How many times I gotta say it?"

"Maybe someone connected to him would."

"What?"

"What do you know about Simon's friends?"

"I'm his only friend. It's hard for him to trust people."

"I don't buy that. I know he's gotta have a guy friend somewhere. Every guy has at least one guy friend."

"Well I don't know. He didn't introduce me to anyone."

"He's been with a lot of women right?"

"I guess."

"Maybe he has a jealous ex or something you know?"

"And she attacked me?"

"Or had you attacked."

Cheyenne played with the remote. "I don't think so, Steve."

"Well hell we gotta think of something. Maybe that was it. Maybe someone was jealous. If he had a lot of women then he might have dumped one or something."

"He hadn't dated in a while. Too long ago for someone to take revenge now."

"If only we knew someone who knows Simon." Steven looked up.

"What?"

"His sister."

"Clara?"

"Maybe she could help us."

"I don't think so. She only pops into Simon's life once in a while. He barely knows where she is."

"How's their relationship?"

"I don't know." She maneuvered the sheets. "Okay I guess. I mean he says she's very protective of him. He adores her. They were very close because of their childhood."

"Yeah Bree told me about that. He killed his stepfather. Signs of someone kinda unstable don't you think?"

"Steve don't. That's not funny."

"I didn't mean it as funny but Simon might be carrying baggage from his childhood. If you can shoot someone you can hit..."

"Simon wouldn't hurt me! You keep saying that then I want you to leave."

"Come on. What else did he say about Clara?"

"That she really looked out for him. It's the typical sibling relationship. As for where she is, I don't know. Simon doesn't know."

"How can he not know? If they're so close?"

"He says Clara is a free spirit. She likes to travel."

"Mmm." He scratched the front of his neck.

"Clara wasn't anywhere around. She wouldn't know anything. I doubt Simon even told her about me."

"Why?"

"I just got the feeling. He told me she's overprotective and is always convinced he'd be hurt."

"By women?"

"I don't know. I guess."

"What the hell's so great about Simon anyway? I mean you giggle every time you say his name and Bree's been doing ballerina twirls at the station."

She smiled. "Simon is one of those men that just has it, Steve."

"What "it"?"

"The kind that renders women helpless."

"Oh yeah." He straightened his shirt. "That "it". I have it too."

"Simon is a man some women only dream about."

"Oh please it's a put on."

"What?"

"He acts like he's so refined and classy." Steven pranced around waving his hands.

"Rich, has traveled everywhere and loves art. Shit everything women fall for. But not Bree."

"Oh I don't know, Steve. Bree's a woman just like everyone else."

"Even Simon couldn't reel Bree in. She's tough. It takes a special man to get to her."

"Bree's a woman just like all of us, Steve. Some men are just too hard to resist."

He mumbled.

"You okay?"

"Do you think she still loves me? I mean at all?"

"Of course she loves you." Cheyenne piled her pillows behind her.

"Just not the way I want her to right?"

She didn't answer.

CHAPTER TWENTY-FIVE

Gene breezed into his office after lunch. He hadn't noticed the small square package on his desk until he sat down.

He dialed his receptionist. "Gloria come in here please."

She walked so hard on those damn heels he was surprised she didn't fall through the floor.

"Yes, Dr. James?"

"What's this?"

"Some package that came for you right after you left."

"With the regular mail?"

"No this was delivered." She approached the desk. "Something wrong?"

"No it's just strange." His wedding ring sparkled under the lights. "I didn't order anything and there's no return address. Just my name."

"Open it."

"Get out then." Gene winked with a grin.

"Come on, Dr. James. I'm just as curious as you are."

He opened the package. A DVD lay in the box.

"A blank disc?" Gloria stepped back and crossed her arms. "What's that about?"

"I doubt it's blank if someone sent it to me." He unlocked the little door by the window. He pushed out a cart with a small television and DVD player he sometimes used in his sessions. "Go close the door."

Gloria did.

Gene plugged up the television and DVD player. He gave the disc another long look.

"Go on." Gloria nudged him. "I wanna see."

"Don't you have some work to be doing?"

"It'll wait." She sat on his desk and crossed her legs.

Gene put the disc into the machine.

The homemade movie started immediately.

"Oh my god." Gloria slipped off the desk.

Gene crumbled the box in his hand.

He watched with smoke flying out his ears. The naked blond tussled in the bed. Howled like a dog in heat. She wore a leather bra with the nipples out. Leather boots that reached her knees and fishnet stockings with holes big enough to stick a fist into them.

"Mmm yeah." The man underneath her rolled his pelvis to her rhythm.

"Ahh!" Stephanie bounced and writhed, absorbing every inch of the man inside of her.

"Ohh. Ohh! Yes."

"Ahh." The man leaned his arms back and pounded until the sound of skin slapping together filled the room.

Gloria touched her collar. "Uh."

Gene took off his glasses. "Get out."

"Dr. James?"

"Get out!"

She ran out.

He turned the sound down but nothing took the disgust away.

The man heaved and moaned.

"Michael." Gene almost crushed his glasses.

"Oh…oh!" Stephanie reached her arms to the ceiling. "Ahhhh!"

Gene's face filled with tears.

She hadn't come that hard since he'd known her.

◆◆◆◆◆◆

"Gene?" Stephanie ran from the couch when he came through the front door that night.

He kept his eyes straight ahead, on anything but her.

"Gene where you been?" She hugged him. "You got off work at least two…" She sniffed. "Have you been drinking?"

He batted his bloodshot eyes. "Yes but don't worry, Stephanie. I'm not drunk."

170

"Gene why would you do that? You stopped drinking after I had the kids."

"Well sometimes a man needs to drink you know?" He tottered into the living room.

"Where's Marta? Where's my baby girls?"

"Marta took the kids to her house tonight. I told her they could stay over. You know how much they love to be with her kids."

Gene wobbled.

"Gene what's wrong?"

"Nothing." He smiled like a Cheshire cat. "I'm glad they're gone." He pulled her close.

"I get to spend some time alone with my wife." He nibbled her neck. "Hmm? Been so long since we made love I can't even remember."

"Yeah well." She swiveled in his arms.

He put all his weight on her.

"Gene hold on."

"Hmm?" He shoved his hand inside her robe.

"Gene wait."

"What?" He chuckled. "I'm just kissing my wife. Wanna be romantic."

"Gene I don't like it when you've been drinking."

"Oh." He let her go. "Well I'm not drunk."

"I know. Where are your glasses?"

"Might be in the car."

"Why did you leave them in the car?"

He stared at the television. Martha Stewart made a chocolate chip cake.

"Gene?" She snapped her fingers.

"Hmm?"

"Why did you leave your glasses in the car?"

"Don't need them." He held her. "I need you. Let's be romantic!" He danced around.

"O…okay."

"Remember what we used to do when we had time alone?"

"Why don't we go out to dinner?"

"Mmm, nah. I want you all to myself tonight."

"Oh I'd love to go to Jayson's. I've been dying for that crab salad." She got on the phone. "I'll make reservations."

"I said no." She froze at the authority in his voice.

"I don't see why we can't go out."

"Because." He hung up the phone. "I want to be alone with you tonight. We can eat something here. Didn't Marta cook?"

"No I told her she didn't have to. I was gonna make some spaghetti but I dozed off."

He took off his blazer. "Well Big Daddy's home now isn't he?"

"Big...Gene what is going on with you?"

"I'm just having fun!" He cackled. "Am I not allowed to have fun?"

"You're usually not so..."

"What huh?" He crept to her. "Out of control and unpredictable? Dangerous?"

"Dangerous?"

"Maybe that's what you really want isn't it?"

"No." She stood by the bookshelf. "You are drunk aren't you?"

"No."

"Why don't you go to bed and rest?"

"Oh, Stef." He held his arms out. "Honey I'm just trying to make you happy. I wanna be with you. A man can't be with his wife?"

"I love you, Gene."

"Oh I know *that*. That's why I want us to take advantage of this time together." He took her hand. "Come, come."

"What?"

He shoved her on the couch.

"Oh! Gene!"

"Now you just relax okay? Let me do the work." He put a disc into the DVD player.

"What's that?"

"Oh we're gonna do what we used to do. Watch a nice movie. Oh." He bucked his eyes. "Let me get the wine!"

"Gene that's okay."

"No it's not. I want this night to be very memorable for you, Stef. I'll be right back."

She shook her head. "Jesus."

"La, dee, da!" He twirled into the room with two glasses and red wine.

"Gene what's gotten into you?"

"I'm just so happy." He poured her a glass then his own. "Oh I wanna make a toast. Pick up your glass."

She hesitated then took it.

"Now I wanna make a toast to the most beautiful woman in the world."

"Gene don't."

"And the best mother and wife in all the land!" He slurped the entire glass in one gulp." Ahh."

"Gene?"

"Drink, drink, drink." He tapped her chin.

She sipped. "Gene?"

He snuggled beside her. "Now where's the remote? Ah I see it."

"Gene I don't…"

"Huh? Honey why you seem so uncomfortable?"

"Because I don't know what's going on here."

"What do you mean?"

"You're acting weird."

"Me?" He loosened his tie. "Nah. I just wanna be with you. Is that weird?"

"I don't wanna watch a movie. I wanna talk."

"Nonsense."

"I mean it, Gene. I don't wanna watch a movie."

He held her still. "You're gonna watch this one."

"Gene let me go."

"Shut up." He pressed his arm across her.

"Gene stop it! Let me get up."

"Not until after the movie."

"I hate it when you drink! I hate it!"

"Oh yeah I bet you hate a whole lot of things about me right? Don't you?"

"Gene stop it."

"Just settle down, Stephanie. Watch the fuckin' movie." He snatched her by the neck.

"Oww!" She punched at his chest. "Gene what the hell's gotten into you?"

"Come on." He tightened his arm around her neck. "Don't you wanna see the nice little movie?"

She tried to pry his hands away. "You're hurting me, Gene! Let go!"

He turned the movie on.

CHAPTER TWENTY-SIX

Stephanie gasped at the sight of her naked ass covering the screen.

"What *is* this?" She shrieked. "Gene!"

"Why it's you, baby doll." He kept her from moving. "Don't you like it?"

"Ahh!" She cried and kicked. "Let me go!"

"No watch it."

"Stop it, Gene!" She poked her elbow into his side. "Don't do this. Please!" She shut her eyes.

"Open your eyes, Stephanie."

"Gene don't!" She wailed. "Turn it off!" She grabbed at the remote. "Stop it!"

"What's the matter? Huh? Don't be embarrassed."

Michael flipped Stephanie over in the bed and rammed inside of her. She held the shaking headboard.

"Yes." She moaned. "Oh yes."

"Gene!" She slung her arms around. "Please turn it off! Please I beg you!"

He threw her on the floor.

"Oh!" She hit her head on the wall.

"So you want me to turn it off?"

"Yes!"

He turned the television up.

"Oh you're hot huh, baby? Aren't you? He's doing you good huh?"

"Shut up!" She punched his leg. "You bastard! Please turn it off!"

"You don't like it do you?"

"No!" She put her face in the carpet. "Please turn it off, Gene!"

"You don't wanna see it do you?" He stood over her. "Well how the fuck do you think it made me feel huh?" He threw the remote into the television.

"Gene!"

"Get up!" He yanked her off the floor and gave her a rough kiss.

"Mmm, stop!" She struggled. "Gene!"

"What huh?" He panted. "I thought you liked it rough."

"No, Gene! Stop!"

"You like it rough but not with me right?" He turned her loose.

"Not with *me*!"

"Gene?" She reached for him.

He pointed to the television. "That's the real you isn't it?"

"No!"

"It's what you were all along right?"

"No!" She touched his face. "Please listen to me."

"Listen to you? I have been listening to you all fuckin' day! Since I got this goddamn DVD!" He turned the movie off. "I don't need to listen to you anymore."

"Gene no!" She grabbed his arm and turned him around. "I love you so much."

He ripped his arm away.

"I do! Wait, just listen okay? I didn't know he was taping us!"

"And that's supposed to make it better? I don't give a fuck about the tape! I care about you fucking another man!"

"Gene I love you." She sobbed and chewed her thumb. "Don't do this please."

"Love me? Stephanie I gave you everything! I loved you!"

"You *love* me. Love!" She shook him. "You *love* me, Gene."

"Let me go."

"Wait."

"I can't believe this. You've been fucking Michael Buchanan and for how damn long huh?"

"Eugene please."

"How long, bitch?"

"Bitch?" She hit him. "Don't you talk to me like that!"

"I'll talk to you anyway I want to. You're a slut, Stephanie! That's all you'll ever be and I'm glad I found out before it was too late."

"I made a mistake! I don't love him! I never did!"

He plopped on the couch.

"Gene he wouldn't leave me alone." She touched him.

He moved her hand.

"Eugene." She put her head on his chest. "I made a mistake but I always wanted you and only you."

He shoved her away. "Funny that movie says different."

"Let me explain."

"Explain?" He jumped up. "You don't need to explain, Stephanie! Shit the movie explained it all! You've been fucking Michael! What the hell else can you say?"

"I don't know how this happened."

"You've been fucking him. That's how it happened!"

"How did you get that?"

"Does it make a difference?"

"He sent it to you didn't he?" She snatched her hair. "That bastard. He promised he'd leave me alone, Gene. I told him I would never leave you and he couldn't take it. He's trying to ruin our marriage."

He turned his back to her.

"Please, baby." She laid her head on his arm. Her tears soaked the sleeve.

"I'm so sorry. I love you so much. I'll do anything if you forgive me, Gene. I'm sorry. I'll even go get counseling."

"No need." He unhooked her fingers from his arm. "I want you out of here."

"Gene. You can't mean that."

"Oh you have no idea how much I mean that. I told you before that if you ever did this again it would be over. I gave you everything and you spit it right back in my face."

"No."

"You didn't appreciate a damn thing I did for you!"

"I do! You're the best thing that ever happened to me. Please, Gene."

He went to the stairs.

"Wait!" She tripped in behind him. "Gene! Where are you going?"

He spoke to her without turning around. "I'm going upstairs and I'm gonna pack you up some shit and your ass is leaving."

"No!" She raced upstairs. She almost knocked him down when she grabbed him.

"Let go, Stephanie."

"No. I'm your wife! Look at me."

"I can't look at you."

"Gene!"

"I said…" He grabbed her hands. "Let go of me."

"Gene don't do this. Please."

He went to the bedroom.

"Gene please!" She knelt on the stairs. "I love you! What about the girls?"

He threw her clothes into the hall.

"Ohh!" She cried into her lap. "Gene! Gene please!"

He continued as if she weren't even there.

♦♦♦♦♦♦

A Month Later

Brianna opened her door to Detective Jayce Matthews. The handsome light-skinned black man laid his foot over the threshold. A few strands of his curly hair shown from underneath the rain cap.

"Hey, Bree." His brown eyes sparkled with urgency and emotion Brianna couldn't understand. "May I come in?"

"Of course." She tied the belt of her robe. "Uh, is something wrong?"

"I just have some news. I needed to tell you in person. Sorry for dropping by this time of night."

"Come on into the living room." Brianna shooed Davis off the couch. She removed her latest Harlequin Romance.

"Oh don't go into any trouble. I won't be here long."

"No trouble at all." She turned the television on mute. "You want something to eat or drink?"

"No thanks." He straightened the pillows and sat down.

"What's up?" She curled on the couch as if she were about to hear a bedtime story.

"Michael Buchanan is dead."

Her feet fell to the carpet. "What did you say?"

"He was killed."

Brianna hit his thigh. "Jayce you're kidding me right?"

"Nope. We just wrapped things up at his place."

"Jesus."

"We think it happened last night. A neighbor called the cops complaining about Michael's dog barking all day. They found it strange.

They said he usually keeps him in the house. An officer was sent out and they discovered his front door was unlocked. They went in and found him dead in his bedroom."

"Oh." She covered her mouth. "I just can't believe this."

"I was shocked too."

"He was probably the only person who knew what happened to Cheyenne. This is horrible."

"So you really think he attacked her?"

"I definitely think he knew what happened if he didn't." She stood then sat back down.

"I just never would've imagined this. How did it happen?"

"Ooh." Jayce played with his cap. "Hacked with some kind of knife. Maybe butcher."

Brianna fought the urge to vomit.

"Someone stabbed him like they were chopping ground meat."

She rubbed her stomach.

"This wasn't a random killing. This person was specifically after Michael. Plus nothing didn't seem to be missing from his house."

"Well I don't understand why you came over here just to tell me this."

"I didn't. There's uh something else." He lowered his head. "And I think it's gonna shock you more than anything."

"Nothing could shock me anymore than finding out Michael's been killed."

"What about if I told you we think Michael was the man stalking you?"

She batted her eyes. "Are you out of your mind?"

"I wouldn't joke about something like this."

"And it wouldn't be funny. Why would you think Michael was the stalker?"

"Because he had this in his wallet." Jayce took out a wallet size picture of her.

"This is the picture that was on my desk at the station." She stared in space. "I realized it was gone after the stalker attacked me in the file room."

"Brianna I'm sorry. Are you all right?"

"I don't know."

"You said you had a weird feeling when you were around him. That you picked up something strange."

"Yes. But I wasn't thinking that he could've been my stalker."

"I can't think of any other reason he'd have that picture can you?"

"No." She put the picture on the table. "But something doesn't seem right."

"Your stalker didn't have an accent did he?"

"No but Michael was American remember? He acquired the accent from living in England."

"Or maybe he faked it in the first place."

"This feels so unreal."

"I'm so sorry, Bree."

"You think Michael really attacked Cheyenne?"

"All we can do is hope something comes up or that Cheyenne gets her memory back."

"And you didn't find any clues in his murder?"

"Well we figure he let the killer inside. There weren't signs of forced entry."

Brianna tried her best to put her anger aside. "So you really think this person knew Michael?"

"Oh I'd bet my life on it from the precision of those stab wounds. I mean this person wanted to make sure Michael stopped breathing and tortured him in the process. Another thing was there didn't seem to be any struggling going on until the murder started."

"What would be the motive?"

"Well, Michael was in a lot of shit. We found bank receipts and all this stuff that suggested he was having money problems. We'll know more probably when we check his phone records. We found stuff for loan companies and papers for declaring bankruptcy."

"Bankruptcy?"

"Yeah and it seems he went to the casino a lot. Probably had a gambling problem which would explain his money problems."

"So you think he was in debt to someone and they killed him?"

"Could have."

"But that's not what you think happened is it, Jayce?"

He tapped his foot. "You've known me too long haven't you, Bree?"

"Just tell me what you think."

"A more powerful motive than money is revenge. That's the only way I could describesuch a heinous crime."

"You've got someone in your mind already don't you?"

"Who's lost everything yet has nothing else left to lose?"

"Oh my god. You mean Stephanie James?"

He nodded.

"Jayce that's ridiculous."

"Is it? Her husband threw her out because of Michael. He's even gonna try to sue her for saying the affair threatens his career."

"You know that doesn't mean she killed Michael."

"She went from a pampered princess to living with her sister. Gene's blocked her from having any money. He won't let her see her kids. Her entire affair has been made a media spectacle yet Michael didn't feel any of the heat. Stephanie was left to face all that ridicule and shame alone and this is partly Michael's fault. You think that doesn't make her angry?"

Davis trotted into the room and stopped by his mistress' feet.

"Bree, if that's not a woman scorned I don't know what is."

"She was so desperate. The last time Steven and I saw her she was so distant. Like her mind was somewhere else. She vowed she wouldn't let Michael ruin her marriage. And if so she'd lose everything."

"In which she did. You take a woman's money and husband away and she might cope with it. But you fuck with her kids, that's a different story."

"It had to be just talk, Jayce. I don't think Stephanie has it in her to really kill someone."

"Then think again."

CHAPTER TWENTY-SEVEN

Three Days Later

Cha Clump. Cha Clump. Cha Clump.

Stephanie jerked from her sleep and threw the covers off. She wore sweat like a jacket.

Her sister hadn't any air conditioning. She appreciated the hospitality but she couldn't stand it here. The bed was right in front of the mirror. She couldn't look at herself. She'd never be able to pay for what she'd done. If only she hadn't slept with Michael then none of this would have happened.

On top of losing her family and money she was a suspect in Michael's murder.

It warmed her to think of his death. She'd wanted it more than anything but she wasn't going to prison for something she didn't do. Even if she had taken part in it.

Cha Clump. Cha Clump. Cha Clump.

She heard footsteps coming down the hall. Her sister had gone to her boyfriend's for the night. No way it could be her.

The steps sounded closer. Right outside the door.

She put on her robe. She tiptoed in the thick carpet. She placed her ear to the door.

It was nights like these she missed her husband the most. With

Gene she never had to worry about protection or security.

Would she ever get used to this?

Panting from outside the door.

She bit her tongue to keep from screaming. The damn bedroom door didn't even have a lock on it.

She grabbed the umbrella from the corner.

Law and Order taught her to be prepared for intruders.

She cut her eyes from the bed to the closet. She opened the door.

"Hello, Stephanie." A man in all black and a ski mask grabbed her arm and threw her into the hall.

"Ahh!"

How could she be so stupid thinking she could trust him? Of course he'd come to kill her. She knew what he'd done.

"Ahh!" Stephanie swung the umbrella. The man ducked.

"Uh-uh!" He snatched the umbrella. "I don't think so." He tossed it down the hall.

"Stay away from me." She backed into the room.

"Stephanie. Now is that anyway to treat a friend?"

"What do you want?"

His mouth moved underneath the mask. "Came to take you outta your misery."

"Don't!" She grabbed the telephone. "Don't lay a fuckin' finger on me. I knew I couldn't trust you. I knew you'd kill me."

"I can't risk you telling the police."

"I won't do that."

"How can I be sure?" He wiggled his gloved fingers. "See, you're the only one who knows I killed Michael. As a favor to you I might add."

"It wasn't for me. You tricked me."

"You did more than that, Stephanie. If it hadn't been for you, I never would've gotten into Michael's place. What did you tell the police the other day when they questioned you?"

"Nothing. I told them I didn't know anything."

"I don't buy that." He came inside.

"Stay back."

"Neither one of us are innocent. You had the motive, Stephanie."

"You killed him."

"I couldn't have without your help."

"What the hell's wrong with me?" She trembled. "To have gone with such a stupid scheme."

"You wanted Michael dead and were desperate for it."

"You used me! You only wanted Michael dead so you could plant that picture of Brianna Morris on him. Why I don't know."

"And it's none of your business. No one's gonna find out what really happened to Michael and they certainly won't figure out what happened to you either."

"Listen okay?" She put the phone down. "You said I could trust you."

"I lied."

"I have kids. I have two beautiful little girls. Please don't do this. Think about them."

"I am. Imagine how they'd feel if they grew up and knew their mother was a slut who set a man up to be murdered?"

"Fuck you!" She slammed the phone into his face.

"Ahhh!" The man fell to his knees.

Stephanie ran down the hall.

"You ain't going anywhere, Stephanie!" The man caught her by the hair.

"No! Let go!" She punched and kicked. "Let me go!"

He clamped his strong arm around her neck. He took out the knife he'd used to kill Michael.

"No! Stop! Please!"

"Don't worry." He grunted. "I'm not gonna stab you, honey. Just be a good girl and fold your fingers over the knife."

"No!"

"I don't know why you care." He laughed. "What difference does it make? By the time they find this knife with your prints you'll be fertilizer."

"Mmm no!" She moved her hands.

"Stop moving, bitch!" He shoved the knife into her hand and held her fingers on it.

"Good girl." He put the knife back in his pants. "Come on, Stephanie. Don't make this hard."

"Please!" He heaved her over his shoulder. "Wait. Please! I promise I won't tell anyone what happened."

"Oh I know you won't, Stephanie." He put her down on top of the stairs.He pulled up his mask and kissed her shivering lips.

"Stephanie? Have a nice trip." He pushed her down the stairs.

"Noooo!" She tumbled like a ragdoll.

Her neck broke before she hit the floor.

♦♦♦♦♦♦

A Week Later

Brianna hadn't planned on having dinner with Simon tonight. She wanted to come home and climb into bed. Simon had the talent of persuasion and she lost the battle when it came to her feelings for him. They always won out.

She'd done her best to return to her normal routine since Michael's murder. She hadn't gotten any calls of course but for some reason she still expected to. It just didn't feel like it was over. People found her distrust with the situation unusual and called her crazy. But she listened to that feeling inside. It never stirred her wrong. Why would it now?

There were still unanswered questions. The prints on the stalker's knife hadn't matched Michael's. Sure that didn't prove he wasn't the stalker. But something didn't add up. Michael's phone records didn't reveal that he'd called Brianna once. But stalkers had a way of calling their victims without leaving a trail. Okay, fine. But Michael's prints weren't even on her picture found in his wallet. She questioned the situation now more than before.

Cheyenne's case also made it hard to celebrate her own victory. She'd get out the hospital soon but still didn't remember anything about her attack.

Things had gotten crazier. Stephanie committed suicide a week ago and Gene was a nervous wreck.

A domino effect.

What strange thing would happen next?

"Brianna are you all right?" Simon ate across from her.

"Yes. I'm fine."

He'd been going on about something for the last ten minutes. She hadn't heard a word.

That's how she'd been lately. Sitting in a room with others but not really there.

Those damn unanswered questions.

"You'd love Venice, Brianna." Simon chewed roast. He'd rushed over when she got off from work and brought the home cooked meal.

She hadn't thought he could get anymore perfect until she found out he cooked.

The roast was damn good. Better than what she'd make.

"Brianna?"

"Huh?" She touched her fork. "I'm listening."

He'd insisted they eat in the living room instead of the kitchen so he'd slapped this silk blue sheet over the table for decoration. He'd slipped in her favorite Erkyah Badu CD. Dressed the little table with her scented candles that smelled like watermelon and cantaloupe.

He cut his meat into chunks. "You'd love Venice. Out of all the places I've been it's one of my favorites. Liberia was fun too. You should go and see Africa. It would be very educational for you."

"Why because I'm black?"

"No because it would be educational and a great place for anyone to visit. Where did that come from?"

"I'm sorry, Simon. I didn't mean to snap. It's just the first thing that came out."

"How about I take you one day?"

That suggestion brought her back to earth. She enjoyed being with Simon and craved making love to him every minute. But she hadn't thought of their relationship in the long term once. Jesus she needed to check the signals she threw out. Seemed to get her in trouble.

"Why are you looking at me like that?" Simon blew into his champagne.

"You're like a book."

"I never had someone describe me like that before."

"No I mean you're so interesting. You've lived things and gone through things most of us only dreamed about."

He straightened the napkin in his lap. "And things most people wished they'd never go through. I try to push them away everyday."

"But your good heart won out, Simon."

"Did it?"

"Yes. You went from that horrible situation with your stepfather to being adopted by one of the richest couples in Great Britain. They treated you like you were their own. Don't you see the happy ending?"

"Of course I do. I loved my adoptive parents. I couldn't wish anything better for Clara and I. But it wasn't the money or what they had. It was the love they provided. If all parents were like they were it would be a much better world."

"Anyone knows they loved you guys I mean..." She chewed. "They left you their entire fortune. Did you expect that?"

"I didn't expect them to die, no."

"Oh hey." She felt his hand. "Shit I win the award for the biggest moment killer don't I? You brought over this wonderful meal and I'm talking about death."

He moved his hand from hers. "It's okay."

"Simon it wasn't your fault they died in that fire. You were in the states. You couldn't have done anything."

"I felt like I should've." He breathed into his fists. "I'll never get over that."

"What happened to your stepsister?"

His mood softened and he continued eating. "Her relatives took her in."

"You and Clara still see her?"

"I don't see her much because I live over here. I can't speak for Clara. She just goes where…" His voice trailed. "You know, where things take her. But I hear from my stepsister from time to time."

"You two get along?"

"Yeah."

"I didn't hear you."

"Yes." He seemed startled at his own voice.

She picked at the crunchy baby carrots and golden potatoes.

"You have something on your mind?"

He dabbed his mouth. "I just wish you'd be less of a cop when we're together and be more of a woman."

"I didn't know I had a choice. I'm both remember?"

"You shouldn't be a cop tonight or when we're alone. Don't you see what I'm saying?"

"Simon I think this is moving too fast."

"Too fast? I don't agree. I think we've been taking things incredibly slow."

"Really? We go any "slower" and we'll be married next week." She chuckled while sipping champagne.

"Would that be so bad?"

"What?"

"I'd marry you if I had the chance."

"Oh Simon stop."

"I'm serious."

"How the hell can you be? We still don't know each other that well."

"That's shite. You know everything about me and I know everything about you."

She swallowed roast. "No one knows everything about everyone, Simon."

"You still don't trust me do you?"

"Of course I do. I just got so much on my mind."

"You always seem to."

She dropped her fork. "Look you wanted to come over here and eat. I didn't ask you to come."

"Fine." He threw his napkin on the table. "I'll leave then."

"No, Simon."

He sat back down.

"I'm sorry. I don't know what's wrong with me. I'm so wound up."

"You seem to have gotten worse since Buchanan's murder."

"Do you think he really was the stalker?"

"I can't answer that."

"I know things point to him but I still feel like it's not over. Why?"

"Well you were traumatized by it. It's only natural to feel that way. Cheyenne said even after the Albany Predator was arrested, she still felt like he was out there somewhere watching her. But when she let go of her fear, that's when she dealt with the rape."

"It's just so complicated."

"Not if you start letting others help you." He kissed her hand. "Lean on me, Brianna, that's what I'm here for."

"How come you never call me Bree?"

"You want me to?"

"Only if you're comfortable. It doesn't matter to me."

"I'd like to just call you my lady." He tightened his hold on her hand. "May I?"

"You mean officially?"

"I don't know if there's another way I could mean it." His eyes sparkled against the candles' glare. "Next time we make love, I'll call you Bree."

She uncrossed her legs.

"Hmm?"

"Not tonight, Simon."

"Really?" He kept his sly expression.

"I'm too tired."

"Oh well I think I can make you feel more relaxed."

She laughed. "No I'd like my mind to be clearer so I can concentrate on you."

He sucked the top of her hand. "Just let me concentrate on you then. Let me pleasure you tonight. I'll get satisfaction from that alone."

Her cell went off. "Damn it."

He let her hand go.

"I'm sorry." She turned the stereo down and got her phone off the banister.

"This is Bree."

"Bree it's Jayce. I got a lot of news, babe."

CHAPTER TWENTY-EIGHT

Brianna excused herself and went into the den. "What's up Jayce?"
"Found the weapon Cheyenne was attacked with."

"What?" She got woozy and sat down.

"Looks like your hunch was correct all the time. Michael attacked Cheyenne."

"Hold on. Go slower, Jayce."

"You remember that little statue I told you we found in Michael's home?"

"Yeah some little copper or gold angel right?"

"We found tiny red spots on it that looked suspicious. Thought it was paint or something but it wasn't. It was blood. We ran it through the lab and it was Cheyenne's blood. It was her DNA."

"You've gotta be fuckin' kiddin' me."

"Yeah and Michael's prints were all over the statue too."

"Jayce I knew it. Just the way he acted the first day I met him. It was like he was playing with us you know?"

"There's something else."

"What?"

"We found more prints. Some we couldn't match but another we could."

"Cheyenne's?"

"No Olivia Delcie's."

"The woman that was strangled last year?"

"Uh huh. Now how would Delcie's prints get on a statue in Michael's house if she'd never been there?"

"Oh my god. You think Michael killed her?"

"Can't say for sure but I think it's suspicious he knew this woman when he was the one who also attacked Cheyenne. I see a pattern here."

"Wait. You think he's done this before?"

"Also, Delcie was a member of a dating service a while back but it wasn't Havana Horizons. We always suspected her killer might have contacted her through this service. Now it looks like that might be true."

"Holy shit."

Simon crept through the hall.

"Jayce you think Michael was a serial killer or something? Like he met women off sites, dated them and killed them?"

"I don't know about all that Bree but he's definitely connected to Cheyenne and Delcie."

"Oh shit."

"Too bad the motherfucker's dead though."

Simon fell against the wall in a sweat.

"You heard what I heard?"

"Leave me alone." He whispered.

"Doesn't sound too good to me. They're getting too close."

"Yeah, Simon." A different voice spoke. *"Might need to take care of that."*

He clamped his lips. "Leave...me...alone." He went back to the living room.

"You okay, Bree?" Jayce asked. "Got quiet there."

"Seems like everything we get lately is only making me think something else."

"What do you mean? You still not sure Michael was your stalker?"

"Yes. I mean, I don't know. It's this feeling I get. And now this. I don't feel like this is right. I feel like there's more to the story."

"What could that be?"

"I have no idea." She bid goodbye and hung up.

"Everything okay?"

"Simon." She clutched her chest. "You scared me."

"I'm sorry. Did something happen?"

"No."

"Your face says otherwise. Wasn't bad news was it?"

"It's police business."

"Does it have to do with Cheyenne?"

"It's not your concern."

"That's not fair. I care about her. If you've gotten news then I deserve to know too."

"That was Jayce Matthews. He told me they found the weapon Cheyenne was beaten with."

She didn't think his face could get anymore pale but it did.

"Simon you okay?"

"Uh just shocked. This is uh great news."

"They saw blood on it and it turned out to be Cheyenne's blood. Michael's prints were on it along with other prints. Let's go back into the living room and finish dinner."

"Hold on." He held her. "Are they sure that Michael attacked her?"

"What other explanation would there be? This thing was found in his house with Cheyenne's blood. I didn't believe a word Michael said from the beginning."

"What's wrong, Brianna?"

"It's just I hate my intuition sometimes. Momma always said I over thought stuff."

"I don't understand." He sat on the arm of the sofa.

"I don't know if I believe all this. I mean I've been hoping we connected Michael to the attack but it just doesn't feel right. Maybe he had something to do with it but didn't attack Cheyenne."

"Then how would you explain him having the statue in the first place?"

Statue?

Brianna gaped.

"You okay?"

"Uh yeah." She shook from her gaze. "Yeah uh what was I saying?"

"You said you're not sure Michael really did this?"

"It's not that I'm not sure it's just that this feeling won't go away. I feel like it's so easy to put all this on Michael when he's not here to defend himself."

"But the evidence has pointed to him right?"

She nodded.

"So what's the problem? He did it."

"Something's telling me we need to keep looking."

"Looking for what?"

They went back into the living room. Brianna took her CD out the stereo.

"Uh can we call it a night? I'm not up to this."

He spun her toward him. "Honey, I don't understand what's going on. Looking for what? You saying you really think Michael's innocent?"

"I'm saying something's not adding up. I mean Michael's dead and suddenly he's the person who did everything. Then Stephanie James who they *thought* killed Michael commits suicide. It's not making sense."

"All this time you've been saying Michael did this."

"I know but…"

"And now he's innocent?"

"I didn't say that. You don't understand."

"You're right I don't. None of this is making any sense. How can you completely change what you thought about Michael being guilty?"

"I didn't change anything." She laid the CD on the table. "I am just not sure okay? Don't ask me why. I'm just not."

"There's something else isn't there? About Michael?"

"It's police business. I told you."

"I thought you trusted me."

"Simon I do but we can't go around blabbing stuff about everything we find."

"Some trust."

"This has nothing to do with you."

"I'm trying to be supportive if you'd let me!"

"I am but I don't have to tell you every damn thing about the case. You should respect that."

"I don't understand anything about tonight." He flung his arms. "You wanted Michael hung by his nuts and now you think he's innocent!"

"And why does that bother you so much?"

"It bothers me because every time I think I've figured you out, I haven't! You're one surprise after another."

"Thought you said you liked that about me."

"Brianna I want you to let down your damn armor and let me love you. You don't give an inch."

"How did this get about you and me?"

"It's been about you and me! This entire thing."

"So you're saying I should just write it off as all Michael and be done with it?"

"Yes!" He grabbed her. "Stop doing this, Brianna."

"What the hell are you talking about?"

"You've been using the case as a way to ignore what's going on between us."

"Oh that's ridiculous! You keep talking this stupid and you won't have to worry about anything being between us because it won't be."

"You can dish it out but can't take it."

"Go to hell, Simon."

"It's like you're obsessed with this case!"

"Cheyenne's my friend and she's supposed to be yours too. I'm not obsessed but I wanna make sure the person who did this is really the one who's dead!"

"I love you, Brianna."

"Simon."

"You knew that the moment we met. I feel like you'd do anything not to deal with your feelings for me. You're so scared to give in."

"What the hell do you call this?" She stretched her arms.

"I mean completely. You've given me your mind and body, maybe even your soul. But not your heart. At least it doesn't feel that way."

"You want every part of me? Is that it?"

"Yes. Every single part."

"Like the stalker did?"

He rolled his eyes. "Good lord. So I'm the stalker now and not Michael?"

"No I was just asking. I know you're not the stalker! I just don't understand what you want from me."

"I just want you, Brianna." He kissed her. "I wish you'd let this go."

"I can't." She opened the front door. "Goodnight, Simon."

He left without a word.

Brianna hopped on her cell and called Steven.

◆◆◆◆◆◆

Simon pulled over to the side of the road once he got out of Brianna's neighborhood. The police were getting too close. Brianna was getting too close. He forced away those thoughts. He'd die if it meant protecting her.

He sweated like he'd taken a shower in his clothes.

He rested his shivering hands on his thighs. He'd better calm down or he wouldn't make it home.

He pulled down the rearview mirror.

"What the hell?"

Instead of seeing his face he looked at some warped jigsaw puzzle. One of his eyes sat in his forehead. The other hung from his chin. His lips were backwards. His ears were turned upside down.

"No." He batted but the image remained the same. "Stop it!"

His hands trembled on the steering wheel.

One eye had disappeared. His ear replaced his lips.

"Mmm!" He slapped both hands on his mouth.

"What's wrong, Simon?"

"Simon, long time no see, buddy."

Oh no. Not now please.

"Simon what are you gonna do, pal?"

"Yeah you gotta do something man. Before it gets out of hand."

"Leave him alone."

"Leave him alone?" A different male voice cackled. *"We leave him alone and he won't know what to do will he?"*

"Stop it." Simon covered his ears.

"You know what you gotta do, Simon. It won't just go away."

"No."

"Simon?"

"Leave me alone!"

A new voice spoke. *"You can't be scared, Simon."*

"Michael?" Simon gripped the steering wheel. "Is that you?"

"Of course. You didn't think death would keep me from my old buddy Simon did you? No we're gonna be together forever."

"What do I do?"

"Gotta get rid of that cop."

"I can't. I love her."

"Get your dick out your ass, man," Another male voice said. *"You think she's gonna give a shit about you once she finds out the truth?"*

"Shut up!" He punched the window. "I didn't do anything wrong!"

"Simon you gotta get rid of her. She knows too much."

"I can't, Michael. I love her so much."

"It's unavoidable, Simon. She's gonna figure out the truth. She's too much of a threat."

The voices poured in.

"Simon you gotta do it. She's trouble."

"Yeah Brianna's gotta die."

"You know it's the truth, buddy."

"Trust in us, Simon. We'd never steer you wrong."

"Yes trust us, Simon."

"Yeah Simon, you can trust us."

"Simon we love you."

"We'll protect you."

"I'll protect you, man," Michael said. *"You know you can trust*

me."

"And me, Simon."

"And me."

"And me."

"Gotta get rid of the cop, Simon. You just got to."

"Simon?"

"Simon? You listening?"

"Don't shut us out."

"Siiiiimmmmmoooooonnnn?"

"Nooooooo!" He rammed his foot on the gas and took off.

CHAPTER TWENTY-NINE

Brianna got to the station in fifteen minutes. Steven was working late and refused to cut it short and head to her place. Jerk.

She hopped off the elevator. He'd be in the file room. She got a chill when she reached the door. She hadn't felt comfortable being in here since the attack.

Her detective eye spotted Steven in the back. He kneeled behind the last file cabinet.

"Steve?" She got on her knees beside him.

"Woo wee." He whistled. "Damn you look fine, Bree."

"What?" She'd forgotten to take off that dress she'd put on when Simon came over.

"Stop looking at me like a piece of meat."

He licked his lips. "Turn around and let me check out the back."

"Steve this is serious."

He sorted through files. "So am I."

"I mean it."

"All right what was so important you couldn't even say it on the phone?"

"It's about Cheyenne's case."

"Jayce must've called you right? He called me too and told me about the statue having Cheyenne's blood on it."

"It's not about that." She sat on her butt. "This is about Simon. He was at my place tonight."

He stuck his pencil behind his ear. "I see. Would that explain the hot-looking dress? Although I should've known you were with him. I can smell that cologne. Can't mistake the scent of dead skunk can you?"

"Funny. His cologne happens to be French and one of the most expensive on the market."

"It smells like a skunk took a shit in another skunk's ass."

"Forget the cologne. Simon was at my place when Jayce called me."

"Oh? Did he call when you were going down or when Simon was?"

"Steven I'll just get my ass up and leave if you don't wanna hear this."

"All right. Go ahead."

"After Jayce called Simon pressured me to tell him what the call was about. I told him that they'd found the weapon Cheyenne was attacked with."

"And?"

"I never told him about the little statue. I never told him what the weapon was."

Steven lowered the folders.

"When we were talking about it, Simon specifically said "statue." I swear I never told him. Not even when Jayce first told me about it the other day."

"You sure you didn't tell him before? Might not remember."

"I'am positive. I never said anything about a statue to Simon. Not one time."

"I told you I thought Simon was involved."

"I didn't say he was involved."

"Oh Bree come on. I know you got the hots for him but you gotta think with sense."

"I know him, Steve."

"Oh please."

"I do know him! He wouldn't do this."

He squinted. "How well do you know him?"

"It doesn't matter right now."

"It matters to me."

"Just that he's shared with me. That's all."

"Don't play with me, Bree. You know what I'm asking."

"Steven."

"Oh jeez." He laid his foot against the cabinet. "Please don't tell me you slept with him, Bree."

She sighed.

"Did you sleep with Simon?"

"That's my business."

"No." He threw the files down and grabbed her.

"Let go!"

"You tell me! Look me in the damn eyes. Did you sleep with Simon?"

"Don't do this."

"Did you?"

"What I do with Simon is my business."

"I don't believe this. I don't fuckin' believe this."

"Steve." She followed him to the table. "Look there's something more important than whether I slept with Simon."

"Not to me."

"If you're gonna hate me, hate me. But do it after we solve this case."

"Oh I see. You're now suspicious of Simon? After I told you to be all along?"

"I trust him."

"Liar."

"You're really enjoying making me feel like a fool aren't you?"

"Well it takes my mind off how you keep breaking my heart."

She titled her head.

"Steve."

"Did you ask Simon how he knew it was a statue?"

"No. I was too shocked plus I didn't want him to realize I picked it up."

"Because you think he had something to do with the attack."

"Stop putting words into my mouth. I said I trust Simon and I do. I know he wouldn't hurt anyone."

"Then why are you telling me all this?"

"Because no matter what I think we need to find out how Simon knows what the weapon is."

"He knows because he did it."

"We still don't know where it happened. Cheyenne still claims not to remember Michael. But if he attacked her, how can she not remember him at all?"

Steven propped his foot in the chair. "Okay I'll bite. Say Michael did do it. Maybe he didn't know her before he did it. Maybe he saw her somewhere and attacked her."

"But why would he beat her like that? I could understand if she'd been sexually assaulted."

"Maybe he got off on it. He was into BDSM. Maybe his violent tendencies were getting to where he couldn't control them. You remember how scared he had Stephanie. He was also stalking you."

"Supposedly."

"Well it looks like he was anyway. It's not a stretch that a man like that would beat Cheyenne."

"Simon got upset when I told him this doesn't add up. I wanted Michael to be guilty so badly. You were right. I was judging him unfairly because I didn't like him and his lifestyle. But I just can't get over this feeling that something is still missing about all this."

"I don't think Stephanie committed suicide, Bree."

She didn't answer.

"What do you wanna do about Watts?"

"I wanna bring him in for questioning."

◆◆◆◆◆◆

Simon showed up the next morning calm as always. He even brought Brianna flowers, embarrassing the hell out of her in the process. She didn't like the officers in her personal business.

She'd explained why they wanted to talk to him on the phone but didn't mention the details. He seemed happy to oblige. Brianna couldn't figure out what was going on but her instinct told her Simon was not dangerous. Or least he didn't try to be.

They showed him into one of the smaller interrogation rooms away from the noisiest areas in the station.

He didn't break a sweat. Acted like he'd come to shop for a new home not to talk about an attempted murder case.

Steven pulled Brianna to the side. "Let me handle this."

"Why?"

"Because we need to get some answers and you'll be pampering him like he's in fuckin' day care."

"Fine, Steve. You wanna handle it?" She sat in the chair in the corner. "Go ahead, Sherlock." She crossed her legs.

"Simon do you know Michael Buchanan?" Steven strutted around the musty room with his hands behind his back. "Or should I say *did* you?"

"No I didn't." Face didn't even flinch.

"Bree and I think you might have."

"*Steven* thinks you might."

Steven muttered at Brianna's dismissal.

"Well that's funny," Simon said. "I don't see why you'd think that. I didn't know anything of Michael until Brianna told me he might be connected to the attack. I hadn't ever heard of him before in my life."

Simon winked at Brianna. She moved her head to hide her giggle.

"Keep your eyes on me, Watts."

"I can't help myself, Detective Kemp. Don't tell me it's not hard for you being around such a beautiful woman and not being able to touch her."

"Watts this isn't a game."

"Just wanna clear the air between you and I."

"And what the hell does that mean?"

"Come on, Detective Kemp. No one here is stupid are they?" Simon moved his fingernail across the tabletop. "Tell me something. Whose idea was it that I knew Michael in the first place? Was it yours?"

"You suggesting I'm doing this out of spite or for some personal agenda?"

"Well maybe. Sure is funny that all of a sudden you're suspicious of me now that Brianna and I have gotten close."

"Simon don't."

"It's okay, Brianna. I mean you can't protect him forever. He deserves to know the truth."

"Simon this isn't the place to do this."

"Seems like the perfect place to me, sweetheart."

Steven made fists and jiggled in place like he needed all the strength in the world to not hit Simon.

"This has nothing to do with whatever's going on between you and Bree. This is my job and I take it very seriously."

"I'm sure you are very passionate about your job. And the people you work with as well."

"You little." Steven lunged at him.

"Steven stop it! Simon you're being rude."

"I apologize."

"Don't blame this on Steve okay? It was my idea to bring you in." Brianna straightened her badge on her belt. "Now I'll ask you again. You sure you don't want a lawyer?"

"Positive. I don't need one. I didn't do anything."

"And you're that sure of yourself, Watts?"

He swung his arm over the back of the chair. "When you're innocent, you can be."

"Simon how did you know the weapon Cheyenne was attacked with was a statue?"

"What?" He put his hands on the table. "I don't understand."

"Oh I think you do." Steven scratched his ear. "Just answer the question."

CHAPTER THIRTY

"Simon last night at my place you mentioned a statue in reference to the weapon."

"What?" He felt his hair. "I don't remember that."

"You did. I didn't say anything, but you did."

"Sure you don't want a lawyer, Watts? Wanna finally admit what's going on here?"

"I don't know what you're talking about."

"Cut the shit!" Steven bent over the table.

"Steve cut it out."

"Don't fuck with me, Watts. I know you think you're so damn clever but you're not."

"Brianna what in the world is he talking about?"

"You." Steven got so close to Simon he blocked Brianna's view. "See the police never mentioned the items that were found in Michael's to the media or anyone. Bree and I just got the call from Jayce last night that the statue had Cheyenne's blood on it. Bree didn't tell you what the weapon was so unless you're psychic, how the fuck would you know?"

"I…" He looked at Brianna.

She turned away.

"How, Watts?" Steven punched the table. "Stop fucking with me or I'll throw your ass in a cell right now."

"Stop bullying him, Steve!"

"Bullying? He might've attacked Cheyenne!"

"Just let him say what he's gonna say." Brianna stared at Simon with hope and fear.

"Simon please tell us the truth. How did you know about the statue? You don't need to be afraid."

"The fuck he doesn't." Steven looked him in the eyes. "Watts I for one don't give a damn what happens to you. I just want the truth right here and now. If you care about Cheyenne then you'd be honest."

"I know you wanna lock me up but I hate to disappoint you, Detective. Yes I did know of the statue. But I didn't know it was a weapon until I heard Brianna on the phone last night."

"How did you know?" Brianna asked.

"Cheyenne told me about the statue."

"What?" Steven rubbed the hairs on his chin.

"She told me about the stuff Matthews said he'd found. I saw Cheyenne at the hospital yesterday morning. Detective Matthews had been there."

"So?" Steven grimaced.

"He told Cheyenne he suspected the spots on the little angel thing was blood. He'd know more once the results came in. I showed up not long after he'd left."

Steven dropped his head.

"Cheyenne told me all of this. And last night I heard Brianna on the phone." He watched her. "Your voice carries, sweetie."

"Bullshit."

"It's the truth, Detective Kemp."

"Well I don't buy it."

"I do," Brianna said. "I believe Cheyenne told him. There'd be no other way for him to know."

"He knows because he did it!"

Simon sat back with a crooked smile.

"He is playing you like a guitar and you're letting him."

"He has an explanation that can easily be verified. All we have to do is talk to Cheyenne."

"I still wouldn't believe it. What the hell is wrong with you, Bree? Open your damn eyes and look at the signs!"

"Look we brought him in to find out how he knew about the weapon. He told us! So what the fuck's your problem, Steve?"

He gasped between words. "It's him. It's you. It's all of this shit! It doesn't make any sense."

"He gave us an answer, Steve. If you can't accept it then that's your problem."

"You'd accept any damn thing he says wouldn't you?"

"I am telling the truth. You can ask Cheyenne."

"And Cheyenne." Steven kicked chairs. "Doesn't she have the sense to keep her big mouth shut?"

"Shut up, Steve."

"How the hell we gonna get anywhere if she keeps blabbing everything to everybody, Bree? This is all just bullshit!"

"Obviously she trusts Simon if she told him. That says something."

"He's fucking with you, Bree. You can't see that? He seduced you to stay in the know about this entire thing. Baby you gotta see that."

"I don't believe that. He saved me from the stalker, Steve. He's been truthful anytime we've needed something. He did not attack Cheyenne. I truly believe that."

Steven snatched her from the chair. "What is it huh? What's so great about Watts? What's this trance he has you in?"

"Let me go, Steven! What's the matter with you?"

Simon put his hand on Steven's shoulder. "Let go of her, Detective."

"You stay the fuck outta this."

"You put me in this." Simon removed Brianna from Steven's hold. "This little charade today isn't about helping Cheyenne. It's about your bruised ego. You would do anything to get back at me because you can't have Brianna and I can."

"You motherfucker!" Steven punched him.

"Ohhh!" Simon fell over.

"Steven!" Brianna pushed him. "Simon?" She helped him up. "You all right?"

"Yes." He hid his nose under his hand. "Ahh."

"Steven you are outta control!" Brianna blocked Simon. "You don't ever put your hands on anyone! You know better!"

"He's a lying shit, Bree."

"It makes no difference what you believe. You can't hit him! This is police brutality Steven and you know better! If Simon presses charges you could not only be kicked off this case but off the force! How many times I have to tell you to control your temper? It's going to get you in big trouble one day!"

Simon dabbed his nose. "It's okay, Brianna."

"Steven how could you?"

"Ah fuck you, Bree." He went to the door.

"What?"

"You claim you care about Cheyenne but Watts is the one you care about."

"You hit him!"

"I know he's lying! You're not using your brain, Bree. Simon is using you."

"Why can't you admit this is all because you're jealous? You don't want to see me with another man no matter who it is."

"You know me better than that." He opened the door. Passing officers peeked in.

"I thought I did, Steve. But I don't doubt that if I wasn't seeing Simon, you'd be more willing to believe him."

"Well if that's what you really think about me after knowing me all these years, there's nothing else I need to say."

"Steve."

He slammed the door.

◆◆◆◆◆◆

After some serious begging and a bit of charm, Steven persuaded Gene's maid to let him talk to him. He'd rushed over straight from work with a ton of questions and hoped Gene could shed some light.

He went upstairs to find Gene sitting in his home office. His intense eyes fell under his glasses as he studied some handheld notebook.

Part of being a good detective was being able to read people. You couldn't read Gene James. Psychiatrists read people's behaviors and actions by nature. Steven was way out of his league. Luckily he hadn't come here for that.

"Detective Kemp."

"I apologize for coming over without calling."

"And you need to talk to me right?"

Steven caught the shine of Gene's loafers.

"I know this is a hard time for you, Dr. James."

"Well when you and your lovely partner stopped by the other day to give your respects you won me over." He showed a faint smile but it didn't take away from the pain in his eyes.

"I thought it was very considerate that you came here when you didn't have to. What did you need?"

"You sent your girls away already?"

"Yeah I sent them to Stephanie's family out of town. I'll be joining them for the funeral." He stared at a photo on his desk.

"Dr. James? You okay?"

Gene turned the photo of Stephanie toward Steven. Kinda chilling how vibrant she looked. Her smile made you feel like she stood right in the room with you.

"Look at the picture, Detective Kemp."

"I am, sir."

"Does the woman in this picture look like she'd ever commit suicide?"

"No, sir."

"No." Gene laid it flat on the desk. "She does not."

"But she wasn't that woman in the picture anymore was she? Stephanie probably wasn't smiling at all after she knew her marriage was ruined."

Gene acted like he wanted to comment. Shit. Steven had a way of putting his foot in his mouth. He hadn't wanted to sound like he accused Gene of deserting his wife. But in a way he had. Is that how rigid the doctor was? Could throw away his entire family over a few meaningless mistakes?

"My wife didn't commit suicide. I know her better than anyone. Stephanie would never kill herself and leave the girls, never. She loved them more than anything." Gene twisted his wedding ring around his finger. "That's what I loved about her the most. She might not have been the perfect wife but she loved her children with every bone in her body."

"I'm sure that's true. And for the record I don't think Stephanie killed herself either. If she wanted to I think she'd done something other than throwing herself down the stairs."

"What did you need, Detective?"

"You sure you're up for it?"

"You're here already. Might as well say what's on your mind."

"Did you know Michael Buchanan well?"

"Well that was one name I could've gone without hearing for the rest of my life."

"I'm sorry."

"I didn't know Michael "well" but I knew him. The first time I met him I distrusted him. He just had ways about him that made him come off as sneaky. You got the feeling he was bullshitting you but he seemed so arrogant that either he thought you were too stupid to realize it, or that you'd just be so charmed by him, you'd take whatever he said."

"Yep that was definitely Michael Buchanan. Did you like him?"

"I try not to not like people, Detective. I wouldn't say he was a bad person but he just had those ways. Like he was hiding something."

"Do you believe he attacked Cheyenne?"

"Why you asking me?"

"Just wanted to know what you think."

CHAPTER THIRTY-ONE

"I couldn't make such a statement. Michael was an acquaintance. He wasn't someone I saw all the time." Gene writhed in his chair. "I knew he wanted my wife the minute I met him. He looked at her the same way I did when I first saw her."

"Well your wife was a very beautiful woman."

"And much younger than me right?"

"No I didn't mean anything by that."

"It's true. I know Stephanie loved me but can I really blame her for having affairs with younger men? Maybe it was my fault. Obviously she missed something I wasn't giving her."

"She loved you. I didn't know her long but I knew that. Anyone could tell. It radiated off her."

"It's funny. I've spent my career listening to people's problems and issues. Yet I couldn't do it with my own wife. I can pinpoint what a stranger needs and how they need it but hadn't a clue about what my wife needed. And didn't have the patience or consideration to listen."

"Dr. James?"

"I was just so angry. Angrier than even the first time she cheated. Why didn't I see the signs then?"

"Stephanie's death was not your fault."

Gene punched the desk. "If she'd been here it never would've happened!"

"You don't know that."

"I do! I kicked her out and that's what made her vulnerable to whatever she got mixed up in."

"What are you talking about?"

"You *know*, Detective. Whoever believes Stephanie killed herself needs a brain transplant."

"I agree but what do you think?"

"She was murdered!" Gene's eyes popped out their sockets. "And I don't know why but that's what happened."

"Do you think she killed Michael?"

Gene scoffed. "Am I seriously supposed to answer that?"

"Just wanted to get your take on it."

"Hell no. Stephanie couldn't kill anyone. She was one of the kindest people you could meet. Besides what point would there be to kill Michael after I knew they'd had an affair?"

"Some folks think for revenge."

"Well some folks need to go to hell. Stephanie wouldn't have done anything to jeopardize her being with her kids. She wouldn't have killed Michael knowing she'd go to prison."

"Then what do you think happened?"

"How the hell should I know?" Gene rubbed his knuckles. "Is that all you wanted? To ask me about Michael?"

"I just thought maybe you could help. How did you meet him? Was he a patient?"

"You think someone as arrogant as Michael would've had a shrink? No I met him through a patient. He's a friend of someone I've been working with for a long time."

"Oh."

"Detective I don't mean to rush you but I'd like to be alone."

"Of course. Thanks for your help."

The phone rang downstairs. Marta ran up.

"Dr. James you have a call."

"I told you I'm not taking any calls today unless it's family. I don't care who it is."

"I'll be going, Dr. James. Take care." Steven went to the hall.

"But it's Simon Watts," Marta said.

Steven turned so fast that he almost tumbled down the stairs.

"Watts?"

Did she say Simon Watts?

"You know how he gets, Dr. James. He says he really needs you."

"All right." Gene went to the back room and shut the door.

"I'll see you out, Detective." Marta ushered Steven downstairs.

"Wait. Uh, is the Simon Watts he's talking about a British dude with long hair and a goatee?"

"Yes." Marta opened the front door. "You know Mr. Watts?"

"How does Dr. James know him?"

"He's one of Dr. James' patients."

Steven's mouth dropped to the floor.

◆◆◆◆◆◆

"Holy shit." Steven lost train of thought when he drove up to Simon's security gate that night. His home looked like a beautified version of the Bates Motel.

He wouldn't let Simon's money and status intimidate him. The man attacked Cheyenne and he was gonna prove it.

He pressed the little button on the speaker beside the gate.

"Yes who is it?" Simon asked.

"It's Kemp." Steven looked at the papers on his lap.

"Kemp who?"

"You know exactly who. Open the damn gate, Watts."

"Why, Detective Kemp. What a surprise."

"Open the fuckin' gate."

"Not until you say the magic word."

Steven gritted his teeth. "If you don't open this gate I'll tear down this speaker and shove it up your ass. Asshole." Steven gripped his papers.

The gate slid open.

◆◆◆◆◆◆

"What are you doing here?" Simon wore nothing but a white towel around his waist. Sweat covered his chest and his skin seemed flushed. His flimsy ponytail hung lopsided.

Steven hadn't heard Simon's question. He couldn't take his eyes off this ridiculous museum he called a home. Shit he wasn't a chick but even he'd be willing to fuck Simon for such riches.

"Detective Kemp?"

"Oh." His mind settled on Simon's lack of clothing. "Can you put on some clothes so we can talk?"

"I could but I'm not going to. Sorry if this makes you uncomfortable but you interrupted my evening."

"Let me guess. You meditating or soaking in your big ass Jacuzzi?"

"And how did you know I had a Jacuzzi?"

"Oh just a guess."

The men exchanged false smiles.

"This is important. I'd expect to get the truth but I'm sure I'd be asking too much."

"You still upset, Detective?"

"Oh I'm steaming."

"Oh I see. You're here to duke it out over Brianna aren't you? Well I'm sorry but I don't have time for this right now. I'm busy."

"This ain't about Bree it's about you, Watts. Now you can play your little game in front of her, but we both know you've been lying left and right."

"What are those papers you have?"

"Oh these?" Steven waved them. "Oh just a little proof that's all."

"Proof of what? I don't have time for this."

"You're gonna make time."

"If you wanna talk to me about this nonsense, call me back down to the station. Now if you'll please excuse me."

Steven stuck his foot in the door.

"Uh-uh. I'm not going anywhere until we talk."

"Simon!"

A woman yelled from upstairs."What's going on?"

"Is that your sister?"

"No."

"It is, isn't it?"

"Leave right now."

"It's her isn't it? What's the matter? Don't want me to talk to her?"

"Get out."

"No way." Steven went to the stairs.

"Detective get outta my house!"

"I have a feeling I won't get the truth outta you, Simon. Let's see if your sister wouldn't mind clearing things up huh?" Steven trotted up the stairs.

"Detective Kemp I'm warning you." Simon ran behind.

"Warning me?"

Simon's antique statues caught Steven's eye when he got upstairs.

"Detective leave right now!"

"Well one thing I can say is you got some taste, Watts."

"Simon!" The woman called from the room at the end of the hall.

"Oh yeah." Steven started for the room. "Now we get some answers."

"You don't wanna do that, Detective!" Simon trekked after him.

"Oh believe me I do. It's about time your lies come to an end. I'm gonna prove to everyone that you had something to do with Cheyenne's attack."

"You're out of your mind!"

Steven pressed on the door.

"Don't go in there! You have no right!"

"Scared, Watts? Ha, ha! Man this is golden. I finally knocked your ass off your high horse huh?"

"Detective!"

Steven opened the door. Every sensation he owned leapt from his body. The giant bedroom stunned the hell outta him but not as much as the woman inside the bed.

Brianna scrambled around under the sheets. She pulled the covers over her naked breasts.

"*Steven.*"

She looked like he felt.

"Oh my god." She shifted as if she couldn't look him in the face. "I don't believe this! What the hell are you doing here?"

Godzilla could've been in that bed and Steven wouldn't be this shocked.

"What in the..." He struggled to breathe.

Simon sauntered in with a smirk that Steven couldn't wait to slap off his face.

"Steven I asked you a question." Brianna hit the sheets. "What are you doing here?"

"I uh..." He stared at his papers. "I..."

"Something wrong, Detective Kemp?" Simon walked to the bed as if he owned the world and knew it.

"Steven answer the question." Brianna squirmed in the sheets. "I can't believe you're even here."

Her being in Watts' bed was bad enough but now she's snapping at *him*?

"What the fuck do you mean what I'm doing here? What are you doing here, Bree?"

"None of your business."

"What the hell are you doing, Bree? I mean what the hell is going on in your head? You can't see who you're dealing with?" He pointed the papers to Simon. "Watts is dangerous. You don't know him."

"I think I know him a lot better than I thought I knew you."

Simon smiled.

"How can you say that, Bree?"

"Because you came here like this! Why are you here?"

"Oh are you asking because you're embarrassed or because you really wanna know why I'm here?"

"I'm not embarrassed, Steve. But you should be."

"Look this is serious. I don't give a damn about you being here."

"Right," Simon said. "Is that why you're red as a beet?"

"Bree Simon is lying. I can prove it."

"Okay didn't we settle this at the station?"

"Apparently not since you're laying up in his bed."

"Truth hurts doesn't it, Detective Kemp? But I tried to stop you from walking in here. I was trying to spare your feelings."

"And you care so much about my feelings huh, Watts?"

"To be honest, no."

"And we both know that's the first time you've *been* honest isn't it?"

"Steven for the last time, why the hell are you here?"

"I need to talk to you."

She raised her hand. "If this is the same song about Simon, I don't wanna hear it."

"Well you're gonna listen!"

"What?"

"You're gonna listen to me Bree if I gotta hold you down and make you."

"Oh yeah?"

"Yeah! Now you wake up! You running around here like you've lost your fuckin' mind!"

"You're the one who hits Simon at the station and now you show up here outta the blue like a mad man. Just admit this is all because you're jealous."

"I am not jealous of Watts."

"Oh really, Detective?" Simon leaned on the dresser. "Isn't that the basis of this rampage you've now got going against me?"

"No." He swung the papers. "But this could be."

CHAPTER THIRTY-TWO

"And I'll ask again. What papers are those?"

"Fuck you, Watts." Steven put them behind his back. "I'm not telling you shit. Bree can I speak with you alone please?"

"No." She rolled her eyes. "Get out."

"Bree you're gonna listen."

"I'd listen if you were being rational but this is getting ridiculous. You're just running around, finding stuff to pin on Simon."

"Would you just give me a chance to explain?"

"Well explain it to us all!" Simon cackled. "I'm dying to hear it myself."

"We'll see how funny you think it is after I tell Bree what's going on and she wants nothing else to do with your stuck up ass."

"Just say it Steven because right now I can't stand looking at you."

"Simon knows Michael Buchanan."

Boy that felt good.

"Oh, ha, ha!" Simon dropped down. "Oh goodness, Brianna! I can't wait to hear this!"

"Well we'll see how long you keep laughing lover boy."

"Steven I don't understand." Brianna scratched her head. "What makes you think Simon knew Michael?"

"Brianna." Simon's amusement faded. "Why are we entertaining this nonsense? Whatever he comes up with is a lie. I didn't know Michael Buchanan. And if those papers say so, he's cooked them up."

"Oh these papers have nothing to do with Michael, Watts. But we'll get to these later. I visited Gene James a few hours ago."

Simon raised his chin.

"Why did you go to see Gene?"

"That's a good question, Bree. I really don't know why but something told me to go over there. Guess God led me to his door."

"Would you get on with this?" Simon tapped his fingers on the dresser. "It's pathetic."

"Simon is a patient of Gene's."

"What?" Brianna looked at Simon.

Yeah. What you think about that, Watts?

"Simon is this true?"

"Sweetheart." He sat on the bed.

"Don't sweetheart me. Is this true?"

"Yes it is."

"What? You mean you knew Gene James and you didn't tell me?"

"I didn't think it mattered."

"Simon all these people connect somehow to this attack in one way or another. You saw me talking about Stephanie and Michael and you didn't tell me you were a patient of Gene's? How could you do that?"

"I didn't mean to hide it."

"Oh you just forgot it huh?"

"Shut up, Detective Kemp. Brianna?" Simon kissed her hand. "You're right. I should've said something but I didn't know what you'd think of me. A lot of people seem to look at you differently when you admit you're seeing a psychiatrist."

"Oh please. This has nothing to do with how you thought Bree would see you. You hid it because you were involved in this from the beginning!"

Simon gave Steven the evil eye. "Happy aren't you, Detective?"

"Are you kidding? I wanna take my clothes off and dance down the street."

"Just because Gene is my doctor doesn't mean I knew Michael."

"Oh please. Yeah right."

"He's right." Brianna fixed the sheet over her bosom. "Just because Simon is connected to Gene it in no way proves he knew Michael."

"The fuck it doesn't. You think all this shit's a coincidence? Michael was fucking Gene's wife. Gene's Simon's doctor!"

"Doesn't prove anything."

"Bree wake the fuck up! What, is he so good in bed that you've lost all mental capacity?"

"You have nothing, Detective Kemp. Why don't you stuff your tail between your legs and leave with some kind of dignity while you still can."

"You really don't see the significance of it, Bree?"

"Steve yes, it's a surprise that Simon knew Gene and didn't tell me. But it does not mean he knew Michael. Just because you're someone's patient, it doesn't mean you know the man who's screwing the doctor's wife."

"Simon knew Stephanie!"

"So! I know my dentist's nephew. But does that mean I know everyone who is connected to him?"

"So you really think this is a coincidence? Is that what you're saying?"

"You're running out of gas, Detective."

"Watts if you say one more word I'll stick these papers down your throat."

"Steven it's nothing. You gotta be able to tie Simon to Michael."

"Which he can't because I didn't know him."

"Gene told me that he met Michael through a patient of his." He gestured to Simon.

"How much more proof do you need?"

Brianna's eyebrows wiggled. "Did he say through Simon Watts?"

"No but..."

"And how did you find out I was a patient of Gene's?" Simon walked around. "Oh wait. I called Gene earlier. That must've been when you were there."

"The maid announced your call."

"And you ran with it didn't you? Oh that's so cute, Detective Kemp. So this is how you gonna tie me to something I didn't do huh? Just piecing together stuff?"

"Bree I'm telling the truth."

"Steven no one's denying that Simon knows Gene. The question is, did he know Michael and I don't believe that he did."

"Okay fine." He swallowed his anger. "Maybe you'll believe what I have to show you."

"Ha, ha! The magic papers!" Simon rubbed his hands together.

"Oh this is great. I'm so glad you showed up, Detective. Who needs cable with such entertainment?"

"Simon you're in no position to be joking around," Brianna said. "You still lied."

"I didn't wanna risk that you wouldn't understand."

"You sure can turn it on and off can't you, Watts? Is there a class that teaches that technique?"

"Steven you're getting on my last nerve too. Right now I don't know if I wanna be around either of you."

"Bree I need to speak to you in private."

"No."

"I wasn't asking you, Watts."

"This is my house. I don't have to leave if I don't want to. If you've got something to tell her, let me hear it."

"I'll wait then. I don't wanna say it in front of you so you can come up with some lie."

"I am sick of those papers! Either show them or get the hell out!"

"Simon!" Brianna got on her knees in the bed.

Steven caught a glimpse of her nipple when the sheets slipped. He held the papers over his crotch.

"Simon let me speak to Steven please."

"Brianna."

"You owe me this don't you think? After you didn't tell me about knowing Gene? I thought we were gonna be honest with each other."

"I didn't intend to hide it. I just…"

"Forgot to tell her?" Steven sat on the bed.

Brianna scooted to the edge and sat beside him.

"Please let me hear what he has to say, Simon."

"Okay." He patted the sides of his thighs. "If that's what you want. Will you give me a chance to rebuke anything he might say? Any lie?"

She nodded. "I just wanna see what he has to show me."

"All right." Simon headed out.

"And don't listen at the door, Watts."

Simon left.

"I didn't see your car outside," Steven said.

"Yeah uh, Simon met me at my place after work and he brought me over."

He clenched his teeth. "My isn't that special?"

"Okay. What did you wanna tell me?"

"You remember the last time *we* made love, Bree?"

She avoided his gaze. "What did you wanna tell me?"

"Do you?"

"Course I do. At the department picnic, a year ago. It was a mistake."

"No it wasn't."

"Yes it was. I got caught up in how we used to be and well we shouldn't have crossed that line."

"You wanted to cross it. There shouldn't even be a line between us. That's what I want you to change."

"Steven please."

He moved the papers when she grabbed at them.

"Remember that night when we made love in the rain, Bree?"

"What does that have to do with anything?"

"Remember what we said afterwards? That we'd always be there for each other no matter what?"

"And that hasn't changed. Look I'm not in the mood to stroll down Memory Lane with you. Now tell me what you got or piss off."

"Piss off? You have been hanging around Watts too long."

"What do you wanna tell me, Steven? My patience is long gone."

"I've been trying to do research on Simon."

"Wow surprising."

"Would you just listen? After I left Gene's, I got on the computer."

"You Googled him?"

"No I Googled his *past*."

"What?"

"Bree you remember you told me his adoptive parents died in a fire?"

"Of course."

"Did it ever seem strange to you?"

"No."

"Well it did to me and it's not because I'm jealous. I did some research. I came across some news articles about that fire. Did you know that the police suspected arson?"

"Arson?"

"It's right here." He passed her the different articles. "See I highlighted the parts about suspected arson."

"Okay but so what? A lot of times they suspect arson and it doesn't turn out to be."

"I know it. But how many times does a fire break out, killing a couple and their fortune is left to their adopted children?"

"Wait a minute. Are you trying to say Simon had something to do with this fire?"

"You can't be that surprised. This man made off with millions when they died. You think Simon didn't know he and Clara would inherit that fortune?"

"No! This is crazy." She threw him the papers. "And I'm not gonna even entertain it."

"Bree listen to me! I know you like him but you gotta think. You know damn well this is suspicious."

"So you really think Simon killed his parents?"

"Yes I do. And I think he beat Cheyenne too."

"No." She shook her head. "Simon would never do anything like that. He adored those people."

"Some folks will do anything for money!"

"Simon isn't money hungry!"

"That's because he has all the goddamn money he needs!"

"He loved those people. He'd gone from having a horrible life to a fairytale! He said losing them almost made him crazy. He almost committed suicide when it happened. He told me."

"And what about his sister? Where the hell is she?"

"Simon did *not* kill his parents. He came from hell and he deserved to have a happy ending."

"Doesn't Cheyenne?"

"He didn't attack Cheyenne."

"And how do you know?"

"Do you think I'd be around a man who would be capable of that? Cheyenne is my friend. If I even suspected Simon was involved I'd have his ass in jail. You know that."

"Why are you refusing to see what I am trying to show you?"

"Simon told me all this before!" She stood. The sheet slipped from her breasts again. "He didn't hide it! He told me all about his childhood!"

"But he didn't tell you that the authorities suspected arson did he?"

"This happened ten years ago, Steven. Simon was well into adulthood. If they thought he'd done this, why wasn't he arrested for it?"

"Because they couldn't prove it was arson!"

"No they didn't suspect Simon in the first place!" She snatched the papers. "I don't see one damn thing where any name but Simon's parents are mentioned. If you showed me something that said the authorities suspected him or his sister, fine. Steven the man lost his entire life and family! Can't you feel pity for that?"

"Not when I know there's more to the story. How come no one can tell me where his sister is? Do you even know?"

"Uh, hello, I don't know where my dad is."

"That's different."

"No it's not. Simon and Clara have been estranged for a while now."

"Oh? Well Cheyenne said they're supposed to be so close. What's the truth?"

"They were close." She straightened the sheet. "But through the years they drifted apart."

"For no reason at all?"

"It's not my business Steve and it sure as hell isn't yours."

"I don't believe this. I could wake Michael Buchanan up from the dead and have him say he knew Simon and you still wouldn't believe it."

"You are doing this out of spite. If Simon is capable of so many things then how come he never *once* laid a hurtful finger on me?"

"Oh I don't know! Maybe it's because you ain't pissed him off yet."

"Take your papers and your worthless theories and get out, Steven."

"You wanted to find out who attacked Cheyenne. Well there he is outside the door."

CHAPTER THIRTY-THREE

"And I'll tell you for the last time that Simon didn't do it. It doesn't add up.

He'd have slipped and let out something about that night sometime."

"Watts is a pro! He's probably been lying his whole damn life."

He grabbed her arm.

"Let me go."

"Listen to me goddamn it. You don't know who he really is."

"And you do? Admit this is all because you're jealous. You'd find anything if you look long enough."

"Watts is a psychopath, Bree."

"Oh ha!" She laughed. "Can you get anymore pathetic?"

"Why did he not tell you he knew Gene James?"

She looked at the carpet.

"I tell you why. Because he knows Michael and he knew damn well we'd put two and two together."

"Please leave."

"So you're just gonna stay here with him tonight? Nothing I've said matters?"

"Simon wouldn't hurt anyone and I want you to back off."

"Me?"

"If you can't then I don't wanna be around you." She tripped on the sheet when she walked to the side of the bed.

"Fine." He straightened his papers. "I don't understand you, Bree."

She got in the bed.

"Don't tell Simon what was on these papers and what I told you. Don't forget you're a cop too."

"I know what I am."

"Promise you won't say nothing, Bree."

"I won't if you leave right now."

"So this is what you want huh?" He gestured to various items in the room. "You want Watts?"

"He's what I want right now."

"Do you love him?"

It took forever for her to answer.

"I don't know."

Somehow that hurt him more than if she'd said yes.

"Oh. Wow. That's something then."

"Get out, Steven! I mean it."

Simon walked in. "Okay that's enough of this. She asked you to leave Detective and now I'm *telling* you to. Get out."

"I just wanna protect you, Bree."

"We'll talk later okay?" She lay on the pillows.

"Get out." Simon held the door open.

Steven shuffled up to him. "You'll never fool me, Watts. I know what all this has been about from the beginning."

"Oh?"

"Yeah it's all about Bree. You don't care about anything else. I think you beat Cheyenne just to have a reason to meet her."

"Stop it, Steven."

"Huh?" Steven got in Simon's face. "Is that so hard to believe? You've already proved how clever you are, Watts. I wouldn't put nothing past you."

"She's in love with me too. I had no control over that no matter what you think about the situation."

"Maybe, maybe not. I get the feeling you manipulate any situation to please yourself. You think you know Bree? You don't. We've gone through shit together that you have no idea about."

"Well that's the past."

"Is that what you do, Watts? Go around stealing other people's women?"

"If she's your woman how come she just made love to *me*?"

"Jeez." Brianna pushed her face into the pillows.

"You're lucky I'm a cop or your ass would be mine."

"Is that a threat, Detective Kemp?"

"You think you know Bree huh? You don't at all."

"I know she doesn't want *you*."

Steven watched Brianna for the longest time then left.

"You okay?" Simon sat on the bed.

"Why didn't you tell me you knew Gene?"

He caressed her arm. "Please don't be angry."

"I'm not angry but I'm not thrilled either. I just can't believe that you didn't open your mouth and say you were connected to Gene James."

"I didn't because I was scared of what you'd think of me. Everyone doesn't understand things like this, Brianna. I was afraid you'd look at me differently when you found out I had a psychiatrist. Thought you'd think I was crazy."

"That's silly. A lot of people have shrinks and they aren't crazy. My mother had a shrink for years."

"She did?"

"Yeah and that didn't make her crazy. She already was crazy."

He laughed and pinched her chin.

"Simon you've been begging me to trust you but then when it comes down to it you don't trust *me*."

"Oh I do." He took her hand. "It had nothing to do with you."

"You claimed you knew so much about the type of person I was before you met me. You should've known that you having a shrink wouldn't matter to me." She touched his knee. "I care about you. I want you to always be honest."

"I didn't mean to hide it, sweetie." He kissed her. "Would never do anything to hurt you."

"Just keep me in the know okay? I hate being in the dark about anything. It's better if you're honest."

"What did Kemp say to you?"

"Huh? Oh uh, nothing of any importance."

"Seems like he was in here forever. He didn't say much of anything?"

"Just trying to get me to believe you're connected to the attack. Like he always is."

"What about those papers?" He played with her toes through the sheet. "What were they about?"

"What?"

"What was on the papers he had?"

"Oh uh just stuff about the case. That's all."

"You sure?"

"Of course I'm sure. Why are you looking at me like that?"

"That little speech you just ran goes both ways I hope. Just like I should be truthful, you should be."

"And I will be." She kissed him. "Can we please stop talking about Steven?"

"Hmm." He dragged his lips down her neck. "Thought you'd never ask."

She pinched his nipple. "So what's this present you've been telling me about all night?"

"Well." He went to the closet. "I'm not so sure you deserve it."

"Simon don't play with me." She yanked up a pillow. "I'll throw this if you don't give me my present."

He laughed. "Okay. I'd be killing myself if I didn't give it to you. Been waiting to for a while."

"What is it?" She scooted to the edge of the bed with the sheet secured around her.

He pulled out a large sack. He lifted a portrait from the top of it.

"*Simon.*" Brianna covered her mouth.

It was a portrait of her and Cheyenne on the beach. As lifelike as the photo it was made from.

"You like it?"

"I don't know what to say." Tears clouded her eyes. "I can't believe you did this."

"Well I didn't do it." He grinned. "A friend of mine. He did it for a favor. It's from the photo Cheyenne gave me."

"Simon."

"And it's all yours, honey." He gathered her into his arms.

"Simon I can't take this."

"Nonsense. I had it made for you."

"Why?"

"Because you're the two most important women in my life." He hugged her. "And I want you both to stay in it forever."

Brianna placed her chin on his shoulder. She admired every stroke of the painting.

Something seemed so familiar about it. Not the actual picture, but the way it had been done. She'd seen this style before. Just couldn't remember where.

"Who painted it?"

"Hmm?"

"Who painted the portrait?"

"Oh just a friend of mine. You like it?"

"Of course I do."

"Good." He laid her down. "Now let's take up where we left off before we were interrupted."

Simon loosened the sheet from her body. He positioned himself between her thighs.

He kissed her chest. "Mmm, I love you so much, Brianna. We belong together. It's so perfect."

She gave him full access to her body. Welcomed every tender stroke.

But she couldn't stop thinking about Steven's accusations or the sense that she'd seen this artist's work somewhere before.

◆◆◆◆◆◆

Two Weeks Later

Brianna ran into the hospital room. "Cheyenne?"

Cheyenne turned the television down.

"Are you all right?"

"If you mean my health, yes. I don't know about everything else."

Brianna studied the lines of worry on Cheyenne's face. "What's going on?"

"Sit down, Bree. This is so hard for me."

Brianna pulled a chair up beside the bed. "What is?"

She burst into tears.

"Cheyenne? Honey what's wrong?"

"I've been trying to come up with a reason that made sense but I can't."

"Honey." Brianna stroked her head. "Did something happen? You can tell me anything."

"I finally remember, Bree."

Brianna touched her hand. "You mean the night you were attacked? You remember the attack?"

"No. But I remember something that might be a key. And I wish I didn't."

"Well this is great news! I don't see why you're so upset."

Cheyenne massaged her temples.

"You getting another headache?"

"Mmm hmm. But not from the injury, from stress."

"Cheyenne you gotta tell me anything you remember."

"Even if it hurts you?"

Brianna hesitated but pushed away her fear.

"How could it hurt me?"

"Tell me I'm wrong." Cheyenne yanked Brianna's hand. "Please, please tell me I'm wrong!" Tears fell on her gown. "Bree it can't be true. It just can't be but I can't come up with a…"

"Does this have something to do with Simon?"

"I still don't remember the attack or where I was. But I had some kind of vision."

"Vision?"

"That's how it's coming back to me, through visions and daydreams. Today was the most vivid of all."

"What?" Brianna held her breath.

"I remember being somewhere pitch black and it was raining."

"So you were outside somewhere? In the dark?"

"It was a room but all I remember is hearing thunder and being in the dark."

"Like maybe you were somewhere and the lights were out."

"I think so." She closed her eyes. "Bree the vision seemed so damn real. Like it was happening today."

"How does Simon fit into all this?"

"In the vision I'm calling out to him. Now why would I be calling out to someone who wasn't there?"

"Maybe your mind's playing tricks on you. It could be the medicine or…"

"Bree it's my memory. Believe me I tried to talk myself into a reason why Simon would've been with me at the time I was attacked and I can't. He was there and he said he wasn't."

"Cheyenne." Brianna walked around. "You've gotta be confused, babe."

"You're dancing, Bree."

"This doesn't make sense!"

"And you think it makes sense to me? I care about him. I don't want it to be true that he lied but he did."

"I just can't believe this."

"I care so much about him too but he lied to both of us, Bree."

"No."

"He did and we both have to admit that. I'm not saying Simon attacked me but he was there. Maybe he didn't say anything because he was scared or..."

"He played us didn't he?"

"Bree."

"He lied. That's the point. Nothing else matters."

"I don't think he hurt me. I mean Simon wouldn't do something like that. I didn't wanna say anything at first because I didn't wanna accuse Simon in case I was wrong."

"But you know in your heart you're not wrong don't you? Wherever you were attacked Simon was there."

"Yes he was."

"He's a world of surprises isn't he?"

"Bree he cares about you very much."

"Just like he cares about you yet he lied about something so important? Something that could've helped you?"

"Bree wait."

She left.

CHAPTER THIRTY-FOUR

"Morris?" Captain Jersey walked from her office that night swinging her umbrella. "Why don't you go on home? You need some rest."

"How can I rest when I can't stop thinking about what Cheyenne told me?"

"It doesn't mean he attacked her."

"That's not the point."

"Then what is? You've been going around in circles all day. You don't even know if Cheyenne really remembers. She's been on so much medication."

"I tried that same excuse too for myself but it didn't work. Damn it." Brianna pushed away from her desk. "What if Simon beat Cheyenne?"

"Bree hold on."

"No he could've right?" She started crying like she had been all day. "We gotta admit that. Nothing else he's said matters because he lied. He was with her during the attack now why would he hide it if he didn't do it?"

"You know Simon better than I do. Do you really believe he did it?"

Brianna twirled her pencil. "Hell why ask me? I seem to be off base with everything. I'm the only person who thinks Michael might not be my stalker and that Stephanie didn't kill him. Maybe my intuition's fucked when it comes to Simon too."

"You gotta listen to your heart. That never steers you wrong."

"But what if I'm wrong about him? Oh god." Brianna threw the pencil down.

"He could've done it. I don't know how or why but he *could've* done it."

Jersey slid her purse on her shoulder. "Don't get worked up until you check things out for sure."

"I kissed him and made love to him." Brianna scrunched her face. "What the hell do I do?"

"Why don't you go talk to Simon huh?"

"He's the last person I wanna see right now."

"You sure about that?"

Brianna laid her head on the desk.

◆◆◆◆◆◆

Simon watched the dark streets from his front door. He jumped at every car that passed.

Where the hell was Michael?

Cheyenne lay by the couch, her head in a pool of blood.

Damn it.

"Come on, Michael. Come on." Simon walked back and forth from the front door to the hall. He wasn't gonna move her. It would be best to let Michael take it from here.

Like he always had.

But this was different. Cheyenne was his friend. He'd never meant for this to happen. Course he never meant for any of it to happen. It wasn't his fault. Clara ran the game.

Blood matted Cheyenne's hair to her head.

He should call the police. Why didn't he? For Clara's sake or his own?

"Why damn *you?" He threw a vase against the wall. "Clara! Answer me!"*

Of course she didn't. Besides, what would she say?

He heard rubber screeching on wet pavement. He'd opened the gate. They couldn't waste any time.

Michael walked in with a rain cap and long coat.

"Ahh fuck." He raised his leg and shook his foot. "Got rain on my shoes." He wiped off his Sean Johns.

How did he always stay so calm during this? Simon on the other hand split in pieces with each passing moment.

"Michael. I..."

"Shh." He noticed the pieces of the smashed vase. "Think I got the idea."

Simon pointed a shaky finger to the battered woman on the floor.

"Jesus." Michael stooped besides Cheyenne. "What happened?"

"You know what happened." Simon twisted his fingers together. "Things just got out of control. I couldn't stop it."

"Never could huh, Simon?"

"Clara. She came at me and we tussled."

"Yeah I'm sure." Michael rubbed his forehead.

"I blacked out and when I came to, Clara was gone and Cheyenne was lying in here. Oh god I can't take this anymore. I can't take it."

"Clara tussled with you." Michael bit his lip. "Right."

He checked Cheyenne's breathing. "She's still alive huh? Guess Clara's losing her touch."

"Course she's still alive!" Simon tugged on Michael's coat. "She won't be if we waste much time."

"Then we finish her off."

"No! You out of your mind?"

"We have no choice, Simon. You wanna get caught?"

"She is my friend! I care about her very much."

"Well our futures are more fuckin' important than your goddamn friends, Simon. I'm not going to prison for something I didn't do!"

"You won't!"

"Oh you goddamn right I won't. It's her or us, Simon."

"No." He covered his ears.

"Listen to me, man." Michael pulled Simon's hands down. "I'm not one of the voices, man. I'm a real person with a real fuckin' life and I'm not throwing it away!"

"We're not killing her. Now if you don't help me I'll do it myself."

"Do what?"

"I want to make this right."

"And how the fuck can you make this shit right, Simon?"

"Couldn't help the others." He rubbed his hands. "But I won't let Cheyenne die. She's too good of a person."

"Look decide something or you're on your own."

"Just hold on!" He grabbed Michael's arm. "I got an idea. Take her to the hospital."

"Are you out of your mind?" Michael looked up. "What am I saying?"

"This is serious." Simon stepped over Cheyenne. "We won't get in trouble and she'll be able to live. If we waste more time she'll die."

"You really care about this little birdie don't ya'?"

"I can't let her die. I just can't, Michael. Please help me."

"That's all I ever do!"

"Please." Michael spotted the small angel statue on the floor. "Is that what she was hit with?"

Simon wobbled.

"You sure you don't wanna finish her off? One more hit might do it."

"Take her to the hospital or take her to the police station," Simon said. "What's it gonna be? This will help both of us."

"How?"

"Free up our guilt."

"I don't have any guilt. I never hurt anyone."

"I didn't either."

"I think the opinions would vary on that, Simon."

"Just do it! We don't have time. You do this Michael and you never have to help me again. I promise."

"What if I get caught?"

"You won't! Just take her in and leave! It's not that hard."

"Then why don't you do it?" Michael scratched under his cap. "What if she remembers what happened and tells? You willing to risk that?"

"I don't care! She's my friend and I don't want her to die!" Simon combed his fingers through his hair. "Take her to Central West."

"I don't know. We've never played it this way before, Simon."

"I am not letting Cheyenne die if I have the power to save her." He sniffed. "You can smell the blood. I'm gonna throw up."

"You should be use to it by now I'd think."

Simon covered his mouth. "Ohh god."

"Just keep yourself together long enough for me to get back okay? Then we'll clean up this blood and stuff." Michael lifted Cheyenne then started laughing.

"What's so funny?" Simon quivered.

"I wonder where Clara went. Don't you? Ah, ha, ha, ha!"

"Oh!" Simon awoke from his dream. He lay on the couch with his arms spread wide.

The glass of Cognac he'd been drinking had spilt onto the carpet.

"Oh, Jesus." He sat up and pushed his face into his hands.

A hand caressed his hair. Clara's cunning eyes glared at him.

"You okay, honey?"

"No." He jumped off the couch. "Leave me alone."

"Oh sweetie what is it? Had a bad dream?"

Simon twitched and batted. "Go away. Just leave me alone!" She blocked him.

"Asking way too much aren't you, Simon?"

"Why are you doing this to me? Why won't you let me have some peace? That's all I ask."

"Because you don't deserve peace, Simon. You think you can just do bad things and get away with it?"

"It was you. You made me. I never wanted to hurt anyone."

"I made you huh?" She traipsed around in her white dress. *"And how did I make you, Simon? I'd love to know that."*

"You know how. Just leave me alone! Stop using my mind as your playground!"

"You put me here, Simon. It's your fault if I can't rest."

"Stop it!" He swatted at her but only hit air. "Just stop it."

"Jesus you think you'd be happy. You're a lucky bastard aren't you?"

"What are you talking about?"

"Well Michael's dead now. You don't have to worry about him turning on you. Doesn't that make you happy?"

"He wasn't perfect but he was my friend."

"Oh, ha, ha, ha! Simon." She put her hands on her waist. *"I knew you were gullible but I never took you as stupid. Michael only hung around you because of the money. You gave him millions, of course he'd have done what you wanted him to."*

"He was my friend."

"Right. You don't know what was going on in his head."

"And you do?"

She swept the ends of her dress. *"I know everything remember? Michael was only inches away from turning on you. He had his own plans. We both know all he wanted was Stephanie."*

"If they ever link me to him they'll think I killed him. What do I do?"

"Oh you know what to do." She sat on the coffee table. *"You're just scared. But you don't have to be. I'm here for you, Simon. We all are whenever you need us to be."*

"Please. I don't want anyone else to get hurt."

"Oh I know, honey. But it's unavoidable. You're in too deep to just walk away. You don't wanna spend your life in prison or worse some hospital. I know you don't want that again."

"I'd kill myself before I go back into one of those places."

"You won't have to if you do what you know you have to. You just have to be like us Simon, strong."

"I've never been strong. You always had all the strength."

"You have to make a new start, Simon. It's getting stale here."

"You mean leave? I love it here."

"You can love it somewhere else if it means keeping your freedom. Leave Albany and all this mess behind. You've got to."

He walked to her. "What did you mean when you said I know what I have to do?"

"You always fall for women who can ruin everything don't you? Just like a fool. You gotta make your life here history, Simon. Leave and act like you never lived here in the first place."

"I don't wanna leave. I can't."

"You can't until you take care of business. There's another person in the way. She's too smart for her own good. She'll start to doubt you and ask questions. She's the enemy."

"No. Don't even think about it. No one's hurting Brianna."

"It's unavoidable."

"No! I love her and nothing you do will change that!"

She got off the table. *"You listen to me, little brother. I make the rules. Now I've protected you all this time and I'll keep doing it but you gotta listen."*

"I am not doing anything to Brianna! Just stop this!"

"You don't have a choice! She's a cop. When it comes down to finding out the truth and being on your side, what do you think she's gonna pick?"

"Me!" He beat his chest. "Brianna would pick me."

"You don't know what you're saying."

"I love Brianna. I'm not gonna let you ruin this."

"The cop goes, Simon. Either you take care of her or I will."

"Simon?" Brianna's voice sounded from the security speaker.

"Hmm." Clara licked her lips. *"Isn't it amazing how opportunities just fall into your lap?"*

"Shut up."

"Simon it's Brianna! Open the gate!"

He pushed the little red button on the intercom by the front door.

"Brianna, honey?" He cut his eyes to the living room. Clara was gone. "I didn't expect you tonight."

"Well is it a problem?"

"Of course not, darling. It's never a problem where you're concerned. I'll open the gate."

CHAPTER THIRTY-FIVE

Brianna counted each breath she took while waiting for Simon to answer the door.

She couldn't come out and tell him what Cheyenne said. She just didn't know what to listen to, her head or her heart.

Her heart won out when Simon opened the door. She melted when she saw his eyes.

His face looked torn. Loose strands stuck out of his ponytail. His pupils switched as if he couldn't focus. His shirt hung lopsided out of his pants.

"Brianna."

"Simon are you all right?" She lifted her hand to touch his face. He pulled her into a suffocating kiss.

"Mmm." His tongue roamed the inside of her mouth. "I'm so glad you're here. I can't get enough of you." His fingers dug into her back.

"Simon, not so tight okay?"

"I'm sorry." He loosened his hold. "I just missed you so much. Seems like the more time I spend with you, the harder it is to let go."

She felt his forehead.

"What?"

"Just seeing if you were warm." She sniffed. "You've been drinking."

"Had a little cognac." He flashed a half-smile. "Needed to relax."

"Why are your clothes all twisted?"

"There you go again." He shut the door. "Being a cop."

The sound of the door closing echoed in her mind. She hadn't been afraid to be alone with him until now. The secret showed in his eyes. Did he love her enough to tell the truth?

"What is it, darling?" He swung her around and dipped her.

"Oh! Simon stop being so silly."

"I can't help it." He shook his hips. "You have no idea what you do to me."

He had no idea what he did to *her*. Damn she couldn't control herself around him.

Even now she could make love to him as if she hadn't even spoken with Cheyenne. Her nipples burned at the tips. Her clit called his name.

Steven had asked her if she loved Simon. She wasn't sure but it became harder to picture her life without him.

She hated herself for it.

"Gonna take you upstairs." He hoisted her up.

"Simon put me down!" She laughed. Her long legs went limp.

"God you're tall." He bounced her in his arms. "Wasn't reminded of it until I picked you up."

"Ha, ha!" She hit his arm. "Put me down. Come on."

He let her go when he got to the main bathroom.

"Wanna get in the Jacuzzi?" He unbuttoned the first button on her blouse.

"Simon, no."

"No? Why no?" He kissed her neck.

"Wait, honey."

She didn't want him to. She *needed* him to.

"Simon come on."

"You're so beautiful."

She took her purse off her shoulder. "You don't have to keep saying that."

"I can't help myself. It's the truth. I could look at you forever."

"Your face." She moved her fingers across his nose and mouth. "It's flushed. You look like you have something on your mind. Eyes look like you're not even here."

"Do they?"

"Uh-huh." She led him into the bathroom. She pulled the toilet lid down. "Sit down."

"Huh?" He laughed. "Brianna what are you up to?"

"You know how you always pamper me when we're together?"

He inched down on the toilet while watching her. "Yes?"

"Well I'm gonna repay the favor right now."

"You don't need to. I love pampering you."

"Simon?" She massaged his face.

"Hmm? Oh that feels good." He closed his eyes. "I am kinda tired. The nap didn't help."

"It didn't?" Brianna got a container of lotion from the cabinet. She poured a dot of it into her palms and rubbed them together. "Why didn't it help?"

"Hmm?" His hand went up her thigh.

"Does this feel good?"

"Oh yes. It's soothing. Loosening up the muscles in my face."

"You're always tense." She pressed her breasts against his shoulder.

"Stressed." His head moved with her hands. "All the time."

"Simon you trust me right?"

"Of course I do, love. Mmm." He laid his head on her stomach.

"I do care about you. I'm sorry if sometimes I don't show it."

"You show it all the time."

"Take off your shirt."

He kept his eyes closed when he did it. Brianna squeezed lotion on his back.

"Mmm. Oh, Brianna."

"You like that?" She circled her palms down the arch of his back.

"Oh god do I? It's been so long since I had a massage."

"You relaxed?"

"Oh yes. It feels too good actually."

"You can tell me anything." She whispered into his ear. "And I won't judge you or get mad. Anything."

He snickered. "What?"

"Seriously." She worked her fingers into his shoulders. "I care about you so much, Simon."

"Why did you fight me at first?"

"Because I was afraid."

"Of what?"

"Of being hurt. But I know now you wouldn't hurt me."

"Oh you do?"

"Yes."

"And how do you know?"

She took the rubber band off his hair.

"Because every time you look at me I know you'd never hurt me. You wouldn't hurt anyone."

"No I wouldn't."

"It's the character that matters, Simon. I know you have a good heart. You're a good person."

He moaned.

"Sometimes good people do things they don't understand or are scared to admit."

"That's what Clara always said when we were growing up. Said I was too scary to do things. I was you know? But I looked to other things and I got strength from that."

"You still close to Clara?"

"I hope so. Sometimes I'm not sure."

"What does that mean?"

He straightened up on the toilet. "She's mean sometimes."

"To you?"

"Always picking at me and calling me names. When we were kids that's all she did."

"I thought you were so close."

"We were but still she has her ways. She gets so angry and jealous. Sometimes it's like she tries to live her life through me."

"Simon you really trust me?"

He nodded.

"What if I told you that you could tell me anything. Would you believe me?"

"Yes. I know you wouldn't lie."

Yeah right.

"And you know I'd have your back."

"Oh yes of course. You proved that when Kemp busted in here like some moron."

"I know you'd never do anything to hurt Cheyenne or anyone."

"No."

"But if you know anything about that night, something that maybe you haven't shared you can tell me. I promise I'll understand."

"I told you all I know. All that happened."

"Are you sure?" She kissed him. "It's okay. I love you."

"What did you say?"

"I said I love you, Simon."

"Oh." He kissed her wrist. "You don't know how long I've waited to hear you say that."

"You want to be with me don't you?"

"More than anything."

"You'd do anything to accomplish that wouldn't you?"

"*Anything*."

Even attack Cheyenne?

She got the red brush from the cabinet and dragged it through his hair.

"Simon I wanna be with you but we can't have secrets between us. I promise I will always love you no matter what you tell me."

"I see."

"Let me prove how much I love you, Simon. Tell me the truth, baby."

"The truth?"

"Don't be afraid to tell me everything. I'll love you more for being honest." She kissed his forehead. "I don't want you stressed and worried."

"No?" He purred from her touch.

"Oh no. I know you got a lot on your shoulders. It's probably killing you to keep it in. It's best if you just confront it. You'll feel so much better if you confide in someone you trust. You don't have to be afraid to tell me."

"I have nothing to tell you, Brianna."

Would she have to fuck him first?

He opened his eyes and looked at his fingers as if he'd never seen them before.

"I care about you, Simon."

"Take off your clothes."

"Come on."

"You know someone used to tell me that you could see inside someone when they were naked. I wanna see inside you, Brianna."

"Now you're being silly." She put the brush down.

"Oh have I offended you?"

"I was just trying to…"

"Oh I know what you were trying to do." He stood by the towel rack. "And it won't work."

"What are you talking about?"

"You think I'm stupid, Brianna? You think I had something to do with Cheyenne's attack don't you?"

"No."

He shook his head. "So much for thinking you never lie." He went into the hall.

"Simon wait."

Shit.

"Goodnight, Brianna." He pointed downstairs. "I'll see you out."

"Wait are you throwing me out?"

"I want you to be here for the right reasons. Not to sneak around and try to trap me!"

"Simon what the hell's gotten into you?"

"You think I'm stupid, Brianna? Don't play with my emotions."

"I'm not. Just calm down."

"I love you. I wanna be with you."

"Okay."

"But I will not be made a fool of."

"I wasn't doing that."

"You can honestly say that you weren't trying to seduce me so that I'd tell you I attacked Cheyenne?"

"You're crazy!" She started for the stairs. He pulled her against him. "Simon let me go!"

"One thing I'm not is crazy."

"Let me go."

He did.

"What the hell is wrong with you?"

"I'm sick of this crap, Brianna! Either you trust me or you don't!"

"I do!"

"Either you wanna be with me or you don't!"

"I told you I do!"

"Then leave me alone about Cheyenne's attack!" His eyes bulged. "I did not attack her and I do not know who did!" He charged her. "Do you understand that?"

"Yes."

He sweated.

"I understand a lot of things now."

"Brianna I'd give you the world if you'd let me. But you have got to let this go. I did *not* attack Cheyenne."

"I shouldn't have come here."

"Yes you should have." He pinned her against the wall. "Either way you did."

"Simon let me leave."

"You don't really want to do you? Did you mean it when you said you loved me?"

Her lips trembled.

"Did you?" His hardness poked her thigh.

"Yes."

"Then prove it. Go away with me for the weekend."

"What?"

"I was planning to ask you anyway. I have a little spot I like to go to in Rhode Island. I want us to go and spend some time together. Alone."

He went in for a kiss. She put her hands on his chest to stop him.

"I can't go away with you."

"Why not?"

"My job for one. Cheyenne's case."

"Cheyenne's case is over with. Michael did it." He locked his arms around her.

"Now come here."

"Simon it's not over for me."

"Just Saturday and Sunday, Brianna. You can take two days off."

"I can't, Simon."

"Damn it!" He punched the wall.

"Oh." Brianna ran downstairs. "I don't know what's wrong with you Simon but I'm leaving."

"Fine." He opened the front door. "I'll go by myself."

She stared at him.

"Maybe that's best. Maybe I should just go off somewhere and be alone for a while."

"How long a while?"

"Oh I don't know. I might go away forever. Would you like that?"

"You can't leave, Simon."

We'd never find you.

"And why can't I leave? You don't give a damn."

"I just told you I fuckin' loved your ass!"

"But you can't go away with me for two days? You know Kemp said I was playing you but look at it from where I sit. Maybe you seduced me to see what I knew."

"Oh you know that's not true."

"But when the heat's on you can't take it."

"Don't talk to me like this, Simon."

"I've put my heart out for you and you can't go away with me for two fuckin' days? How can you love me if you're afraid of me?"

"I'm not afraid!"

"Then come with me. If not I'm going alone and I can't promise I'll be back."

CHAPTER THIRTY-SIX

"That isn't fair, Simon. You're trying to blackmail me into doing what you want."

"You damn right I am. It's the only way I can get you to admit what's really going on between us."

"And what's that?"

"You said that you loved me, Brianna. But you know what's funny? I don't think you realize that you really do."

"If you really love me then why would you wanna leave?"

"I don't. I want you more than anything but not if you're gonna accuse me of something every time I turn around. Now this is the last time I'm gonna have this conversation with you. If you trust me, fine. If you don't then leave and we can call it quits right now."

"So you can turn your feelings off like that?"

"No but I won't deal with this every fuckin' time we're together. I give and give and give to you and now I want something back."

"My heart right?"

"I want all of you and if I can't have it then there's no reason for trying."

She put her hand on the doorknob, on top of his.

"I don't want you to leave."

"If you don't want me to leave then give me a reason to stay. We need to spend time together without this damn case hanging over us.

I'm sick of Cheyenne's case, Michael, Stephanie, Gene, all of it! I'm cracking and I need a break. You do too. We need time alone together. It's the only way we will truly know where we stand and where this can go."

She hadn't a choice. Simon had enough money to disappear. If he left she'd never find out what happened to Cheyenne.

"Okay I'll go away with you this weekend."

"Oh." He kissed her. "You mean it?"

"Yes." She fondled his chest. "You're right. We need to get away from all this."

He picked her up.

"What are you doing?"

"Taking you to the bedroom."

"No, Simon."

"Shh." He kissed her.

"I can't."

"Oh this weekend's gonna be wonderful. I'll have you all to myself." He stopped at his bedroom door. "We'll come back knowing all we need to about each other."

She hoped so.

◆◆◆◆◆◆

"I mean it, Bree." Steven followed Brianna from her hallway to her front stoop Saturday morning. "You're not going."

She set her suitcases on the porch. "I don't have time for this, Steve." She went back into the house. "Simon's gonna be here in a minute. I don't want him to see you."

"I don't give a damn what you want." He followed her upstairs. "Where's Davis?"

"Next door." She checked her bedroom and bathroom in case she missed something.

"Susie's gonna watch him for me." She looked in her top dresser drawer. "Making sure I have my moisturizer."

"I couldn't believe what Captain Jersey told me. Where'd you get such a stupid ass idea?"

"I don't think it's stupid to go off with Simon if I can get information from him." She brushed past him. "Move."

They went downstairs.

"And you think Watts is just gonna hand you information?" Steven admired the portrait of Brianna and Cheyenne. She'd hung it on that section of the wall leading to the kitchen.

"You think Michael painted that?"

"I don't know." Brianna moved dishes from the table to the sink.

"Well I'm glad you finally admit that Simon knew Michael."

"I didn't say he did but..."

"You know he did."

She wiped off the table and put the dishrag in the sink. "So what do you want? To say you told me so?"

"No but it hurt that you believed Cheyenne and not me."

"This isn't your business." She marched down the hall with Steven on her heels."This is the only way I can find out what he's hiding. I thought that's what you wanted."

"Not like this." He stood in front of her.

"Move."

"I sure as hell don't want you going off alone with Watts. You know how dangerous and dumb that is?"

"I don't have a choice!" She shoved him. "Simon said he wants to leave town. If I don't go with him now and convince him we'll be together, then he'll run off. He does that then we'll never find out the truth."

"Watts isn't going anywhere."

She turned off the television, computer and closed the shades.

"Wake up. He just said that to get you to go off with him."

"And what if you're wrong?"

"I'm not."

"I forgot, you never are right?"

He put his hands on his waist. "Act like you got some brains would you?"

"Excuse me?"

"You think you can seduce Watts into telling you something? You've already been sleeping with him and he's still been lying."

"If I get him alone, away from all this shit then I can get to him. I know I can."

"Ha!"

"And I don't plan on seducing him." She fluffed the couch pillows.

"No you don't have to right? I mean he's already getting the cow and the milk."

"Go to hell."

When she turned around she ended up right in his face.

"I'm not gonna try to convince you that this decision is smart or not. But it's the only one I can make. I have no choice, Steve. Do you get that?"

"Well I have a choice!" He threw her on the couch.

"Steve! What the?"

He got on top of her.

"Get off me! You crazy?"

"I'm not letting you leave, Bree."

They scuffled.

"Steve! Ohh! Get off! This is the most idiotic thing you've ever done and that's saying a lot!"

"I'm not letting you go to end up like Cheyenne."

"Ohh! You are a moron!"

"Maybe so."

"Get off me!" She kicked at his shins. "Steve he'll be here in a minute! You're gonna ruin everything! You're just jealous!"

He held her down.

"You just don't want me to go off with Simon!"

He grunted. "It has nothing to do with that."

"Bullshit! I gotta do this for Cheyenne!"

"Uhh!" He pinned her arms behind her head. "Cheyenne wouldn't want you to risk your life!"

"I know what I'm doing. Let me go!"

"Simon might be taking you to Rhode Island to off you."

"Oh you're out of your mind!"

"You don't know he isn't!"

"Get off me you jackass!"

"You can't trust him, Bree." Sweat fell from his face onto her blouse. "He's dangerous. He's way out of your league."

"It's not about me trusting him but him trusting *me*!"

"I won't let you go off to your death."

"Steven please."

He settled down and looked in her eyes.

"Please. This is for Cheyenne. This might be the only chance to find out the truth. If I don't go, Simon will leave."

He loosened his hold on her wrists.

"You know he will. If that happens how could we ever forgive ourselves?"

"So it's either your life for the truth? I don't like that bargain, Bree."

"I don't either but I am not letting the person who hurt Cheyenne get away. Whether it's Simon or not, he knows something. You know I'm the only one who can get close enough to find out. Please let me up."

"Shit." He got off of her.

She patted her curls down in the back. "You messed up my hair."

"I don't give a fuck about your hair. I'm trying to save your life!"

"That's not your responsibility." She went to the front door. "You need to go before he gets here. I don't want him to see you."

He crossed his arms. "Well I wanna see *him*."

"I need him to trust me. If he sees you here it'll ruin everything."

"Shit I'm still your partner in case you've forgotten." He trekked to the door. "We should be doing this together."

"I'm doing this for the last time now please leave."

"Bree."

"Steven I've taken all the precautions. I have my gun. I'll be all right."

"You gonna sleep with him?"

"That's none of your business."

"Answer me."

"I'll do what I have to do."

"Of course you won't mind it either will you?"

"Steven go." She pushed him onto the porch.

"I hate you're doing this, Bree."

"I can't say I'm thrilled myself. But whatever happens, I'm not coming back until he tells me the truth."

CHAPTER THIRTY-SEVEN

Saturday Night
(Providence, Rhode Island)

One word would describe Providence for Brianna, "heaven". The charming city and the charismatic Brit she toured it with swept her away beyond control. Before she left Albany Brianna didn't understand her feelings for Simon. Now she did. She was falling in love with him. The responsible, well-contained side of Brianna fought hard against it. But that wasn't the side that showed up when she spent time with Simon.

With him she displayed the part of an adoring and obedient lover. Most would refer to it as the "love fool". The love fool could be a bitch because you couldn't control your emotions in this state. It opened the door to your heart. Exposed your vulnerability. Showcased your wants and desires. Tinkled around with your dreams and fantasies of living happily ever after, truly in love.

She sat at the center table of the four-star restaurant with diamonds draping from her ears and wrist. Dazzling couples laughed and danced underneath the rotating lights. To her right she smelled chalamari and steak. To her left she caught a hint of *Bond No. 9* cologne. The restaurant's sexy atmosphere rounded out an already perfect day.

Simon had treated her like royalty when they got to Providence. They spent the entire day sightseeing. They toured Kennedy Plaza and

City Hall. They went to Roger William Park, the Museum of Natural History, Waterplace Park and toured homes on The Mile of History. After only a twenty-minute breather they visited the Cathedral of St. John.

They shopped after finishing the tour. Simon ignored Brianna's protests to his spending.

He bought her clothes, jewelry, and the best time she'd ever had at the spa. He said she'd enjoy herself if he had to force her. Simon believed that you had to spend a little money to have fun.

Brianna grew guiltier with each dime he spent.

A flower swayed over her right shoulder. She jumped, being taken back to memories of being stalked. A young man in a white long-sleeve shirt and black apron walked around the table.

"I'm sorry if I frightened you, Miss."

"Oh no. I'm fine. It's okay."

"Would the lovely lady like a rose?"

Simon came from behind Brianna before she could answer.

"Yes she would." He sat down with that charismatic smile she'd gotten use to. "What do I owe you?" He asked the man.

The man did a double take. "Mr. Watts?"

Brianna sat up.

"Oh uh." The blood rushed from Simon's cheeks.

"How are you, sir?" The man shook Simon's hand. "It's lovely to see you again."

"You know each other?"

"Uh I might've forgotten for a moment." Simon laid his napkin in his lap. "But yes, I remember him from the last time I came."

"Well who could forget you when you tip with such appreciation." The man touched Brianna's shoulders. "He's such a sweetheart. Makes me jealous how he treats his lady friends."

"Oh really?"

Simon pulled on his collar. "That's uh sweet. Now if you'll excuse…"

The man flounced around Brianna's chair. "If you're Mr. Watts' new lady then you are very lucky. He'll dote on you from head to toe."

Simon cleared his throat.

"Well you seem to know a lot about Simon. He must come here more than I thought."

"Well he's the kind of guy that makes an impression." The man blushed.

"That's sweet." Simon coughed. "Will you please excuse us?"

The man dug in his flower basket. "If you need anything." He stroked Simon's ponytail.

"Don't hesitate to let me know."

"That's very kind of you thanks."

The man took Brianna's hand. "It was lovely to meet you."

"Thanks." Brianna spoke to the man while looking at Simon.

"I'll see you." He twisted away with his hand in the air.

"Wow." Brianna's dress strap fell off her shoulder. "You make an impression with both genders don't you?"

"He's a little fruitcake with a crush."

"I'd say more than that. He obviously paid a lot of attention to you when you came before."

"Well I did tell you this is one of my favorite little hideaways."

Brianna crossed her legs under the table. "Did you bring all your women here?"

He held his fork in midair. "Not *all*."

"And what does that mean?"

He guzzled champagne. "Nothing, honey. Eat before your food gets cold."

"Oh my food's fine."

"Don't tell me I forgot to tell you how lovely you are in that dress."

She twirled her glass. "Oh you've told me a thousand times already. I'd like you to answer my question though."

"Yes I have brought a few women here before."

"What's a few?"

Simon smiled at the couple at the next table. "*Some*, Brianna. That's what a few is." He ate a piece of chicken breast. "It was the past. It doesn't matter."

"Oh?" Her food caught in her throat. "Is this the normal treatment?"

"What do you mean?"

"Here I am thinking you brought me here because I'm special."

"You are and you know it."

"Am I?"

"Don't I prove that every time we're together? Just because I brought someone else here in the past doesn't mean you're not special."

"Uh-huh."

"I'm sure there are places you've gone with other men that you used to go to with Steven. It's the same thing."

"Really?" She scooted her chair from the table. "I bet you told every woman you brought here that didn't you? Did they all buy it?"

"Don't do this please. We're having an excellent time."

"Sounds like a man with a guilty conscience."

"I have nothing to be guilty about and you have nothing to be worried about." He lowered his voice. "You don't have to be jealous. I never felt for those women what I feel for you. You know that."

"Do I? I feel like some toy you bought and dressed up like you probably did every woman you brought up here. Don't you understand how this makes me feel? I feel like none of this was authentic."

"It is." He grabbed her hand. "The other women are the past and they mean nothing to me now. Stop it okay?"

"I shouldn't have come here." She tore her roll in half.

"Look at me. I love you. The past doesn't matter."

"I'd like to go back now." She put her silverware on the plate. "I'm not feeling well."

"You're not going anywhere."

"Take me back to the cottage, Simon."

"No."

Her diamond necklace hit the tip of the champagne bottle when she bent over.

"I'm going back to Albany."

"No. I brought you here for something very important. Please."

"I feel like a fool, Simon."

"Why? You know how I feel about you. You also knew about my past. You know I've had a lot of relationships. I never hid it."

"Yeah well it just sucks to be reminded on a night that was supposed to be so special."

"Brianna what do you want? Just tell me."

"I want to go back to the cottage and go to sleep."

"Well I want to dance with the lady I'm in love with."

"No."

"Yes." He led her to the raised platform in front of the piano player.

Simon whispered into the man's ear. He nodded and began playing Celine Dion's "My Heart Will Go On."

He pushed his chest into her. "This song fits us you know? It's exactly how I feel about you."

His glorious eyes made her second-guess everything. She put her head on his shoulder and swayed to the music.

The flower guy laughed with customers as he left the restaurant. She'd talk to him again very soon.

◆◆◆◆◆◆

The door opened. The hall light shined into the dim bedroom. Brianna placed her earrings on the table by the bed. Simon's warm breath penetrated her neck. She worked the bobby pins from her French roll. He lowered her hand and unraveled her hair for her.

"Mmm." He pushed his nose into her hair and ran his hands down her arms.

His sticky tongue sent an electrical spark all over her body.

She clenched when he spread his arms around her.

"No." She tried to move his hands. "Simon."

"Come on, darling." He pushed his crotch against her backside. "Can't you feel how much I need you? I can't stop myself, Brianna. It's beyond my control."

"Simon please."

He sucked her neck. "Don't say no to me." He panted. "Don't refuse me. Not now." He turned her around. "I need you more than I've needed anyone." He thrust his tongue into her mouth. "Mmm."

She lowered to the bed under his body weight.

"No wait." She turned from his kisses. "Simon please."

"Don't refuse me."

"We need to talk. Please."

"Later." He unzipped the back of her dress and slid it off her shoulders. The chilly air hit the top of her breasts. He started to unsnap her bra.

"No." She went to the window. The moonlight set against the fabulous yard that surrounded the little chalet.

"Oh. You're still upset aren't you?" He stood behind her. "Wanna punish me? Is that it?"

She caressed the lace of the colonial-style curtains.

The room smelled of caramel with a tinge of ash.

"I know you more than you think." He kissed her shoulder.

"Don't. Don't touch me okay?"

"Why can't I?"

She went to the other side of the room. "Because I don't want you to right now."

"You're not angry just because of the other women are you?"

"You don't get it. I'm not mad because of the other women. I'm mad because I'm mad about it."

"You're still scared of your feelings for me aren't you?"

"That's not it."

He approached her.

She moved in front of the china cabinet full of mini porcelain animals.

"So you still think I'm hiding something don't you? Answer me."

"Yes." She stared at the tiny elephant in the cabinet.

"But you don't like doubting me do you?"

"No. I want to be on your side. I really do."

"Because you're in love with me."

"I don't know what I am." She leaned on the cabinet.

"It's okay." He held her. "To love me. Let your heart make the decision."

"It's not that easy."

"It can be." He sucked her earlobe. "Brianna I only wanna make you happy. Give me a chance to do that please."

"Let go."

"I can't. And I don't think you want me to."

She turned around.

"You can't run from this, Brianna. Your heart won't let you." He walked her to the bed. "*I* won't let you."

"No, Simon."

"Shh." He started to unhook her bra.

Ring! Ring!

Simon glanced at her purse on the dresser.

"I have to get it."

"Ignore it."

"It could be important." She got it. It was Steven's number. "Hello?"

Simon curled his fingers into a tight fist.

CHAPTER THIRTY-EIGHT

"Bree, are you all right?"

"Yes." She spoke low. "It's not the best time right now."

"Is Watts with you now?"

"Yeah." She watched Simon from the corner of her eye.

"I just wanted to make sure you were all right. I still hate you went with Watts."

"It's really not a good time to talk. I'll call you tomorrow okay?"

"That's Steven isn't it?" Simon reached for her phone. "Hang up."

"Stop it, Simon. What's the matter with you?"

"Hang up right now."

"Bree are you all right? Bree?"

"I'll call you tomorrow, Steve. I…"

Simon snatched the phone and cut it off.

"*Simon*. You had no right to do that. Give me my phone!"

"No." He put it behind his back.

"No? Are you crazy? Give me my phone!"

"No." He snatched her waist.

"Simon cut it out."

"I just want you to get the point, Brianna. You're with me now not Steven Kemp." He threw the phone on the bed and shoved his lips on hers. "Mmm!" He pushed his hands under her dress.

"Simon wait okay? Just wait."

"I've been waiting." He snatched her bra off her shoulders. "I love you and I want you."

"Simon."

"Right now."

He pushed her on the bed and climbed on top of her. He didn't take his pants off just pulled them down with his underwear.

Brianna flinched as he entered. She stared at the overhead light, wondering how the hell she'd get the truth from him.

"Uhh." He gyrated inside her. "Ohh!"

◆◆◆◆◆◆

"Ahhh!" The man threw the phone. He'd gotten Brianna's answering machine for the hundredth time that day.

"Fuck!" He stomped across the hardwood floor. "Where are you, Brianna? Where the fuck are you?" He threw a chair at the wall.

"Hey!" His neighbor from the apartment next door knocked on the wall. "Keep it quiet in there! I've had it with you!"

"What?" The man kicked the wall. "You shut up or I'm gonna come over there and cut your dick off and shove it up your ass!"

"You asshole! I'm gonna report you to the landlord again!"

"Do it, fucker!" The man banged his head against the wall. "Do it, do it, do it! I don't give a fuck, you cocksucker!"

He sprawled out on the floor and propped his arms under his head.

"Where the fuck are you, Brianna? *Where?*"

He'd find her. He'd worked too hard to let her get away. He'd go around this whole fuckin' city if he had to.

He loved her *that* much.

His anger settled when he looked at the photos of her enchanting face. He'd wallpapered his bedroom with them.

"You won't get away from me." He lifted his hand and moved it into the air as if he were feeling her lovely face for real. "I've worked too hard to get you." He took out his pocketknife. He pressed the point to his index finger. He smeared his blood over her photo.

"I will have you, Brianna." He kissed his blood from her lips. "I will."

◆◆◆◆◆◆

Simon was gone when Brianna woke up Sunday morning. He'd left word that he'd gone into town on a "secret mission". Probably buying her something else. He'd rented a driver for their tours and his note instructed Brianna to call the man when she got ready.

He'd left his debit card and insisted she spend every cent of it. The card couldn't give her what she really wanted.

Answers.

But maybe someone could.

Brianna headed over to the restaurant from last night. The manager informed her all she needed to know about the feminine flower guy. His name was Fabian and he frequented the *Pappa Q's* outside restaurant on Sunday mornings.

The waitress slapped a menu on the table before Brianna sat down. She had nervous stomach and didn't feel like eating but the waitress made the crab cakes sound so delicious she couldn't say no. And she didn't even like seafood.

After ordering the crab cakes and lemonade, Brianna sat at one of the tables facing the busy streets. There wasn't a sheltered area for customers to sit. Everything took place outside except for the booths the staff prepared the food in and the restrooms.

A breeze drifted through the trees and soothed the customers as they ate.

Pappa Q's was located on a corner across from Providence's most popular tourists' spots.

People could enjoy their meals and take advantage of the serene weather and breathtaking view.

A rose fell over Brianna's shoulder just like last night.

"Would the lovely lady like a flower?" Fabian smiled in a pair of *Christian Dior* shades.

Wow. *He can afford Dior?*

"Hello again." Brianna took off her drugstore shades.

"Well hello." His hand slanted in the air. "I thought that was you. If I got your name, I apologize because I don't remember."

"Detective Brianna Morris."

"Fabian." He shook her hand. "Stop. You're a real detective?" He flounced into the seat across from her. "Girl I never would've guessed. You look so fashion forward to be a cop."

She smiled. "Well this isn't my normal wear."

"Well girl you wear it well." He flicked his hand. "Ohh." He kicked off his flip-flops.

His toes shined with clear nail polish. "Well I've been on my feet all doggoned morning selling these damn roses."

Brianna grinned.

"Oh, I don't know why I bother. If I didn't have a sugar daddy I'd ditch it altogether."

"Oh I see. Got someone taking care of you huh?"

"Girl do I?" He took out a pack of cigarettes. "Mind if I smoke?"

"Go ahead."

"Oooh thanks." He crossed his legs and shook his foot. "Hell you can't smoke anywhere these days. It's so republican."

Brianna chuckled.

He winked while sucking the cigarette. "Isn't it a small world that we meet again? Girl." He patted her hand. "Oh you are so lucky to be dating Simon Watts. You talk about a catch."

"He makes quite an impression on you huh?"

"I'd like to make an impression on him if you get my drift. Too bad he's straight." He fanned. "All the good ones are."

"I don't know about that. Us straight girls have a hard time finding men ourselves."

"Why do we even bother?" Fabian dabbed sweat with a napkin.

"Actually it wasn't a coincidence that I showed up here."

"Oh?" He batted his long, mascara-filled lashes.

"Yes I came to talk to you. It's important."

"Little ol' me? Well I'm intrigued. What can I do for you?"

"Well…"

The waitress brought Brianna's food. "Here you go. Crab cakes with tartar sauce, hush puppies and a large lemonade."

"Thanks." Brianna took the drink from her hand.

"Enjoy your meal." The waitress stopped at the next table.

"Mmm." Brianna sipped.

"Taste good?"

"Well it looks better than it tastes but it'll do. Uh, do you know Simon well?"

"I wish I did. We're just acquaintances." He puffed. "He comes to the restaurant whenever he's in town and that's how we met. He's not the kind of guy a gal can ignore."

"So uh, has he brought a lot of women here?"

"Now Detective do I look like the kind of girl who sticks her nose in someone else's business?"

Brianna smiled.

"Okay I am. Well like I said you can't ignore someone like Mr. Watts. Oh he's rich and gorgeous. Perfect. That accent and that long hair I just wanna…"

"Fabian please answer my question."

"Yes he's brought some women here from time to time. Providence is one of his favorite places to visit."

"From what you've seen…" Brianna tasted the crab cake. "Was he serious with the women he brought?"

"Well I can't remember all of them."

"All? So it was that many?"

"Look I don't wanna throw shade on anything you and Mr. Watts have going. Girl just be glad you got him now."

"Is there anything you can tell me about any of the women?"

"Well I know he was very serious with the last one. He brought her here at least ten times."

"Really?"

"Yeah." He flicked ashes on the ground. "Every time I turned around they were here. She was a photographer or something. I ran into them when they hit the tourists spots and they always came to the restaurant."

"Photographer huh?" Brianna swallowed the crab that lodged in her throat along with her nerves. "How do you know it was serious?"

"Well you could just tell. The way he looked at her. The same way he looked at you last night. Also, you don't bring a woman somewhere a bunch of times if you're not seriously dating. They seemed to really care for each other, that's why I found it strange when he offered me that money."

"What?" She sat up. "What are you talking about?"

"Well the last time he came back he was alone and looking for me. I didn't know what was going on but I knew something was up."

"Why?"

"Well he offered me one hundred dollars to forget I ever saw him with the woman. And from what I heard, he offered other folks money to do the same. Money talks."

"Wait. Why would he offer you money to say you'd never seen him with this woman?"

"I dunno." He scratched his big toe. "I guess they broke up or something because I never saw her again. One minute he acts like she's his world and the next it's like he's trying to erase his relationship with her."

"And you didn't ask him why? Just took the money?"

"I was struggling okay? I also didn't wanna know because I didn't wanna get in trouble. Course I'm not stupid. I knew something was strange when he asked folks to act like they'd never seen him with this woman. But not a lot of folks will turn down money."

"This doesn't make any sense."

"She was gorgeous too. Looked like a model." Fabian blew smoke out his nose. "I'd killed her for that hair."

"And you say she was a photographer? Like professional?"

"Yes. She took pictures of the tourist spots and other places around town. When I saw her in the square, I asked. She said she was putting together a portfolio because she does landscape photography." He chuckled. "She said it was a fluke how she and Simon met."

"Uh huh?"

"Said she'd been avoiding dating services because she thought all the men who used them were jerks."

"Dating services?"

"So uh, she said Simon was the most perfect man she'd ever met and that she wished she'd tried it sooner."

"Dating service?"

"Uh-huh, girl. What's wrong?"

Brianna reran Fabian's words in her head.

"Oh it's okay." He waved his cigarette. "Don't be upset with him. Obviously he's moved on with you. Olivia Delcie's the past."

The fork fell from Brianna's hand. "Olivia Delcie?"

"Yes. I looked up her photos online. She's very talented."

"Olivia Delcie from Albany, New York?"

"Yeah. Is something wrong?" He fanned her face. "Girl you look like the devil just sat on your lap or something. What's wrong?"

"I don't believe this." She knocked her plate over when she stood. People gawked but she didn't give a damn.

"This can't be true. It couldn't have been Olivia Delcie."

Fabian puffed. "What's the deal with Olivia Delcie?"

Brianna darted off through the tables.

CHAPTER THIRTY-NINE

"Hey, babe?" Jerry flopped into Susie's kitchen in shower shoes.

"Damn it, Jerry." She almost dropped the tray of corndogs. "You scared me."

"Meow." Davis crept in and sat beside Jerry's feet.

"Babe."

"Just hold it. I said the food's almost ready." Susie dumped the corndogs in a Tupperware container.

Jerry grabbed a beer from the fridge. "There's some dude outside." He scratched his butt.

Susie took off her oven mitts. "Well who is he?"

"I was gonna ask you the same thing." He belched. "Better not be cheating on me."

"Oh please." She filled a cup with ice and grape soda. "You're the last one to mention cheating. What's the guy look like?"

He scratched under his arms. "Shit a dude. He's an impatient son-of-a-bitch I know that."

Susie picked Davis up. "I'll be right back. Don't eat everything in sight okay, Jerry?"

He opened another beer. "Get rid of him so we can fuck." He belched.

"Wow. Romantic huh?" She scratched Davis' ears on the way to the front door.

A handsome guy in fitted jeans, a navy blue tee and shades stood against a Camaro.

She walked out. "May I help you?"

Davis wiggled in her arms.

"Well, I hope so."

She couldn't see his eyes but felt them on her breasts.

"Do I know you?" She asked.

"No. I know Bree." He pointed next door. "I was looking for her and I thought you might be able to help me."

"Oh well I'm Susie." She shook his clammy hand. "So you're a friend of Bree's? I've never seen you before."

"I don't come around much. Anyway, I really need to talk to her and I don't know where she is. I've been looking everywhere and calling her house but no one answers. I see her car's in the driveway so I'm a little worried."

"Oh no need to be worried. She's fine."

"Meow."

"Glad to hear it. Where is she?"

"Uh, you've known Bree long?"

"Yes." He patted Davis' head.

"Did you try her cell phone?"

"I don't have her cell number. Can you give it to me?"

"Uh." She looked at Davis then into the stranger's shades. "You're a good friend of Bree's yet you don't have her cell number?"

"No she never gave it to me."

"That's kinda strange isn't it? I mean all my close friends have my cell number."

"Well I guess Bree never got around to giving it to me. Where is she?"

"What's your name?"

He pushed his hands in his pockets. "Does it matter?"

"Yes I think it does."

"Look I told you I'm a friend. Bree would be very upset if she knew you were treating me this way."

"I'm not treating you any way but this is odd to say the least. You show up at my house claiming you're a friend of Bree's and I'm supposed to trust that?"

"Yes. I don't see what the big deal is."

Davis licked Susie's wrist.

"I'm sorry but you'll have to come back when Bree gets back."

He spit in the grass. "What's your problem, lady?"

"My problem?"

"Yeah. You on your period or something? All I want is to find out where Bree is. I said it's important. What's your fuckin' problem?"

"If you don't see why I'd be cautious than something's wrong with you."

"Hey." He grabbed her arm.

"Let go of me."

"I'm not playing you little slut. You tell me where Bree is and you tell me right now."

"Oww! Let me go!"

"Hey motherfucker!" Jerry bolted out the door. "Get your hands off her!"

"Oh yeah?" The man held her tighter. "Come make me, man."

"Motherfucker!" Jerry took out a gun.

"Jerry no!" Susie wrestled with the stranger. "Put the gun down before you get in trouble! It's okay."

He walked to the edge of the porch with the gun pointed straight at the man.

"Get your hands off her and get your ass outta here right now."

The man stared at him.

Jerry cocked the gun. "You think I'm playing? You won't be the first motherfucker I've shot."

"Jerry don't!"

The man let Susie go. She ran up the porch.

"Now get the fuck outta here!" Jerry hollered.

The man spit at them. "Fuck both of you. You better hope you guys don't see me again. I mean that." He jumped in his Camaro and sped off.

"Shit." Susie hung onto Jerry's shirt. "Think we should call the police?"

"He gon' now." He lowered the gun.

"I got a bad feeling. Something was wrong with him." She followed Jerry to the door. "Wonder who he was."

"No telling." Jerry scratched through his greasy hair.

"And put that gun down." She hit him on the back of his head. "You know you're on probation!"

"Hey this gun saved your ass."

They went inside.

Sunday Night

After many times of secretly driving by Simon's home in hopes to catch something out of the ordinary, Steven got his wish. Maybe patience won out. Maybe he'd prayed enough to get this case over with that God put pity on him. He didn't care the reason. He'd just been lucky to find the gate open and the lights *on*.

Who would be in Simon's house?

Steven parked and tiptoed inside the gate. He expected to be blasted by security lights but it didn't happen.

He patted the gun on his side. He got another surprise when he got to the front door.

It was unlocked.

If he'd been a woman he'd listen to the voice telling him to be careful. But he was a man so he told it to fuck off and eased inside. It started raining as soon as he shut the door.

He tiptoed to the stairs. A lady stared down at him.

"Whoa!" He fell back. "Shit!"

"Who are *you?*" She grabbed a vase off the banister. "Don't come near me."

She had a slight British accent that became more apparent at the end of her sentences.

Her oval face blushed with shock. She had long blond hair and eyes wide as soccer balls. Her old-fashioned features and that deer-caught-in-a-headlight stare reminded him of those pale women in them Botticelli paintings Bree always swooned over.

A woman that wasn't that pretty to him but one that men who were into the art scene would probably try to claim was beautiful.

Jeez how he remembered Botticelli's name he had no idea.

"I asked you a question." She placed one hand on the railing and kept the other one occupied by the vase high in the air.

She had French tips on her nails and wore an entire jewelry store. She smelled good too. Probably some French cologne like Simon wore that Steven couldn't pronounce.

"Stay away from me."

"Clara?"

She lowered the vase.

CHAPTER FORTY

"Who *are* you?"

"Why don't you just put the vase down huh?"

She raised it higher. "I'll put it down when I feel like it. What do you want?"

"Hey." Steven approached the stairs with his hands up. "I'm not gonna hurt you."

"Like I know that. You stay there."

"We can be nice right? And just talk."

"Get out. Don't come near me."

"Just calm down. I'm not gonna hurt you okay?"

"Get out and leave me alone."

"No need for us to play games, Clara."

"Clara?" Her eyes got even bigger. "You're crazy. Who are you?"

"Someone who's tired of getting the runaround all right?"

"I said stay away from me!" She threw the vase.

"Ahh!" Steven ducked.

"Help!" She ran to the door. "Help me someone!"

"Come here!" He hoisted her off the floor.

"Let me go! Help me! Someone help!"

"Shut up!" He swerved her around in his arms. "Let's not play games!"

She kicked him in the crotch.

"Ooh!" He let her go. "Ooh shit."

"Come on. I got more." She threw up fists.

"You kicked me in the nuts you psycho!" He clutched his middle. "What the hell's wrong with you, woman?"

"You still haven't answered my question!"

"Just hold it okay! I'm a cop."

She lowered her arms. "*You're* a cop?"

"Yes." He grunted.

"Why didn't you just say that in the beginning?"

"You didn't give me a chance!"

"How do I know you're telling the truth?"

He groaned and pulled out his badge. "That enough truth for you?"

"Detective Steven Kemp." She looked back and forth at him as she read his name.

"I'm sorry but you should've said something first."

He put his badge in his back pocket.

"Are you all right?" She helped him stand up straight. "Did I hurt you?"

"I don't know if I'll ever have kids but that's another story."

"I'm sorry."

"It's okay." He shook away the pain.

She wasn't anywhere near his type of woman but her voice captivated him.

"I like your voice."

"What?"

"I like your accent. Ahh." He stretched. "Sounds a little different from Simon's."

"So you know my brother."

"I wish I didn't. I'm so glad to see you. Maybe you're the only person who can help me figure out Simon."

"Why do you think I'd be able to help?"

"Well you two used to be so close. Wouldn't you know things about him no one else would?"

"Wait a minute. You called me Clara didn't you?"

"Yes."

"I'm not Clara. I'm Darien."

"Who?"

"I'm Simon's stepsister."

"Wait a minute. Are you fucking with me?"

She shook her head.

"Is this another game?"

"No." She showed him her identification.

"Well shit I need to speak to Clara."

"Well that's not gonna happen unless you have a Ouija board with you."

"Excuse me?"

"You know any other way to talk to the dead?"

"What?"

"Clara. She's been dead for years."

The blood rushed from his head. He felt like his feet were on air.

"Detective Kemp?" He fainted in Darien's arms.

◆◆◆◆◆◆

Brianna turned the television off when she heard Simon's car outside the cottage.

She straightened up on the couch. She'd do her best to act like everything was okay. She still couldn't believe what she'd learned earlier that day. Had to be a mistake. But there weren't that many coincidences in the world.

She shivered as she heard his car door close. She'd be alone, far away from safety with a man who could be a murderer. She took a deep breath.

Why the hell hadn't she stayed in Albany?

Simon walked in with sacks of food that smelled up the entire house.

"Hi, darling." He kissed her cheek. "Mmm I missed you. Been watching television?"

"Simon."

"Hope you got out and had some fun today because that was my intention."

She followed him into the little kitchen that had been constructed to look like one you'd find in a genuine log cabin.

"Simon where have you been? You claim we came up here to be alone and you just ditch me for the whole damn day?"

He set the sacks on the table. "Just wanted to give you some space. Didn't want you to think I was smothering you." He took two Styrofoam containers and a bottle of wine out of the sacks. "I hope you're not angry."

Disgusted and sick to my stomach is more accurate.

"I got you a present that I think will lighten your mood. It's the reason I've been gone all day. Wanted to make sure it was perfect."

"Where is it?"

"Oh you'll get it when it's time." He pinched her cheek.

She followed him to the sink and back to the table. "Where you been?"

He read the bottle of wine. "Nineteen-eighty-five. Man that was a fun year for me."

"Simon answer me."

"Have you eaten? Hope you got your appetite."

He opened the food containers. One held piles of crab legs along with lobster soup and garlic breadsticks. The other had a mountain of shrimp fried rice, fish fillets and butter sauce for dipping. "I hope I got enough to last for the night."

"Looks like you got enough to last for the week."

"Boy I love your sense of humor." He got candles from the cabinet. "How about we light these? Makes it more romantic."

"Simon the last thing on my mind is romance. You have no idea."

He continued as if she hadn't spoken.

"I hope this satisfies you. Now I know you're not big on seafood but you haven't tasted seafood until you've had it in Rhode Island. I got this from one of my favorite restaurants up here."

"Simon."

"At first I was gonna take you but I thought it would be more romantic to eat alone."

"Simon."

"The lobster soup ooh." He dipped in his spoon and sipped some. "Delectable. They use real lobster too. Not fake crabmeat like at Jayson's."

"Simon would..."

"I had lobster soup all the time when I traveled. It's amazing how many places can cook the same thing so differently." He put the empty sacks in the trash. "We've gotta go traveling together as much as we can. You need to see the world, Brianna."

"No right now I need to talk to you about something very important."

"You know what I was thinking would be a great idea?"

"What?"

"Why don't we visit your mum and stepfather, huh?" He laid out the plastic utensils.

"Excuse me?"

"I think it's about time I met them don't you?" He got matches from the cabinet.

"You told them about me yet?"

"No."

"I see. Guess I should be a little offended."

"Simon this isn't about my folks."

"All I'm saying is that it won't take but a hop and skip to check on them in Hartford. I'd love to meet them."

"Well maybe it's time you realize you can't get everything you want."

"Okay did I do something wrong? I don't see your gratitude at all."

"My gratitude?"

"Yeah I get the fact that you're not easily impressed by money and status as other women. It attracts me to you believe me. But could I get some kind of appreciation? I mean, I bring you up here for a wonderful weekend." He smoothed down the tablecloth. "I leave you with my debit card so you can do whatever the hell you want with it and what do I come back to? Bitching."

"Simon fancy dinners, debit cards, and you buying me clothes is not gonna change what's going on here."

"And what's that?"

"No see you playing the fool worked in Albany. But I'm not settling for the BS anymore."

"BS? What has gotten into you?"

"Oh anger, disgust and impatience just to name three things, Simon. I can't even explain the emotions I have toward you right now."

"I see. Well I'd like to know what I've done to put you in such a mood." He slammed the table when he sat down. "Especially when I haven't been here all damn day."

"You said we came down here to share well damn it, I want to more than anything."

"I wanted us to get closer."

"Part of becoming close with someone is being honest. So we need to get the shit all out now because I can't take anymore of you walking around and acting like I'm stupid and will just take everything you say because you're charming."

"God you're sexy when you're angry."

"I'm not playing with you."

He whistled. "Okay I see." He filled two glasses with wine. "You're stressed and need to relax." He sniffed the wine. "Did you start your period?"

She gaped.

"I didn't mean that mockingly I just wondered."

"You don't get it do you, Simon? This isn't about me but you. All about you."

"So changing the location doesn't change the song you sing right?" He set his glass down. "And even though I doubted it would I hoped we could move on past all this."

"There's no way as long as you don't trust me enough to tell me the truth."

He stood. "So now it's all about trusting you huh, Brianna?" He gripped her face in his palms. "I do trust you and I love you very much."

"Sweet words won't do it this time. You have to prove to me that you love me. There's only one way to do that."

"I can do that, Brianna." He kissed her nose. "You wanna know why I've been gone? I already knew my purpose for inviting you here. But still I had to search to find the item that made it perfect. Something worthy of you."

She stood against the refrigerator.

"And even though I searched every goddamn place in Providence and found something almost as beautiful as you are I don't think it will ever show you how much I love you. Nothing could show you that because I love you too much to even describe it."

"Simon."

"No." He raised his hand. "You wanted me to prove it and I'm glad you asked. Now it gets me off the hook because I didn't know how I was gonna do this in the first place."

He got down on his knee.

CHAPTER FORTY-ONE

"God, Simon. What are you doing?"

"After this I hope there will be no more doubt about how much I love you."

He took a tiny black box from his pocket.

Brianna shoved her hands together to keep from shivering. It didn't help.

Surely he wasn't gonna.

He held her hand and kissed it. "This is your proof. Brianna Elaine Morris?"

"Simon don't." She closed her eyes.

"Would you do me the honor of becoming my wife?"

Her heart dropped to her feet.

He opened the box. An oval-shaped diamond sheathed with tiny rubies shimmered on a gold band.

"Brianna?"

"Simon stop it." She started crying without warning. "Just stop it." She pushed the ring away. She couldn't bear to look at it.

"What's wrong?" He rose. "I just asked you to marry me."

"I know." She sucked in tears. "I…"

"Honey?" He held her shoulders. "Sweetie I hope these are tears of joy."

"They aren't."

He lowered the ring.

"I didn't want things to become so complicated. I didn't. I came up here for the truth, Simon. I didn't come up here for this."

"This is the truth. The only truth we both need."

"Stop it!" She turned away from him. "We have to stop this now, Simon. I can't go on like this."

"What is the problem? I don't understand it. Did something happen today?"

"Please." She cried in her hands. "I can't do this anymore. No one's strong enough to do this shit! And I didn't mean to lead you on but tell me the truth, damn it! That's all I want, Simon. I just want the truth!"

"This is the truth!" He shoved his lips on hers.

"Mmm, no!" She slapped him.

"Brianna?"

"Just stop it! I want the truth right now! I don't want a ring! I don't want your sweet words or your promises! I want the fuckin' truth right now!"

"*What* the fuck do you expect me to say?"

"You bastard you know!" She hit his chest. "Stop this game once and for all! Just stop it!"

"What do you want from me? What the fuck do you want?"

"I want you to stop lying! Admit the truth! Admit you knew Olivia Delcie! You dated her didn't you? Admit you knew Michael and admit you attacked Cheyenne!"

He stared with his mouth opened.

"That's where you can start or stay the hell away from me!" She ran upstairs.

◆◆◆◆◆◆

"Mmm." Steven awoke on Simon's couch with Darien holding a cool rag on his forehead.

"You all right?"

"What the?" His stomach swirled when he moved. "Ohhh. What the hell happened?"

"You fainted."

"What? That's impossible. I don't faint."

She snickered. "Well you did. Either it was from what I told you or your blood sugar is low."

"Shit." He ran the towel down his face.

"You feel okay? Need something to eat?"

"No. Clara."

269

"I told you she's dead."

"She can't be dead."

"Why would I lie?"

"I don't know. Maybe you're trying to protect Simon."

"Protect Simon? How would lying about Clara protect Simon?"

Rain slapped the roof.

"Do you know what's been going on? There was a woman attacked and I think Simon was involved. Her name's Cheyenne Wilson and she's a friend."

"I don't know what you're talking about."

"Look Simon's been acting like Clara's still alive. He's been telling everyone he doesn't know where she is. Now can you explain that?"

She stared straight ahead.

"Darien please tell me what the hell is going on."

"I knew something was wrong when Dr. James called me."

"Gene James?"

"Yeah. He called me and told me he was worried about Simon. That's why I'm here."

"Well how'd you get in?"

"Simon gave me a key a while back. I just got in town. I live in LA. Simon doesn't even know I'm here."

Steven folded the rag.

"Our relationship is estranged at best."

"Why?"

"Because I'm the only person left who knows the truth."

"Darien am I wrong to think Simon is dangerous and that he could've attacked Cheyenne Wilson?"

She shook her head.

"I knew it. Then how come everyone keeps acting like Simon could do no wrong?"

"It's not that simple. Simon is a good person but he's sick."

"Sick?"

"God where do I start?" She laid her foot on the coffee table. "I love Simon like he was my real brother and I can't believe I do after what he took away from me. What he took from everyone."

"You're losing me here. Does this have something to do with your father killing his mother?"

"I can't believe he talked about that to you."

"Well not to me but my partner. See he's been seeing her. He said he shot your father by accident when he killed Simon's mother."

Darien shut her eyes and hugged herself.

"What? Is that not the truth?"

"Maybe Simon wants to believe it but that's not what happened. I bet he said my father was on drugs and was abusing his mother right?"

Steven nodded.

"Gave you all that story about how he wanted to save us so he shot my father only he didn't realize it?"

"Well yeah."

"None of that is true."

Steven got butterflies in his stomach.

"My father didn't shoot Tara Watts, Simon did."

"What?"

"And when my dad ran into the room, they fought over the gun and Simon shot and killed him."

"Whoa, whoa. Wait a minute."

"It's the truth. I know it's hard to believe. Simon killed his mother and my father. We were then thrown into the child protective system. Simon wasn't charged with murder because they realized he really couldn't control himself."

"And why not?"

She covered her eyes. "I'm sorry. It's just so hard to talk about it even now. I close my eyes and I see my dad lying on the floor. His eyes pleading for help and none of us knew what to do. Simon was so scared. Clara was hysterical and I was in shock."

"Fuck *me*."

"He said the voices made him do it. We protected him because we didn't understand what he meant. We were kids. We believed he really was hearing voices."

"Hold on, voices?"

"Simon is schizophrenic."

Steven stared at the wall.

"Course Clara and I didn't understand until we were older and Simon was finally diagnosed. Up until then he was thrown into mental hospitals. I don't know what the hell the doctors were doing but they didn't solve the problem. They just pumped him up with drugs and said he was fine. That he'd recover."

Steven lowered his head.

"So they finally found places to put us after we spent time in foster care. Relatives took me in. The McMillians adopted Clara and Simon. The very *rich* McMillians."

"Did that bother you? That they were taken in by rich people?"

"I'd be lying if I said I wasn't a little jealous. What kid wouldn't want to live in a mansion with servants and getting everything they want? I realized though that money couldn't buy the home I'd been lucky to find. I loved living with my aunt and uncle. They weren't rich but they loved me."

"Did Simon have something to do with the McMillians' death?"

"Why?"

"I found these articles about the fire and how the authorities suspected arson. Nothing came of it."

"Simon set that fire. I'd bet my life on it. But whether he did it for the money, I can't be sure."

"Do you think the voices told him to do that too?"

"The voices tell Simon to do everything. He's completely delusional if he doesn't take his medicine. I mean he's come a long way but Simon will never be like everyone else. He'll have to take medicine and be on his guard the rest of his life. There's no cure for it."

"Now I feel like a bastard. I hated Watts and I had no idea he had these issues. I knew he was a patient of Gene's but I had no idea this was the reason."

Thunder.

"Shit and my partner's alone with him. She's not safe."

"If Simon's on his medicine then he's all right."

"But he probably attacked Cheyenne! Now that I know this, Bree's not safe with him at all. And she doesn't even know what he's capable of."

"I don't think Simon even understands what he's capable of."

"And Clara?" Steven touched her hand before he asked the question. "How did she die?"

Darien dropped her foot. "Her car sped out of control one night. Brakes weren't working and she smashed into a tree."

Steven covered his mouth.

Darien wiped tears. "Police said it was an accident."

"Do you believe that?"

"All I know is that Clara was suspicious about the fire. She told me many times. She might have confronted Simon."

"You believe he killed her don't you?"

She looked at him. "With all my heart."

CHAPTER FORTY-TWO

"Brianna?" Simon knocked on the bedroom door.

She turned over in bed. "Go away."

"Come on that's not fair." He stopped at the end of the bed. "You put something out there and I have a right to confront it."

"Oh so now you wanna be honest?" She sat against the headboard with tears gathering under her eyes.

He sat on the edge of the bed. "So you think because I knew Olivia Delcie that I attacked Cheyenne? Better yet, you think I killed Olivia don't you?"

She kept her eyes on the miniature animals in the china cabinet.

"I didn't kill her. It hurts me that you'd even think that."

"Then why the hell didn't you tell me you knew her? Simon how many fuckin' coincidences could there be? Come on! You knew Gene James and Stephanie but you claim you didn't know Michael. Now you knew Olivia Delcie who somehow knew Michael and I'm supposed to just take this too?"

"Let me explain."

"For you to lie?"

"I loved Olivia damn it. I thought she was the one for me. I danced in the air she breathed. She broke my heart and I lost myself. I've been with a lot of women but only a few I've really loved and wanted to spend my life with."

"Me and Olivia right? Did you propose to her too?"

"Yes."

"Here in this cottage like you did me?"

"Yes."

"Damn it." She coughed between tears. "So much for being special."

"I am with you now and I love you now! Olivia is history."

"Olivia is *dead*!"

"I had nothing to do with that."

"If not then why didn't you say you knew her?"

"Because it didn't matter! I didn't know you were even concerned with Olivia's murder. I can't help it that a woman I used to date was killed. Does that mean I did it?"

"You're nothing but a manipulative liar."

"Watch your mouth, Brianna."

"Fuck you!" She threw the pillow at him. "Don't tell me to watch my mouth. It's the truth. That's why I came up here, to get the truth from your ass finally."

"Oh I see so you being here was just a fuckin' game? It wasn't because you really cared and you have the nerve to say *I* haven't treated *you* like you're special?"

"Steven was right. You played me like a fool. What's so bad is that I let you."

"I'll come back when you're willing to talk sensibly."

"Oh don't leave now."

He stopped at the door.

"My stance won't change no matter how long you wait. It's over, Simon."

"And what does that mean?"

"I'm not playing with you anymore. You can seduce me and buy every diamond ring in the world and nothing will get me to stop until you finally tell me the truth."

"I've been seducing you?" He marched to the bed. "You seduced *me*."

"I'm such an idiot!" She pulled her hair. "I trusted you. I believed you even when Steven said I shouldn't."

"Brianna?"

"I wasn't using my damn head. I was going on what I felt for you. I really believed you couldn't hurt anyone."

"I wouldn't hurt anyone!"

"Well you hurt me when you lied."

"I never lied to you."

"Oh yes you did. You said you didn't know Michael and I know you do."

"I didn't."

"Stop it!" She jumped from the bed. "Stop lying! That picture you gave me of me and Cheyenne, Michael painted it!"

"You're losing it, Brianna!"

"I know he did! You forgot how much I love art? I pay attention to details too, you forget that? That portrait has Michael written all over it down to the stroke of the brush! Artists have their own identity and Michael painted that portrait. I've seen his work. I know his style. Tell me the truth! Admit it!"

"All right!"

She jumped back.

"I knew Michael! I knew him!" He shoved the items off the dresser. "He was a friend of mine. You happy now?"

"You son of a bitch."

"But it's not what you think! I had nothing to do with Cheyenne's attack."

"Oh so this is another coincidence? Boy how lucky can one man get, Simon?"

He grabbed her. "Listen to me."

"Let me go."

"None of this matters, Brianna. What matters is you and me."

"Get the fuck off me!" She swung at him. "You're a liar and you attacked Cheyenne!"

"I swear I didn't! Believe me!"

"*Believe* you? That's like asking a porcupine not to stick me! What's the chance of that?"

He fidgeted. "I wouldn't hurt Cheyenne."

"I want your ass to admit you did it. If you really love me then that's the least you could do."

"How can you treat me like this?" He sobbed. "I love you more than anything. I wanna be with you. I would never hurt Cheyenne!"

"Then who did?"

"It was Michael! I swear it was!"

"Oh." She turned from him.

"Listen to me."

"Stop lying!"

"I didn't do it, Brianna. Please believe me."

"Then tell me the truth. If you don't it's over between us for good!"

"All right! I didn't attack Cheyenne!"

Brianna held her breath.

"It was Clara!" He threw a candleholder across the room. "Clara did it!"

Brianna took a few steps toward him then backed up. "Simon."

"That's the truth. It's what you wanted isn't it?"

"What about Michael? How did he end up with the weapon?"

"Michael was the one who took Cheyenne to the hospital."

Brianna walked around, shaking her head.

"So now you know the truth, Brianna. I lied to protect my sister, not myself."

"But why would Clara beat Cheyenne?"

"She wants to be the only one I can depend on. Every single time I fall in love, she's there. Trying to ruin it."

Brianna wobbled.

"Still I can't turn my back on her no matter what she's done."

"How do you know Michael?"

"Met when he lived in England."

"If you care for Cheyenne how could you hide this?"

"You don't have siblings, Brianna."

"That doesn't make a difference. Clara could've killed Cheyenne. Would you be taking up for her if she had?"

"Clara's not perfect but she's all I had. She's the one person who was always there."

"That doesn't excuse what she's done."

"Do you still love me?"

"That doesn't matter."

"Yes it does."

"Simon you just told me that your sister attacked Cheyenne and you hid it. What am I suppose to do? Hug you and kiss you and say it's okay?"

"Yes and say you'll marry me."

"You're not living in the real world. Can you see how much trouble you're in? You covered up a crime."

"I don't care about that right now. All I care about is you." He took her hands. "Brianna please don't end this. If I don't have you I got no chance of a better life."

"What?"

"Before you I needed Clara but now I don't. You're all I need and all I want. I wanna be with you forever. Please say you feel the same."

"Simon how can you even say that? How can I get over what you've done?"

"I didn't hurt Cheyenne."

"But you knew who did all this time. You think I could ever trust you again? Think I could possibly be with you after this?"

"What are you saying?"

"I'm not gonna marry you, Simon. In fact it's over between us. When we get back to Albany I'm gonna do my best to make sure your sister is found and arrested."

"Brianna you can't leave me."

"Simon how the hell could I be with you?" She laughed. "Are you living in a fuckin' fantasy world? I can't be with someone who lied about an attempted murder and who I cannot trust!"

"But you said you loved me! You can't change that just because you get angry."

"Simon you are not thinking. Look at me. There is no way I will ever be with you after what you've done."

His lips shook.

"I'll probably always care for you but I cannot be with you and just the thought of it is unbelievable to me. I will never trust you again."

"I'd do anything for you." He broke into tears. "Anything."

She moved from his touch.

"Just tell me what I can do. Please. I love you so much."

"It's over, Simon. The only thing I want from you is to tell me where Clara is."

"Don't do this. You love me. You said it."

"Simon stop it."

"Brianna you said it. You made love to me last night and I felt how much you wanted me."

She looked at the floor.

"Come on look at me." He touched her chin. "Let me hold you."

"No."

"If I hold you it'll make everything all right."

"I said no." She went to the window. "I can't be with you, Simon. You're the last man I could..." She shook away tears. "The last man I could be with."

"Simon?"

He looked toward the hall.

"What is it?" Brianna asked.

"I told you didn't I, Simon? She's just like the others. You can't trust her. You know that now don't you?"

He batted his eyes.

"Simon?" Brianna touched his arm. "What's wrong?"

He ran down the hall.

CHAPTER FORTY-THREE

❝Bree come on." Steven paced in Simon's entrance hall on his cell. "Shit."

Darien came from the living room. "She's still not answering?"

"No. Can you call Simon's cell for me?"

"I don't have his cell number."

"Fuck, man. I gotta tell Bree what's going on."

"Keep trying. She probably has her phone off or something."

Steven tried to push away the horrible thoughts that flooded his mind.

"Better be the only reason." He dialed again. "I swear Darien, if Simon's hurt her I'll kill him." He blew into the phone. "I will fuckin' kill him."

"Simon?" Brianna chased him to the other bedroom. "Simon what is it?"

He slammed the door and rested against it.

"Simon?" Brianna turned the knob. "Simon are you all right? Don't do anything crazy! Simon!"

"You can't be with me? Is that what you said?"

"Simon open the door!"

"No! Leave me alone!"

"Don't do anything stupid, Simon! Open the door so we can talk!"

"Oh now she wants to talk." Clara drifted out the bathroom. *"Wow she deserves an Academy Award huh?"*

"What do you mean?"

Brianna banged on the door. "Simon!"

"It was all an act. Don't you get that now?"

"Simon please!"

"She never cared about you. Just like I told you."

He slid to the floor. "That's not true. She's just confused because I didn't tell her the truth."

"She used you to get the truth. I keep telling you that no one is gonna love you like I do. I'm the only woman who stands by you. Everyone else is gone."

"Simon open the door!"

"See she cares." He broke into a cold sweat. "If she didn't then why would she be worried that I'd do something to hurt myself?"

"Guilt." Clara sashayed around the bed. *"It's all about her, Simon. Just like with the others."*

"No. I tell you Brianna is different!"

"Simon?" Brianna yanked on the knob. "Simon?"

"Tell her to go away."

"Go away, Brianna!"

"Are you all right?"

"I'm fine! I'm just gonna lie down!"

"Are you sure?"

"Yes!"

She left.

"See? If she really cared she'd have beaten the door down. I know I would've."

"Go away." He got his bag out the closet. He pulled out his pills.

"What are you doing?"

"It's time for my medicine. Leave me alone."

"Simon look at me."

"No." He wrestled with the medicine cap.

"You know you don't really wanna take that medicine."

"Go away and leave me alone."

"You're not thinking, little brother. You know what has to be done now. She knows the truth. You see how she threw you away just now? Think of how she's gonna treat you when you get back to Albany hmm?"

She swayed in her white dress.

"She took you for a fool, Simon. All you wanted was for her to be on your side and she can't even do that."

"Then she mocked me when I asked her to marry me. And all the time I spent trying to make this perfect."

"And she's never satisfied. You give her an inch and she always wants more. She kept hounding you about Cheyenne's attack. She never trusted you." She swept her finger under his chin. *"How does that make you feel?"*

He tightened his fingers around the bottle. "Like a bloody fool."

"That's what she obviously thinks you are. You gotta show her you're not. We gotta show her."

"I'm so sick of jumping through hoops for her. What does she want from me?"

"Nothing would be enough for her. Besides, she just said she couldn't be with you.

She dumped you like a pile of sewage. She wants to tell on you and you'll end up in prison. No, you'll end up in one of those hospitals again."

"No way in hell will I."

"She's the only one who knows the truth. Michael's dead and no one else knows. You get rid of her and everything will be okay."

"I can't, Clara."

"Shh. I know. But I'm here to help as always." She smiled. *"I'll do it. You know I don't mind helping you out."*

He sniffled. "I don't know."

"Shh. You know.*"* She went into the bathroom and lifted the toilet lid. *"Let me in, Simon. I'll make everything better again. Like I always do."*

He stood by the toilet.

"The pills, Simon. You don't need them."

He titled the bottle over the toilet.

"Yes." Clara's eyebrows flexed into thin lines. *"That's it. Yes."*

He shook the pills into the toilet.

◆◆◆◆◆◆

Captain Jersey rushed downstairs with her gun. Those sounds she'd heard by the den a minute ago had stopped. She stood in the front hallway. The smell of sawdust hit her like a fist to the face. She'd been having her den remodeled for months and was sick of the entire process.

She trotted on bare feet careful not to trip over some tool or sharp object. She wasn't turning on the light yet. If someone were here she'd let their ass be shocked like they'd done her.

Thunder crackled. A beam of lightening busted through the curtains. She stood in the doorway of the den.

Silence.

Her stomach turned from the smell of sweat and underarms. The workers had been at it for four months and their scent seemed imbedded in the walls. She'd gotten so sick of Timberland boots scuffing her tile and tools scattered around.

The humidity was more insufferable than last night.

When the hell would all this rain stop once and for all?

Why Mother Nature continued her wrath of storms on Albany she didn't understand. But she was sick of it.

Something creaked in the darkness. She swung her gun around.

Her loose banana clip bobbed in her hair. Who could hold a decent style in this heat?

She stepped over wooden planks that had been cut for who knew what. A hammer lay in a pile of debris. Tape measures, screwdrivers and pliers had been thrown in the corners.

"Damn it." She stepped around the ladder that they'd left in the middle of the room *again* after she'd told them not to.

She hadn't been in here since they began working. She'd crammed half the furniture and the television in that walkway area by the kitchen.

A makeshift den she liked to call it.

She got the drill off the floor and placed it on the table.

Good lord let them be finished soon.

She searched every inch of the dark den and came up with nothing.

"Shit." She giggled. "I gotta stop watching *Ghost Hunters* reruns before bed."

"Funny."

"Ahh!" Jersey turned around and stared him straight in the face.

The man smiled. "*Ghost Hunters* happens to be one of my favorite shows."

◆◆◆◆◆◆

Clara parted the bedroom door where only an inch of light shined from the hall. Brianna slept with her back to the door. She wore a tank top and shorts instead of the flimsy nightgowns Simon's girlfriends usually wore.

Nothing excited Clara more than murder. But this wouldn't be easy. She'd never killed a cop. The other women were weak and unable to fight back. One wrong move could put Clara on the wrong end of this equation.

She lifted the hammer over Brianna's head. Killing brought forth an incredible high. Made her feel like she was in her own little world where anything could happen. The more she killed, the more powerful she became. With the increase in power she gained more control over Simon. She smiled. One day she'd have enough to take over.

She brought the hammer down.

"Oh!" Brianna threw the sheet at Clara and ran out the room.

"Shit!" Clara cornered her in the hall. "Ahh!" She swung the hammer at Brianna's face. Brianna kicked her in the stomach.

"Oh!" Clara toppled with the hammer.

Brianna raced downstairs and flicked the lights on.

Clara stared from the top of the stairs. Brianna displayed that famous mixture of shock and confusion all her victims did when they first laid eyes on her.

"Oh my god it can't be." Brianna wobbled with her arms swinging. "It can't be!"

Clara started down the stairs. "It *is*."

CHAPTER FORTY-FOUR

"Ryan?"

"Having some work done I see." He stalked around Captain Jersey's den.

"What the hell are you doing here? How did you get into my house?"

"How the fuck you think? I broke in. Isn't that usually the way it works?"

"I'm calling the police."

He blocked the doorway. "I don't think so. I'm trying to find Brianna and I know you know where she is. Tell me because I don't have time for games."

"I'm not telling you shit. You're gonna get out of my house right now."

She almost stepped on a nail when she backed up.

"Careful." He picked it up. "You could get seriously hurt in here. And put the gun down. You won't use it."

"The hell I won't." She held it up.

"Don't you trust me?"

"Hell no. I can't believe this."

He shrugged.

"You're the stalker aren't you? This is goddamn unbelievable."

A chilling smile cruised across his lips. "Not really if you think about it."

"I had a funny feeling about you the minute you started working at the station."

"Really?"

"I knew something wasn't right about you. The way you always seemed to be lurking around and listening. The way you always seemed to pop up around Bree, being so concerned. Shit we should've known."

"Well I guess that's why they say you should always go with your gut huh?"

"And you were right there trying to comfort Bree when the stalker got into her home."

He smiled.

"You put the alarm in her house. You weren't doing it to make her safe but to give you more control over her. And she thought you were a nice guy."

His damp combat boots squeaked on the planks. "Going from carpet to hardwood huh? My apartment's got hardwood floors."

"Why, Ryan? Why were you stalking Brianna?"

"Because I love her."

"It has nothing to do with love." She steadied the gun. "I just can't believe no one knew how sick you really were."

"I'm not sick. I got a job to do. I don't care if you understand but Brianna knows the deal. No one can keep us apart. It's in the heavens and the stars. So why don't you put the fuckin' gun down and tell me where she is before I get mad?"

"I'm not telling you shit."

"Sure about that?" He picked up the drill. "Don't wanna end up like Michael and Stephanie do you?"

"What?"

"I got rid of them both."

"It was you?"

"Yep."

"Why? How?"

"More questions huh?"

"It couldn't have been you."

"Oh really? What, don't think little weak ass Ryan could do something like that?"

"What would be the reason you'd kill Stephanie or Michael? Did you know them?"

"Nope. Actually Stephanie just got mixed up in my plans. I didn't wanna hurt her but had no choice. Michael, well that had to be done. He was trying to get in the way."

"Of what?"

"What do you think? Of me being with Bree."

"What the hell are you talking about? Your mind's so warped I bet *you* don't even know what you're saying."

"Michael had an interest in Bree too. He'd been following her around."

"What? That's crazy."

"It's the truth. I caught him lurking around the station one day. Then saw him driving past her house. I also heard you and Bree talking about him making passes at her or whatever when she went into his bedroom. So I knew he wanted her for sure."

"I thought he was in love with Stephanie James."

"Yeah but when he realized he couldn't have her I guess his interests switched. I mean Bree's the kind of woman who can charm any man. Just ask Steven, or better yet Simon Watts."

He picked up a box of nails. "So I decided to get rid of him but I was gonna make sure there was no way I could be tied to it."

"Well you didn't know them did you? How could someone suspect you?"

"I've learned to be very prepared, Captain. Never know what's gonna happen."

She backed up. "How did you do it?"

"Ah interested are you? One night I followed Michael to a bar. We started talking and throwing down drinks. We talked about all kinds of shit he was going through. Ain't it funny how folks will open up to a perfect stranger?"

"I guess."

"So uh he told me about this "collection" of his he had at his place."

"Collection?"

"Yeah home movie collections he'd made. Man you should've seen it. He was a sick cocksucker. He had all these pictures and shit and magazines. And those homemade movies." He shook his head. "We watched some of them. He actually got hot watching them with me. I guess it gave him a thrill to show them off to someone else."

"You sent Dr. James the DVD of Michael and Stephanie."

"Bingo. Clever?"

"Sick and sadistic."

"But clever I know. Hey admit it was a damn good idea."

"Yes it was clever but it doesn't make it any less disgusting."

"So. I'm not trying to get a Boys Scout badge here. Can I get back to the story?"

"Please do. The most interesting I've heard."

"Michael got so loaded he passed out. I wanted to kill him then but knew it wasn't the right time. I snatched up the movie of him and Stephanie and left. I wondered how I could make this work for me. I'd heard some things about Stephanie's history about having affairs when Bree and Steve were talking in the file room one day."

Jersey held her tired arm up with the other hand.

"So then it clicked. I knew if James found out Stephanie cheated one more time that it would be over. She'd be left with nothing and desperate. So desperate I might be able to get her to do anything. I was right. James kicked her out and Stephanie lost everything."

"And like cancer you just slid on in when she was most vulnerable."

"I guess you can say that. I did what I had to do."

"No you didn't."

"That's your opinion. So I made my presence known to Stephanie. You know, played with her a little bit." He dragged his tongue over his front teeth. "I didn't have to do much. I put the idea in her head and she couldn't say no."

"And what was the idea?"

"I told her I needed to get back at Michael for something he'd done. I made up some lie but she bought it. I asked her to help me get in the house, act like she would seduce him. At first she said no but then that hate for him set in and she agreed. We went over to his place one night. She dressed up in this sexy outfit and got him to let her in. She made sure he kept the door unlocked and moments later I went inside."

"Then what?"

"Well when I got upstairs he was trying to rape her like I thought he would. He saw me, recognized me and tried to fight me. But I had him. There was no way he was going anywhere."

"So you hacked him up."

"Yep and Stephanie and I left. She was hysterical too." He grinned. "Kept saying, "You weren't supposed to kill him! You weren't supposed to kill him! Oh god! Oh god!" Man you should've seen her. I calmed her down and told her we wouldn't get caught and I reminded her she wanted it just as much as I did."

"She trusted you and you killed her?"

"The police thought she killed Michael but I had the feeling she'd sell me out. I couldn't let that happen. So I pushed her down the stairs. I'd worked too hard to let that little slut ruin things."

"In a roundabout way all this was to get Bree all the time?"

"Yep."

"And that's how her picture got in Michael's wallet? You put it there as a decoy when you killed him."

"Mmm hmm."

"Did you beat Cheyenne?"

"No. I followed Brianna to the hospital that night. That's how I knew."

"Bree thought you were her friend. She thought you were a nice guy."

"I think we've done enough talking, Eleanor. Tell me where she is." He held onto the drill.

"No what I am gonna do is arrest your ass for stalking and murder."

"I don't think so. Someone's gonna tell me where Brianna is. Now if it's not you it's gonna be someone else. Steven, Cheyenne."

"You stay away from them. Cheyenne's been through enough."

"Not compared to what you're gonna go through now, bitch!" He pushed her down on the floor.

"Ohh!"

He kicked the gun out of her hand. It slid under some boards.

"No!"

"Shut up!" He got on top of her with the drill.

"Ahhh no!" She clawed at his face. "Stop! Get off me!"

"Guns seem worth shit these days huh? So easy to knock 'em outta folks' hands."

"Stop!"

He pushed the tip of the drill to her forehead. "Well don't you find yourself in an awkward position, Eleanor?"

"Ryan think!" She wrapped her fingers around his wrist. "You won't get away with this."

"We'll see won't we?"

"Ahh!" She pushed him off and ran behind the ladder.

"Whoo wee!" He blocked every switch and turn she made. "I had no idea this would be so fun."

She held the ladder in front of her. "Ryan listen to me okay?"

"Hmm?"

"You're not thinking."

His voice deepened. "All I do is think. It's time I start *doing* what

I think about. Bree doesn't have a choice in this and neither do I. This is gonna happen whether she wants it or not. It's fate."

"I won't tell you where she is."

"You old bat!" He kicked the ladder over. He snatched Jersey by her gown and threw her against the wall. "Ever wondered how it felt to get your brains drilled out your head?"

"Oh don't. Please."

He held the drill to her cheek.

"Please don't do this, Ryan."

"I gave you the options, Eleanor. You had your chance to be nice and you didn't wanna do it."

"Wait!"

"I get so sick of having to show people when I'm serious. I guess I'm gonna have to do the same to you."

"No!"

"Tell me where Brianna is." His hands crushed her neck. "Or this is the last breath you take."

CHAPTER FORTY-FIVE

"Stop!" Brianna pointed her gun. "This can't be true. It just can't be."

"It is, hon." Clara jumped onto the glass table and twirled. "It's me, Clara Watts in the flesh."

"Put the hammer down." Brianna shot at her.

"Whoa!" Clara dove off the table. "That's not nice, Brianna. Thought we could talk."

"Put the hammer down right now!" Brianna shot at her feet. "Put it down!"

Clara stood up straight and composed. "Fuck you."

"I don't wanna hurt you. Don't make me do this."

"Aww isn't this sweet?"

"We can get you some help. Just listen to me okay?"

"I don't need any help!" Clara chucked the hammer.

"Shit!" Brianna fell and dropped her gun.

Clara landed on top of her with the hammer raised high. "Ahh!" She slammed the hammer toward Brianna's face.

"No!" Brianna turned to the left, missing the blow.

"Be still." Clara swung the hammer again.

Brianna switched her head to the right. "Awww!" She slapped her hands on Clara's wrists and pushed her knees into Clara's chest.

"Uhh. Let go!" Clara wriggled her wrists underneath Brianna's grip.

Brianna kicked her off and grabbed the gun. She leapt to her feet.

"You're not getting away!" Clara swung the hammer inches from Brianna's face.

"You don't wanna do this!" Brianna dodged the hammer. "I wanna help you!"

Clara chuckled with sweat rolling down her cheeks. The only help she needed was this bitch dead.

"Ahhhh!" She flung the hammer so hard her shoulder snapped.

Brianna flipped onto furniture and ducked behind shelves. She threw a vase and lamp. Clara foiled every attempt she made.

"You don't know what you're doing!" Brianna hollered from behind a shelf of antiques.

"Damn it you're fast sister." Clara waved the hammer from left to right. "I figured killing you would be tough but I had no idea!"

"It's not gonna be easy. Ugh!" Brianna tossed a bowl of peppermints.

"I'll make it easy!" Clara ran toward her.

BANG!

"Ohh!" Clara felt the odd stinging in her chest.

BANG!

"Uhhh! Oooh!" The second shot knocked *Simon* to the floor. His body tensed. His breathing slowed. He tried to raise his head but didn't have the strength.

Brianna laid his head in her lap. "Breathe damn it."

His fingers went limp. The sensation took over his body.

"No come on!" Brianna rocked him with tears in her eyes. "Stay up okay?"

Simon clutched Brianna's hand.

"I'll call nine-one-one."

"No." His voice fought through his trembling lips. "Let it be, honey."

"Please." She kissed him. "Let me call them please."

"No, Brianna." His warm fingers clenched her chin.

"Don't do this, Simon. Please! Let me call them."

He coughed up blood. "It's time, honey."

"*No.*" She laid her head on his chest. "I'll help you with your problem. I promise."

He circled his finger on her cheek. "This *is* the only help, Brianna."

A haze fell over Simon's vision. He fought to make out her beautiful face for the last time.

"No please. Come on." She caressed his face. "Look into my eyes and remember how much you love me. How much you wanna be with me. Please."

"I do. More than anything."

"Then fight for that damn it!" She punched his chest. "You said you loved me! You said that! Fight, Simon." She kissed him. "Please."

"I never knew how to fight. That was one of my problems."

She sucked tears from her lips. "I love you, Simon."

"I know." His hand tightened on hers. "I knew that all the time."

"Simon?"

He stopped breathing.

◆◆◆◆◆◆

"You get one more chance, Eleanor." Ryan pressed the drill into her face. "Tell me where Brianna is."

"She's with Simon Watts! Uh!"

"Where? I'm not fucking around."

"Go to hell!" She kneed him in the crotch.

"Oww!" He rolled off of her.

The room went black after another clatter of thunder.

Jersey shimmied across loose boards.

"Get back here!" Ryan grabbed the ends of her nightgown.

"Let go!" Jersey kicked his face.

He rolled over.

Jersey's gown ripped up the side as she crawled over the planks. She shuffled and felt for her gun.

"Where are you, bitch?" Ryan stomped in darkness. "Oww!" He tripped and fell. "You ain't getting away!"

Jersey found her gun under the boards. She couldn't see him but she knew the room better than he did even in the dark.

"I'll kill you when I get my hands on you! Tell me where Brianna is!"

The lights came on.

Ryan stood over her. "Gimme that gun!"

BANG!

"Ohhhh!" He flew backwards. He grabbed his shoulder. Blood bubbled underneath his clothes. "You fuckin' bitch. Ahh."

"What did you say?"

She shot him in the leg.

"Owww!" He brought his leg to his chest. "You fuckin' ooh!"

"Aw you okay?"

"No I'm not okay you stupid bitch!"

292

"Oh don't worry. You're not going to die. I only bruised you."

"Oh that's what you call it?" He panted. "Finish me off then! It's what you really wanna do."

"Actually it's the farthest thing from my mind." She shifted her weight to one foot. "Brianna deserves true justice. The only way she'll get that is if you go to prison. Dying would be the easy way out and there's no way I'm letting you take the easy way."

Blood ran down his arm. "I'm not scared of prison if that's what you think. I got God on my side. He'll protect me."

"Nothing will protect you from the shit you're about to experience. I promise you that."

"So you think you won something?" He laughed. "The game's not over."

She hobbled to the doorway. "This wasn't a game in the first place. You were the only one who thought it was."

She left the room.

◆◆◆◆◆◆

Two Weeks Later

Brianna made it to the little room right after the guard brought Ryan from his jail cell.

"Hello, Detective Morris." Benny straightened his uniform.

"Leave us." She almost puked from that corrupt smile on Ryan's face.

He sat in a chair with his hands cuffed behind his back.

"You sure you want that, Detective? I think I should stay."

"Oh don't worry, Benny. He's not gonna do anything to me."

Ryan smirked.

"Don't underestimate him, Detective Morris. Cuffs or no cuffs he's a slick son of a bitch. He stabbed a guy in the neck with a pen this morning. Then had the nerve to say God made him do it."

"Well I'm on my way to the big jail house downtown, Benny." Ryan winked. "So you can go on back to your boring life when I'm gone."

"Good riddance." Benny fixed his belt. "You can spread your "good cheer" around there and let them deal with ya'."

"Hey, Bree?"

She got queasy just looking at him.

"Ol' Benny loves me. Don't let him fool you."

"See I should stay in case he tries something."

293

"It's okay, Benny. He's a coward. He only does things to people behind their backs."

"Is that right?" Ryan crossed his feet at the ankles. "Take the cuffs off and let's see how much of a coward I am."

"Shove it, Cummins. I'll be right outside that door, Detective Morris. If he even looks at you wrong come get me." Benny left.

Ryan's eyes lurked on her breasts. "Well you look good enough to eat. Did you ever see that *Skinemax* flick where the detective gave the inmate a blowjob? Always been one of my favorite fantasies where you were concerned."

She raised her hand to slap him but stopped herself.

"Go ahead." He stuck his face in the air. "Hit me. As long as you touch me I don't care what you do."

"I wouldn't waste my time giving you the pleasure."

"I like it when you're angry because it means I'm inside you."

His revolting tone took her back to that night in the station.

"Ooh, being inside every part of you."

"I could stand here all day and tell you how sick you are but what's the use? It wouldn't make a difference. You'd act like you did nothing wrong. You have no remorse. You don't care about all the fear you caused. How you almost made me insane day after day."

"I love you, Bree."

She spit on him. "You don't *love* me. How can you love someone else when you obviously don't love yourself? I don't wanna hear your sad story okay? I don't care if you had a bad childhood or if someone abused you down the stretch. I just wanna know why me. What did I do to deserve what you put me through?"

"If you really wanna know then get down on your knees."

"What?"

"God will show you the answer the same way he did me. That's your problem. You don't love the Lord."

"I do love the Lord."

"You don't go to church. You don't pray."

"You don't know shit about me, Ryan. After all the time you spent watching and following me you still don't really know who I am."

"I know you better than anyone."

"You just can't tell me why can you?"

"I told you why before." He laid his right leg over his left thigh. "It was just supposed to happen. I didn't make that decision. It was willed by God or whoever."

"Don't blame God for what you did. It's one thing to be sick in the head but it's another not to admit it."

"Oh I'm no more sicker than Simon Watts was. You fucked *him* didn't you?"

She lunged at him.

"Don't you dare compare yourself to Simon. He wasn't like you at all."

"Watts was a freak of nature. I mean come on. He was a schizophrenic murderer and on top of that he was so fucked in the head he thought he was his own sister." He laughed. "You're right. I can't compare to Simon Watts can I?"

"Simon couldn't help what he did. You could."

"So is that how you justify falling for him, Detective? I bet you say that a hundred times before going to bed just to sleep at night."

"I cared about Simon."

"Is that why you killed him?"

She forced away the sting of his words.

"Hey it's okay, Bree. I mean even an intelligent woman like you couldn't know what Watts was really like."

"Know what your problem is, Ryan?"

"What's that, darling?"

"You'll always believe you had a reason to do all the horrible things you did. I mean you pass judgment on Simon but you murdered a couple of people yourself if I'm not mistaken."

"That was different. I told you I was picked to do that. I couldn't control that you and I were supposed to be together. I had no choice."

"And I bet you don't regret it do you?"

"No not really. I'd do anything to have you."

"You'll never have peace until you admit what you've done."

"God brings me peace everyday. I'm comfortable when I lay my head down in my cell. I'm content when I walk around in handcuffs. I'm still free, Bree." He wiggled in the chair. "I'm free *within*. That's something you'll never be. I tried to help you though. But you fought me tooth and nail. You can judge me all you want but at least I'm being *put* in prison. I'm not putting myself in one."

"There's so much shit I always wanted to say to you. So much I wanted to say to your face. About how you made me feel. But I see now there's no need to because you really don't care. So I wasted a trip for nothing."

"Oh don't leave, darling."

She turned from the door. "What's so fucked up about this was that I really liked you, Ryan. I thought you were a nice guy. I thought you were my friend."

"Oh baby I can be so much more. If you let me."

"I will never forgive you for what you did to me. I'll pity you but never forgive."

"You're just angry because I broke you down. That's what you didn't like."

She covered her eyes to hide her tears. Didn't wanna give him the satisfaction of knowing he still got to her even now.

"Oooh." He closed his eyes. "You smell so good. Just like peaches."

He scooted his chair toward her.

"Stay back there." She put her hand on her gun.

"Come here and give me a kiss. I wanna remember this moment forever."

"I don't know why I even came in here." She turned the doorknob but didn't open the door.

"Oh I know why. You couldn't resist seeing me face to face." He exhaled. "Say, what color panties you have on?"

She lunged at him. "You bastard!"

"Yeah hit me. Go on. It's okay." He poked his face out.

She put her hand down. "I wouldn't touch you if it would save my life."

"You wet huh?" His eyes went to her crotch. "Your pussy wet? I know I made you feel better than Watts and Kemp ever could. Did you touch yourself when you heard my voice? Just like I touched myself?"

"Shut up! I hope you rot for the rest of your life you asshole!"

"I'm not giving up on you, Bree. It doesn't matter how long I go away. God's picked this mission for us. We're destined to be together and we will be. Might not be now but it'll happen. You don't have the power to stop it. I was put on earth to be with you."

"What do you really want from me? What did you expect from all this?"

"To love you and make you happy. To make every wish you have come true."

"I hate to disappoint you but I don't think you can do that, Ryan."

"Don't doubt me. Give me a chance to make you happy."

"What I mean is that no amount of wishing will change what I want the most."

"What's that?"

She leaned over him. "That you had been the one who died instead of Simon."

"You don't mean that."

"It's over, Ryan."

"No it's not. It never will be."

"Go to hell." She left.

He stared at the door. "I'm already there."

CHAPTER FORTY-SIX

"Bree!" Steven caught up with Brianna down the hall.

"Oh hey." She wiped tears on the inside of her blouse. "Something up?"

"Captain Jersey told me you wanted to talk to Ryan before his transfer."

They went upstairs. He stopped her at the doors of the stairwell.

"Wait. You okay?"

"I didn't expect him to care but I had to confront him for myself. He doesn't give a damn. Just as cocky and disgusting as before."

"It's okay." He hugged her.

"You think I'm stupid for seeing him don't you?"

"No I know why you did it. You felt it would help you move on."

"I just feel like this will never be over with."

They started down the hall.

"It'll be all right, Bree." He pulled her back. "Hey." He put his finger under her chin and turned her face to him. "Is something else wrong? Something other than Ryan?"

"I can't stop thinking about him."

A fat cop titled his head to them as he passed.

"Simon?"

She nodded.

"You can't blame yourself. You did what you had to do to protect yourself."

"Didn't sound so noble when Ryan threw it in my face that I killed him."

"So what do you care what that psycho says? If you hadn't killed Simon you'd be dead. You know that in your heart right?"

"I don't know." She looked off to the side. "I could've helped him get through what he was dealing with. His sickness."

"You kidding me right? That wasn't your responsibility."

"I still blame myself."

"Baby you didn't have a choice. Simon was gonna kill you. You know that."

"But I feel like I should have done *more*."

"Like what?" He held onto her shoulders.

"I could've been there for him more, understood."

"You didn't know Simon was schizophrenic. And no one but Gene knew he suffered from Dis…Dis…"

"Dissociative Identity Disorder."

"I mean who the fuck could know Simon thought he was Clara? Even Darien didn't know."

"He shouldn't have died, Steven. Simon was a good person. He had a good heart."

"He was going to kill you. By the time he came to his senses it was too late."

She wiped tears. "He was kind and gentle. He really loved me, Steven. I know it."

"You regret he's dead?"

"Of course I regret it."

"But that's not all you regret is it? You were in love with him weren't you?"

"I can't answer that because I don't know."

He walked in a circle. "You think I'm stupid? I can tell by your face and how you've been acting that you were in love with him."

"What difference does it make now? He's dead."

"He proposed to you."

"Well I had no control over that."

"You miss him don't you?"

She moved a loose curl out her face. "Does that make you angry?"

"Doesn't make me happy."

"I'm sorry but you asked and I had to be honest."

"So if Simon were still around you'd probably be with him?"

She caught the pain in his eyes. "I don't know."

"Really? Well that's good to know."

"Steven." She slipped her arm inside his. "I care about you. You know that. I never wanted to hurt you."

"For someone who doesn't try to you sure do it a lot, Bree."

"Steven?"

"Come on." He headed down the hall. "We got work to do."

THE END

CPSIA information can be obtained at www.ICGtesting.com

225765LV00002B/48/P

9 780982 967256